TH

PUPPET

MASTER

Sam Holland is the award-winning author of the Major Crimes series, following detectives as they investigate murders committed by brutal serial killers in the south of England. Her debut, *The Echo Man*, shocked and enthralled readers and reviewers alike with its sinister depiction of a serial killer copying notorious real-life murderers of the past.

Her books have been published in 11 countries worldwide, including the US, Germany and the Netherlands, where she became the first author to win the Bronze Bat for her debut and the Silver Bat for best thriller in consecutive years at the Nederlands Thrillerfestival.

The Puppet Master is her third novel.

Sam can be found on Instagram and Twitter at @samhollandbooks.

Also by Sam Holland

The Echo Man
The Twenty

THE
PUPPET
MASTER

SAM HOLLAND

HEMLOCK
PRESS

Hemlock Press
An imprint of HarperCollins*Publishers* Ltd
1 London Bridge Street,
London SE1 9GF

www.harpercollins.co.uk

HarperCollins*Publishers*
Macken House,
39/40 Mayor Street Upper,
Dublin 1
D01 C9W8
Ireland

First published by HarperCollins*Publishers* 2024
1

A catalogue record for this book is available from the British Library

ISBN 978-0-00-861506-2 (B-format PB)

Set in Sabon LT Std by HarperCollins*Publishers* India

Printed and bound in the UK using 100% Renewable Electricity by
CPI Group (UK) Ltd

For Dom

Death is the wish of some, the relief of many, and the end of all.

Lucius Annaeus Seneca, 4 BC–AD 65

Part 1

DAY 1
MONDAY

Chapter 1

In the battle of human versus 127-ton diesel locomotive, there can only be one winner.

Cara stands on the edge of the platform, looking along the railway track. A hundred metres to her left, a gaggle of PCs wearing latex gloves and clutching yellow biohazard bags peer beneath the wheels of a stationary freight train. Disgruntled commuters gather around her. Some voices are sympathetic, shocked. Others moan about the delay, consulting their smartphones.

'Why can't they do this at home?' a woman says next to Cara's shoulder. 'Selfish, isn't it?'

Cara turns slowly. The woman is staring at her, expecting a response. Cara's black jeans and smart coat are deceiving; she's not an early-morning traveller, about to offer something agreeable – what an inconvenience it is to be standing here, freezing to death, in the dim light at seven-fourteen a.m. on a cold January morning.

'DCI Cara Elliott,' she says, flashing her police warrant card. 'And I'd say the selfish one is you. Take a look at yourself. In your cashmere scarf, your leather gloves. You can't get to the office. So what? Instead, you'll work from home, in your twenty-two-degree central heating, a mug of Fairtrade coffee by your side because you pride yourself on doing the right thing, don't you?'

The woman gapes, speechless.

'Think, as you drive home,' Cara continues, getting into her stride now, 'about how lucky you are, compared to this poor sod, spattered all the way from the platform edge to where those coppers are, on the tracks. Do you realise that the force at which he was struck knocked his head clean off? It's over there.' She points, the woman still open-mouthed. 'His hair caught in the brambles. While the rest of him ...' Cara makes an expansive gesture with her hands. 'When the driver got out of the train, he stood on the guy's intestines. Had to be taken to hospital, hysterical. So, when you think about who might be worst affected this morning, maybe, just consider, it isn't you.'

'Boss?'

Cara is distracted by the large man appearing at her side, awkwardly clearing his throat.

'They're waiting for us,' he says.

He turns to the stunned woman as they leave; Cara hears him give her a mumbled, 'Sorry for the inconvenience. Have a nice morning,' as he ushers her away.

'You went a bit hard on that one,' Jamie says as they duck under the cordon. 'Bad night?'

'You could say that.'

'Here.' He hands her his coffee; she takes it gratefully.

'I owe you one.'

'You owe me five,' Jamie replies with a smile.

They walk in silence down the deserted platform, yellow line to their left, white paint marking the edge to their right.

On the tracks, the massive class 66 diesel-electric locomotive is quiet, the line of freight containers on flatbed wagons stilled behind it. A dinosaur, put to sleep. Chances are it'll be there for a while.

Cara notes overhead lights, but no cameras this far along. A metal fence separates them from the car park. Six feet high, not easy to scale.

They step over black rubber pyramids, designed to deter people from leaving the end of the platform, down to paving slabs then gravel. She approaches the main gathering of people cautiously, looking at her feet as she walks. Cara has no desire to tread on something nasty – there are pieces of their victim distributed down this entire stretch of track.

The call had come through at half six that morning. A likely category two, a violent and unnatural death at Southampton Airport Parkway station. Normally an accident on the railway would fall under the BTP; Cara's in the dark as to why they're there.

Hopefully all will become clear soon. Cara and Jamie stop next to the uniformed officer, British Transport Police emblazoned on his fluorescent yellow vest. He smiles, an apologetic grimace.

'You must be DCI Elliott. I'm Sergeant Pearson. Sorry to bring you out. I'm starting to think it's a wasted trip.'

'We're here now,' Cara replies. 'This is DS Jamie Hoxton.' The two men shake hands although Pearson's gaze stays locked on Cara. 'Tell us what you know.'

'Well,' Pearson turns and scowls at the uniforms as they pick their way around the track, depositing what can only be described as 'samples' into yellow plastic bags. 'It seems that our victim was stood at the far end of platform one, waiting for the six-oh-four to London Waterloo. The normal announcement went out about the non-stopping diesel, and while everyone else moved behind the yellow line, he stepped forward.'

Cara's eyes narrow. 'So, a suicide?'

'Yes, but ...' Pearson pauses. 'Our initial witness statements were confused. It was a full platform, rammed with commuters. Still dark. A girl was doing some filming. Everyone was looking at her.'

'Filming?' Jamie repeats. 'We'll need that footage.'

'A YouTube thing, she said. I'll help you find her. But everything's ... muddled. So we called you. Your team is more accustomed to dealing with such matters. Murder, and—'

He stops abruptly. *Serial killers* is what he was going to say. Cara's used to it. The slight nervousness, the reverent way she's treated. She's DCI Cara Elliott. The senior investigating officer from the Echo Man case. Infamous, in her own way.

'Plus, we're understaffed,' Pearson finishes apologetically. 'We cover a huge area and there's a potential jumper at Basingstoke. My team's been deployed up there. Better if we can stop one before ...'

His voice trails off as his gaze drifts to the ground. Between them, resting in among the crushed stone ballast, is a single white tooth. Jamie takes a glove out of his pocket, puts it on and picks the tooth up, letting it rest solemnly in his palm. Cara looks at it for a moment. A piece of gum is attached, blood leaving a trail on the blue latex. Jamie closes his fingers around it then trudges towards one of the PCs.

Cara watches as he drops it into a double-layered yellow bag, thinking that she should feel something other than bone-deep weariness. This is a piece of a human, after all.

She sighs and tips the last dregs from Jamie's cold coffee into her mouth. 'Fetch me another one of these,' she concludes to Pearson. 'And we'll see what we can do.'

An hour later, Cara is warm, hyper-caffeinated, and sitting in front of the CCTV surveillance screens in the station office. On the array of monitors she can see Jamie outside, nearly six inches taller than the majority of the people around him, taking a preliminary witness statement from a uniformed woman on the platform.

Her new right-hand man for ten months now, Cara's become accustomed to his calm, solid style. His reliability, his steadfast approach. She appreciates having him around.

The footage from that morning loads, and Cara cranes forward as people mill about on the platform, drinking coffee, chatting, waiting. A train comes through, passengers get on, some disembark. The roster changes.

'There he is,' Pearson says, pointing to the far left of the screen. Cara squints. The man's clearly nervous, circling like a caged dog, his hands fluttering.

'The station staff spotted him, went over to see if he was okay.'

As Cara watches, the man is approached by a woman in uniform. He's agitated, rendered panicky by the conversation.

'She tried to persuade him to come with her, but he refused. She left to fetch someone who could help.'

'What was he wearing?' Cara asks. He stands out from the rest of the commuters in their smart suits and business attire.

'That's just it. It seems to be a tracksuit.'

7

'Or pyjamas,' she comments.

She continues to watch as he paces, until he moves out of the range of the CCTV and the view is lost.

'Is there a better angle on this?'

'No, that's—'

Pearson pauses as the diesel comes racing through the station. The moment of impact isn't caught, but Cara can tell what happens from the shock and panic on the faces of those waiting.

The door opens behind her, and Jamie enters. He has a woman with him – Cara recognises her from the CCTV. She's young, in a light blue shirt and navy fleece. Her badge says, *Sharon. Happy to Help.* She shrinks in the face of three staring police officers.

'I couldn't stop him,' she says immediately. 'I should have … I dunno.'

A droplet of snot trickles from her nose; she sniffs.

Jamie gestures to one of the chairs and she reluctantly sits down. Cara edges closer so that their knees are nearly touching. She leans forward, hands together.

'Sharon, I'm DCI Elliott,' she begins, her voice soft. 'You can call me Cara. And you've done nothing wrong. But could you tell me what you've been discussing with DS Hoxton? With Jamie here. I'd like to hear directly from you what happened this morning.'

The girl nods. Sniffs again. Jamie hands her a tissue.

'What was it about this guy that made you talk to him?'

'I've just been on my training. You know. The suicide prevention programme. And I thought … he looked how I was told.'

'And how was that?'

'Nervous. Out of place – he didn't have a bag with him

and he was dressed all casual. He was by himself, and he wouldn't look at me. He seemed … random. And—' She sits up, getting into her stride. 'He didn't have a coat. He must have been freezing.'

'What did you do?'

'What I was taught. I went up to him, said hello. Asked if I could help. But he stared at me, fidgeting, his eyes all glassy. Like a zombie.'

Cara glances up at Jamie. He meets her gaze, reading her mind, but both stay quiet.

'And then what?' she asks Sharon.

'Asked his name. And then I didn't know what to do so I thought I'd better get someone. I told him to stay there and I'd be right back but then I heard the train coming in and the screams and …' She starts crying again, messily, tears streaking through her mascara. She raises a shaking finger to swipe it away, only making the smudging worse. 'I should have …'

'You did all you could, Sharon,' Cara says gently. Jamie passes across another tissue; the girl dabs at her eyes. 'Did you see anyone around him? Anyone with him?'

'No. Just the usual commuters. If anything, he was trying to get away from them, like he was scared. Can I go now? There's all these people here and I need to help my boss.'

'Yes, of course. But what was his name?'

She pauses. 'I dunno. I didn't catch it. I should have asked again, but I thought it was more important that I get someone. I—'

Cara reaches out and touches her arm. 'You did everything you could.'

Sharon nods, her eyes pleading, desperate to believe her. Cara thanks her and she hurries out of the room.

Jamie moves his chair next to Cara. 'Drugs?' he says, articulating her thoughts.

'Maybe.'

Cara wordlessly rewinds the CCTV footage, leans back so Jamie can see.

When the final act has played out for the second, awful time, Cara turns to him.

'What do you think? Suspicious death or suicide?'

'That's all we have?' Jamie addresses Pearson. Pearson nods. Jamie tips his head to and fro, considering.

'Based on this, and the statement from the desk clerk, my inclination would be suicide. He was agitated, panicked. He clearly wasn't there for work. He gave all the warning signs of someone about to kill themselves.'

'But?' Cara says, pre-empting.

'But,' Jamie says with a nod in her direction, 'if he was on drugs, and confused, it could have been an accident. And our budding Spielberg is AWOL.'

'Bloody fantastic. You can't get a better angle on the CCTV?'

Pearson looks apologetic. 'Not yet. Sorry.'

Cara sighs. It would be too easy to leave it with the British Transport Police. But she wants to cover all bases. Be certain nothing shady's going on before she hurls it back over the fence.

'Take a formal statement from this witness,' she directs to Pearson. 'Send me all the footage. And we'll need to interview the train driver. When he's in a fit state to talk,' she adds grimly.

'Understood, boss,' Jamie replies. Pearson looks relieved.

'Let's take it all back to the nick. We'll go from there.'

Chapter 2

The incident room of the Major Crimes Unit is a shrunken shell of its former self. Once bursting with detectives and analysts and admin, it's now down to a few DCs and one DS, all working quietly behind aged computer screens. So many have left.

After the events of last February, nobody's keen to join Major Crimes. The team where they catch serial killers, the dangerous and the psychotic. But also where detectives die. Stabbed, drugged and mauled to death in the worst possible ways. Who would want to work there?

The job has always been hard, but more so now only the dedicated remain. The most loyal of these, DC Toby Shenton, looks up from his desk as Cara and Jamie return.

'Press are reporting it as a suicide,' he says. He sweeps his blond fringe out of his eyes with long, delicate fingers. 'Apparently the victim was depressed.'

Cara slumps down next to him. She gestures, and Shenton turns the screen around so she can read it. Sure enough, the *Chronicle* has churned out the standard phrases – 'train not able to stop in time', 'severe delays' – as well as a few remarks about the victim. Colin Jefferies, thirty-one. Unemployed.

'How did they get an ID so fast?' Cara asks Shenton. 'And how do they know about his mental health?'

'They interviewed a witness. Heard him talking to the clerk on the platform. And they've spoken to his mother. "Much-loved son",' Shenton quotes.

'Have we got the mother in?'

'No. It's—'

'It's what?' Cara snaps.

'Thought it might be dealt with by the BTP. It is their area?'

'Get her in,' Cara concludes, and leaves him to it.

She instantly feels ashamed of her bad temper; she's been the same for months now. No tolerance for sluggishness; fed up with waiting for her officers to read her mind.

Her other DC approaches her tentatively, holding out a mug of coffee as a peace offering.

'So, it's ours?' DC Alana Brody asks. She's new. Black hair, nose piercing and an array of holes up her ear. From her appearance, Brody doesn't seem conventional, but her work has been meticulous. Cara was wary of anyone requesting a transfer in, but Brody's grown on her, steadily tackling the backlog of cases that had built up while Cara was barely functioning.

Cara takes the coffee with a grateful smile. 'For now. There's nothing cut and dried. I'd like to know for certain how this man died.'

'CCTV and witness appeal, then?'

'Please. With a special request for anyone who might have been filming that morning.'

'Will do. And Halstead wants to see you.'

Cara winces. Their new Detective Chief Superintendent

12

has been in role for two months but is making her presence known, albeit remotely from her office on the fourth floor. Cara had been summoned almost daily in her first week, generally for small infractions or policy decisions that could have been communicated – and ignored – in an email. Cara thinks about her last boss, Marsh, with his omnipresent cigarette stench and barked orders. Dead now for nearly a year. He was a detective who knew what he was doing – when to intervene and when to leave her alone. Usually the latter. She misses him.

Cara swigs back the coffee and plods up towards Halstead's command centre. She's glad it's in a different place to Marsh's old office; the memories and grief would have been hard to bear.

As it is, she greets Halstead's suffering secretary quickly, and is ordered straight through. Halstead gestures to the seat in front of the desk with an abrupt flick.

'I've heard about this suicide,' she begins, steepling her fingers on the meticulously tidy desk in front of her.

'We'll get rid of it as soon as we can, ma'am—' Cara begins, but stops as she sees Halstead's frown.

DCS Halstead is young. Too bloody young to be doing this job, in Cara's opinion. The words 'fast-tracked' and 'nepotism' had been bandied around when her name was announced, but whatever the reason, she's here. She has severely straightened hair, carefully manicured nails, and a penchant for brightly coloured jackets over black vests and trousers. It's a shocking pink today, with a gaudy necklace to match.

'Treat it as suspicious,' Halstead says. 'The BTP called us for a reason. They are our esteemed colleagues, after all.'

Cara waits. That can't be what this is about.

'And the PR department has been in touch.'

Ah, okay.

'We can't be seen to be anything but thorough. The mother has already been on the phone, screaming about how her darling son would never kill himself. The perception of our department isn't shining at the moment,' she pauses, pursing her lips, 'and that's an understatement,' she continues. 'Two serial killers in two years across the county, both running rings around the detectives. Mistakes were made—'

'Two detectives were murdered!' Cara exclaims.

'As I said, mistakes were made. Evidence missed.' Halstead gives Cara a warning glare. Cara knows what she's saying. *By you.* 'And we need to be seen to be doing everything we can to make sure there are no more unsolved murders on our patch. Resolve this quickly and efficiently.' She leans forward. 'I know things have been hard for you, Elliott. But I need both my chief inspectors at full speed – DCI Ryder's just started up at Basingstoke HQ, have you met her?'

'No, ma'am.'

'A fantastic officer. Full of energy. Capable of more,' Halstead adds, the implication clear. *Taking over your command, too.*

Cara's face flushes. She needs this job. She needs to be working.

'I'm fine, ma'am. I'll get my team on it right away.'

Halstead's gaze remains judgemental. 'How's the recruitment going?'

'Slowly,' Cara replies tentatively. That's a lie. Non-existent, more like.

'Well, double down on your efforts. It's rare I'll say this, but we need more detectives. Make the most of this unique situation and recruit as many as you can.'

Cara pauses, thinking. A glimmer of an idea flickers.

'Anyone?' she says.

'Anyone that's qualified,' Halstead replies.

Cara utters more reassurances, and, dismissed, she backs out of the room. She hurries out of the office, down the stairs, towards the car park. She has to leave now or she'll talk herself out of it. Rational, sensible thought will intervene and she won't follow through.

She gets in her car and drives a few miles out of town. Houses evolve from nice semis to run-down terraces. Fenced-off waste ground, fly-tippers, vape merchants and sex shops.

She pulls up outside a second-hand car garage. The vehicles on the lot haven't changed since the last time she was here, six months ago. There's a Portakabin on the right, a light on, and someone moving about inside. But that's not who she's there for.

On the far left is an office block. She follows the rough brick wall around to the side, to a large, rusted blue metal door. She bangs on it with her fist, the clang reverberating around the car lot.

There's no answer. She bangs again, waits; the faint bass line of nineties rock thuds close by. She's about to pull her phone out and call, when she hears heavy footsteps echoing up the metal staircase within.

The door is pushed open. A man stands there. Six feet. Dark, uncombed hair. Needs a cut and a shave. All in black: tracksuit bottoms, a T-shirt tight across his chest. Battered trainers, laces trailing. He scowls at her from light brown eyes, similar to her own.

'What do you want, Cara?'

She tries a small smile.

'Nice to see you, too, Griffin,' she replies.

15

Chapter 3

'Are you going to invite me in?'

'Depends on what you're going to say.'

'Griffin ...' Cara warns, and he sighs, opening the door so she can squeeze through the gap.

She goes down the dark industrial metal stairs, Griffin's footsteps behind her, and pushes into the basement flat.

Inside, she wishes she hadn't bothered. The music is deafening: Rage Against the Machine, his tastes haven't changed since he was a teenager. The air inside is freezing, tinged with the musky smell of male sweat; a large barbell sits in the middle of the floor, two huge weights either side. He picks up a towel and runs it down his face, his inaction challenging her to do something about the din.

Cara reaches over to the speaker and turns the music off.

'How are you?' she asks.

'How do you think?' he replies gruffly, heading across to the kitchen in three long strides. He fills a glass under the tap and downs it. Clicks the kettle on, then holds up a jar of instant coffee. 'You want one?'

'Do you have milk?' Cara replies.

'Fresh from the cow this morning.'

His tone is sarcastic, but he takes two mugs from the cupboard; a truce of sorts. While she waits she surveys the room, notes the spotless kitchen, the tidy bed.

'You've been looking after yourself.'

'You don't need to sound so surprised.' He gives her a look. 'But yes. Working out, doing my physio.'

'I can see that,' she replies, his biceps on full view as he makes the coffee. 'Have you been getting enough sleep, eating well?'

'You're my sister, not my mother. Give it a rest.' He stirs the coffee then carries both mugs across to the battered wooden table, sitting down and gesturing for her to do the same. 'What do you want, Cara?'

'I—' But before she can say any more, a flurry of black fur leaps onto the table. She jumps with a squeal, almost laughing as the cat sits gracefully in front of her, regarding her outburst haughtily with amber eyes.

'Since when do you have a cat?' Cara says, catching her breath.

'Since Frank decided this was where he wanted to live.'

'Frank?'

'It suits him.'

Any other name in this world would be more appropriate for this delicate creature, but Frank doesn't seem to mind. Cara reaches out to stroke him but the cat moves away, curling his tail high into the air before lying down languidly next to Griffin. Griffin ignores it.

'What do you want?' Griffin repeats.

'Come back to work.'

He stares. 'I thought I made myself clear. I'm done with that.'

17

'And what are you doing instead? Six months you've been here. Mouldering away in this basement flat. Doing bugger all—'

'I have a job.'

'Security for a second-hand car garage? It's hardly a job. What does he pay you? Apart from letting you use this place?'

Griffin's silent. Not much, Cara surmises.

'You're wasted here,' she continues. 'You must be going out of your mind with boredom. Behaving like a teenager, sulking over a failed relationship.'

'You never liked her. But it's not about Jess.'

'What then?' Cara knows Griffin is disappointed things didn't work out – his move up to Manchester to be with Jessica Ambrose was doomed from the start in Cara's opinion, but who is she to judge? Her own love life isn't exactly spectacular.

'Griffin?' she prompts. 'Is it the oxy—'

'I'm off the painkillers. I told you.'

'The counsellor signed you back—'

'What if I don't want to go back? I can't face that again.' He frowns, scratching the top of the cat's head then looking at Cara properly for the first time. 'Why are you so keen anyway?' he asks. 'You never liked me working with you in the past.' He squints at her, thinking. 'You're fucked, aren't you? Marsh has gone, what's the new detective chief superintendent like?'

'Halstead. She's … a bitch,' Cara acquiesces.

Griffin laughs. Cara smiles, despite herself.

'Nobody wants to work in your team,' he continues. 'And I can't blame them. What's the retention rate? Pretty low, despatched via the serial killers you're supposed to

18

catch.' He pauses, and she knows he's thinking about his dead wife, Mia, murdered three years ago by the Echo Man. A killer Cara failed to find, missing the signs right in front of her nose.

But Griffin doesn't mention it, suppressing the anger in the same way he has since they last worked together. He continues on his rant.

'You've got Jamie Hoxton, a year out of his own personal tragedy. Shenton, although his mind is on his profiler thing. Is he still doing that PhD?'

Cara nods, miserably. 'Part time.'

'Who else?'

'Brody,' Cara replies. 'DC Alana Brody. Transferred from the Met.'

'What's her problem? Why's she there with you?'

'She said she wanted a challenge.'

Griffin cackles again. 'She's got that. Fucking hell.' He leans over, selects a cigarette from the pack and lights it. He catches her disapproving glance. 'What? I'm not drinking, I'm off the painkillers. I'm not allowed one vice now?'

'The fags will kill you.'

'So will a lot of things. I'm not dead yet.'

The cat gets up and jumps silently off the table; Griffin grunts, stubbing the half-smoked cigarette in the ashtray, the cat's displeasure seemingly holding more sway than Cara's.

'Why are you here, Cara?' he asks. 'There are thousands of good detectives out there. Why do you need me?'

Cara sighs, irritated with her brother.

'I need someone I can trust. Everyone, with the exception of Shenton – they're new. And we've got cases up to our ears. Take this suspicious death this morning. Body on the railway tracks.'

19

'What's that got to do with you? That's BTP.'

'Witness statements are a mess.' Griffin pulls a face. 'Yeah, yeah. I know. They don't have the resource, and the papers are screaming suicide.' She tries one last attempt. 'I need your help. Come back, Nate. Please?'

'I'll think about it.'

'Nate—'

'That's as good as you're going to get from me today, Cara. Let it go.'

'Fine.' She gets up, waving the lurking cigarette smoke away. 'I would give you a hug, but honestly, you stink. If you're going to resurface, have a shower first.'

Griffin rolls his eyes and waggles his fingers in a patronising goodbye. She swallows the annoyance, almost regretting her offer.

She'd forgotten how insufferable he can be. What a pain in the arse. Even if he is a brilliant copper.

Chapter 4

I don't smell *that* bad, Griffin thinks as he closes the door behind his sister with a thud. He waits, listening to her footsteps clang up the metal steps to the outside, then the growl as her car's engine fades away.

He looks around his flat, seeing it from her perspective. Sure, it's tiny – a room with a bed on one side and a sofa on the other, the large wooden table taking up the space in front of the door – but it's clean and tidy, and his home.

And it's free, in exchange for his watchful eye over the garage at night. Not that anyone ever wants to steal the assorted shitty Fiestas and Corsas on the lot. It makes for a quiet life, priceless right now.

His ego is bruised. His pride mangled. He'd tried, put his heart on the line, and it hadn't worked out. But why is he surprised?

His brief foray with Jess came to a predictable end within less than a year in a cacophony of shouting and slammed doors. Eleven months wasn't bad, all things considered, but what had he been thinking? He's not suited to family life. To a home with a girlfriend and a child and trips to

Tesco every Saturday morning. No, he belongs here. By himself.

With Frank.

The cat arrived a few months ago, following him on his patrols around the car lot, curling itself between his legs as he made his way down to his flat. He ignored it, didn't feed it, but that made no difference. The small black cat took up residence, whether Griffin liked it or not.

And now he has a name, a favourite spot on the sofa, and food and water bowls – although he drinks out of the sink and eats whatever takes his fancy. He comes and goes when he pleases, treating the top window as his cat flap. Griffin rarely closes it now.

He feels a kinship with this independent soul. And he's come to rather like the small warm body next to his at night, the loud purr as they eat their dinner side by side, the soft fur rubbing against his face first thing in the morning.

Frank is watching him now from his position, curled up on Griffin's bed.

'So that's Cara,' he says to the cat. Frank lifts his head, curious. But Griffin's under no illusion: it's food he's after, not therapy, and Griffin opens a can of tuna, tipping it into his bowl.

While Frank eats, Griffin considers their conversation. He hadn't liked the look in Cara's eyes. That he is someone pathetic, to be pitied. He's fine. *Fine*. Always has been: self-sufficient, happy in his own company. He doesn't need much. He likes his life simple. A few saucepans and plates and mugs, a half empty wardrobe. A place to work out and somewhere to lay his head.

His sister was right about one thing though: he is bored. He considers Cara's offer. But a return to the Major

Crimes team means death and murder and everything he'd like to put behind him. Plus, working with his sister again. A daily reminder of how she'd let him down, failed to notice what was going on under her own nose. A killer who murdered his wife. And put him in hospital. Three times.

Three fucking times.

He rubs that most recent scar now, almost subconsciously, his hand tracing the line of the surgeon's knife under his T-shirt. Recovery took months; it pushed him into sorting his life out, but where has that left him now? Here. Alone. Back in this basement flat.

He pulls his T-shirt down decisively. No point dwelling. He considers returning to his workout but his motivation has gone; he feels grimy and cold, sweat drying on his skin. Maybe a shower wouldn't go amiss.

Fifteen minutes later, clean and clothes dumped in the washing machine, he debates lunch. Pop to the shops, buy something fresh and nutritious he can ignore for a curry later. But as he's picking up his jacket there's another knock on the door. He wonders if it's Cara again, but it's lighter, more tentative.

He knows who it is. He stands for a moment, motionless, until it repeats.

'Griffin?' the woman says, her voice muffled. 'I know you're there. You can't ignore me.'

He sighs and opens it.

'Issy, we've talked about this.'

The girl sashays into the room with what she thinks is a sexy walk. In reality she's pissed, and she catches her hip painfully on the wooden table. She pauses, swaying, her eyes unfocused, then swans up to him, pushing her body against his. She's wearing tight blue jeans, a cropped white

23

vest top. Her eyeliner is black and wonky. Goosepimples stand out on her near translucent skin, cold from outside, bones jutting from her shoulders.

'You smell nice,' she says.

She reaches up to touch his face, but he stops her, his fist enclosing her wrist.

She smiles. Struggles weakly. 'It's like that, is it?'

Quickly, he lets go and takes a step back. She is undeterred.

'Griffin,' she wheedles. 'Come on—'

'No, Issy. I told you. No.'

'Is it because of my father? Fuck him.'

'He's my boss. And anyway, it's not him.'

She scoffs. 'So what's the problem?'

Griffin is only too aware of what the problem is. She's nineteen. Half his age. Her father owns the garage. But her advances have been going on for a few months now. Ever since he arrived back, stupid, pride-bruised, and vulnerable to the charms of a hot young woman who never holds back making her desires known.

But he turned her down then. He'll turn her down now.

She presses herself against his chest, slides a gentle hand up his T-shirt. It's been a while since Griffin got laid. And she's soft, smells nice. Something floral, feminine. She stands on her tiptoes, lifts her lips to his neck. He forces himself to take a step back; her eyes flare. She pulls her vest off in one swift movement, revealing a lacy bra. And then she slaps him, hard.

His cheek stings. He winces, feeling blood rush to his face. His teeth grit together. She lifts her hand to do it again and he grabs it, tightly. He looks down, and she's smiling. A smug, satisfied grin as she punches him hard in the stomach.

He's had worse hits; this one barely leaves a dent. But

24

Griffin doesn't appreciate the discomfort, the bruise it will invariably leave. He takes her other hand in his, holding both above her head.

'Hit me,' she says.

Griffin lets go like he's been stung. He forces himself to unclench his jaw as she slaps him again, as hard as she can. He feels his ears ring, but he does nothing.

'Punish me,' she repeats.

'Issy—' She slaps him again. 'Isabel, I'm not going to hit you.'

She lifts her hand, he blocks it this time, her wrist bone jarring against his forearm. Angrily, she tries again, and again. Desperate to get a response.

That first time, he'd been drunk. A relapse – a bottle of Jack down, judgement and good sense out of the window. They didn't kiss, but it was close. And she'd punched him. Square on the jaw. An inept attempt, but enough to raise his hackles, for his muscles to tense automatically in response. She'd tried again and again, until he'd scrambled away, quickly leaving the flat. Logic prevailed just in the nick of time.

She's tried, many times since. Each time he's walked away.

Now, she strikes him again, but in her frustration it turns into kicking and punching, her nails scratching at his face. He grabs her wrists again, holds her firm. It's not hard to stop her, she's small, and after a while he feels her crumple.

'Isabel, I'm not going to hit you,' he repeats. 'I'm not going to sleep with you—'

'Fuck you!' she screams. 'Fuck you! Don't pretend to be this nice guy. I know what you are. You sad old man.'

'I can get you help—'

25

'Help? From you?' Her lip curls with disgust. 'How can you help? I've seen you. A washed-up junkie with no life!'

'You've been watching me?'

'Sometimes. I hang out in Dad's office. At night. A bottle to keep me company. I thought you … You could give me what I need.'

She says this coquettishly, trying to be sexy again.

'I need to be told, Griffin. I need to be punished.'

'Not by me.'

'You know you want to. Show me who's boss. Fuck me like you're the man in charge.'

But whatever she thinks she's doing, it's not working. Griffin's horrified.

'No.'

Her eyes turn dark again. 'I'll tell him. If you don't do what I want, I'll tell him.'

Griffin stays silent.

'I'll tell my dad that you hit me. That you forced me to have sex with you. He'll kick you out. You'll be homeless. That's if he doesn't call the police.'

In two long strides, Griffin's by the door. He holds it open. 'Get out.'

'I'm leaving. Just think about it. You know where I am. You might enjoy it.'

She slinks past him in her bra, her top in her hands. He shuts the door with a wave of repulsion. He may end up homeless or arrested. He may be an ex-addict, a failure. But nothing will make him do *that*.

Chapter 5

Colin Jefferies once had brown hair and blue eyes. He'd been slight, single, with a love for fantasy novels and classic black and white films. But all Cara can think, as she sits opposite his mother in their family liaison room, offering tea and tissues, is that everything that made him human has gone to waste. He's now scattered under the wheels of a train.

She keeps these thoughts to herself. His mother is small and crumpled, her body folded in as if grief has punched her in the stomach.

'You were saying?' Cara prompts. She glances to Brody, notepad in hand. Mrs Jefferies had been telling them about Colin's mental health issues before she'd dissolved into an avalanche of sobbing.

'It started when he was in his twenties. We suspected something wasn't right before that, but it got worse once his father died.' She sniffs wetly and wipes her eyes with the tissue. 'His dad collapsed, in the street. Nobody around. If he'd been at home with me, he might have been saved, the doctors said after. That's probably what started it.'

'Started what?' Cara asks.

'The agoraphobia. He refused to go out. At that time Colin was living by himself, in his flat, and I didn't twig for a while. Everything nowadays – you can get it delivered. And he could work from home, his boss didn't mind at the beginning. That was five years ago. But you have to go out sometimes, don't you?' Mrs Jefferies dabs at her nose, her reddened eyes searching Cara's for understanding, sympathy, anything. Cara's not sure she's giving it. Whether she's even able to.

Mrs Jefferies continues: 'His boss got grumpy. He wouldn't come in for team meetings, nights out. Made up excuses. Too proud, like his father, to tell the truth. And he got fired.'

'Colin never left the house?' Cara glances to Brody. 'Ever?'

'No. Never. That's what I can't work out. How he even got to the train station. He'd have a panic attack just thinking about it.'

Cara sits forward. 'We've received his medical records from his GP. Colin was on medication. For anxiety and panic disorder. Maybe he took some of those?'

But Mrs Jefferies is adamant. 'No. We tried that once. He couldn't get past the front door of his block of flats.'

'What if he was determined?' Brody interjects.

Mrs Jefferies' head snaps around to face her. 'Determined to kill himself, you mean? No. My Colin wouldn't have done that.'

'How can you be so sure?' Cara asks gently.

'He'd started talking to someone new. Said it was helping. New drugs. He was optimistic, when I spoke to him last. Almost happy. There was the prospect of a new job. He

28

could see a future for himself – and it'd been a while since he'd said that.'

She grabs Cara's hand; Cara starts. Mrs Jefferies' skin is hot and greasy, desperation pushing through the pores like sweat.

'You'll keep looking, won't you? The papers, they say he killed himself, but I know you wouldn't be asking me questions if that was the case. You're a murder detective, you think it's murder.'

'I'm investigating, Mrs Jefferies.' Cara extricates her hand. 'But tell me, if he was at the station to catch a train, where might he have been going?'

'I don't know,' she snaps. 'Isn't it your job to find out?'

Mrs Jefferies departs, leaving Cara and Brody standing in the corridor.

'A man with a fear of public places goes to a train station in the middle of rush hour?' Cara says. 'Even with my cynical hat on, it doesn't make sense. If he was trying to kill himself, he didn't need to go then. He must have known the platform would be packed.'

'Perhaps he was hoping someone would stop him?' Brody proposes as they walk to the incident room. 'Or he was genuinely trying to get somewhere.'

'But where?'

Back in the room, Cara pauses next to Shenton. 'Toby, pull up the footage from the station. Let's see if we can trace where our victim came from that morning.'

Brody and Cara sit either side of him at his desk. He pulls up the files – the CCTV from the platform, from the booking office, from the waiting room. The latter shows no more than a few bored businessmen, and the shots from the platform pull them to the fateful moment before he fell to his death, the actual leap missing. A vital omission.

'Take the footage back,' she instructs. 'How did he arrive? Did he buy a ticket?'

The booking office is busy. The cameras show him stumble through the packed foyer. He doesn't glance at the departures board; he doesn't stop at the ticket machines or the windows.

Shenton swaps views, to the outside of the station. He estimates the time of arrival, people walking backwards as Shenton rewinds. It's hard to see on the grainy screen, and Cara's frustrated.

'He must have got there somehow. He doesn't own a car.'

'Bus stop?' Brody suggests. 'Or changed from a connecting train?'

'Suicidal precursors often include swapping platforms or station hopping,' Shenton adds, but his attention is diverted. 'Here, here,' he says, pointing to his screen.

Silently they watch a car draw up. It's small, old. Blue. The passenger door opens and Colin stumbles to the kerb, as if pushed from the front seat. He looks dazed, wobbly. The car quickly departs.

Colin stands on the pavement, his eyes darting around, his hands fluttering.

'What does that look like to you?' Cara says.

'Confused. Scared.'

'Like the car dumped him and ran,' Brody suggests.

'Can we get a plate?'

Cara waits as Shenton scrolls the footage. 'Maybe a partial. We'll get the digital guys to work their magic.'

'Let's do that. And fast. I want to speak to that driver.'

30

Cara sits back in her seat. They have nothing that indicates Colin Jefferies was pushed. He had a history of mental health problems. It looks like a suicide.

But studying that footage, her skin had crawled. Every cell of her body, telling her that it's not.

Chapter 6

The train driver's hands tremble as he sits in front of DS Jamie Hoxton on the sofa. A large man, in his late fifties, whose thread veins on his nose and unkempt grey beard make him look much older. He's introduced himself – Stan – with hands of sandpaper; a life lived of hard work and toil.

'Do you take sugar? I'm sorry, I didn't ask,' the wife says as she places a cup of tea in Jamie's hands. 'I can get you some. Or biscuits? Would you like a Hobnob?'

'Susan,' Stan snaps, 'the man doesn't want a Hobnob.'

Susan reels, then scuttles away.

'I'm sorry,' Stan says wearily. 'She fusses.' He glances behind him to where loud crashing noises emerge from the kitchen. 'I'll pay for that later,' he mutters.

'It's good you have someone to take care of you,' Jamie says, with an understanding smile. 'And I'm sorry to make you relive this again. But if you could tell me what happened this morning?'

Stan nods slowly. 'It's my fourth. Did you know that? For my first one, over thirty years ago now, they didn't even give me the rest of the day off. "Get back on that horse," my boss said. Like it was nothing.' He picks up the mug of tea, but his hand quivers so much it slops over onto the carpet. He puts it down again quickly. 'Nowadays, it's all about counselling and welfare visits. I don't know what's worse.' He looks up to Jamie with watery eyes. 'That kid. He was young, right? The papers said he was young?'

'Early thirties,' Jamie confirms. 'Did you get much of a look at him?'

'Hardly at all. We were going at quite a lick. I'd slowed for the station, but I didn't even …' He looks up, taking Jamie in properly for the first time. 'You're not from the BTP. Why'd they send a detective?'

'We're exploring all possible angles—'

'You're not here for me, are you? Because I did nothing wrong. That kid—'

'I'm not here for you, Stan. You have my word.'

Stan meets Jamie's gaze, then sags again, the fight fading as quickly as it arrived.

'I didn't even have time to hit the brakes,' Stan continues. 'I didn't think … He wasn't even facing the right way and … and … That was it.' He spreads his hands out in front of him. 'Splat.' He attempts a chuckle, but the laugh turns into a sob and he puts his head in his hands, shoulders heaving.

Jamie gives what he hopes is a reassuring pat on his arm and waits. He thinks about the counselling this man will be offered, and wonders whether it'll provide the help he needs. Jamie doubts it.

The man's sobs fade and he wipes his eyes with fat, gnarled fingers. Jamie looks down to where he's been scribbling the man's account in his neat handwriting, and something niggles.

'Sorry,' Jamie says. 'You said he wasn't facing the right way. The right way for what?'

Stan looks up. 'To jump.' He clears his throat. 'You notice them normally. The ones that are going to do it. Some leap. Almost spring in front of the train. Others just sorta … tip. This guy. His back was to the rails.'

Jamie sits up straight. 'He was facing away from you?'

'That's right. Yeah.'

'Excuse me, I need to make a call.'

Jamie jumps up, pulling his phone out of his pocket. Cara answers on the first ring.

'Boss, I've got something strange here.' And Jamie tells her what Stan has told him.

'Backwards?' Cara parrots. 'Nobody jumps backwards.'

'Do you think he fell? Got too close to the edge, and slipped?' There's a long pause at the end of the line. 'What are you thinking, boss?' Jamie prompts.

'That there must be better footage of what happened this morning. That YouTube woman. Have we found her? Can you …' She stops. 'It's late, don't worry.'

Jamie glances at his watch. Five past eight. 'It's fine. What do you need?'

'Can you follow up on our witness appeal? See if she's called in?'

'No problem.'

'And Jamie, how are you—'

But he hangs up. Never a good idea to cut off your boss, but he knows what she was going to ask. *How are you doing? Are you okay?*

Questions he doesn't like to answer.

Jamie finishes up with Stan, says his thank yous to the wife, then heads home. He makes calls on the hands free,

34

eventually speaking to someone on 111 who confirms that they've had a few people get in touch. Even one with mobile phone footage. And yes, it's all on the server.

Jamie lets himself into the house, picks up the letters on the mat, throws his keys on the table, and loads up his laptop. While he waits, he flicks through the post. All addressed to Dr Romilly Cole or Mr A Bishop – nothing for him. Seeing those names makes him wish they were here. Friends he could talk to. About the case. About anything. But instead, he's alone, in a house that doesn't belong to him. Night after night, listening to cars pass on the road, to the sound of his own exhausted breathing.

He doesn't mind working. Cara tries her hardest, she doesn't want cases to bleed into their free time, but he doesn't mind. What else would he be doing? Drinking a few beers and watching football until he falls asleep on the sofa? Only to wake at two in the morning, freezing cold with a dry mouth and a head full of *her*?

This way he's doing something useful.

The laptop has sprung into life and he clicks on folders, trying to find the right case number. Eventually, he finds them: hastily typed witness accounts, infused with hyperbole. He scans them quickly; nothing new. People searching for their five minutes of fame, desperate to recount how they were close to *that* guy who died on the tracks.

He moves on and clicks on the .MOV file and a video loads. This is it: a girl, front and centre, with shiny painted lips and bright, cartoonish eyes, animatedly talking about where she's going. 'A train to London, it's soooooo early.' The word is annoyingly elongated, her excitement jarring. He mutes the video, trying to ignore her.

And then, there he is. As the desk clerk described, Colin

35

Jefferies is agitated, panicked. Behind the self-absorbed girl, their victim rakes his hands through his hair then wraps his arms tightly around his body. He turns, twirls, flinches at the people gathering around. Some jostle him, nudges and shoves, the platform packed. Jamie watches the crowd move together, backwards from the yellow line, and he puts the sound back on, listening to the repetitive announcement of the non-stop cargo train on the overhead speaker. But Colin doesn't hear it; doesn't notice.

The next few events happen so quickly Jamie has to rewind. For a fraction of a second, Colin looks right into the camera. But his eyes are glassy, his focus split with terror and confusion. He takes a step back – as the blur of the freight train races into the station.

Jamie winces, although there's nothing graphic in shot. That was limited to the front of the train, the wheels, the rails. The onlookers react slowly. Exclamations of horror, sharp screams, hands over their mouths in shock. The film distorts as the phone is moved in quick jerks, then the video ends.

For a moment, Jamie stares at the dead screen. Colin Jefferies hadn't meant to die; he hadn't jumped. This proves it. He had fallen.

Kate

A body without a brain is no more than a shell. A receptacle; no soul. No rational thought, no emotion, no love. Nothing that makes them human.

Kate considers these thoughts as she stands in the doorway of her mother's bedroom. As she watches her sleep, a gentle wheeze with each rise and fall. She does this more since the dosage increased. Keep an eye out for bed sores, the nurse said. Keep her warm and dry. Bathe her regularly.

Easy for them to say.

They're not surviving on three hours' sleep a night, interrupted constantly by her mother waking, confused. Calling her dead husband's name, or that of her own mother. Taking hours to soothe her back into slumber.

They're not carefully counting the pennies. Living off benefits, unable to work. Buying from the yellow-striped shelves. Dropping meals, in an attempt to keep this draughty place warm.

And they're not worrying about their own health. Their own descent into oblivion.

She thought the nurse was coming today. Monday

afternoon, same as it always is. But nobody showed, and when she phoned the nurse said, 'No, Kate. You emailed me. You changed it to Wednesday.'

Kate blustered, apologised. She couldn't remember doing such a thing. She tried to log on, password not recognised. Had she forgotten that too? She didn't have the energy to reset it. The nurse must be correct. Surely?

She called the doctor again last week. Was put on hold for an hour before she gave up. The NHS is overstretched, she'd seen that first-hand when she asked for help with her mother. *Waiting lists, no beds available. No home help, we're sorry.*

And what use would a doctor's appointment be, anyway? She knows what's going on, despite what the tests said, what the scans showed. She doesn't need that tired GP looking over his glasses at her. Thinking she's yet another hysterical woman.

She knows.

Her mother has Kate to rely on. For ten years now, she's been looking after her, day and night. Kate lost her job. She never goes out. What sort of a life is this?

Earlier, she'd risked the trip to Tesco. Second time in two days – the first, yesterday, walking miles home, shopping bags cutting into her hands as she trailed in the pouring rain. She'd stood in the hallway as water dripped from her coat, from her hair, forming a puddle on the mat. Her boots were sodden and cold, her shoulders and collar wet from where the rain had seeped under the hood.

And she'd felt nothing but despair. An aching sadness that sucked at her soul, making her so exhausted she could hardly move.

The car's gone. Lost, yesterday. She could have sworn

she'd left it to the right of the entrance. Two down, like she always does. But when she'd arrived back, pushing her trolley, there was nothing there. She'd scanned the row. She'd taken her keys out of her pocket and pressed the button, looking for the orange flash, but nothing.

She'd started walking. Annoyed circles at first, evolving into a panicked stomp, up and down the lines of parked cars, an anxious sweat prickling under her arms.

'You okay, love?' an older gentleman had asked. Bent over with age, liver spots freckling his skull. A gentle concern that made her want to cry with frustration.

'I can't find my car,' she'd replied.

He'd chuckled. 'I do that all the time.' He tapped one finger against the side of his forehead. 'Sign of old age. But you're a bit young for that, love.'

With a final friendly smile, he'd left her, frozen, his words drilling into her brain.

You're a bit young for that.

She thinks upon that now. Her mother wasn't too young. Her mother, upstairs, drugged, sleeping, rotting away in that bed. Runs in the family, doesn't it? And the lost car, the postponed appointment, the forgotten password – they aren't the only things Kate has noticed.

Walking into a room and forgetting why she's there. Misremembering names, dates. Birthdays that used to be ingrained in her memory, now lost, in a fog of incomprehension. Things going missing. Keys. Her wallet. Found again in the most ridiculous of places. She'd forgotten to order new prescriptions for her mum, couldn't remember if she'd administered her drugs that morning or not. Small, inconsequential moments, but added together, something.

He was right. Her friend, the only one who listens. He

said this would happen. It's come for her, too.

This afternoon, she'd given up. Again, she'd paced the rows, to no avail, then walked home. An embarrassed phone call followed, to the police, reporting it as stolen. Maybe.

'Maybe?' the woman at the end of 101 had said. 'Has it been nicked or not?'

'I can't find it,' Kate confessed, her voice withering into a whisper.

The details were taken, despite the scepticism at the other end of the line. And now, dully, she thinks about dinner. She opens the fridge – and there are the keys to the back door. Lost a week ago.

Kate knows why.

The gradual creep; her brain rotting. How long will it take? Before she forgets to wash, to eat, to turn off the gas. Before she can't follow simple instructions. Before her life becomes a fog. The shell.

She has no one to look after her. Nowhere to go. She'll die, decaying slowly, in a care home. Fed porridge, with bed sores. Lying in her own stench and faeces – and that's if she's lucky.

No.

She wants control of her life. What's left of it.

Their house is in the middle of nowhere. An old cottage, part of what used to be a farm. She knows what she needs to do.

She pushes her feet into wellingtons and trudges across the farmyard, dodging the puddles left after yesterday's downpour. She opens the door to the barn, unlocks the safe on the back wall. She pulls it out, the weight solid and calming – and the small box alongside.

She leaves it on the kitchen table while she goes upstairs.

While she's been gone, her mother has soiled herself. But not just that. She's pushed her hands into her clothes, gathered a handful and thrown it across the room. Shit streaks the far wall, smears across the bed, her clothes, her skin. The whole room stinks.

Kate gags, but it's nothing new. They do this, apparently. At the end. Losing control of what makes them civilised. Human.

Her mother is sleeping again, worn out by her rebellion. Kate fetches disinfectant, warm water, cloths. And slowly, methodically, she cleans the room. Wipes her mother's skin, arid paper over sinew. Gently dabs her dry. Lifts her old bones, changes the bed, dresses her. She puts the soiled clothes and sheets in a bin bag. Makes sure her mother is warm. It doesn't matter now, but she won't have people saying she wasn't a good daughter.

She regards her mother's face. She brought Kate into the world, but now, she doesn't even know who her daughter is. A devastating blow with each misnomer.

Reports will be sympathetic, maybe even understanding, when they hear. *She coped so admirably, but it was too much. In the end.*

Kate picks up a pillow, slips on a clean white cotton pillowcase, then takes a step closer to the bed.

She doesn't think, doesn't dwell. She doesn't feel anything. Not regret, not sorrow. Nothing but a sense of inevitability. This is what was always going to happen.

Kate tenderly tucks her mother into bed, her arms folded across her chest, her eyes closed. She pushes a tendril of silver hair away from her forehead, kisses her lightly on her cheek.

She takes one last look, then leaves the room, closing the

door with a quiet click.

She goes back to the kitchen. She looks at the parcel, brought in from the shed, and unwraps the swathe of material from around it. A shotgun. Double-barrelled, break-action, side by side, twelve gauge, right-handed. A wooden butt, needing a varnish, followed by a sleek black barrel. Old, but should be working fine. She picks it up. It's heavy. Reassuring.

She loads it, as her father showed her how, all those years ago. Two cartridges, although she only needs one. It's bigger than she remembered.

She carries it into the living room and sits in her old armchair. The same one she always chooses, a groove worn into the cushion from repeated wear. She places the butt of the gun on the carpet, holding the barrel in one hand, then removes the sock from her right foot.

She disengages the safety.

The gun rests between her legs. The cold of the metal presses against her skin as she places the barrel in her mouth. Being so close to the gun conjures a distinctive smell. Winter shoots on the farm as a child. Her father in a waxed Barbour jacket, wrapping his arms around her in the cold. An old black Labrador gundog called Bessie. She holds the memory as she lifts her foot and rests her toe against the trigger guard. Her leg shakes. Last chance. Last opportunity to change your mind, Kate.

But for what?

Soon, Kate will be no more than a shell. No soul. No love. Nothing that makes her human.

DAY 2
TUESDAY

Chapter 7

Griffin's woken by a hammering. A fist, thumped repeatedly against metal. His door. His stomach sinks.

'Okay, okay,' he shouts as the banging continues. 'I'm coming.'

He pulls on a T-shirt and a pair of jeans, then steels himself for the inevitable. The eviction and dismissal from this shitty job, maybe even an arrest – whatever Isabel has set into motion.

He opens the door. Sure enough, it's Ron. But the look on the garage owner's face isn't what he expects. Not anger or hatred. It's tears. Desperation.

'Griffin. You need to come. It's …' He trails off, his voice breaking into wracking sobs. Griffin doubles back into the flat, pulling boots over his bare feet.

'What's happened?'

'It's Issy. She …' Ron straightens up, looking at Griffin with bloodshot eyes. 'You were a cop. You can tell them.'

'Tell who what?'

But Ron's gone. Racing up the stairs to the garage forecourt, the door slamming against the wall as he pushes through.

Griffin emerges into chaos. Blinking in the sudden daylight, he pauses, gathering his bearings. Blue lights flash – from a police car, from an ambulance. Fluorescent yellow and black uniforms merge with the green of the paramedics. A boundary has been set up around the Portakabin of the second-hand garage; the door is open, more uniforms inside.

Ron grabs his arm and drags him to the nearest policeman.

'This is Detective Sergeant Nate Griffin,' Ron pants. 'He'll tell you. He knew Isabel.'

Knew? Past tense. Griffin glances over to the Portakabin, the dread intensifying.

'What's going on?' Griffin asks. 'PC …?'

'Tweedie, sarge.'

'Tweedie, please give me a summary?'

Griffin's not been an active police officer for near two years, but he keeps that to himself. The uniform escorts him across, Ron following.

'We had a 999 call at half seven this morning,' the uniform explains. 'Mr Warner here. I'm sorry to say he'd discovered the body of his daughter, Isabel, in the office of these premises. The paramedics were first on scene but there was nothing they could do.'

'What's your initial assessment of cause of death?'

'All signs point to an overdose. I'm sorry, sarge. We believe she took her own life.'

'She didn't!' Ron shouts from behind them. 'Tell them, Griffin. She wouldn't!'

Griffin looks back at Ron and nods. 'Can I take a look?' he asks the officer.

'Be my guest. It would be good to get your expert opinion.'

Griffin's not sure whether the PC is being sarcastic, but he dons shoe covers and gloves anyway, and climbs the two metal steps into the cabin.

He's been in here before, with Ron, over the years. Paperwork on every surface, discarded newspapers, coffee cups growing mould. A large desk is on the far side, where Ron completes documentation with whatever poor sod is about to buy one of his doozies.

The mess is normal. But the body ...

She's lying on the sofa. Sprawled on her back on the worn brown fabric, her eyes staring glassily upwards. The same jeans as when he last saw her, the same crop top. Skin pale, hair lank and dishevelled.

Griffin knew Issy came here at night. He'd notice the light go on, hear the giggling, the whispers, the clink of bottles in a plastic bag as she unlocked the door. He'd done his job – mentioned it to Ron, who'd given an indulgent smile.

'At least if she's there,' he'd said, 'I know where she is. Better that than drinking in a park.'

There was nothing valuable kept in the Portakabin – no money or keys, they all went home with Ron – so if he didn't mind, Griffin had no objections. But he always kept an eye out. Made sure the music didn't get too loud. He knew she took men back there – but she was nineteen. Not his problem.

Except now, it is.

Isabel looks undisturbed. The body hasn't been moved to the floor; there is none of the medical detritus he would usually see around a victim when paramedics attempt resuscitation. He can see why they haven't tried.

All of the usual signs to verify death are present. Her mouth is open, her lips blue. A line of white-yellow vomit

45

makes its way from her head to the floor. He touches the body. Cold. Stiff. Griffin can clearly see the pink pooling underneath the skin on her back – the hypostasis of blood settling to the lowest points. All together it tells Griffin she's been dead over eight hours. No coming back from that.

And as for cause? He glances around. Takes in the empty bottle of vodka, the popped blister packs of pills around her. He picks up a few – amitriptyline, tramadol, diazepam. Xylazine, ketamine, Ritalin. Some prescribed, some not, Griffin assumes. He leans forward, as close as he can bear – there are small flecks of white in the vomit. Half-digested drugs.

She was tiny, no more than eight stone dripping wet. This lot would have finished her off nicely, assuming she hadn't choked on her own puke.

'What do you think, sarge?' the PC says from the doorway.

'G28. Category two,' Griffin says. A violent or unnatural death, but not involving a suspected offence. 'Hard to say whether it was suicide. Have you found a note?' Tweedie shakes his head. 'Her phone?'

The PC ducks outside, then returns clutching an iPhone in an evidence bag. He passes it to Griffin; it demands an access code. One he doesn't have.

'Get this to digital. See if they can recover the data.'

'For a cat two?'

'The coroner's going to want to know. Kids do everything on their phones nowadays. Perhaps even leave suicide notes.'

Tweedie nods and backs away. Griffin stays a moment longer, looking down at Isabel, feeling the heavy pull of failure and regret he's so used to. In life, she was a ball of energy, so much future ahead of her. And in a second, it's gone.

46

He wipes his eyes, vision distorted, and turns away.

Ron grabs him the moment he emerges from the Portakabin.

'What do you think? It's not suicide, is it? She wouldn't,' he repeats.

Griffin doesn't know what to say. He's experienced first-hand how fucked up Isabel could be. He'd known about her issues. She'd threatened many things, but never suicide.

'Why are you so sure?' he asks.

'She ... she said ...' Ron rubs a hand down his face. 'She'd signed up for college. A diploma in counselling.' He smiles with misplaced pride – it fades as soon as it arrives. 'She was excited ... She wouldn't have ...'

'Isabel had ... problems,' Griffin says, choosing his words carefully.

'You need to find who did this to her,' Ron pleads.

'There's nothing that indicates anyone else was here last night.'

'But someone sold her the pills. The alcohol. You can find them.'

'I'm not a serving police officer—'

'You were. You know what you're doing, Griffin. Please.'

Griffin pauses. Cara's words from yesterday linger. He could. It wouldn't take much to investigate this case. Check CCTV. Get into that phone. Follow up on cause of death. It might give Ron some peace – and put his mind at rest too.

But that's not him any more. He's not a detective – he's a security guard, an ex-addict. His life is quiet, dull. Exactly what he wants. It's better like this.

He turns his back to Ron, ignores his protestations, and walks away. Across the car lot, down the stairs to his flat, where he closes the door firmly behind him. He kicks his boots off and slumps on the bed, disturbing the cat and pushing his head hard against the pillow to block out the noise of the radios, the chatter, the blue flashing lights.

He left that life behind. And nothing, not even a dead nineteen-year-old girl, will drag him back.

Chapter 8

Cara wakes early. Sleep is impossible, has been for a while. She wants peace and quiet. Forgiveness, maybe even retribution. Failing that – a few hours of oblivion. But it all eludes her. As soon as darkness falls, her thoughts whir. Clues overlooked; the ache in the pit of her stomach where the memories of the people she failed reside.

She got a few hours, maybe three. She gives up and climbs out of bed, wandering the house aimlessly with a cup of coffee as the heating clicks on.

With the kids absent, the house is quiet. She pauses in the doorway of Tilly's bedroom. She takes in the empty picture hooks, the cardboard boxes, ready to go. She wonders what the next owners will do with the colourful animal frieze on the wall. Paint over it, probably. She hopes the new people coming in will be a family who will love it. Too many happy memories, dashed into nothing.

She turns back into the hallway, closes the door behind her with a quiet click. Outside, the world is slowly coming to life, a glow of orange and amber on the horizon. She sips at the dregs of her now cold coffee, watching the nurse next door go to work, a heavy coat over her crisp blue tunic; squares of light pop on as the house across the road wakes up for the day. She's contemplating a shower, when something catches her eye. Or is it a someone? A shadow, moving quickly, ducking out of the way. Hiding? From her? She focuses now, all her senses on alert, her eyes scanning the street. But whatever it was, it has gone.

She laughs to herself. Foolish, getting het up over nothing. A fox or a cat, no doubt – this case going to her head already. The sooner she gets to the bottom of this suicide, the better, if this is how she's going to react.

She has a shower, washes her hair. Gets dressed; hair blow dried; smart. Battle armour, for whatever the world throws at her today. The bell rings as she's putting the last dab of mascara on.

She heads downstairs.

She knows who it is before she opens the door, catching a glimpse of his car through the window – the ostentatious red Mercedes she always hated. She pulls the latch across, a sigh resting in her lungs.

'Hello Roo.'

'Cara.' Her husband – soon to be ex – pauses, waiting. 'Are you going to let me in?'

She takes a step backwards; he walks into the hallway, taking his coat off.

'You can't stay long,' she counters. 'I was just leaving.'

'We need to talk. You've been ignoring my calls.'

'What's there to talk about?' She glances up at the clock. 'Where are the kids?'

'Sarah's taking them to school.'

'I'm not sure I'm comfortable with that.'

'Why, Cara? Because it's Sarah?'

50

Cara doesn't reply, pulls a face. Sarah – Roo's girlfriend of six months – only has to exist to annoy her. *Girlfriend* is the operative word – can't be older than late twenties. She should have expected it. Roo may be forty-three, but he's looking good. The grey at his temples suits him. The unfairness of societal expectation on the ageing genders grates. That Roo is considered a catch when Cara is over the hill.

Roo sighs and walks past her to the kitchen, taking a mug out of the cupboard and switching the Nespresso machine on. He puts a capsule into the machine. It whirs and gurgles. She waits, irritated by him making himself at home in a house he discarded eighteen months previously.

Coffee made, he turns to face her again. 'I see the For Sale sign is up.'

'That's what you wanted.'

'You know neither of us can afford this place alone.'

'Not on your shit chef's salary, no.'

It's a petty dig. Roo doesn't react.

'Has there been any interest?'

'Some. I'll call if we get an offer.'

The conversation is pinched and abrupt, deliberate on Cara's part.

'Have you found somewhere?'

'Nice of you to be so concerned about my well-being, Andrew.'

'I'm worried about the kids,' he continues, ignoring her sarcasm. 'They're going to need somewhere to go.' He takes a chair at the bare dining table, the table that hasn't been used to eat at since the kids left. 'Sit down.'

She stays standing. 'Sit down, Cara,' he directs.

51

She scowls, but does as she's told.

'They've been asking when they're going to see you. We always said we'd share custody, that we could be civil for Josh and Tilly, but you haven't seen them for weeks.'

Cara feels the familiar burn of guilt. 'I've been busy.'

'You've been avoiding them.' His face softens. 'Cara, you need to do something. See someone. You look like shit.'

She doesn't even bother stirring up indignation. 'I haven't been sleeping.'

'So get some help. For your kids' sake, if nothing else.' He pauses. 'They miss you.' He leans forward, placing a hand over hers. 'I miss you.'

She stares at it for a moment. How easy it would be to take him back. To fit snugly into the roles they had assumed when they were happily married. But how happy had it been? Roo had cheated on her, with more than one woman. Cara had been buried in work, spending all hours at the nick. And then everything that happened – with the Echo Man. Hard to call it water under the bridge when it had been fast-flowing rapids of blood.

She pulls her hand away. 'We've been over this, Roo. And you have Sarah.'

'I do.' He takes his hand back, wrapping it around his mug and drinking the last of it with one final swig.

'This weekend, please? You said yourself work had been quiet—'

'I've got a new case—'

'These are your children, Cara,' he says, bitterness creeping into his voice. 'Bollocks to your new case.'

And with that he stands up and sweeps out of the room, the front door slamming behind him. She waits for the rev of his engine, then slumps as it fades into the distance.

As much as her husband annoys her, he's right. And that's the worst feeling of all.

Heads turn as Cara arrives in the incident room. She almost walks straight out again at the sight of their eager faces – the responsibility, the burden to get things sorted almost too much to bear – but needs must. A man is dead.

'Mrs Jefferies called,' Shenton says, standing in the doorway to her office before she's even sat down at her desk. 'She found the spare keys to her son's flat so we can take a look. She's going to meet us there.'

Cara sighs. 'Let me guess. She's been in already.'

'No. I told her to stay away. That if she wants us to treat her son's death as suspicious then she has to respect the crime scene.'

'That's something.' Cara looks through the open door to her paltry team of detectives. Jamie Hoxton has arrived and is taking his coat off; Alana Brody is hard at work already, face craned forward, staring at her computer screen. And Toby Shenton? He's paused, waiting in her doorway, his strange light blue eyes locked on her.

'Get me some coffee, then we'll talk,' Cara concludes.

She logs in to her computer, runs her eyes down the emails she's received overnight. Nothing of interest, bar for one from Charlie Mills with the subject: *Number Plate*.

She clicks on it; it's short. *We have it. Come down when you're free. C.*

Cara remembers Charlie from a few years ago. Not your average head of digital services, although she wonders why he's working on something so trivial as image enhancement when he has a team to do it for him.

She goes out to the incident room and the detectives swivel their chairs to face her. She perches on the edge of a desk, next to their whiteboard. It's covered with black scrawling from an old assault, and with a few defiant gestures she wipes it clean.

Fresh case. Fresh start.

'If Halstead wants us to investigate,' she begins. 'Then that's what we'll do.' She writes *Colin Jefferies* on the board with a flowing script, then hands the pen to Shenton. 'Our Southampton train victim. Suicide, accident or a suspected offence, that's the question. And one I want us to find the answer to, fast. Views, please. Brody?'

'Accident,' she says, decisively. 'I watched the footage Jamie found. Looks clear to me.'

'Do we have anything new on that front?'

'No more witnesses,' Brody confirms. 'No more footage – CCTV or otherwise. And I spoke to his GP first thing. He was cagey. Said that yes, he was seeing Colin for agoraphobia and anxiety, among other things. And no, he hadn't noticed any warning signs for suicide.'

'What about this new person he was talking to? Therapist?'

'Not via the NHS. If he was seeing someone it was private.'

'So if we're all agreed it was an accident' – she scans her detectives' faces, nods, no dissent – 'then the big questions are why was an agoraphobic at a station in rush hour and how did he get there?' Cara diverts her attention to Jamie Hoxton before anyone answers. 'Jamie – the mother is meeting us at Jefferies' flat with the keys. Head down there. See what you can find.'

Jamie nods.

'Shenton, keep going with the CCTV – track his movements from his flat to the station. I've had a message this morning from digital, I'll head down there next. Hopefully we'll have a number plate and an ID for whoever dropped him off.'

Shenton nods, but his attention is diverted as a figure appears at the back of the room. Jamie looks confused, Brody eager. Shenton jiggles in his chair with excitement.

Cara can't help but smile.

'Nice of you to join us. Team, meet Griffin. My brother, and former detective from this department. Or are you here to tell me otherwise?'

Griffin gives a reluctant shrug. 'Current detective sergeant, if that's all right by you?'

'Couldn't be happier,' Cara replies. And she's surprised to realise that's the truth.

Chapter 9

'You could have at least brushed your hair,' Cara remarks to Griffin as the team head off on their assigned tasks.

He runs his hand through it. It doesn't help. 'I washed it. And I shaved.'

'Good enough.' She smiles. 'You're here to help?'

'Frank thought it would be a good idea.'

It takes Cara a moment: he means the cat. An attempt at humour; he looks sheepish and her enthusiasm fades. She should have known better. 'What have you got yourself into this time?'

'A category two. Isabel Warner.'

'I thought you were here to reduce our workload, not add to it.'

'It won't take me long. Drug overdose. I need to be sure.'

Cara purses her lips. 'And why is a DS involved with that?'

'I knew her.'

'Right.'

'Don't give me that look.'

'What look? The look that asks, "How well did you

56

know her?" Or the raised eyebrow that says, "Did you sleep with her?"'

Griffin stays silent. 'Yes, then,' she says.

'No, for what it's worth. But Cara … She's Ron's daughter.'

'Ron – your boss? Who owns your flat?' Griffin nods. 'You're personally involved, Griffin. You can't be investigating her death.'

'I owe it to him. I owe it to her.'

His voice is pleading. Almost desperate.

She's too weary to argue.

'Okay, okay.' She steps backwards, accepting her fate. 'Keep me updated. I need to go to digital.'

At that, Griffin's eyes light up. 'Could you take something down for me?' He pulls a rose gold iPhone in an evidence bag out of his pocket. 'Isabel's mobile. I need to know if there is any evidence of suicidal ideation.'

'They're going to want a case number.'

'Give them yours. Please?'

She sighs. 'Fine. Just don't cause any trouble while I'm gone.'

'Would I?'

Cara doesn't dignify the comment with a response and leaves him to settle in. The digital department is in the bowels of the building, down five flights of stairs and an unlit corridor to the far door at the end.

She rings the buzzer. After a moment the door is opened. A man peers out, glasses resting on the end of his nose, posture stooped. He peers inquisitively at her, silent.

'DCI Elliott to see Charlie Mills?'

'A DCI?' the man says. He looks almost scared; Cara's not sure whether it's her rank or her gender that's causing the problem.

Luckily, the door is pulled open and Charlie stands there. 'Thanks, John. I can help DCI Elliott from here.'

John grunts and retreats to the sanctuary of his workstation while Cara stares at Mills. Slightly curly brown hair, the right side of tousled. Kind, dark brown eyes behind his glasses, that crinkle at the edges when he smiles, as he is doing now. He holds out his arm and gestures her inside.

Suspicious faces look up as they pass, the bright light from the computers reflected in their thick glasses. Cara knows why Griffin was pleased to avoid them – techies are at the opposite end of the spectrum to his act-first, think-later ideology. These guys don't speak without giving every option a full risk assessment, including ranking and percentage distribution.

Charlie shows her inside the glass-panelled office. He gestures to the seat next to his. 'Tea? Coffee?'

'I'm good.' Cara sits down. She recognises the footage on the screen – the CCTV taken outside the station. 'I'm surprised you're working on this. I assumed your time would be taken up with reports and budgets.'

'It usually is. I like to keep my hand in.' He clicks on the file and it plays – the car driving into the station, Colin being pushed out, then it heading away.

'Did you have any luck?'

'It wasn't a simple one. As I'm sure you know, it's not a question of zooming into an image. If the pixels aren't visible, they're just not there.'

'But you have something?'

'Would I have called you down here if I hadn't?' He grins. 'And I'm surprised you came yourself. I would have thought you'd be busy with reports and budgets.'

He waits. He's got her there. But she's damned if she's

58

going to admit that she likes the distraction of a handsome man. 'I like to keep my hand in,' she replies, echoing his words with a smile, then running her hand through her hair.

He chortles. 'Fair enough. And it's a fairly simple process. We take multiple frames that contain the licence plate from the video and run these through a machine learning system. This identifies a shortlist of plate numbers that could potentially match all the frames.' Cara doesn't understand all the technicalities, but her brain can make the next leap.

'Then you compare those to the same make of car pictured …' She cranes forward at the screen. 'Which is?'

'A late nineties Renault Clio,' Charlie answers. He notices her surprise and laughs. 'I can't take the credit for that one. I spoke to my guy at the Transport Research lab in Wokingham and he took ten seconds to identify it. So …'

Charlie clicks a few more buttons and two full number plates appear on the screen. 'These are the only two blue Renault Clios on the road matching that description. And this second one was just north of Birmingham at the time. Caught on the M6 toll.'

'That's brilliant.' Cara beams at him, thrilled. They have a car. And with a jolt she realises that she's flirting. *Pull yourself together, woman,* she tells herself. *You're a forty-one-year-old Detective Chief Inspector and you have a case to solve.*

'Don't get excited,' he replies, reading her mind. Her cheeks flush, compounding her embarrassment. 'The downside is I've already run this final plate through the system. And it's been reported stolen.'

'When?'

'Yesterday. I'll send you the details now.'

Cara stands up. 'Thank you. Seriously, Charlie. Thank

you. For moving so quickly.' Then she remembers the iPhone in her pocket and passes it to him. 'And sorry. Another one. Griffin asked me to give you this.'

'Griffin's back?' Charlie asks, taking the phone. He presses the screen through the evidence bag and it springs into life. 'No unlock code?'

'No, sorry. And yes. For my sins.'

'We need more coppers like Griffin.' He taps again on the screen. 'No worries. We have ways of getting these guys to talk.' Cara giggles, then catches herself, clearing her throat awkwardly and backing out of his office, jarring her hip on the doorframe in the process.

'Shall I email Griffin the results?' Charlie asks.

'Yes, do.' She starts to close the door, but can't help one last look back at him. He's staring after her, his smile broad, enjoying watching her leave. 'You could have just emailed me, you know?' Cara says.

'But where's the fun in that?' he replies.

Feeling her face graduating from pink to beetroot, Cara turns swiftly and marches through the department, focusing on a dignified retreat without falling over any of the trailing cables or abandoned equipment. But even as she's well out of eyeshot and climbing the stairs back to her office she feels a warm glow. Rare, inconvenient – but nicer than anything she's experienced in a while.

Chapter 10

Shenton is glad to see him, at least. The infamous Jamie Hoxton disappeared out of the door before Griffin had a chance to say hello, and while Alana Brody is initially friendly, she went straight back to work.

Still. He's not here to make friends. He's here to find out what happened to Isabel.

It hadn't taken long for his resolution to waver. Lying in the semi-darkness on his cold bed, emotions of regret and failure whirred in his head.

He'd been right there – barely fifty metres away when she died. And he had done nothing. He'd wanted to keep away from her after their altercation the night before so he hadn't even patrolled the lot, as he sometimes would. What if he'd gone after her? What if he'd persuaded her to get the help she so desperately needed. Would she still be alive?

His cat regarded him silently. Then he got to his feet, tail in the air, showing Griffin his bumhole as he nimbly jumped to the floor, then up on the kitchen counters and through the open window.

Frank's opinion echoed his own.

The least he could do was look into it. The least he could do was go back to work. And be a police officer again.

Now, Shenton directs him to the desk next to his, and Griffin logs on, happy to discover that his old username and password still work – the IT department as inefficient as ever. His email box is full of crap about car park spaces and canteen price changes, and he does a quick Ctrl-A-delete, then clicks onto the network.

As the reluctant head of security for the garage, he's already logged into the CCTV system and uploaded the footage from last night to the police system. He didn't want to look at it with Ron hovering; there was no guarantee Ron wouldn't notice Isabel going down to his flat earlier that day, and what state of undress she'd emerge in. Enough for him to ask questions, that's for sure.

Griffin clicks on the first file. It's the view from outside the Portakabin – looking across the car lot. He glances at the timestamp: 20:19. Six hours after Isabel had been to visit him. He scrolls through. Not a lot happens. The forecourt remains in darkness; a few people walk by. And then, two minutes after eleven, Isabel appears. She's wearing the same jeans and top as earlier, her arms twisted across her chest in the cold. She's holding a plastic bag in one hand; it looks heavy. Griffin guesses with alcohol.

She glances around, and her gaze rests on his basement window. At that time it would have been dark behind the glass. He hadn't been asleep, but staring into the black, lost in his own contemplations. She lingers for a moment, then pulls a key out of her pocket and pushes into the Portakabin. Lights switch on. Nobody else appears. Nobody leaves.

Griffin fast-forwards. A slow creeping dawn throws a grey light across the lot. Ron arrives – about to discover the

62

terrible fate of his only child. Griffin freezes as Ron goes inside. He emerges mere moments later, his mouth open, screaming for help.

It seems there was nobody with Isabel when she died. But the next video would show that for sure.

The inside of the Portakabin.

He selects the correct file and moves the footage to the time of Isabel's arrival. She steps into the Portakabin, turns on the lights. Takes the bottles out of the carrier bag and rests them on the desk. She doesn't hesitate to pour a large measure into a glass, swallowing it without hesitation. Then another.

She stops. She looks as though she's crying and Griffin's heart wrenches. She was a nice kid. At nineteen she should have been at university or starting a new career – having the time of her life. Instead, she was drinking alone in a cold Portakabin. Going to see Griffin. Demanding sex, and who knows what.

The video continues to play. Griffin forces himself to watch as she takes a few small boxes out of the carrier bag. She lines them up on the desk and stares at them.

'What's she doing?'

The voice comes from behind him. Brody, peering over his shoulder.

'Drinking,' he replies. He suppresses the urge to cover the screen; she is his new colleague, and may be able to offer some insight. 'And about to kill herself.'

'Poor girl,' Brody murmurs.

She sits down next to him, leaning forward towards the monitor. As they watch, Isabel methodically takes the pills from the blister packs, making a small pile. Then she sweeps them into her hand and into her mouth, washing them down with the vodka, straight from the bottle.

She gags, but clamps her lips shut and swallows again, wincing. She repeats the procedure with the other packets.

Griffin reads from his notebook. 'Amitriptyline, tramadol, diazepam, xylazine, ketamine, Ritalin. I found the boxes at the scene.'

Brody frowns. 'Xylazine and ketamine bought off the street, nicked from a vet's?' Griffin nods in agreement. 'The tramadol and diazepam might have been hers. Looks cut and dried to me. What makes you think otherwise?'

'Nothing yet,' Griffin admits. 'But I'm wondering whether she was coerced. I'm waiting for digital to come back on her phone.'

'You'll be waiting a while then. Unless you can get the boss to work her magic. Only Elliott can get next day delivery.' She raises her eyebrows, then realises who she's speaking to and colours. 'Sorry,' she mutters.

But Griffin dismisses it. 'Here she's my boss. And as much of a pain in my arse as she is in yours. Possibly more.'

The video's still playing. Isabel's movements are slowing. She lies down on the sofa, everything laboured. Even with the quality of the video they can see her movements slow, her eyelids droop. They're watching her die.

'It never gets easier,' Brody says, her voice catching. He risks a look at her. Her face is scrunched up, blinking back tears. 'Watching this stuff.'

'Textbook female suicide,' a voice says from behind them. Shenton's hovering, a few dirty mugs in his hand. 'Women typically have higher rates of suicidal ideation and behaviour than men, but their mortality is lower. It's thought that men structure their suicidal act in such a way that means they are less likely to survive, while women default to less lethal means, such as poisons.' He points to the screen. 'Or overdose.'

'Shenton, do you want something?' Griffin snaps.

Shenton flinches. 'Coffee?'

'No. Thank you,' Griffin replies, as Brody shakes her head.

Shenton shuffles off to the kitchen.

'He hasn't changed then?' Griffin asks.

'He was always that weird?' But she waves the question away. 'Who am I to talk?'

Griffin takes in her black hair and undercut, the line of piercings marching up her ear, and guesses Brody's had her share of unfair judgements in her time.

Griffin sits quietly, staring at the screen and the now dead girl. 'I was less than a hundred metres away from her,' he says, quietly.

Brody regards him for a moment. 'You weren't to know. We can't save everyone.'

And she gets up, leaving him to his misery.

But he should have.

He watches Brody head back to her desk. And he remembers the things Isabel wanted him to do. Hit her. Hurt her. All caught up in the fucked-up mishmash of sex and desire. Griffin may have done some weird things in his time, but not that. He just wishes he had done more to help.

Curiosity flashes, and he pulls up the PNC, typing in her name. She has a record. Cautions for shoplifting and petty theft. Penalty notices for drunk and disorderly, possession of class B drugs – probably pot or speed – all minor offences but pointing towards a disturbed teenager. What led her to go off the rails so spectacularly? Griffin doesn't think that Ron would tell him much – or even know – but maybe her friends can shed some light.

He picks up the phone. Dials a number he knows off by heart, department extensions indelibly carved into his mind.

Charlie answers on the second ring.

'Mills? Is Cara there?'

'Just left. Nice to hear from you, Griffin. Cara said you were back.'

'Did she give you the phone?'

'Yes.' There's a long gap, then a sigh. 'You want us to do it now, don't you?'

'Give me her five most frequent contacts. The rest can wait until tomorrow.' Griffin pauses. 'Please.'

'Since you asked so nicely. Ten minutes. I'll get my guy on it.'

Griffin hangs up and twiddles his fingers. He doesn't need to wait ten minutes; the call comes back almost straight away.

'I've only got one name for you,' Charlie says. 'But they talked every day. Texted constantly. Dougie. That's all it says.'

As Charlie recites the number, Griffin scribbles it down in thick marker on the pad.

He hangs up, then taps his pen. If anyone knew what was going through Isabel's mind, it would be this guy. Her best mate.

Chapter 11

Colin Jefferies' flat can hardly be described as such. A studio, with a tiny wet room off to one side, the shower practically hanging over the toilet.

Jamie gently extracts the key from Colin's mother and asks her to wait outside.

'Shouldn't you have all those crime scene people?' she asks. 'The ones in the white suits?'

'Only me for now,' Jamie confirms, pulling on the gloves and shoe covers. 'I'll be in touch,' he adds, and waits. Mrs Jefferies luckily gets the hint and leaves.

But now he's inside, Jamie's not sure what he's looking for. It's clean, tidy. Minimal belongings, meticulously ordered. A small shelf, with all the Harry Potters, the Game of Thrones series, and an assortment of other fantasy books, unicorns and dragons on the front. His clothes on a rail, matching hangers facing the same way. Jamie opens drawers, finds carefully folded clothes, socks and boxer shorts in neat lines. Obsessive compulsive, or making the most of his small space? Impossible to know.

His kitchen is one small hob and a microwave, a neat

cupboard above. He ate mainly pasta and pot noodles, as far as Jamie can tell. A single glass has been left in the sink, the dregs of what looks like orange juice in the bottom. He takes a sample; the glass goes in an evidence bag. He turns his attention to the bed – single, duvet and pillow all in place, all clean – and opens the drawers next to it. Ear plugs, blue inhaler and an assortment of pills. Jamie rifles through and bags up the drugs to look at later. But nothing illegal, all in his name with the pharmacy labels intact.

He stands in the middle of the room and frowns. There are no red flags, no hastily scribbled notes. No letters from therapists or new appointments with the doctor. Nothing that makes Jamie think the man was suicidal.

A knock on the door interrupts his thoughts. Jamie sighs, praying it's not the mother returning, but when he opens it it's an elderly woman. She squints behind Jamie, into the flat.

'Where's Colin? Who are you?'

'My name is DS Jamie Hoxton. I'm a police detective.' He shows his ID. She peers at it, suspiciously. 'And you are?'

'Gloria. Gloria Maxted. I'm Colin's neighbour. Where is he?' she repeats, her voice rising.

'I'm sorry to have to inform you, Gloria, but Colin's dead. He died yesterday morning.'

'Dead? He can't be dead. I've got his prescriptions.' She says it forcefully, as if that will bring Colin back.

The woman wobbles, and Jamie takes her arm, steadying her. 'Would you like to sit down, Mrs Maxted? It must be a shock.'

Jamie guides the dazed woman back to her own flat, across the corridor. Like Colin's, it's no more than a small room and bathroom, except the woman has stacked her whole life in this tiny space. Belongings are heaped on top of each other, balanced on furniture, with little order. Jamie guides her to the only clear area – the armchair across from the ancient television – and she slumps down, stunned.

'Would you like a cup of tea?' Jamie doesn't wait for an answer but crosses to the kitchen. Moving two saucepans out of the way, he boils the kettle and takes a mug out of the stack, locating the teabags and milk.

When he rejoins Gloria she has some of her colour back. She takes the tea gratefully.

'How did he die?' she asks.

'That's what I'm investigating. We suspect it was suicide.'

'He killed himself? Colin?' She seems surprised.

'Does that sound out of character?' he asks. 'We heard he had some problems with his mental health.'

'He never left his flat, if that's what you mean. And I think he was lonely. I went around there a lot. Me and Colin, we liked to chat. I know what it's like being alone.' She pauses, thoughtfully. 'Guess it's just me now.'

'And you did odd jobs for him?'

'I collected his prescriptions. Got him some bits from Lidl when I went. But he usually had Tesco bring it to his door. Accommodating, they were. No, he had a good set-up. He was resourceful, that lad.'

'There was nothing that made you think he might kill himself?'

'He said he would like to meet someone. I know he was online a lot, not that I understand those things. The Twitter, and that. Although …' She pauses.

'Mrs Maxted?'

'Oh, Gloria, please.' She takes a sip from her tea. Smacks her lips together with appreciation. 'I don't like to gossip.

But I wonder whether he wasn't a fan of the ladies. It's only occurring to me now, but he had a visitor a few times. A chap. I heard him, in the corridor.'

'You didn't see him?'

'No, just his voice. I would have checked but I don't move so fast.' She frowns. 'Last time was ... I don't know ... a few days ago?'

'Could you describe this man's voice for me?' Jamie asks.

She frowns. 'Nothing significant. No accent. Sorry. Maybe if I heard it again.'

'You didn't hear him Monday morning? Before six? Or maybe Sunday night?' He might have stayed over, Jamie thinks. But who knows where, given the size of that single bed.

'I don't know. Sorry, love. Sunday nights I stay at my brother's. Try to help him out. He's getting on too. I don't get back until Monday lunchtime, and I was late this week. There was an awful delay on the trains. Some lad tried ...' Her hand flies to her mouth, realising. 'Oh. That wasn't Colin?'

'I'm sorry. But yes. It was.'

'Oh,' she whispers. 'What a way to go. Poor Colin. I guess you never know, do you?'

Jamie's about to answer when his phone rings. A number he doesn't recognise. He apologises and moves into the corridor to answer it.

'Jamie Hoxton?' the voice at the end of the phone asks. Jamie agrees. 'This is PC Braxton. I thought I'd give you the courtesy of a call, given you're job.'

'How can I help?'

'I'm sorry to say that your house was broken into last night. Nine Robertson Avenue?'

'That's mine, yes.' Jamie feels a sinking dread at the address. 'I'm not living there at the moment.'

70

'No, I thought it might be empty. Someone smashed their way through the back door. We were called by one of your neighbours. I had a good look around and I couldn't see any other damage or anything nicked, so I think you were lucky. We must have disturbed them. But you'll want to take a look. Make sure.'

'I'll come when I can.'

'The back door's swinging open, DS Hoxton. I'd make it sooner rather than later.'

Jamie thanks him for the call and hangs up. He pauses in the corridor. He hasn't wanted to go back. Not for nearly a year. Not since …

He shakes his head, pulling himself out of his trance. It was always going to be a possibility; he couldn't leave the house empty for ever. He goes back to see Mrs Maxted, saying his goodbyes and leaving her with a final cup of tea. He calls Cara from his car. When she answers he relays what he's found.

'Nothing that proves either way?' she clarifies.

'Not that I can tell. Sorry, boss. I've just had a call. Someone's broken into my house. Not the one I'm living at. The other one.'

She knows instantly what he means. 'That's fine. Check it out.'

'It can wait—'

'We can live without you for a few hours, Jamie,' Cara confirms. 'Go and have a look.'

He hangs up, sitting in his car. He doesn't want to go back there. Not ever.

But now it's calling him. He starts his car's engine and drives. Some things can't stay buried. However hard you try.

Chapter 12

Dougie Morgan is shocked. Stunned into silence, his mouth opening and closing wordlessly, because nobody had told him that his best friend had died. Until Griffin showed up at his door.

'What do you mean? Dead?'

'Last night,' Griffin says, as if that makes any difference. 'Can I come in?'

Dougie nods and shows Griffin through to his lounge.

It's a rough place. Cheap and well loved, with retro posters of Nirvana and Bob Marley pinned to the wall. Brightly covered throws on the sofa. It's chilly, and smells of cigarettes and takeaways, the remnants of one lying on the coffee table, a stubbed-out fag in the middle of a piece of naan like a mast on a sinking ship.

But Dougie doesn't see it. He slumps on the sofa, then takes a packet of fags out of his pocket and tries to light one with shaking fingers.

'Let me,' Griffin says. He takes the lighter from him – an old Zippo, worn to a dull, dented grey – and flicks it on, holding it up so Dougie can inhale deeply. He takes two long lungfuls before he speaks again.

'How did she die?'

'She killed herself. Overdose. Pills and alcohol.'

He nods slowly. 'Issy always said that would be the way to go. I would have done something more dramatic. Go out with a bang.' He catches himself. 'Not that I would. I mean ... You talk about these things, don't you?'

Griffin never has, but kids are different nowadays.

And Dougie does look like a child. With spotless pale skin, a few freckles across his nose, cherubic blue eyes and a flop of dark curly hair, Griffin has to hold back from asking for his ID.

'Do you know where she might have got the pills from?' he says instead. He opens his notebook and reads the list. 'Any ideas?'

Dougie sighs. 'Some of those were hers. Doctor prescribed them – not that she always kept them for herself. You can make a bit of cash if you know the right people. And Issy did. The others she would have bought, no problem.'

'Did she often buy prescription drugs?'

'Yeah. All the time.' He assesses Griffin, in his black jeans, his T-shirt and scuffed jacket. 'You don't look like a cop.'

Griffin shrugs. 'I'd rather be comfortable.'

'I bet you've seen some things, right?' Dougie smiles, conspiratorially. 'Tried some things?'

'I've had my fair share.' Dougie holds the silence and Griffin senses he's not going to open up until Griffin does the same. 'Nearly died a few times. Ended up in rehab.'

'Rough,' Dougie says with a nod. Seemingly trusting him, he continues. 'Everyone does it. The drugs. Uppers to combat your downers. A bit of ampho to get you up in the morning, oxy to sleep at night.'

73

'She took these regularly?'

'Every day. She had a permanent rattle, that girl.' He starts crying then. 'I thought she was over the worst of it.'

Griffin leans forward. 'The worst of what?'

'The shit from her childhood. We all have it. But she had it worse than a lot of us.'

'How?'

Dougie wipes his eyes wearily. 'So – me.' He points the lit cigarette to his chest. 'Kicked out by my dad when I was fourteen. Caught me blowing off one of his best mates on the sofa. Not my finest moment. But Dad wasn't keen on faggots so out I went. Homeless for a bit. Until I met up with the gang I live with here.'

Griffin can't hold back from asking. 'How old are you?'

'Twenty-two.' Dougie exhales a long plume of smoke, amused. 'You thought I was younger, right?'

'Take it as a compliment. And who does live here?' Griffin can hear people moving about upstairs.

'A real mishmash. People come and go. Needing a place to stay. Ex-cons, a few students. The beautiful and the damned,' he adds with a grin. 'Saved my life. And now look at me. Got a job and all.'

'And Isabel?'

'Issy ... well. She didn't like to share, but I know something happened. To do with her stepdad, that shitbag her mum left for. He wasn't the violent type. Not to her, anyway. She used to say that was the best thing about him, but he was one of those incels, you know? The type that think they're entitled to sex. Any time, all the time. Fucking heteros. And if her mum wasn't around, he'd turn to Issy.'

'How young was she?' Griffin asks, trying to keep his voice level.

'Young. *Young,*' he stresses. 'Barely teens, I reckon. Fucked her up. Eventually she left. Went to live with her dad, and that did her the world of good, but the damage was done by then. Oh, Issy …' He trails off, and tears run silently down his cheeks. 'You should go and find that stepdad of hers. Give him what for. He's who killed her. But you know …' The cigarette pointed in Griffin's direction this time. 'I wouldn't have imagined her killing herself. She said she'd met someone. Someone older, who was going to help. I reckon she was fucking him, but as long as he was nice about it that's okay with me.' Griffin flushes. Luckily Dougie doesn't notice. 'And she was going for a job. Her dad was going to pay for her to go to college, maybe uni after. She was hopeful.'

He pauses, staring at the floor, his face pensive. 'No. I've seen people about to kill themselves. And I've done everything I could to get in their way. Issy was not one of them.'

And yet, Griffin thinks.

The CCTV shows that's exactly what she did.

Chapter 13

How could a house this innocent hold so many horrors? Jamie sits in his car, his hands locked on the steering wheel. He stares up at the bland brick facade. It looks normal – the curtains closed across the windows, the front door securely bolted. He should leave. Walk away.

But the house has been broken into. The police officer had given him the courtesy of calling, he can't abandon it now.

He climbs out into the cold night. He opens the gate, steps onto the path. The front garden is a mess. Grass long, flower beds overflowing. The neighbours must hate him but the tragedy renders them mute. What can they say? Nothing works.

The key is still with his others and he pushes it into the door. A gust of stale, cold air greets him; the heating hasn't been on for months. Since the last time he went back. Shut the door and never returned. Until today.

This was his home. The place he lived as a happily married man; the house from which his wife was abducted. Later, murdered, the body found by him, staged in the upstairs bedroom.

After that point, nothing was the same. He packed a few belongings and moved out – to the home of his best friend and boss, DCI Adam Bishop, and his wife, Romilly Cole. And there he stayed. But Romilly and Adam were long gone, leaving him alone.

Life-changing decisions had been made in a split second. In the course of the murder investigation last February, Adam had been stabbed. Life threatening injuries – three wounds to his abdomen, paramedics only just getting to him in time. One perforating his small bowel, one lacerating his liver, and the last, a lucky superficial wound. Hours in the operating theatre, complicated medical terms thrown around like emergency laparotomy, small bowel resection, that neither Romilly nor Jamie understood in their fog of worry. Adam lost three and a half litres of blood, the doctors said, mostly from his liver. But the rest was uncomplicated; he was home in two weeks.

Recovery took time. Wounds healing – physical and mental. Hours of physio. And once Adam was well enough, they left. For Australia, and beyond. Warmer climates. A whirlwind of excitement. Their new life, without him.

Jamie didn't blame them. It wasn't up to Romilly or Adam to look after him, he wasn't their responsibility. If he wanted someone to take care of him he could go and stay with his mother, but bloody hell, not that. She gives him that look. *That look*. The one that said, my poor boy. The sympathy he can't bear because he deserves none.

At least at work, nobody gives a shit. They all have their own problems. Hell, Nate Griffin even has his own murdered wife. He isn't unique.

Now, Jamie steels himself and steps inside. He closes the door behind him. He feels ridiculous. How could a house, especially one painted in beige and white, have such a hold over him? He walks through to the kitchen, running his hand gently across the walls. It's quiet. He pushes the door open and the afternoon light catches dust motes gently spiralling in the air. Cold and damp, an air of abandonment and neglect. What would Pippa say about leaving the house for this long? Would she disapprove? Or would she understand that it's not the house he fears, but her ghost.

As described, the back door is open, blowing in the breeze. He bends down and peers at the lock. Splinters of wood are exposed, the metal bent and broken. A crowbar, he assumes. It wouldn't have taken them long. But what were they after?

Jamie walks the ground floor, eyes scanning the furniture and belongings abandoned in this tomb. The officer said there was nothing taken, nothing else damaged, and Jamie has to agree. He can't even see footprints. No mess. He walks up the stairs to the main bedroom.

He steels himself as he opens the door, but to his surprise he feels nothing. Just numb. The bed has been stripped of sheets; the denuded duvet and pillows lie in a neat pile. He knows he has clothes in the wardrobe but Romilly went back in those early days, packed some up, and those are the ones he still uses. He opens the door to the en suite. Nothing. It is as he left it.

He heads back downstairs, resolving to sell this place. Buy somewhere new, before Romilly and Adam are forced to throw him out onto the street. It's ridiculous it has held this grip on him for so long.

He wanders through to the living room, completing his tour. The television is there, not that this one would be worth much second-hand. The cushions are plumped and artfully angled. The blanket that Pippa used on cold evenings is meticulously folded, as if she had done it herself.

And that's the thing that breaks him. This blanket. Not the room where Pippa was left, dead. Not the hallway she was dragged through, leaving bloody handprints across the paintwork. Not even her books, her ornaments, her photos. This fucking blanket.

He lived his life, in this room, with her. Watching television while she made her way through her marking, exercise books piled in her lap. Always the diligent teacher. Curled up together, watching a film. Or listening to music, drinking wine. *Here you are,* she would say as he arrived home from work. *Here you are.* And they would talk, laugh, make love. Their life, those memories, here.

All that has been taken away.

The numbness dissipates, obliterated in the avalanche of sorrow and hate and self-pity. But most of all the loss. That the love of his life has gone. Any semblance of an existence without her is meaningless. He's going through the motions. Living one day at a time. Without thinking. Without loving.

He drops onto the sofa and picks up the blanket. He holds it to his face, and for a moment he catches a scent of her perfume. But not just that. A slight aroma of salt and vinegar crisps. Of the washing powder they used. Of her skin, and her warmth and how he felt when she was next to him.

And with that blanket in his hands, Jamie curls into a ball and cries. Tears he hasn't shed in a long time. Tears that bring it all back, in one mournful howl.

Chapter 14

Cara sits in her office and drums her fingers on the desk. Now they have a number plate for the car, Shenton is plugging it into ANPR and the traffic systems – anything to get to the bottom of Colin Jefferies' last movements.

She can't work it out. A man who hasn't left his house in years finds himself at a busy station in rush hour, then plunges under a train. Is it as simple as it seems? If they could track down the driver of the stolen car, they might be able to get some answers.

Jamie hasn't returned from the break-in at his house, and Griffin is out – doing his own thing as usual. She knows he works best like that. Alone. Unchecked. And once he's satisfied his curiosity with this dead girl, maybe he'll focus that energy onto one of their live cases.

Brody appears in the doorway. 'Shenton's got something. But I don't know if it helps.'

Cara gets to her feet. 'Show me?'

Brody leads the way to Shenton's desk; Cara recognises the footage on his screen – from one of the many traffic cameras across the city. Cara sits next to him as Shenton explains.

'If we work backwards from the railway station, we can follow the route of the car down the A335, then joining the M27 at junction five. From there it's a short hop and jump to Colin's flat – off at junction three and into Ashfield.'

'They don't deviate from that route at all?'

'No. It looks like whoever picked him up at home drove him straight there.'

Cara frowns. 'But why? Did they know he was suicidal?' Brody opens her mouth to answer but the question was rhetorical. 'Did you get any clues to the driver?' she directs to Shenton.

'There's not much.' Shenton flicks screens and a grainy black and white shot appears. 'This is the best view. It could be anyone, but there's clearly two people in the car.'

Cara cranes forward. He's right. But it's impossible to make out features, let alone enough of a face to run through the recognition software. 'Have you spoken to the owner of the stolen car?' she directs to Brody.

'No answer,' she replies. 'I have an address, so I'm going first thing tomorrow.'

'I'll come with you.'

Brody looks surprised. 'You will? I mean, it's only a routine enquiry.'

'I'm interested,' Cara replies, and Brody looks disgruntled. She's probably assumed that Cara doesn't trust her to do her job properly, but it's not that. 'Pick me up at eight,' Cara adds. 'I'll message you the address.'

Brody nods.

Shenton glances between them. 'I know where the car went after the station?' he says.

Cara's attention snaps back. 'Where?'

'Out of Southampton, towards Durley and Bishop's

Waltham. But I lost it. Too much countryside, not enough cameras.'

'Put out a BOLO, alert Response and Patrol. I want to know where that car is now.'

Shenton nods and picks up the phone; Cara spots Griffin returning. She raises a hand and points to her office; he sees her and heads across.

'And?' she says once they're inside. He slumps in the chair opposite her desk; she sits behind it. Anything to reinforce her status.

'I don't think she killed herself.'

'Griffin ...'

'Hear me out. Yes, Isabel was a troubled teenager, but her best mate says she was on the up. She was happy living with her dad. There was even the possibility of college.'

'You knew her,' Cara says. 'Did she strike you as happy?'

'No, but—'

'Griffin—'

'Look, the post-mortem's tomorrow. And the digital team should have accessed more of her mobile by then. If that all points towards suicide, then fine. I'll let it go.'

Cara frowns. She doesn't want to ask, but a thought niggles. 'Griffin,' she begins.

His head goes up at her tone.

'Are you sure it's not ...' She starts softly. 'Are you sure this isn't about ... him?'

Griffin's jaw tightens. 'No.'

'Nate. All this talk of people killing themselves. It's bound to stir something up.'

'I could ask you the same question. You're the SIO on this "murder".' He draws air quotes around the words. 'Why are you so keen on investigating it into the ground?'

Cara considers Griffin's question. And she realises that this case, however strange, is giving her a boost. A return to when her brain felt something other than insecure and numb. Odd as it may sound, she yearns for that feeling – the burn of determination and intrigue, motivation to get out of bed in the morning.

But she keeps that to herself.

'Because I was told to,' she says instead. 'By my boss.'

'Since when have you been so compliant?'

'Since people died when I got it wrong!'

There's a long pause. She hadn't meant to shout, but her brother brings out the worst in her: the defensive child, the sulky teenager. After a moment, she risks a look at him: Griffin's expression has shifted from guilty to hostile.

'You won't make the same mistake again,' he tells her, bluntly.

Cara swallows. She focuses on a spot on her desk, clenching her hands into fists. 'I won't. I promise you that,' she says, defiant. But this is her brother, and she's desperate for some reassurance, however small. 'Why didn't I see it?' she says quietly. 'I should have noticed.'

She gets nothing from him. He stays motionless, his brows lowered as he stares at her across the desk. 'We all have our blind spots,' he says at last. 'He was yours.'

He gets up, leaving her office. The answering question echoes in her mind, and she whispers it then, knowing he would never answer her truthfully.

'And who is yours, Nate? Who is yours?'

Chapter 15

It's the closest Griffin and Cara have come to openly discussing what happened with the Echo Man, but Griffin hasn't got time to reflect on it now. Shenton jumps up from his seat the moment Griffin returns to the incident room, the phone clamped to his ear.

'They've got it,' he squeaks. 'The car. They've got it.'

Griffin's unclear what he's referring to, but it's obviously important – Cara is out of her office in seconds, Brody gathering her coat and keys.

'Griffin, go with Brody. See what you can find. Brody will update you on the way.'

He nods and follows her out of the office, talking as she goes.

'Call last night. Criminal damage. Uniforms attended the scene with two fire units.'

'Fire?'

'Yeah. The car was left in the middle of nowhere, doused in petrol and lit. Dog walker spotted the smoke, called it in.' She glances back as she holds a door open for him. 'Response and Patrol were falling over themselves to hand it over.'

'I bet. No witnesses, no forensics?'

'Got it in one.'

They take a car from the pool; Griffin is annoyed that Brody turns down the offer of his Land Rover.

'I want heating,' she grumbles as they climb in. They head out of town, east down the M27. Conversation is brief; Griffin switches the radio to a local station. He appraises Brody as she drives.

One hand on the wheel, she's relaxed, tickling the upper edge of the speed limit but never going over. She indicates, smoothly manoeuvres around slower cars, then politely returns to the slow lane, as instructed by the Highway Code.

And she's attractive, albeit unconventionally so. The black hair and piercings make him assume the image is deliberate, clashing with the rule-abiding driving and career choice. He's intrigued.

But Griffin's never been one for forcing conversation, so he sits back, enjoying being chauffeured for a change. Darkness settles into the evening, the street lights flicker, lulling him into a stupor. So when he jerks upright, he's surprised. It's ink-black, no lights except for the beam from the car.

'We're here,' Brody says as she pulls on the handbrake. She gets out and he follows, shaking his head to wake himself up.

They're on a single-track country lane. Grass sprouts down the middle of the road; hedges line either side. The burned-out car is in front of them, conveniently left in a lay-by. No sign of an investigation except for the patrol car behind.

The uniformed PC approaches them. Brody holds out her warrant card.

'DC Alana Brody, this is DS Griffin.'

Griffin shows his ID. 'What can you tell us about the car?'

'Not much to say, sarge. A 999 call after eight last night. Units arrived to find the thing smouldering. The hot spots were dampened down, then the fire team left.' He regards them curiously. 'What's your interest? Seems an odd choice for Major Crimes.'

'We believe it's linked to a suspicious death,' Griffin explains. 'Did you get forensics to take a look?'

'Yeah, but they didn't hold up much hope. The whole thing's a wreck. You know it was stolen?'

'We saw. What were your plans from here? You were going to leave it?'

The uniform shrugs. 'Clean up has been requested. What else can you do? The dog walker said he didn't see anyone. No CCTV around here.' He shuffles his feet, desperate to make his getaway.

'Leave it to us,' Griffin says with a sigh. The uniform almost runs back to his vehicle, doing a quick three-point turn and heading off into the night.

'What do you think?' Griffin directs to Brody.

She frowns. 'He's not wrong – there's bugger all we can do. But it's suspicious. If someone was a friend of Jefferies, innocently dropping him off at the station, why would you be in a stolen vehicle? And why would you dump it?'

'Perhaps he was dodgy and when he found out about Colin's death he knew it would draw attention to him and the nicked Clio?'

'Perhaps.'

Griffin does a circuit of the car. It's a blackened shell. The insides have burned away, leaving the smell of molten plastic and rubber. Only the metal frame remains and that's twisted and bent, a ghostly skeleton of the Clio they've been studying in the CCTV. With a gloved hand Griffin carefully pushes at the boot. It swings open, revealing an empty space. What was he expecting? A dead body? It's absurd.

'Let's go,' he says briskly to Brody. 'There's nothing here.'

Griffin calls Cara on speaker as they drive back. Cara's frustrated, but what can they do?

'Go home,' she commands. 'Griffin, you've got the PM, first thing? Brody, I'll see you at mine.'

'Roger that, boss,' Brody replies.

'What's that about?' Griffin asks once Cara has signed off.

'We're going to see the owner of the car.'

Griffin detects her frosty tone. 'And you need a DCI to do that?'

'What do you think?'

Griffin pauses. 'I think maybe cut Elliott some slack. She's not normally like this. She's finding her feet, after ...' He pauses. 'You know.'

She nods slowly, and they finish the drive in silence.

They go their separate ways once they arrive at the nick. Griffin to his Land Rover; Brody upwards to another level of the car park. She's a funny one. Most police detectives are desperate to know about the new guy, especially one with Griffin's reputation, but she's disinterested. To the point of rudeness. Perhaps she resents the ease with which Griffin has returned to the team. Perhaps she assumes nepotism, expecting he'll be given an easy ride.

Still. That's her problem, not his.

He arrives back at his flat, glad to see the garage quiet and in darkness. 'Trading suspended. Family bereavement,' a note on a car says. The crime scene sticker on the door of the Portakabin is the only sign of an active investigation. He can't see Ron around, and for that he's glad – the conversation would have been short and disappointing. He'll update him when he knows more.

Frank appears and curls around his legs as Griffin lets himself into the flat, switching the lights on. The chaos that he'd left that morning greets him. The mug from breakfast, his clothes abandoned across the sofa.

He hangs his coat up, pours some biscuits for the cat, then rolls up his sleeves, starting work on the kitchen. Washing-up done, he digs through the freezer and finds the last pizza – throws it in the oven. He feels better already, from gathering that tiny bit of self-respect. He was never a slob. Even though his living conditions are less than salubrious, he takes pride in the tiny space.

Pizza cooked, he eats it at the table, flicking news sites on his laptop, looking for any mention of the suicides. There's not much. Only the initial reports on Colin Jefferies yesterday, and a brief mention in the local rag about Isabel. *Much-loved daughter*, he reads. *Tragic overdose. Assumed suicide*. There are no quotes from Ron, no mention of Dougie. Seeing those words in print take him back to his own childhood, the event Cara alluded to earlier.

For the first time in over twenty years Griffin feels the need to dig. Pick at a scab he's left festering for too long.

He leaves his dinner half-eaten and goes across to his wardrobe. He reaches up – his fingers touch the small package hidden at the back and he pulls it out, placing it on the table. An old shoebox. Wrinkled cardboard, pocked by damp and dust, its contents are more significant than the bland outside.

88

The cat has made the most of his unattended pizza and has settled on the table, chewing a corner. Griffin shoos him away.

'That's yours,' he says, gesturing to the untouched bowl. The cat ignores him and Griffin sighs, pulling off the gnawed piece and giving it to him. Frank delicately nibbles at the cheese, purring.

Griffin turns his attention back to the old box. He bites off a piece of the remaining pizza and chews, pensively. He hasn't given it much thought in years but maybe Cara's right. Maybe this is the spectre lurking over Isabel's death.

He blows dust off the top and opens the box. An assortment of paper and photos stare back. Newspaper clippings, cards, sepia stained shots. He takes one out. He's young here, standing with Cara, her arm protectively around his shoulders. He turns it over. *Cara and Nate. Nov 1987*. So, he was four, Cara was six. He had the scowl down pat, even then.

It's written in his mother's handwriting, that neat, looped cursive that makes him sad even though she's still with them. In a care home, on the other side of town. He needs to go and see her, but each visit is harder than the last, as her memories slip away, lost in the grip of dementia.

Griffin slowly sits down at the table, ready for the next jolt down memory lane. A newspaper article is next. The photo is of two middle-aged men, standing together, grinning. The headline: *Local Businessman Tragic Death*. His car, wrapped around a tree. Splintered metal; smashed glass. No seat belt. No airbags, in those days. Just an uninterrupted glide through the air at seventy miles an hour. If the windscreen hadn't killed him, the impact of the tree would have. His crumpled body had lain there, in the freezing cold, for five hours until a passing car found a phone box and called 999.

By then the man was dead.

Griffin turns his attention to the caption on the photograph. *Neil Lowe,* it says. *Local lawyer and his business partner, now deceased, Mark Griffin.*

Mark Griffin. Nate's father. Died 1999.

By suicide.

DAY 3

WEDNESDAY

Chapter 16

Griffin can't sleep. Unleashing the memories of his father has been like unlocking Pandora's box, the curse of the emotions he's kept imprisoned for so long swirling around his head.

Growing up, Griffin's mother had been the one that provided all the childcare for him and Cara. Like many mothers at that time, she was there at breakfast, opening the door at the end of school. She soothed their fevered brows at night, she fed them, cooked with them, laughed with them. She was their constant.

Their father was a different matter. A man of many faces. Life and soul one moment: arrogant and outspoken, with grand plans to develop the business, advertise, network. He'd talk his way into parties, come home at all hours of the morning without the car, having left it by the side of the road somewhere. And that was on a good day. Other times he'd roll them, speeding, until finally his licence was taken away. Not that it stopped him.

And then he'd change. Up one moment, down the next. Days, weeks in bed. Often to their shed at the bottom of the garden, living there with a grubby old sleeping bag until their mother tempted him back for food. Or he'd go, and nobody knew where.

Either way, he was oblivious to his children.

Griffin stares at the ceiling all night, the memories churning his brain until he can bear it no longer. He gets up, the world dark, the cat sleeping, and makes a pot of coffee, carrying it to the table. He drinks mug after mug, his hands shaking, as he reads everything he can find, both official and unofficial, about Isabel and Colin – expanding his search to other sudden deaths and suicides across the country.

As the sun comes up, he notices the time. He downs the last of his coffee, his mouth gritty, his stomach acidic, and heads to the shower.

He has a post-mortem to attend.

Dr Ross almost double takes when he sees Griffin in the doorway.

'Well, well,' he says. 'The prodigal brother returns.'

'Sorry to disappoint you.'

'And this is your case?' Ross shifts his gaze to the body on the table, the early stages of the PM already completed.

Griffin has so far deliberately avoided looking, but now he can't help but take it all in.

The sight makes him immeasurably sad. That this once beautiful woman is now reduced to a shell: pale, eyes glassy, lips white. Laid out, naked, to be cut into.

Griffin knows the body will have already been examined. External appearance noted, the presence of any distinguishing features – such as the scar on her stomach, the tattoo on her arm – recorded. Injuries will have been documented;

samples of tissue and blood will have been taken.

He tries to apply a passive eye. There are no noticeable bruises around her wrists or the tops of her arms – indicators of restraint. Her nails aren't broken or ripped, defensive injuries absent.

There's nothing that points towards the involvement of someone else in her death.

'I have some initial observations,' Ross begins, pulling Griffin out of his grief. 'Whether or not they have any bearing on cause of death, I don't know, but they could be significant.'

'Go on,' Griffin says as he steps closer.

Ross reaches over and raises one of her arms. He turns it over so the delicate skin of her forearm is exposed. A criss-cross of silvery lines scatter over her skin, some barely noticeable, some red raw. Griffin's seen these scars before – both on Isabel and on others.

'Self-harm?' he says.

'By the look of these it's been going on for some time. On both arms. Plus there's this.' He stands behind her head and opens her mouth. He shines a penlight inside. 'Considerable damage to the tooth enamel and erosion to the surfaces, especially at the back.' He pauses. 'A common indicator of bulimia. These two indicators alone point to a woman in the grip of considerable mental problems. I had a look at her medical records. There's not much there. A few GP appointments. Prescriptions for amitriptyline and diazepam. You say you found them at the scene?'

'Yes. And Ritalin and ketamine. Although I suspect she wasn't getting hold of them legally.'

'You're probably right. Her GP had referred her for counselling, but the waiting list is ridiculously long. He notes

93

depression and anxiety, but no more than that.' He picks up a scalpel from the tray and moves around to the side of her body. 'Give me a few hours, I'll see what else I can tell you.'

Griffin nods and moves to the viewing platform, taking a seat. The lack of sleep from last night is taking its toll and he resists closing his eyes, instead taking his phone out and scrolling through the latest messages from Cara.

He feels a bubble of guilt that he hasn't been there for his sister over the last year. But he'd had his own demons to fight. An addiction to prescription painkillers – oxycodone specifically – obtained through the debilitating back injuries inflicted by the man who killed his wife and later tried to kill him.

It had scared him – that dependency – and he'd felt pathetic begging the GP for a prescription when he'd failed – again – to beat it by himself. He couldn't be a partner to Jess, or a father figure to her daughter the way he was, so a trip to a private rehab facility followed. He was fortunate, Jess had paid. But that luck faded fast once the withdrawal symptoms started.

The vomiting, the headaches, the shaking. Feeling so agitated he could do nothing but pace, well into the early hours of the morning. Replacement medication could only do so much; for days there was nothing Griffin could do but ride it out, sweating until his sheets were soaked, wishing that Cara were there to soothe him but being too proud to call. Counselling, therapy and group work followed. CBT and mindfulness, overcoming years of ingrained pride and stubbornness to finally talk about Mia and what had happened.

He'd left with two resolutions. To make it work with Jess, and never to return to that awful place again.

He'd already failed at the first.

True to his word, Ross is done in under two hours. He leaves the body to be sewn up by his technicians and beckons to Griffin to join him at the side of the room.

'I'll do all the usual tox work-up but her stomach contents was as I expected. Booze, and a few partially digested pills. She took the motherload for those to still be floating around.'

'So, suicide?'

'Unless you find something that contradicts it, that will be my recommendation to the coroner.'

Griffin nods his thanks and leaves with a heavy heart. There is no reason to think otherwise from what he's seen on the cameras, so why was he hoping for something else? Because it would let him off the hook, that's why. That his actions, his rejection of her, would have nothing to do with her death. Someone else he failed.

He climbs into his car, fastens his seat belt. But before he starts the engine his phone rings. It's the central police station. He answers it.

'Griffin? It's Charlie Mills.'

'You didn't need to personally call. You could have emailed.'

'Are you on your way back to the nick?' There's a long pause, Griffin waits. 'You're going to want to see this.'

Chapter 17

Alana Brody collects Cara at eight on the dot, her car idling at the kerb. Cara waves from the window where she's been standing guard, grabs her coat and heads out to the car.

Last night, she'd had that strange feeling again as she'd arrived home from work. A prickle on the back of her neck as she'd got out of the car, a sixth sense – that someone was watching. Waiting. For what? She'd hurried inside, locked the door and peered out through a gap in the curtains. There was nothing there – bar Trevor from three doors down being walked by his dog. She'd chastised herself for her foolishness, but hours later, heating on and warm dinner eaten, she couldn't shake the unnerving chill.

This morning, fears forgotten in the fresh winter air, Brody gets straight to the point.

'I had a look at the address. It's a farm, outside Braishfield. Should take us about half an hour.'

'Excellent,' Cara replies. 'Can we stop for coffee?'

Brody glances across as she pulls away. 'I shouldn't think there's a Costa nearby. Do you want me to detour?'

'No, no. It's fine.' Brody's shoulders are practically

around her ears with annoyance; Cara needs to put her constable's mind at rest.

'Listen, Alana,' she begins. 'Me coming with you this morning has no reflection on your ability as a detective.' Brody doesn't reply, she continues anyway. 'I want to be involved in this investigation. I'm fed up with sitting in my office, staring at paperwork. I know you're an excellent DC, that's why I hired you.'

Brody manages a small smile. 'That's the only reason you hired me?'

Cara laughs. 'That, and the fact that nobody wants to work for us.'

'It's nice to have the company, boss.'

'You do your stuff. I'll lurk in the background. Don't worry about me.'

That small glint of excitement she experienced yesterday still buzzes in her brain. That this could be something. A case that could bring her back to life.

Brody's shoulders return to their usual level, her eyes on the road. As they drive away from the town centre the roads turn rural. Fields peppered with sheep. Hedgerows and fences, the houses becoming more sparse. The coffee isn't forthcoming, but at least Brody's relaxed. Maybe even smiling.

'So, Griffin's your brother,' Brody says. 'Younger or older?'

'Younger. By two years.'

'And you both ended up in the police force? As detectives?'

'I know. Odd, isn't it? I guess something drew us to the darker side of policing.' Or some*one*, Cara thinks. That desire to get to the truth, to find out what happened to a victim at the final and darkest moment of their life – instilled in them the moment their father killed himself.

'And yes, he's single,' Cara adds, pre-empting the question that always comes next. 'But I wouldn't go there.'

Brody laughs. 'I didn't say a word.'

'You didn't have to. The first time you've willingly instigated a question about something personal and it's about my brother.' She looks at her DC, smiling knowingly at the flush creeping up from the collar of her T-shirt. 'Besides, you're not his type.'

'Why do you say that?'

Cara grins. 'You're normal.'

Brody snorts in reply and they continue their journey in good-natured silence, until a sign directs them off the road. *Bracken Farm*. The gate is open. A bumpy track leads them towards a set of farm buildings – barns, stables – a house beyond. It feels empty and disused. No signs of life.

'Did you call ahead?' Cara asks.

'I tried again, but there was no answer.'

Brody pulls up outside the cottage. It's a sweet place. Ivy up the outside walls, framing old white sash windows. They get out and push through the squeaking metal gate to the red front door. Paint peeling, the iron fixture is rusty and worn as Brody knocks. There's no answer and Cara takes a step back, looking up at the darkened windows. The curtains are open, but there is no light behind. Her skin crawls, sensing something amiss.

'I'm going to head around the back,' she says, and Brody nods, knocking again.

Cara steps through overgrown grass, shoving an open gate to get through. The garden, if it could even be described as such, has the same air of neglect. A twist of brambles latches onto her trousers, she tugs herself free then pushes through tall grass to stand next to the window. She puts her hands up against the pane and peers through.

It's a kitchen. Dated, but clean and tidy, surfaces bare. She moves on. A back door. Locked. She can hear Brody's knocks at the front, calling out now, trying to attract someone's attention. Cara moves to the next window. It's the same as the last, cast in darkness, and she squints through. The shape of an armchair, the back towards her, but she can make out a hand, drooping, limp, over one side. It looks female, delicate. Cara knocks on the glass, as hard as she can.

'Ma'am? Hampshire Police. Please come to the door.'

The arm doesn't move.

That's reason enough. Saving life or limb, section 17, PACE 1984. Grounds to force entry, in Cara's opinion.

She takes two steps to the back door and aims a swift backwards kick at the old, rickety lock. It splinters easily. She shouts out to Brody as she heads inside.

Cara makes her way through darkened corridors, hearing her DC's footsteps behind her. It smells of damp. Of cold, unheated rooms. Of …

'Check upstairs,' she directs.

She knows before she gets there. There's no mistaking that smell, ignoring the flies buzzing past her ear, the feeling of cold dread as her skin rises in goosebumps. The door to the living room is closed, she pushes through it, hearing thuds from Brody on the floorboards above. Then she stops dead in her tracks.

There is a woman in front of her. She's wearing a navy blue woollen jumper and jeans. A hole in the knee, white threads visible. A discarded sock lies on the carpet. Her hand dangles loose to her side, the other one – the one Cara saw through the window – is draped over the arm of the chair. Her manner is relaxed, her body slumped. She could be sleeping, except for the fact her face is nothing but a mass of blood and splintered bone. Dark red blood paints the wall behind her, drips running down the white patterned wallpaper to the skirting board beneath, pooling on the carpet. A double-barrelled shotgun lies at her feet. One is bare, her toes pinkish-red.

'Shit,' Brody says from behind her.

The buzz she felt earlier, the excitement at the prospect of a new case, disappears in an instant. Replaced by absolute dread. She can't do this again. She can't.

Cara turns, takes in Brody's pale affect. 'Call Control,' Cara says. 'Get a team sent down here. Including firearms. I want this shotgun made safe.'

'How long do you think she's been here?' Brody asks, motionless.

Cara turns back to the body, making an initial assessment. There are no signs of putrefaction, none of the marbling of the skin she's seen in the past as bacteria spreads through the nervous system. Cara pulls gloves from her pocket, puts them on then gently presses with two fingers against the woman's hand, testing the joints in her fingers.

'A while. More than twenty-four hours, maybe even thirty-six. No rigor present.' Brody's still staring. 'Alana?' she says gently.

Brody shakes her head, rousing herself. 'That's not all.' Her eyes look skyward. 'There's another one in the bedroom.'

Chapter 18

Jamie feels out of sorts as he drives towards the location sent by Cara. Last night he'd sobbed until his eyes ached, until he was raw and sore throated, eventually falling asleep on the sofa, covered with the blanket that smelled of her.

And when he'd woken that morning, he'd been disoriented. The living room that was once so familiar felt worse as he'd remembered anew. He doesn't live here. Can't.

He'd driven home – his other home – and had a shower before forcing down toast and a gallon of coffee. And now he's in the car and away from there, he feels better. Wobbly but better. At work he can forget. Push all thoughts of his dead wife out of his mind and focus on the investigation.

Another dead body. Another suicide. Two, in fact.

By the time he gets to the farmhouse the place is swarming with police cars. No ambulance, he notes. Only the mortuary van needed for this one. A cordon has been set up; he shows his ID to the scene guard and is waved through, suiting up in full PPE as he goes.

'They're upstairs,' the uniform says. 'It's better up there.'

He soon understands. The first body is visible through

the front door. Her face blown off by the shotgun, head and skull and brain matter spattered on the wall behind.

'Bloody hell,' he mutters.

'Complete disruption of the cranium,' a voice says from behind him. 'Brain turned to mush in seconds.'

Jamie turns and blinks at Dr Greg Ross. His tall, slim build and deep-set eyes make him easily recognisable at any crime scene, even in the full white coveralls.

'Jamie, good to see you,' Ross says.

'Greg,' Jamie acknowledges in greeting. 'We're keeping you busy.'

Ross grunts in agreement then turns away. Jamie notices a lump of something indescribable next to the body. A matted clump of hair, connected to the piece of skull that once made up her head.

'Get it wrong and you're fed through a tube for the rest of your life,' Ross concludes darkly, and squeezes past Jamie into the room.

Jamie leaves Ross to it, and heads upstairs. At the top there's a small landing. A bathroom in front of him. The pattern on the tiles is dated, the lino worn. But it's clean. Tidy. One bedroom to the left, and another, to the right, where a murmur of quiet conversation can be heard.

He edges inside, bending his six-foot-three frame almost in half to get through the door. It's not a big room, low ceiling, one small window. Sunlight shines down, illuminating the woman in the bed.

'Eileen Avery,' Jamie says. 'Seventy-four.'

Faces in their white suits turn. Despite the hoods and masks, Jamie recognises Cara and Brody.

'And?' Cara asks.

'Her daughter, Kate Avery. Forty-nine. Unmarried, no

102

children. No criminal record. Are we assuming murder-suicide?'

'I think so, yes,' Cara replies.

She gestures to the pillow, lying askew at the bottom of the bedclothes. 'Ross has already been up, taken a quick look. Petechial haemorrhages to the skin and eyes. Damage to her inner lips where her mouth was forced against her teeth.'

'Suffocation,' Jamie confirms. 'I spoke to her GP. Eileen was diagnosed with early-onset dementia ten years ago. Specifically, Alzheimer's. Her daughter was looking after her.'

'I'm guessing she didn't want to any longer,' Cara says softly.

They all turn back to the dead woman on the bed. Take in her sunken cheeks, skin barely covering bones. But also, the scent of talcum powder, of disinfectant.

'Boss,' Jamie begins tentatively. 'This all seems a bit … much.' Cara looks back to him, her eyes questioning. 'We're all used to call-outs for sudden deaths like this one, and the guy with the train on Monday – but so close together? How many suicides would we normally see in a week in this area? One at most? This is three in as many days, if you factor in Griffin's dead girl …'

His voice trails off as Cara fixes him with a steady glare.

'What are you suggesting?' Her eyebrows lower. 'Sometimes it's simply a cluster. Anomalies. It's winter, the days are short. We've just had Christmas. Statistically more suicides occur at this time of year.'

She turns and leaves the room, pushing past Jamie and taking the stairs at a rapid clip. He follows her.

'But this many?' Jamie repeats once they're outside. 'And

you have to admit there's something suspicious that the car seen dropping Colin Jefferies at the station on Monday led us here?'

Cara pulls the mask from her face, angrily. 'I know what you're saying, Jamie. And don't.' She removes the white suit with sharp pulls, the material ripping. 'Do your job. Investigate Kate and Eileen here. Finish up with Colin. See where the evidence takes us. Was the shotgun hers?'

'Registered to Richard Avery. The father. Deceased.'

'Good.' She pauses, looking back at the house. 'For the last few years all we've experienced are serial killers. You're hearing hooves and thinking zebras,' she says in a tone that tells Jamie to drop the subject. 'Sometimes it's just a fucking horse.'

But Jamie can tell her resolution is faltering. Her shoulders are slumped, her head bowed as she strides back to her car.

Jamie doesn't like that he's on first name terms with the pathologist, but as he watches Cara he can't help but think: it's happening again.

Chapter 19

Griffin sits next to Charlie Mills, down in the digital lab. On the monitor, a blue screen shows an odd illegible type, Isabel's rose gold iPhone plugged in on the desk, the wire trailing back to the computer.

'Everything you'd expect to see from a teenager's mobile phone is here,' Charlie explains. 'Apps for TikTok, for Instagram, Snapchat. Even one for Facebook although she doesn't use it often. When you click there's the usual stuff. Except for this.' Charlie selects Instagram and one of her posts loads. A smiling selfie next to a beach. Griffin's heart aches. 'But here.' Charlie clicks again and Griffin reels with surprise. 'She was inundated by messages like this.'

Below Isabel's photo are 237 comments, each one a variation of the same.

You're worthless, why aren't you dead?
Why are you here, haven't you topped yourself yet?
Set a time. Send out invitations. I want to see you die.
Some of them repeated multiple times by different users.

'She was being spammed?' Griffin asks.

'Yes, by literally thousands of messages. In the early days

she blocked them. But a month ago she gives up and stops using social media entirely.'

'When did it start?'

'End of November. Two months ago. And that's not all. They were sending her texts. Multiple numbers sometimes several times an hour. Addresses for suicide ideation websites, or message boards where people discuss how they'd like to kill themselves. These things don't just happen on the dark web.'

'Don't you guys shut them down?'

'We try. But as soon as one disappears, another pops up. And they're impossible to trace. IP addresses that start somewhere in Russia. Fake names, fake logons.'

'And they were targeting Isabel?'

'It could be one guy. It's similar to a distributed denial of service attack – when someone tries to take down a server or network with a flood of internet traffic. All you need to do is buy a number of bots off the dark web ...' He trails off in the face of Griffin's blank stare. 'Basically, hacked devices – or in this case, social media credentials – that can then be controlled remotely. Write a code to point those bots in the right direction, tell them what to say, and voila. Messages like these that look like they're coming from genuine accounts.'

'Can you trace it back?'

'Not without some difficulty,' Charlie replies. 'I'm guessing someone who knew how to do this also knew how to cover their tracks. We could try ...'

'But it'll probably be a waste of time,' Griffin concludes.

Charlie shrugs apologetically.

'So, what you're telling me,' Griffin says slowly, making sure he's understanding Charlie correctly, 'is somebody set up a code to send thousands of messages to Isabel Warner. Across social media, and when that didn't work, texts directly to her phone.'

Charlie looks up and nods slowly, meeting Griffin's horrified gaze. 'Telling her to kill herself,' he finishes.

Griffin leaves Charlie and heads back to the incident room. When he gets there, Cara is in her office, Shenton and Jamie are at their desks, and Brody is nowhere to be seen. He heads straight to Cara.

'It's criminal,' he states. 'Encouraging suicide.'

'Where have you been?'

'At Isabel Warner's PM. And then to see Charlie Mills.'

'And?'

'Someone was targeting Isabel. Systematically goading her with suicide sites, messages taunting her to kill herself. I know what you're going to say, that I'm imagining things, but speak to Mills. I'm not making this up.'

His sister is uncharacteristically quiet. 'I know,' she says at last.

Griffin stares at her in shock. 'What do you mean, you know?'

She gestures to the seat in front of her desk; he slumps into it.

'Colin Jefferies,' she says. He frowns, taking a moment to remember it's the victim on the train tracks. 'A confirmed agoraphobic, who hasn't left his house in years and gets chronic panic attacks, is picked up by a blue Renault Clio on Monday morning and dropped at Southampton Airport train station. In rush hour. Where he falls under the wheels of a freight train heading north from Southampton docks.'

She's speaking slowly, her words measured. 'Isabel Warner. A nineteen-year-old with apparently everything to live for, is bombarded with messages telling her to kill herself. And now this. Today.'

Cara pushes a crime scene photo towards him. He winces at the graphic image. 'That's Kate Avery. Devoted daughter. Owner of said blue Renault Clio. Who spent the last ten years looking after her mother with dementia. And then, out of the blue, she suffocates her mother and puts a shotgun in her mouth.' Griffin scowls. 'And do you know why?'

Griffin stays quiet as Cara shunts another image his way. There's no blood in this one. Only a sheet of lined A4, punch holes down the left-hand side, covered in strokes of small, neat handwriting. He reads a few words, but Cara saves him the trouble.

'She says she loves her mother. That she was always happy to look after her.'

Griffin reads the next line on the page. *It's come for me.*

'She thought she had dementia too?' Griffin says.

Cara nods. 'But she didn't. Ross confirmed. She had the full raft of cognitive assessments a month ago. Blood tests, even an MRI. Kate Avery was in perfect health.'

'She didn't believe them …'

Cara pulls the photo of the note back towards her then stares at it miserably. 'Four deaths within the same five-mile radius, all within the last three days.' She pauses. 'What does that say to you, Griffin?'

He blinks. He takes his time, not wanting to articulate the thought racing through his mind.

But Cara says it for him.

'We've got ourselves a serial killer.'

Peter

The wind whips Peter's hair, turning his hands to ice. He's bitterly cold, in only jeans and a T-shirt, and he pauses, assessing the best spot. The middle. The furthest to fall.

He stops on the pavement and turns, looking out across the River Itchen to the docks in the distance. A cargo ship chunters on the horizon; beneath him, a crowd of sailing dinghies meander, their fluorescent yellow sails at odds with the murk of the day. A crane towers above the skyline; a cruise ship lurks in the distance. Is this my last sight, he wonders? Tatty townhouses and industrial buildings?

It's as good as any.

A feeling overwhelms him. A desperate urge to find peace; knowledge that this is the only way to make that happen. For weeks now the thoughts have whirred – repetitive, painful – leaving no space to consider options, any other life than the one he is faced with today.

Cars zip past behind him, heading for the Woolston toll. Giving more thought to the coins in their pocket than the man looking at the view. It's a bright day, although rain clouds are fast putting paid to that. Two p.m. Finished the early shift at a job he hates, returning home to a flat that won't be his by the end of the week.

He glances down to the water. A long way beneath him, cobalt waves chop to and fro, the river churning, pulling. A summons. He's confused. Is this who's been talking to him?

He doesn't know what's real any more. Friend or foe, a man who says he's there for him, will help him – can he be trusted? The voices that chatter every hour, every night. He just wants them to stop.

A man runs past – a jogger in tight shorts and a long-sleeved T-shirt, headphones shoved in his ears. He gives him a look but doesn't pause. There's a white plaque in front of him. Phone numbers, next to a large blue and red buttoned emergency help point. For those that reconsider. Those that hesitate.

Not him.

He knows he needs to be fast, or someone will intervene. Press that red button, grab him, pull him back. Do-gooders, not understanding the lengths someone will go to.

He doesn't want their help. Nothing works. Not the drugs, the brand names now as recognisable to him as his own family's. The new ones, his tongue rolling them around in his mouth as he discussed them with his GP. They make him feel worse. A different type of bad.

He's executed his detailed plan. He's wrapped things up at work, diligently signing off calls for someone else to follow up. Even a will, witnessed and countersigned by his neighbour. Not that he has anything to give, but his nephew might like his old football sticker collection. His brother – his grandfather's war medals.

The only thing he has left. The only thing he hasn't sold.

He's been here too long. No point waiting.

He steps to the concrete wall. It comes up to his chest, the iron railing above. It won't take much.

He puts his fingers on the cold metal. The post with the help point, conveniently positioned so he can pull himself up. One leg, then two. He stands there, on the narrow concrete ledge, using the pole for support. The wind pushes, persuading. He senses cars stopping. A screech of brakes, a beep of horns.

He glances back. A man is out of his car, the Volvo askew on the pavement. Running towards him.

The horizon gapes. He is on top of the world.

He lifts his hand in a half-wave. Then he tips from the bridge.

Part 2

Chapter 20

Cara's hands shake; she presses her palm against her breastbone for a moment, trying to temper the quick thuds of her heart.

Dread, worry, but also something else.

Anticipation.

Murder detectives might have one serial in their lifetime – and now she has two. Three if you count the events of last year, although she wasn't the SIO for that. And she's still not a hundred per cent certain it is one. It's ridiculous. Almost insane. But she doesn't believe in coincidences: this is a pattern.

Griffin has gathered the team outside her office. They're waiting and she stands, trying to ignore the cold sweat prickling her back. This is a case where she won't fail.

There's a light knock on the door; Griffin tentatively pushes it open.

'Boss?' He pauses, looking at her with concern. 'Cara?'

'I'm fine, I'm fine.' She gets up, debating what she's going to say.

Outside in the incident room, the team look up

expectantly. Her first thought is that there needs to be more of them. Barely enough to run one investigation, let alone a serial. She makes a mental note to speak to Halstead; ask for transferred resource. Anyone that will come.

She feels all eyes on her. She leans back, rests against one of the desks, her arms folded, trying to assume a casual look she doesn't feel. She glances behind her where Shenton has already updated the whiteboard. Four names across the top, the bare bones of what they know.

'As ridiculous as it seems,' she begins, 'I am taking the position that these cases are related. That somehow, the deaths of Colin Jefferies, Isabel Warner, and Kate and Eileen Avery are connected.'

'But …' Brody says. She looks nervously at her colleagues. 'But how? Are we saying that someone is manipulating them?'

'That's exactly what we're saying. Putting them in such a position that their suicide is inevitable. Does anyone disagree?'

They're all quiet. Cara scans their faces. Griffin and Jamie look stern; Brody – frowning. Shenton is unreadable as usual, but is sitting up straight, all his attention on Cara.

'Good,' she continues. 'We have a few lines of enquiry to follow. Firstly, I want to know what we've missed. I'll get an analyst from Intel to join us and work through the available data on suicides and open verdicts from the last few years. See if this guy's been operating for a while. I also want to know what connects these victims. Why *these* people? Why now? What do we know about them?'

'They were a mixture of ages – from nineteen to forty-nine,' Brody says. 'If we don't include Eileen. Different demographics. Different ethnicities.'

116

'There must be something that links them. Some path they crossed.' She turns and writes the words in large block capitals on the board: *WHAT CONNECTS OUR VICTIMS?*

'Weren't they all on antidepressants?' Shenton says.

Griffin sits forward. 'Kate Avery wasn't.'

'But they were all ill? Jefferies and Warner had mental health issues. Kate Avery too, given she decapitated herself with a shotgun.'

Cara winces at his turn of phrase. 'They were definitely all vulnerable in some way,' she says. 'But we need more than this. Something that leads us to our killer. Keep digging. Note what you find. Something will connect. Griffin – are digital still working on Isabel's phone and social media?'

'Yes. Mills is.'

'Good. And I'm guessing there's nothing more on the CCTV for Jefferies?'

They spend the next ten minutes running through the evidence to date. Apart from the mysterious driver of the stolen car, and the conversations on Isabel Warner's phone, they have little to go on. The newest case – the supposed murder-suicide – looks open and shut. A lonely woman and her ill mother. Cara struggles to make sense of that one.

'Have we been through the initial report for the stolen car?'

'Not yet,' Jamie confirms.

'Do it. Go down to where it was nicked from, if needs be.'

Jamie nods. He seems quiet today. He's not normally chatty, but he looks paler than usual, his back stooped. Maybe it's the case. He shouldn't be working this – another serial killer so soon after the last one. But he's an excellent detective – they'd be substantially worse off without him on the team.

117

'Are we going public?' Brody asks.

'Not yet,' Cara replies. 'The last thing we need is a panic. Or relatives coming forward, desperate that their loved ones haven't killed themselves. Run the appeals for witnesses on the suicides, but keep it on the downlow. Once the media get on to this they'll be sharks in a feeding frenzy.' She pauses. 'Can I trust you all to stay quiet?'

Nods from the room.

'Then, thank you, everyone. Keep going. Keep pushing. Follow your instincts. And report back to me as soon as you have anything.'

They get up and move back to their desks. Their movements are sluggish; Cara recognises the feeling. Slow creeping dread.

Shenton comes over to her, his cheeks pink.

'Boss … Do you want me to …' He's tentative.

'What, Toby?'

'Do a psychological profile?'

It's Shenton's passion; the subject of his PhD. *The prediction of offender personality traits based on the modus operandi of a kill.* She's seen his proposal, developing the theory espoused by the Behavioural Analysis Unit at the FBI that studying a crime scene gives vital clues about your killer. He's insightful, smart, but Cara always gets the feeling that he's hoping for more deaths like this; an opportunity to practise his craft.

She catches herself; she's being unfair. He's lacking in social skills, that's all. He's always been a diligent detective.

'Yes. Do,' she replies, forcing a smile. 'But don't let it distract you from your day-to-day work. We're light on the ground, so I need you to follow concrete leads.'

She notices him flinch, obviously taking offence at the

118

implication she doesn't see the profile as concrete. 'Thank you,' she finishes. 'I know you'll be thorough, and your insights are always useful, Toby.'

He flushes at her compliment and goes back to his desk.

She turns and faces the board, looking at the faces of the dead four.

'It's bad, isn't it?' Griffin says, standing at her side.

Cara knows what he's getting at. Most murders are obvious. A knife, a gun. A shove, a strangle. But this. This feels worse.

'The killer was miles away when these people died,' Griffin continues. 'Yet somehow responsible. How do we get ahead of that?'

'Every contact leaves a trace,' Cara says, quoting Locard's principle. 'He'll have left his mark. Take this stolen car. Why did he steal one from his next victim and use it to kill Jefferies? Because he knew we'd trace it to Kate Avery. And we'd find her body.'

She looks up at Griffin. His eyebrows are low, forehead furrowed.

'He's playing with us. He wants us to pay attention. And those smug bastards are the easiest to catch.'

Griffin nods slowly. 'But how many people will die before we do?' he finishes.

And he leaves her, staring at the board, his words sinking in.

They have no idea who will be next. Or who might already be dead. And that's the scariest thought of all.

Chapter 21

Cara has worked fast: their new analyst is a studious looking kid, glasses, floppy hair. He is stylish where Griffin is rough and ready; slim and neat and smiling. He arrives with a laptop under one arm and a friend carrying a large monitor.

'We have computer screens,' Griffin comments.

'Not like this one,' the analyst says. He introduces himself cheerfully with an outstretched hand. 'Oliver Maddox. At your service.'

Griffin shakes it, baffled by the guy's buoyancy. 'Griffin.'

The monitor is placed down and connected within seconds. And Griffin sees what he means. It's massive, almost the width of the desk, with a pixel quality you could use to screen movies at the cinema.

'So, what do you need?' Oliver asks.

Griffin sits down beside him. 'All suicides, and anything that could be considered a suicide.'

'Unsolved murders? Accidental deaths?'

'If they fit the MO.'

Oliver pauses. 'And what is the MO?'

'Someone that kills from afar. Who manipulates people

into taking their own lives.'

He takes a moment to digest Griffin's words, then turns back to the screen. 'I'll include coroner court verdicts then. Anything left open.'

It's not a question – he's already moving at speed. He's typing, his fingers flying over the keys, his eyes flicking between the dual images on his laptop and the screen above.

Griffin leaves him to it, going back to his desk and the exchange of messages that Mills has sent through from Isabel's phone. They're exhausting. Each one as abusive and relentless as the last. He can't imagine how Issy felt receiving these. Young, vulnerable, already prone to depressive thoughts and destructive tendencies.

Griffin remembers the first time he met her. He was alone, grieving, homeless and jobless. He'd answered an ad in the local newspaper: *Night security guard. Accommodation available.* The interview with Ron had been quick and to the point. The pay was low. Even less if he was going to use the basement flat.

'The heating's shit. The plumbing's dodgy, and for God's sake don't tinker with the wiring,' Ron had grumbled as he showed him around. It took all of thirty seconds to gesture at the one room and the dirty bathroom. Ron eyed Griffin's scars, the cuts that hadn't healed across his face. 'And you used to be a cop?' he'd asked.

Griffin nodded, but Ron hadn't asked any more as a skinny kid came to stand at his elbow. She chewed on the ends of her hair, staring up at him with big, astonished eyes. Her face was heavily made up. White foundation, black wonky eyeliner and dyed red hair.

'My daughter, Isabel,' Ron had said.

'Nice to meet you, Isabel.'

'Issy,' she'd replied, and that was the extent of their conversation. She turned then and walked away, matchstick legs in black tights poking out from underneath a very short skirt.

'Fifteen,' Ron had said. 'Tricky age.' Griffin nodded, like he had any idea. 'Job's yours,' Ron concluded. 'If you want it.'

Griffin had seen her around over the last four years, but hadn't spoken until that fateful day when she came on to him, just after he returned after his break-up with Jess. She'd looked different. Less of a child, more of a woman. He'd said no, but still. He should have done more. Offered her help. But he'd been too drunk, too selfish, too caught up in his own problems to try.

'Done, boss,' Oliver says now, pulling Griffin out of his musings.

'Sarge,' Griffin corrects. 'Your boss is in there,' he adds, pointing to Cara's empty office. 'And that was quick.'

'Yeah. It's not refined though. Give me a few more parameters and I can narrow it down for you. Gender? Age? Dates?'

'Nothing as yet.'

'Then here it is. Shall I zip it across?'

Griffin nods and he hears the whizz from the computer as the email's sent.

'And the boss' – Oliver looks pointedly to the office – 'said you wanted some comparison analysis doing.' Griffin looks blank. 'Check the personal information of all victims against each other. Look for correlations?'

'Oh. Yes, please. Shenton has all the details. The blond guy there.' Griffin pauses. 'That going to take you half an hour too?'

Oliver laughs. 'You haven't seen the report yet. Raw is

122

an understatement. And no. It'll take a while. Scrape the data from all the various databases and social media, write a programme to work through it all.'

Griffin nods in pretend understanding and turns back to his screen. He loads the email; Oliver wasn't kidding. It's pages and pages, line after line of information. Names, dates, locations. Some going back years. There must be a way to reduce it into something manageable.

His rudimentary grasp of Excel enables him to sort the data into type. He filters by location, rules out anything where someone had been tried and convicted. The open verdicts are probably the best place to start – any deaths that look like suicides but without enough intel to rule conclusively at the time.

And, with a cup of coffee by his side, his chin cupped in his hand, he starts to read.

Chapter 22

Cara's meeting with DCS Halstead has not gone well. There was a long pause once Cara had explained.

'I didn't expect you to discover it was a multiple, Elliott. How do you know they're definitely connected?'

'We don't yet, I …' Cara had trailed off in the force of Halstead's glare.

'I need more than this. More than mere coincidence before I take this higher. A concrete link.'

'On Monday you told me to recruit, ma'am. Now you're saying I can't? I need a bigger team. Four victims, there are a lot of lines of enquiry to pursue.'

Halstead gave Cara another withering look. 'On Monday, you were working your full case load. Now you're saying you're focusing all your energy on this? Absolutely not. As it is I've had to move all other major investigations to the MCIT in Basingstoke. DCI Ryder's champing at the bit.' She looked at Cara over the top of her glasses. 'And I have to say: there are whispers, Elliott. From on high. That you're not up to the job.'

Cara reeled. 'I can assure you, ma'am, I'm on it. One

hundred per cent.'

'I sincerely hope so. Keep me informed,' she directed, dismissing Cara.

'Yes, ma'am,' Cara had muttered, retreating out of her office.

Now, back behind the safety of her own desk, she castigates herself for being so pathetic. She was never like this in the past. She and Marsh would have regular run-ins, heated debates, enjoyed by them both. She feels tears of loss and self-pity threaten. That was then. This is now.

Jamie appears in the doorway. 'Can I come in?'

Cara gestures to the chair and he steps through. He shuts the door behind him. This must be serious.

'It's about my promotion,' Jamie begins. 'I know you put in your recommendation, but I haven't heard. And you were just with Halstead …?'

Cara glances at the date. 'I'm sorry, Jamie. It's been weeks since your interview. I'll chase. I'll get Halstead to come back to you. I'm sorry, I've been … There's a lot on my mind.'

Jamie gives her a weak smile. 'It's fine. Thank you. I know you're doing your best.'

Am I? Cara thinks. If so, it's not good enough. This promotion means a huge amount to Jamie. She needs to try harder. But before she can say anything else a knock interrupts them.

It's Shenton. And Cara's worked with him long enough to know what the flushed face means.

'I've been speaking to Response and Patrol,' he says in a garbled rush. 'They had a call-out this afternoon. There was a man on the Itchen Bridge.'

'And where is he now?' Cara asks.

But she already knows the answer.

It might have been weeks before the body was found. Maybe never. But they've been lucky – for want of a better word.

The unidentified man had to float past Ocean Village and more than a few boats on his way out to the Solent – and that's where he got stuck. Hit by a small day cruiser, his body caught in the propeller. The subsequent crunch attracted the attention of the occupants, who stopped the boat in seconds, convinced they'd killed the guy.

Cara and Jamie head out to the Weston Shore, arriving at the local beauty spot within half an hour. A group has gathered on the shingle. The boat is moored offshore, and Cara can see the bustle of the dive team in the water. Black sleek drysuits, scuba gear, masks and protective equipment – they're used to coming face to face with corpses. And this won't be their worst, by a long shot.

Bodies degrade fast in water, saline particularly. Skin peeling, organs putrefying, causing the body to bloat and rise to the surface. But this guy, if the reports are correct, hadn't been in the river for longer than a few hours.

Police vehicles have taken over the small car park; crows and seagulls jostle for attention; it has the smell of the seaside with zero of the charm. A rusty camper van is parked by the water's edge, the residents within watching the show, mugs of tea in their hands. Cara wishes for a coffee of her own.

From here, Cara can't see the Itchen Bridge, but she knows it well. It's a preferred location for jumpers in Southampton – campaigners have been asking for years to have better barriers erected. The hopeful Samaritans sign and help call point is limited in its effectiveness; the most determined know what they're doing.

'Do we have an ID?' Cara asks the officer in charge once introductions have been made.

'Peter Jessop,' he confirms. 'If it's the same guy, which we should know soon, a rucksack was left behind when he jumped. Contained his wallet, driver's licence and not much else. Caused a right pain. Had to close down the bridge.'

Cara gives him a quick glance but keeps her thoughts to herself. She needs this guy onside if she's to get access to the case. 'Where's the rucksack now?'

'In evidence, back at the nick.'

'Have it sent over to me, please. As soon as you can. And the witnesses? They say he definitely jumped?'

'One hundred per cent. Clocked that they were coming to stop him and threw himself over.'

'Nobody with him?'

'No one.' The OIC gives her a look. 'Why are you so interested? A DCI and a DS from Major Crimes, sniffing around a suicide? Haven't you got better things to do?'

The two of them glance to where Jamie has his notebook out, interviewing someone in a life jacket. The witness from the boat, Cara assumes.

'We're making sure,' she replies, but leaves it at that, heading over to Jamie.

He's finished with the witness and turns to her as she arrives at his side.

'Not the sort of thing you expect, out for a nice cruise around Southampton Water. One of ours?'

'I think it's worth checking, don't you? That's five dead, in less than a week.'

There's a shout; a black body bag being pulled in. Cara and Jamie head to the shoreline as the diver and his

127

unpleasant cargo surface.

The black bag is unzipped; water and a sour odour emerge. The OIC crouches, checking the photo on his phone with the pale face of the dead man.

'That's him. Don't you think?'

Cara looks at the proffered image. Peter Jessop was attractive. Mid twenties, dark hair. Stark contrast to the man in the bag now. His hair is wet, his skin pimpled from the cold. There are several deep gashes across his face, one on the top of his skull, running down his forehead, the other almost splitting his chin in half. Inflicted by the propeller. She knows that many of his injuries will be internal: entering the water from a height like the one from the Itchen Bridge, twenty-eight metres from the surface, is no better than hitting concrete. Depending on the way he entered the water, he might have sustained a pneumothorax, massive pulmonary contusions, cardiac lacerations, a splenic rupture and innumerable broken bones. If he was lucky, he would have died on impact. Unlucky, and you add drowning or hypothermia to the mix. Ross will be able to tell them more, once Jessop arrives at his mortuary.

Cara nods and the body bag is zipped up. She takes a step back and sighs, looking out across the river. How is this happening? One thing she does know is that the key lies in whatever connects these victims. The killer is getting to them somehow. And once they know that, they'll have their answer.

Chapter 23

Raking through the report is slow and boring. Griffin stretches at his desk, raising his arms and twisting his head so his neck cracks. He feels an ache working up from his lower back; his physio has warned him about this. Sitting for long periods on crappy office chairs.

He's been doing this for hours. Taking each line and looking through the facts of the case, and the majority are so different to what they've been dealing with he can rule them out straight away. But some ... Some could be possible.

Take this one, for instance. A woman, died at home. Diagnosed with stage four cancer, she had been bedridden for a while, until she was found dead by her husband. The GP raised concerns and a post-mortem was completed, but the outcome stated cause of death was natural.

So, maybe an assisted suicide. Not relevant to this.

Brody sits on the chair next to him.

'Anything?' she asks.

'No.' He scrolls down the massive Excel spreadsheet, demonstrating the extent of his problem. He can see cases from 2005, more dating back to the nineties. 'Not so far.'

'Cara called from the river. She said they have another one, but they won't have anything definitive until tomorrow, so to go home.' She shouts across to their new analyst. 'Go home, Ollie.'

He raises a thumb and grins.

'How is that guy so cheerful?' Griffin mutters. Brody smiles.

'Night, Griffin,' she says, and collects her bag and leaves.

Shenton seems to have ignored the instruction: he's buried in a mountain of case notes and textbooks. Griffin doesn't need to ask what he's working on. He's intrigued, mixed with concern, about what Shenton might discover about whoever is behind this. Shenton's interest in such crimes has always been the psychological; for Griffin it's retribution.

He picks up his laptop, pushes it into his rucksack. He may be going home – to eat, to shower, to sleep – but there is work to be done.

Lights are on in the Portakabin when Griffin arrives back. He parks the Land Rover in the street, but the rattle and growl of the old truck is easily recognisable. Sure enough, Ron's waiting for him at the door as he passes.

He sways, slurs a greeting.

'They said they don't want it any more,' Ron says. He gestures inside. 'What does that mean? Not a crime scene.'

Griffin walks across to him slowly, biding his time.

'It means the SOCOs have gathered all the evidence they need,' Griffin says. The wind is cold, it whips between the cars, turning Griffin's hands to ice. 'Can we talk inside?'

Ron goes into the Portakabin and slumps in his usual

seat, knocking against the desk as he goes. Griffin follows; he can't help but glance at the sofa where Isabel died. It's bare, the covers and cushions taken away in evidence bags. He chooses a different seat, opposite Ron.

'Do you want one?' Ron says, gesturing to the bottle of whisky.

'I'm fine. Thank you.'

Ron pours himself another. 'You're back at work?'

'I am. And we're investigating. I'm sorry, Ron. But there's nothing definitive yet.'

'She didn't kill herself,' Ron mumbles to his glass. 'Not my Isabel. I blame that bastard, you know. Her stepdad. He's the one that did this. My poor Issy.' His voice breaks and Griffin feels for the guy.

'I heard she had troubles,' Griffin says.

'But she didn't kill herself!' He shouts this, his rage, fuelled with sadness and anger, getting the better of him. 'You promised. You said you would find out.'

'And I am,' Griffin replies, his tone placating. 'These things take time.'

'All the papers are saying she killed herself. They're blaming social media, her friends, me. Anything but say the truth.'

'What is the truth, Ron?'

'That someone killed her. Someone forced her to take those pills.'

Griffin doesn't want to tell him that she was alone when she died. That the one thing he knows for sure is that she put those pills in her mouth and swallowed them down. Even if, as they suspect, she was goaded into it.

Ron takes his silence as disagreement.

'You said, Griffin. You promised me.' His face turns

131

nasty, and he leans across the table. 'You think I don't know, don't you?'

Griffin feels a thud of dread drop in his stomach.

'I saw. I check the cameras. I know – about you and Isabel. What you were doing.'

'Whatever you think, you're wrong,' Griffin replies. 'Nothing ever happened between us. But I'm sorry. I should have done more to help.'

Ron's not listening.

'I know you weren't the only one. I saw her. With all those men, in here.' He gestures to the bare sofa. 'I tried to stop her, but what would my disapproval have achieved? She would have run away from me, too. At least here, she was safe.' A sob erupts from his chest and he buries his head in his hands.

Griffin stands up. There's nothing more he can say at this point, nothing he can do to assuage Ron's grief. He makes his way out, but as he puts his hand on the door, Ron lifts his head.

'You find who killed her, Griffin. Or I go to the police – about your relationship with Isabel.'

Griffin scowls. 'Even if we had, there was nothing illegal about it.'

'You met her when she was fifteen. Who knows what you were doing then.'

'I wasn't …' But Griffin stops himself. There's no point in arguing. 'I'll find out what happened to Isabel,' he says. 'But for her sake. Not yours.'

And with that, Griffin opens the door, pushing it back so hard it bangs on the Portakabin wall behind. He strides across to his flat, takes the metal stairs down two at a time. Inside the basement, he shuts the door hard, then stands

132

behind it. He needs to get out of here. Put his life back together.

But for now: Isabel.

He takes his laptop out of his bag and leaves it on the table while he gets something to drink. He opens the fridge looking for a beer, an automatic reaction from his past, and closes it again with disgust when it stares back empty. He fills the kettle instead, spoons instant into this morning's dirty mug, and makes coffee. Black, no milk. It'll do.

He drinks it, scalding mug in one hand, scrolling the report with the other. The years flick down; he's not sure what he's looking for. Something that will leap out. A pattern. A cause of death. Anything.

He drinks. He scrolls. His mind drifts to self-pity. To the mess he's made of his life. Bad decisions, impulsive, detrimental. Ending up here, now. A tenuous relationship with his sister. A stalled career. And a life, alone. Where everyone has left, one way or another. Even the cat is absent tonight.

He realises in his daze he's gone too far. He's in the early 2000s now, before Isabel was even born. But the date resonates. It makes him stop.

Dregs of coffee forgotten, he scrolls further, looking for the one name that he wishes wasn't here. For the one word next to it: suicide. Back then, the case had been straightforward. Griffin had existed in a strange fog, a blurred existence of grief and confusion, but one thing he'd known for sure. His dad had killed himself. That had never been up for debate.

He scrolls further. And there he is.

Griffin, Mark. Age 42. DOB: 31/01/1955. Died: 24/02/1999.

But the word in the column isn't the one he expects.

Coroner's verdict: Open.

He sits back, his mind reeling. He forces himself to look again. To check his sore eyes haven't skipped a line. But no.

His father's death hadn't been declared a suicide. Everything he'd assumed, since the age of sixteen, is a lie.

Chapter 24

Cara's only been home for half an hour before the knocking begins. Loud enough to make the walls shake.

She heads to the door with trepidation, evolving to bafflement when she sees Griffin through the spyhole. He bangs again; she opens it, glaring.

'What's got into you?' she says, as he pushes past her into the hallway.

'How did Dad die?' he snaps.

She stares at him with confusion. 'You know how he died. Car accident. He drove into a tree.'

'But it wasn't suicide, was it? I found him. On a report. Open verdict. The coroner declared it an open verdict, not suicide.'

He's almost hyperventilating in her hallway. She puts her hand out to guide him into her kitchen, but he shrugs her off.

'Tell me, Cara.'

'I will. But inside. Please.'

He acquiesces, and she follows him into the kitchen. He sits at the table, waiting.

'Do you want tea? Coffee?'

'Cut the crap. What happened?'

Cara sighs. She walks to the kettle and clicks it on, taking two mugs out of the cupboard. She regards him from here – stiff and prickly and glaring – and he reminds her so much of the teenaged boy from that time.

Griffin was skinny then. A sixteen-year-old, tall, barely needing to shave. And so full of pent-up rage and frustration he'd punch walls, kick cars. Anything to let it out.

'Yes, the coroner declared it an open verdict,' she begins, turning towards him, the kettle burbling next to her. 'But he killed himself. Everyone knew he was depressed. That he was on a down, and the worst one we'd seen. Mum, me, you. Even Neil knew.'

'Neil said he'd killed himself?'

'He agreed it was likely. Dad had been drinking, the tail end of a week-long bender. He'd been in the shed. You remember?' Griffin nods. 'Only coming out so he could go to the offy. And then he got barred, flew into a rage. The last thing he said was there was no point if he couldn't even drink. Mum left to go and see Neil, and the next thing I knew I came home from the pub and Mum was crying.'

'Why didn't the coroner declare it suicide?'

'Dad didn't leave a note. Plus, the alcohol – a terrible combination on top of his usual meds. It could have been an accident.' Cara sags, miserable. 'And it worked in our favour. Dad's life insurance wouldn't have paid out if he'd killed himself. We desperately needed the money.'

'What do you mean? We had the business. Dad's share would have passed to Mum.'

But Cara shakes her head. 'It went to Neil. That was one of the conditions when they set it up – if either of them died, their share went to the other.'

She pauses. She doesn't like the look on her brother's face.

'It was in Neil's interest for Dad to die.'

'Griffin ...' Cara begins. 'Come on. Your head is so full of murder that you're seeing conspiracies everywhere. It was Neil's best interest to keep Dad as a partner. You know how brilliant Dad was at his job.'

'But you said yourself – Dad was on a down. And he was useless to Neil when he was like that.'

Cara doesn't reply. She turns to the now quiet kettle and pours two mugs of tea, pushing the bags down with a spoon. There's no arguing with Griffin when he gets like this. She adds milk and carries them across to where his head is resting on his hands.

'Why didn't I know?' he directs to the tabletop. Then he lifts his head and looks at her. His eyes are red. 'Why am I only finding this out now?'

'You were sixteen—'

'Old enough.'

'But you were ...' She doesn't want to say it.

'What?'

'Unstable. Going off the rails. We didn't want to make that worse.'

'We?'

'Mum and I. We assumed you would find it easier if you thought it was suicide.'

'Easier?' he explodes. 'None of it was easy!'

Cara blows on her tea, taking the moment to keep her emotions level. 'So how much worse would it have been without that closure? If we'd shrugged and said, "Sorry, Nate. But we don't know how Dad died." Don't you

137

remember? You were out all hours, barely coming home. Drinking, hanging out with the wrong crowd.' His head drops. She feels bad. Maybe they should have told him. Later. But Nate's always been hot-headed. There was never a good time.

'Have you eaten?' she says gently. 'Can I cook you something?'

He shakes his head. She's not sure whether he's saying no to food or not, so she gets up and heads to the fridge. Pulls out eggs, mushrooms, cheddar.

'I'll make you an omelette,' she replies.

He nods, slowly. He looks tired.

She starts cooking, her stomach rumbling as the aroma of melted cheese fills the air. She glances back to Griffin; he's sitting back now, looking around the kitchen. Taking in the bare walls, the packing boxes. It's been a while since he's been here.

'What's happened?' he says. 'Where's Roo?'

'Roo moved out,' she replies, staring at the frying pan as the eggs cook. 'Took the kids.'

'Took the kids, where?'

'To a new place. He's renting.' She tries to sound light but she feels her voice catch. 'It wasn't working. We argued all the time. The kids are happier there.'

'The kids … What?' Griffin's incredulous. 'The kids are happy with you.'

'I'll sort it out. This place is up for sale. I'll get somewhere smaller. It'll be fine.'

She dishes the omelette onto a plate and puts it in front of him. He looks up at her, his eyes wide with disbelief. She ignores his expression and starts cooking one for herself.

'That reminds me,' she continues, as casually as she can

138

manage, 'some of your boxes are in the loft. You'll have to take them away.'

'Why didn't you tell me? About Roo.'

'You had enough going on. Your break-up with Jess. Rehab.'

'I should have been there for you.'

'You weren't speaking to me.'

She says it without thinking, but it's true. The barrier between them since the Echo Man was caught. The unspoken accusation: *You should have known.*

That her partner, Noah Deakin – who she'd worked alongside for three years, who she spent more time with than anyone else – had been the serial killer they'd been searching for.

A man who put Griffin in hospital. Who'd killed his wife.

'Nobody knew,' Griffin says. He's put his cutlery down and is looking at her. 'Nobody guessed. I was in the same room as him, day after day. If anyone should have worked it out, it should have been me.'

She swallows hard. 'I'm sorry, Nate,' she says, staring at the frying pan.

There's silence. She risks a look over at him. He's poking at his supper with his fork.

Then: 'I'm sorry, too,' he says. 'I shouldn't have blamed you.'

The apology is so out of character that she stares until he looks up. Points with his fork at the cooker.

'The eggs are burning,' he says.

She turns back quickly and whips them off the heat, attempting a laugh. She wipes, frustrated, at the tears prickling her eyes.

She joins him at the table, her dinner only marginally

139

charcoaled. They eat in silence. A simple meal, but the best thing she's tasted in months. A reconciliation, of sorts. The uneasy feeling that's been hanging over her for the last few days shifts. Safe and secure, with her brother beside her.

'No more secrets, please?' he says, mouth full.

'I promise.' Cara pauses, takes a bite of her own. 'And no more digging?' she adds.

He nods, but she detects the slightest pause as he puts a forkful of egg in his mouth. A hesitation that nobody else would have noticed, but a tell she knows only too well from their childhood.

Griffin with a nagging doubt is a dog with a bone.

He's not going to let it lie.

Chapter 25

Jamie's spent the afternoon standing outside a Tesco Superstore, staring up at lamp posts and CCTV poles. At first, the security manager was impressed – a murder detective! At his store! – but he quickly transitioned to annoyed when he realised the amount of video he was going to have to wade through. But the footage has now been secured, for what it's worth. A hazy image of what Jamie assumes is a man, walking straight towards the blue Renault Clio, opening it with a flash of orange indicators, and driving it away. All in a matter of seconds.

Jamie sits in his car and makes a call.

'He had a key, boss,' Jamie says. 'That car was targeted.'

'It all feels very deliberate,' Cara responds. That specific car, owned by that specific woman. All adding weight to the theory of a methodical offender. She continues: 'I've spoken to Halstead. About your promotion. She wants to see you.'

'Now?' Jamie asks. He looks across the car park, filling up steadily with post-work shoppers.

'Yes. Sorry. Now. Face to face.'

And Cara's tone tells him it's not good news.

'Ma'am?' Half an hour later Jamie pokes his head around the corner of DCS Halstead's office.

'Jamie, please sit down.'

He does so. She continues to read the memo on her desk for a moment, then signs it with a final swoosh. She puts it to one side, taking off her glasses.

'Your promotion,' she says. Her voice is stern; his instinct confirmed. 'You're going to have to wait a little longer before we move you up to detective inspector.'

The disappointment bites. 'May I ask why?'

Halstead shuffles paper; pulls out a file. Jamie has an excruciating wait while she puts her glasses back on and reads.

'The feedback from your interview panel was exemplary. Your annual reviews from DCS Marsh – before he died – and the recommendation from DCI Bishop – before he left – were glowing. Elliott has nothing but good things to say about you.'

But? Jamie thinks.

'But the investigation into the murder of your wife has thrown a spanner in the works.'

'In what way?' Jamie snaps. He consciously tells himself to calm. 'If I may ask?' he adds, words measured this time.

'As you know, the circumstances around your wife's death were … unusual. Before that point you were one of the lead detectives on the investigation, and the IOPC are worried that your involvement may have compromised the case.'

A thousand questions tickertape through Jamie's head.

He pushes them down, desperate to contain his emotions.

'I was excused from duty the moment Pippa was taken. In line with protocol,' he adds.

'You returned less than four days later.'

'Because Adam was kidnapped!' he exclaims. 'We needed all hands on deck.'

He can't help the disbelief creeping into his tone. That this woman, who – by all accounts – hasn't been face to face with an offender for at least five years, could criticise what happened.

'Even given the fact that *Adam*,' she says pointedly, highlighting his closeness to his senior officer, 'had been abducted, you shouldn't have been involved. It was personal to you.'

Jamie swallows his reply, choosing to stay quiet.

Halstead looks at him over the top of her glasses, then shuffles more paper.

'And we've had a complaint.'

'From whom?'

'From … relatives of the victim.'

'Which victim?'

'That's confidential. It's being investigated as we speak, but there may be repercussions. Rules weren't followed. Protocol wasn't adhered to. Breaches which may have resulted in the death of officers in this very team. So it goes without saying that we can't promote you while this is going on. What sort of message would that send?'

That you have faith in your officers. That we did nothing wrong. That DCI Bishop is an incredible detective and that the investigation was conducted in the best way we knew how, under unimaginable stress. But Jamie doesn't say any of those things.

He tenses his jaw, grips the armrests of his chair so tightly his knuckles blanch.

'And when will we know the outcome of this investigation?' he manages.

'In due course,' Halstead concludes. 'And then we can revisit the matter of your promotion.' Jamie doesn't move. 'Thank you,' she says, and looks towards the door.

Jamie gets up and walks with stiff muscles out of the room.

'Close it behind you,' Halstead says, her head already bent over her paperwork.

He does as he's told, then stands in the hallway gulping deep breaths. Someone complained. Who? About him, about Adam. About Marsh – a dead man, for fuck's sake.

He can't imagine who would be so callous. But he is sure as hell going to find out.

DAY 4

THURSDAY

Chapter 26

First thing, Griffin should be heading to the nick, but instead he finds himself on a detour. Towards the outskirts of town, a route he'd taken a million times as a child, as a passenger in his mother's car. A treat – to visit a magical world. To see his father, at work.

The solicitor's office is down a side street. In those days it was lined with shops – clothes boutiques, gift emporiums, privately owned businesses who knew them all by name. Now the fronts are boarded up; there is nothing except two betting shops and a Help the Aged charity store. He parks the Land Rover in one of the many empty spaces and gets out. It's starting to rain; he pulls the collar up on his coat as he walks towards where the office used to be. But it's gone. Like the others, the solicitor's office is closed, the shutters down. The letters above are faded. *Griffin and Lowe Solicitors*. He stands outside, barely able to believe his eyes. It was once thriving, too many clients, they never turned anyone away. But that was over twenty years ago. A lot has changed. Neil Lowe must be in his sixties now, maybe even retired. Griffin wonders what happened.

He huddles in the doorway taking shelter from the drizzle, and takes his phone out, hoping the archives of the internet will provide some answers. But to his surprise a different entry comes up.

Griffin and Lowe Solicitors, 63 Carlton Crescent, Southampton. And a website. He clicks on it – glossy, well made. Using buzzwords like *empower* and *deep sector* and *synergies*. He recognises the address and, curiosity getting the better of him, he gets back into his truck and drives into town.

This office is a far cry from the one he knew. He looks up at the impressive white facade, the shiny glass doors. The logo, displaying his name. He pushes through, and a woman with sleek blonde hair looks up with a saccharine smile.

'How can I help you?' she coos.

'I'm here to see Neil Lowe.'

'Mr Lowe's about to go into a meeting. And he doesn't see clients any more. Can I book an appointment with one of our lawyers?'

'So he's here?' Griffin takes his warrant card out of his pocket and shows it to her. She glances at it, unsure. 'Please tell him that DS Griffin is here to see him.'

Her smile falters. 'Griffin?' she says.

'He'll know who I am.'

She hesitates, then picks up the handset. 'Please take a seat,' she recovers smoothly.

She gestures to the line of classy black armchairs, but Griffin ignores them, choosing to peer through the glass wall to the office on the other side. Rows of open-plan desks, men in smart corporate suits; woman the same, their hair shiny, lips glossy. All designed to convey the same message: we are upmarket. And we charge top dollar for our services.

'Nate?' The voice from behind him grabs his attention. 'Nate Griffin?'

He turns and is immediately transported back twenty years. The man in front of him is older, fatter, greyer, but unmistakeably his father's ex-business partner. He stands, his hands on his hips, appraising Griffin.

'You must have been sixteen when I saw you last. You look just like your father.'

Neil steps forward and grabs Griffin in a warm embrace. Griffin's speechless, still struggling to come to terms with the change in premises, let alone a hug from his father's best friend.

'How are you?' Neil asks, once he's released Griffin from the bear hug.

'I'm good. And you …' Griffin sweeps an arm around the expansive reception. 'You're doing well.'

'We are! I know. It's been a shock to me, too. Come through, I'll give you the grand tour.'

He walks ahead of Griffin, using his security pass on the access door. Inside, there are more desks, more see-through walls. Frosted writing on glass, advertising the lawyers that work within.

Neil catches Griffin's surprised expression. 'Over fifty employees, half of those solicitors spanning residential, family, commercial, dispute resolution. You name it, we've got it.' He stops at the door to his office. *Neil Lowe, Founding Partner.* He shows Griffin through but he eschews his desk, directing Griffin to two armchairs at the side of the room. They sit down, Neil grinning.

'But how did you … How did it get like this?'

'I don't know. After your father ... died,' he finishes awkwardly, 'there was more work than I could handle alone. I took on new blood. Younger recruits. And ...' He smiles. 'Here I am. I don't do much actual lawyering nowadays. I'm more about business development.' He pats his stomach. 'And by that I mean long lunches and drinks. Entertaining clients.' He pauses. 'How can I help you, Nate? This visit is ... unexpected.'

Griffin opts for the truth.

'I wanted to talk about Dad,' he says.

'Okay ...' Neil starts, warily.

'I found out yesterday that the verdict on my father's death was left open.'

Neil nods slowly. 'That's true. I'm sorry, I thought you knew.'

'I always assumed it was suicide. And Mum and Cara let me believe that.'

Neil sits forward, his face sympathetic. 'It was, Nate. Just because the coroner refused to put a label on it doesn't mean it wasn't true. We all know what he did.'

'Do we?' Griffin snaps. 'What do you think happened?'

'Your father was drinking. He was depressed. He drove into a tree.'

'Something that could have easily been an accident.'

'Look.' Neil sits back, his hands folded across his sizeable belly. 'I'm going to tell you this now because I want to stop this rabbit hole you're going down. Before it gets worse.'

'I know how he was.'

'You know what your mother chose to show you. But your father wasn't around much, right?' Griffin nods reluctantly. 'And when he wasn't at home, he was with me.'

Neil gets up, walking across to his desk and opening

148

a bottom drawer. He takes out a glass bottle half full of brown liquid, and two crystal tumblers.

'Glenfarclas twenty-one-year-old Scotch whisky. I normally save this for when one of our solicitors makes partner, but it feels like it might be required today.' He pours two large measures before Griffin can stop him and holds one out. Griffin raises his hand in refusal.

'I don't drink.'

Neil pauses. 'AA?'

'NA. Prescription drugs. Alcohol is a substitute. One I try to avoid.'

Neil pulls the glass back, putting them both in front of him. 'You're so like your father,' he mutters. 'He drank. You knew that? All the time. Except in those days it was easier to hide. A pint at lunchtime. A shot, a few shots, at the end of the day.'

'But,' Griffin counters, 'his medication …'

Neil gives a short cackle. 'His medication – you're assuming he was on it. He said the lithium made him confused, blurred his thinking. So it was touch and go that he'd take it. And he loved the highs.' Neil laughs again. 'God, how he loved them. He thought he was unstoppable, but the reality was he'd turn into a right arrogant bastard. I'm sorry, because I know you remember him fondly, but Mark was an absolute nightmare when he was on one of his highs. I kept this place afloat. I picked up his case load. I kept him away from new clients, knowing he'd freak them out with his outlandish ideas.'

Griffin shakes his head. 'I don't believe you. Dad was larger than life sometimes, but—'

'But nothing. He always had these grand plans. Clients we were going to seduce, wealthy businessmen. So he bought a boat. An actual yacht. Forged my signature. Or at least he tried to, luckily the loan didn't go through.'

'So why did you stay in the partnership?' he asks.

Neil sighs. 'Loyalty, I guess. All through university, this place was our dream. The two names next to the door. To go on without him, seemed … mean. And he did try. You were too young to remember, but he was in and out of hospitals all through his twenties. I hoped …' Neil shrugs. 'I hoped he'd sort himself out. But the highs got longer, the swings more pronounced. He had no idea about the pattern of the day. He'd be up all night, calling me, trying to get into the office. But what could I do? I knew his salary was the only thing keeping your family afloat. I couldn't do that to your mother.'

'How selfless of you,' Griffin snaps.

Neil glares. 'I'm sorry, but that's the truth. You were good kids, you and Cara. And your mother.' He stops abruptly. 'So yes. When I got the call that he'd ploughed his car into a tree, I hated it but it made sense. He killed himself – either with that car or as a result of his mental state. But this way, Angela got the life insurance.'

'You know about that?'

'Of course. Angela and I, we were friends.'

Griffin detects an undertone. 'More than friends?'

'No.' Neil stops and looks him right in the eye. 'Never. I wouldn't have done that to Mark.' He sags now. 'I'm sorry you had to find out this way, but you should leave it alone. You've done well for yourself. You're a detective, right?'

A knock comes before Griffin can reply; a younger man pokes his head around.

'Neil,' he says. 'Your ten o'clock is here.'

Neil nods, then turns to Griffin. 'I'm sorry, I am. If you

150

want to talk again, here's my number.' He holds out a matt-white card, shiny gold lettering. 'Call me. Any time.'

He stands; Griffin takes his lead and shakes his hand. He's introduced to the waiting assistant.

'Otis will show you out,' Neil says.

Otis smiles and gestures down the corridor. Griffin starts walking, Otis talking as they go.

'So, you're a Griffin,' Otis chatters away. 'Any relation to …' He points up, gesturing towards heaven, but meaning the signs above the door.

'His son,' Griffin grunts.

'Oh, that's fascinating.' And Otis babbles as they head down the corridor. But before they go out of sight, Griffin takes one last look back.

Neil Lowe is watching him leave, his face dark. They lock eyes, and for that one moment, Griffin sees into his soul. He sees the same as he does every morning when he looks in the mirror.

Regret. Sorrow. But something else, too.

Fear.

Chapter 27

Cara watches the tiny figure jump off the bridge. Over and over again. Scrolling, searching for something that will give her a clue as to what is going on.

It's dashcam footage. A camera on a passing car, watching Peter Jessop as he climbs the railing, stands for a moment, then drops.

'I hate to say it,' Brody says slowly, 'but maybe he just killed himself.'

'Just?'

'Rather than someone killed him. There was a lot going on in this man's life.' Brody checks her notepad. 'He was about to be evicted from his flat. He'd been dumped by his girlfriend—'

'Who told you this?'

'His landlord. I called him. Apparently, he'd trashed the place, having some sort of episode. The neighbours had to call the police and after that the landlord wanted him out.'

'What a gent,' Cara growls sarcastically. 'Jessop had been having problems for a while?'

'About a month or so.'

'So why choose yesterday. To jump off the bridge?'

Brody shrugs.

'Find out,' Cara says. 'Something triggered him.'

Brody leaves; Cara shouts after her, out of the door of the office. 'Have we got his bag?' Shenton looks up from his desk. 'Jessop's bag. The officer at the scene said he had a rucksack with him. Where is it?'

'Down in evidence, boss,' Shenton replies and turns back to his textbooks.

'So go get it for me,' Cara mutters, but accepts defeat and gets up, heading to their evidence store in the bowels of the police station.

It's good to get away. Space from the facts of the case, whirring in her head. Is it possible that someone could be killing people in this way? And if so, how do they prove it? She's convinced the answer lies in the victimology, in the lives of the dead. There's something in their killer's psyche that is driving them towards these individuals, whether they know it or not.

She's glad she's got Oliver Maddox, her analyst, churning his way through all their data, and it's this thought distracting her as she rounds a corner, straight into Charlie Mills.

He drops his files, paper goes everywhere. She apologises, repeatedly, and bends down to help him gather the pages. But when they stand up, he's smiling.

'Are you okay?' he asks. 'You were going at speed.'

'Yes, yes. I'm fine. I'm sorry.'

She can feel her face flushing as she hands the last piece of paper back to him. For a moment their fingers touch. She pulls away quickly.

'I'm glad you're here, Cara. I was hoping to see you.'

153

'Have you got something new from Isabel Warner's phone?'

'Just data, but ...' He grins. 'I've sent that to Griffin. I wanted to talk to you.'

There are now two red circles in the middle of Charlie's cheeks. He's nervous; it's sweet. Cara's puzzled.

'I was wondering if you wanted to go out some time?' he says. He stumbles over the words, they come out in a rush.

'Me? Out? With you?'

He laughs, awkwardly. 'Yes. Us. On a date. But if you don't want to—'

'No, I would.' Cara returns his smile, feeling a warm glow in her stomach. 'But I have my kids with me this weekend, so ...'

'Tomorrow night? Friday?' He stops himself. 'Is that too keen? I'm supposed to be playing this cool, aren't I?'

'Okay. Tomorrow. You've got my number.'

'I'll message you.'

Charlie grips his files tightly to his chest, then turns, continuing down the corridor. But before he gets to the end he glances back. He smiles, one last time, then is gone.

She pauses, savouring the moment. How odd. She hadn't seen *that* coming. But it's kind of wonderful. Someone finding her attractive. And she likes him. The dimples on his cheeks as he smiles. The way his shirt is never tucked in, poking out the bottom of his jumper. He seems ... nice. Normal.

That makes a change.

She laughs, then remembers what she's doing. Evidence store. Serial killer. How strange life can be, she thinks, the mixture of good and evil, of excitement and dread. And she heads down the stairs to find the rucksack.

Chapter 28

Griffin ignores the calls from Cara. She's wondering where he is, but he's certain she doesn't want to know. Reception cuts out as he walks. She'll get nothing but answerphone from here.

He's in a warehouse. Tall racking lines the huge room, boxes piled on shelves higher than his head. A man keeps pace in front of him, checking the numbers against the piece of paper in his hand. Automatic lights burst into action as they walk.

He stops. 'There you go. One-twenty-slash-four.' He pauses. 'Why do you need this? It's closed.'

'Could be related to a current investigation.'

Griffin waits. After a moment the man gets the message and sighs. 'I need written permission if you're going to take anything. Sign out when you're done.' He walks away, his heavy boots echoing into the distance.

Griffin looks up at the shelving. At the single brown box, puckered and soft from years in the cold and damp. He reaches and pulls it down. It's light; a sign sparse attention was given to the case at the time.

He rests it on the dusty ground, crouches next to it and removes the lid. Inside, a few files lean against each other. He pulls the first out. Beige cardboard with an array of photographs, all showing his father's light blue Ford Focus, mashed into a tree. Winter sunlight dapples through leaves, green shoots of spring contrast with the faded brown mulch on the ground. The shot would be almost picturesque if it weren't for the lines of blood on the paintwork. And the body lying half in, half out of the windscreen.

Griffin closes it quickly. He shouldn't be looking at this. He wants to remember his father as the joyful man he knew. Making a game out of trips to the supermarket, giving him and Cara pretend lists and leaving them squealing with laughter as they looked for *gobbledegook soup* and *oojamaflip chips*.

But Neil was right. Later on, the bad times outnumbered the good. Griffin remembers one Christmas – their mother maintaining forced cheer while their father refused to emerge from the shed, eating canned fruit and listening to country and western music on the radio. On a high – although Griffin hadn't recognised it as such then – his father behaved like a child. Arrogant, out of control. Stubborn.

And on a low, as he was in the weeks before he died, he'd simply disappear. Retreat to the spare room, emerge stinking and silent for food. He was oblivious to Cara and Griffin. An absent father, one present in body but not mind.

But that man is dead. And if Griffin wants to find out how, he needs to brave the photographs.

He opens the file again. He steels himself for what he's about to see. View him as an unknown victim, he tells himself. Not as your father.

His legs are aching in the uncomfortable crouch, so

156

he drops to the floor, sitting cross-legged in the dust and resting the file in his lap. He flips through quickly. Different views of the car, the body in situ. Blood matting brown hair. Flesh torn. Broken glass. The car is almost a part of the tree, the driver's side front corner concertinaed around the trunk while the bark remains fully intact.

The next photos – the road. Worn, grey tarmac. Paint, showing potholes, where rainwater had puddled. Small red markers where debris had fallen. Glass, blood, rubber.

He doesn't need to see any more. On to the next file – reports this time. He hasn't got time to read all of it now so he skims the headlines. *Mechanics intact. Car in a good state of repair before the accident.* The post-mortem: cause of death was blunt force trauma. Consistent with RTA. Blood alcohol level: 0.15 BAC. Well over the legal limit and substantially impaired. His father was wasted when he got behind the wheel that night. Deliberately or otherwise, it's no wonder he ended up ploughing into a tree.

Griffin lays the reports down on the concrete and takes photos with his phone. He can read them in detail later. On to the final file. The interviews.

There are three. The dog walker who found the car. Griffin's mother, Angela. And Neil Lowe. He takes photos of them all for later, but notices they're short, only a few questions were asked. Mainly about Mark Griffin's state of mind before the accident, both Neil and Griffin's mother stating he was 'fine, nothing out of the ordinary'. It jars. If what Neil told him earlier was true, then they'd both lied. And in the same way. Almost as if …

Griffin sits back, glancing from one statement to the other. Almost as if they'd colluded. He frowns. He looks back to the photographs, to the report from the PM and the garage. There was no evidence of anyone else being in the car. Bottles of single malt, his father's drink of choice, littered the footwell. Griffin flicks again. The forensic report: the bottles had Mark Griffin's saliva on the lip, his fingerprints down the sides. Nothing seems inconsistent with the assumption of an accidental death or suicide.

His phone beeps, making him jump. A text somehow getting through. It's Jamie.

Elliott wants you to meet me at the Avery farmhouse. Got a search to do.

He needs to go. The last thing he wants is for Cara to realise what he's up to; she has enough on her plate without worrying about him.

He hurriedly takes photographs of the last few reports, then throws it all back into the box. But before he does, he flicks through the small notebook included with the files. It's the type used by PCs countrywide, and includes all pertinent decisions and actions related to deployments. Without further thought, he replaces the box on the shelf, disturbing the dust in a cloud.

And slips the notebook into his coat pocket.

Chapter 29

Jamie hears the old Land Rover before he sees it. A grumbling engine, metal rattling as it jolts its way up the potholed track. It pulls into the farmyard in a shower of dust.

Before this week, Jamie only knew Griffin by reputation. Fists and brute force. Not a man of subtlety. To Jamie he seems perpetually grubby, dressed today in his usual black trousers, heavy boots and dirty black jacket. A man with the potential to put someone in hospital. Much like his Land Rover.

'Two DSs to do a house search?' Griffin mutters once he's out of the truck. 'What's Cara thinking?'

'Shenton's on the CCTV for the bridge jumper, tracing his movements. Brody's going through his rucksack. That leaves us.'

'And what does she think we're going to find here?'

'Evidence that someone persuaded Kate Avery to kill.'

He notices a side-eye from Griffin as they make their way into the house. Jamie knows Brody has her doubts about Elliott's theory, he wonders about Griffin.

The scene has been released. The bodies taken away;

159

SOCOs have done all they can for the time being. 'I'm not doing a full search for a murder-suicide,' the crime scene manager had stated, bluntly. 'Until you find firm evidence there's another party involved and formally upgrade it to a category one, we're clearing out.'

Jamie relays this conversation to Griffin.

'And how did the CSM think we would find firm evidence without the team that is supposed to find the evidence?' Griffin grumbles as Jamie hands him shoe covers and gloves. 'It's a bit chicken and egg. It feels like we're looking for a ghost.'

Jamie has to agree. But they have their orders. 'Bedrooms or kitchen?'

Griffin points upstairs and Jamie leaves him to it.

The kitchen is neat and tidy. The draining board is clear, everything put away. Even the sink is empty of the normal dregs that get washed into the plughole. He opens a few cupboards. They're largely bare: pasta, beans, canned veg and tuna. All the essentials range. Saucepans are old but functional. This was a woman who didn't have much money but looked after what she had; in life, Kate Avery was meticulous and careful. Was that how she had approached her death?

He opens the fridge. A carton of yellow banded eggs. Half a loaf of bread. And a set of keys. He picks them up, looking closely. Large, possibly for the back. He replaces them and closes the door.

There's nothing here.

He makes his way into the sitting room, trying hard not to look at the armchair in the corner, coated with the woman's blood. The worst of the bodily fluids have been scooped up and removed, but red spatters up the wall, some

160

hair remaining stuck in the dirt-brown pools on the back of the chair.

There's a battered novel on the side table, a bookmark neatly tucked in halfway through, and the sight makes Jamie feel inescapably sad. *The Bell Jar.* Maybe it's good she didn't get to finish, and he wonders how much the fate of its author influenced Kate Avery's own mind. He opens the front cover. There's a stamp for a Dog's Trust charity shop, *50p* written in pencil underneath. Even someone living frugally considered books an essential, something Jamie can respect.

There's a small notebook underneath, and Jamie picks it up. It's old, with flowers on the front, and he opens it. The first few pages contain mundane details – a shopping list, measurements of what must be a window, *curtains* written next to it – but the next page grabs his interest.

Each line details an action. *Had a shower. Had breakfast – porridge. Gave mum her meds. Washed mum.* With a time in the margin. Some are descriptive. Others simply one word. *Dinner. TV.* Jamie assumes this must be Kate, detailing her life. Notes in case she forgets – worried about her encroaching dementia. He pops it into an evidence bag. The last remnants of her life, catalogued for nothing.

Her handbag is lying to the side of the chair and he picks it up, transferring the contents to the side table, piece by piece. A leather wallet: cards, cash inside. A pack of tissues, tampons, a pen, a few receipts. Nothing out of the ordinary. He gives the empty bag a final shake and something moves in one of the side pockets. He digs again: it's a small plastic bright blue tile.

'Anything?' Griffin says from behind him.

Jamie holds up the two books in their plastic. And the tile. 'GPS tracker?' he says. 'In her handbag.'

161

Griffin holds out an evidence bag, Jamie drops it inside.

'Looks like it. Was she concerned she'd lose it? Fits with the theory that Kate Avery thought she had dementia.'

Jamie nods.

'I've bagged up all their meds,' Griffin continues. 'But apart from that it's just a simple house belonging to two women who didn't have much money, and even less going on in their lives.'

'Did you see any evidence of visitors? Friends?'

'Nothing. No drawers with birthday cards. No old postcards or letters.'

Jamie wonders what someone would find of his existence, if they looked. A life on indefinite hold.

'I went through the notes this morning,' Griffin continues, as they walk out, Jamie closing the place up behind them. 'Gunshot residue was recovered on the deceased, pillow fibres in the old woman's mouth. Evidence supports what we found at the scene.'

'I know,' Jamie says miserably. He pulls the front door shut, the slam echoing around the farmyard. He reaches out; Griffin passes him the evidence bag with the medicines from the two women. Jamie swallows, nervous. 'Listen, Griffin? You know … people, don't you?'

Griffin turns, tilting his head with interest. 'People?'

Jamie feels his cheeks flushing, wonders anew whether this is a good idea. 'People who can find you information, if you need it.'

'You mean, dodgy information? What are you implying about me?' Griffin's expression is dark and Jamie's about to backtrack when his face breaks out in a big grin. 'What do you need to know?'

'Someone's complained to the IOPC. About the investigation last year.'

'About you?'

'Not directly. The way it was run.'

'That's no good. Hate those cunts.' Griffin taps his hand against the door of his Land Rover, thinking. 'I might have someone who owes me a favour. What do you need to know?' he repeats.

'Who raised the complaint. Don't do anything illegal,' Jamie adds quickly, but Griffin laughs.

'You crossed that line the moment you asked,' he says, hauling himself into his truck. 'Don't you worry. No one will get into trouble.'

Griffin closes the door with an enthusiastic slam.

Jamie watches as Griffin reverses in a cloud of diesel exhaust, then drives out of the farmyard. He feels a twinge of nerves at the events he's put into action, almost phoning Griffin there and then to tell him to forget it. But he doesn't.

He's furious. At whoever has stirred up the memories from that awful February last year. And this anger needs a focus. Someone to blame.

He gets into his own Vauxhall Corsa, the car starting on the third try, the starter engine wheezing until it finally springs into life. No. He's glad he's asked Griffin. He wants to know.

But what he'll do about the information when he has it, he has no idea.

Chapter 30

The team crowd Shenton's desk as he takes them through the last movements of Peter Jessop. Brody has finished emptying the contents of his rucksack, now reviewed and catalogued and lined up on her desk in evidence bags, and Jamie and Griffin are back from their foray to the Avery farmhouse. They are all sombre, the atmosphere jaded. It worries Cara, that the energy is this low, so early in the investigation.

'I have to say,' Shenton is saying, flicking between screens on his computer at an alarming speed, 'I didn't find any surprises. Jessop left his flat at six-fifteen that morning. Took the bus into the centre of Southampton, to his offices at Easy Windows.'

'Let me guess, they sell double glazing,' Griffin says dourly.

'Jessop worked in telesales. Big call centre there.' Griffin nods in satisfaction; Shenton continues: 'He stayed in that building from seven, until thirteen hundred hours, when he left for the day. Headed straight there, on foot. Never returned.'

Brody consults the file in her lap. 'Uniforms took a

statement from his boss. Says he seemed the same as usual. Spoke to a few co-workers, but otherwise spent all morning on the phone. Made three leads, apparently less than normal. He listened to a few of his recordings. He seemed distracted, but no massive red flags.'

'Except he then walked to the Itchen Bridge and jumped off,' Cara says. 'What have you got from the rucksack?'

'Bugger all.' Brody's face reddens at her lack of professionalism. 'Sorry,' she mutters. 'Packet of chewing gum. Receipts from Tesco. His wallet, containing ...' She checks. 'Two pounds and fifteen pence.'

'No suicide note?'

'No, but he might have left it at the flat. Landlord's going to give us access this afternoon.' She pushes the evidence bags around the table. 'Two prescription drugs. I googled them. An antidepressant, and an antipsychotic.'

Cara sits up straight. 'Really?' Brody passes them across. Cara examines the foil blister packs through the plastic bag. Olanzapine and sertraline. She hands them back to Brody. 'Let Dr Ross know what we've found. And chase him on the results from the PM.'

Brody's forehead furrows, but she stays silent.

'After, head to the flat,' Cara says. 'Griffin, go with her. Speak to these tenants. The ones that made the complaint. Find out what was going on.'

'Boss,' Brody says in agreement, although her face is closed off.

She thinks it's a fool's errand, Cara can tell. 'Ollie, where are you with the connection between these victims?' He's not listening, his eyes scanning the massive screens on his desk, focusing on the flashing data. 'Oliver?' she says, louder, and Brody nudges him.

Their new analyst jumps. He swivels on his chair, removing his earbuds.

'Yes?' he asks. Cara repeats the question. 'Getting there, boss,' he says with a grin. 'Feeding in the data, defining parameters.'

'How long?'

'A few days?'

Cara utters a groan of frustration.

'But I did find something. With the exception of Isabel Warner, all our victims' – Cara notices Brody bristle at the word – 'had little interaction on social media. All were on Facebook, but none of them had used it for at least six months. No accounts on Twitter or Instagram or Snapchat or TikTok. They were all incredibly isolated people – in every aspect of their lives.'

'Making them easy to target?'

'Isolation and the absence of social support are established correlates of suicide risk,' Shenton chips in, 'and are important components of many of the modern models of suicidal behaviour.'

'Meaning they were less likely to ask for help, with fewer people to notice if they were struggling,' Brody finishes.

'And another thing,' Ollie says. 'I ran a brief analysis on the suicide rates in Hampshire. Last year, 113 deaths were ruled a suicide. And that was across the entire county. There were only seven in Eastleigh, twelve in Winchester and twelve in Test Valley. In this week alone we have seen five deaths. I'm not a mathematician, but that seems significant.'

'More than usual for winter months?' Brody asks.

'Much more.'

'Doesn't help us prove the case though, does it?'

'Just shows we have more work to do,' Cara says. She

pulls her shoulders back, mustering confidence. 'Thank you, Ollie. This is a great start. Shenton, work with Ollie, see what new information you can find on the victims to assist the analysis. Jamie – we still don't have the reports from R and P from the neighbours or friends of Kate Avery. Get them. And Griffin and Brody, you know where you're going.' She nods. They start to move off. 'Alana,' Cara says softly. 'A word?'

Brody follows Cara into her office and closes the door behind her. Cara stays standing, Brody in front of her. Face to face.

'If you have something to say about this investigation I want to hear it now,' Cara says.

'Boss?' Brody feigns bafflement but her cheeks are flushed.

'You're clearly not happy about what we're doing and I want to know why.'

Brody pauses, stuttering. 'I'm … It's …'

'Yes?'

'Are we sure these aren't just suicides?'

'You heard Oliver. There are more than you'd expect.'

'But someone killing them? Targeting them? It's ridiculous.'

She blurts this out then stops, pushing her lips together.

Cara sighs and leans back on the edge of her desk. 'A few years ago, I would have agreed with you. The killers we're used to seeing, day to day, are obvious. Men, murdering their wives. Boys stabbing boys on the street. You and I both know we solve the majority of these within forty-eight hours.'

She pauses, waiting for a response. Brody nods.

'But the things I've seen over the last few years? It makes

167

you believe the impossible. And I've questioned myself, I promise you, so many times over the last few days. That I'm being paranoid. That I'm seeing serial killers everywhere. But my gut tells me that something is going on here.'

Brody opens her mouth, thinks better of it, and closes it again.

Cara knows what Brody didn't dare say. 'And yes, my gut has been wrong before. But it has taught me one thing – that I sure as hell don't want to miss something again. So we'll investigate this. And we'll drill down every line of enquiry until we hit hard rock. But what if, Alana? What if we hit oil? What if someone *is* manipulating these people? Wouldn't you prefer to know we did everything we could, rather than let someone get away with it?'

Brody nods. 'Yes, boss.'

'Now, go with Griffin. Investigate the shit out of this,' she adds, trying to inject some humour into her voice. 'And let me know what you find.'

Brody nods one more time then hurries out of Cara's office. Cara watches her go, head down, walking fast in front of Griffin as they leave.

She doesn't like dissent in the ranks, and knew she had to nip it in the bud early. But Brody's thoughts only echo her own. There's nothing here to indicate foul play. Not definitively.

A blip in the statistics. Five people dead. And an ache in her stomach that tells her that something's going on. Something very wrong.

Chapter 31

Brody's quiet on the drive, even letting Griffin take his Land Rover.

'Did she bollock you?' he asks, when they're rattling along the road.

Brody pauses, chewing her lip. 'Do you think she's right?' she says after a moment.

'Doesn't matter if I think she's right or not, she's my senior officer.' He glances across; she's staring down at her hands. 'But for the record, yes. You've only been working for her for a few months, but I've had thirty-nine years of this crap. She's always right. However much you believe otherwise.'

'She's only human. She has … blind spots.'

'That's true. But she's aware of them. Especially now.' Brody nods seriously, but looks unsure. 'Let me tell you a story. Two years into being a cop, I come across this guy. Absolute shitbag. Tatts on his tatts, a right fat fuck. Spouting All Cops Are Bastards bullshit, you know the type. Deployment to his home. When I arrived, I found the wife bloody on the ground, face smashed in. Arrested him for

169

GBH. Open and shut, right?'

'Right …?'

'Mentioned this to Cara over dinner that night. Even showed her the file. She had a few more years' experience than me, but we were the same rank and I thought I knew it all. Do you know the first thing she said after she'd read the first page?' No answer from Brody, but Griffin continues anyway. '"Look at the wife again."'

'But you'd taken her statement?'

'She told me to read it again. Even quoted the ABC principle at me.'

Brody snorts. She knows what he's referring to. Assume nothing, believe nothing, challenge everything. 'And?' Brody asks.

'And – I did what she said. Seemed fine. Passed it across to her – all full of bluster and arrogance. She pointed to the first word. "We." "We were watching TV when he came home." Who was the "we"? They didn't have kids. There was nobody else on the scene when I arrived.' Griffin has Brody's attention now. 'Turns out she had a bit on the side, and he was the one that had beaten her black and blue.'

'But she set up the husband?' Brody says incredulously.

'She wanted the husband to get sent away, then she could move the lover in to their house. Apparently …' Griffin says the next part with a one-handed air quote. '"He'll be a lot nicer without my hubby around."'

'What a pair.'

'Absolutely. So, my point is: Cara listens. She picked up on that within ten seconds when I would have just charged the husband. She's measured, careful. Smart. And I trust her.' He pulls the car to a stop and puts the handbrake on. He looks over at Brody. 'You should too.'

She ignores him, climbing out of the truck and slamming the door behind her. He joins her on the pavement outside the block of flats.

'I don't trust anyone,' she says, almost to herself, then starts walking decisively to the entrance.

Griffin watches her go, feeling a bizarre bond to the woman. Then he follows.

Divide and conquer. There are four flats, including Peter Jessop's. They take two each. Griffin starts with Jessop's – and it doesn't take him long.

The place has been cleared out. At first he thinks the landlord has already been in, readying a vacancy for a new tenant, but then he spots the sheet of paper left in the middle of the spotlessly clean table. The note is written in blue ballpoint pen. Straight to the point.

It hurts too much. This is the only way to make them stop. You can't save me. I'm sorry. Pete.

Griffin photographs it in situ, then picks it up with a gloved hand and gently places it in an evidence bag.

There's a white A4 envelope underneath it, unsealed. He opens it and pulls out the document. *This is the last Will and Testament* … It's short, barely two pages, but witnessed and signed. It all looks legal and above board.

He continues his search. The bins have been taken out; the fridge is empty. Brody's doubts take root in Griffin's mind. It strikes Griffin as the last actions of a man taking care of business. Peter Jessop knew what he was about to do.

He bags up a few boxes of drugs – the same ones found at the scene – and takes photographs. He puts all the evidence together in his bag, ready to go. He closes the door with a heavy heart.

Onto the next. Brody is nowhere to be seen so he moves to the neighbour. He knocks, and it's opened by a man, warily peering out of the gap.

Griffin holds up his warrant card. The door closes, the chain is slowly removed and the man comes out. He stands in the hallway, the door half-closed behind him.

'Do you mind if I come in?'

The man looks hesitant.

'What are you doing in there, Mr ...?'

'Ladbrook. And nothing.' Griffin tries to peer behind him into the flat. 'Look, I was watching porn, all right?'

'Normal porn?'

'Yes ...'

Griffin sighs. 'Then I don't give a shit. I just want to know about your neighbour. Peter Jessop? He lived next door. He died yesterday.'

Ladbrook hesitates, then pushes back into the flat. Griffin follows and can't suppress a small smile as the man hurries to the remote and points it at the television. The paused image, of an eighties permed woman being efficiently serviced by a skinny bloke in a plumber's outfit, disappears to black. This porn has been around for a while.

Ladbrook turns, regaining his composure. 'Did he kill himself? Jessop. Is that how he died?'

Griffin blinks. 'Why do you say that?'

'Because that's all he ever said.' He points at the wall that links Jessop's flat to his. '"Leave me alone, or I'll kill myself." Full volume. After a few weeks of that, I wished he would.'

Ladbrook has the grace to look ashamed.

'When was this?' Griffin asks.

'The last month or so? When he moved in, he seemed fine. Kept to himself, quiet. I'd meet him in the corridor as he went to work and we'd say hello but nothing else. Distant, but that's a good quality in a neighbour. And then he went nuts. All night, loud music, shouting. Banging. Like he was having a party.'

'And was he?'

'No! That's what was so weird. By the third night of this I knocked on his door. And it was just him. His whole flat in darkness, music blaring out. He poked his head around, apologised, and then went back in. The music turned off straight away but the shouting continued. Like he was having a conversation with someone.'

'Are you sure there was nobody else there?'

'Certain. I only ever heard his voice. Shouting at himself.'

'And that's why you complained?'

'Did it again the next night. And the next. Had enough and told the landlord. Turns out I wasn't the only one that had a problem with it. I was glad he was going to leave. I don't like to be disturbed …' He stops. Flushes. 'Is that all?'

'For now. Thank you.' Griffin glances at the black television, at the line of VHS tapes, the box of tissues. Ladbrook stares, an obstinate expression on his face. 'Keep the porn legal, right?' he finishes.

'Yes, officer,' he replies and watches Griffin leave the flat. Griffin closes the door behind him and waits. After a moment the television starts up again. Faked moans and groans. Griffin smiles to himself. At least someone's having a good day.

He meets Brody on the stairs. He relays what he's found out; Brody smirks at the neighbour's choice of daytime pursuit.

'Much the same here,' Brody says. 'Minus the porn. Shouting. Thuds. Crying. The bloke I spoke to thought he was having a bad trip.'

'Every night?'

She shrugs. His phone rings. He holds it up apologetically and she walks in front of him to the car.

'Thanks for phoning me back, mate.' It's started raining and Griffin takes shelter under the roofline. 'I need a favour.'

'Figure you weren't calling for a friendly catch-up,' the man says at the other end. 'What do you want, Griffin?'

Griffin first met Rick on a drug bust when they were both PCs. Walked in as Rick was pocketing a bundle of twenties, his face guilty, surrounded by the dirt and grime of the cottage industry.

'Don't turn me in, Griff,' Rick had said, his voice desperate. 'I need it. My mum's sick. My wife's taking me to the cleaners.'

Griffin knew a liar when he saw one. And housed in that dark basement, he made a decision.

'Pick an excuse,' Griffin growled. 'Do what you want, it's no skin off my nose.' But they both knew the contract they'd entered into. Tit for tat.

He kept an eye on him; like most of the shitbags Griffin knew, he needed to be watched. And, ironically, Rick had ended up as an advisor in the hallowed halls of the IOPC. More to the point, it was useful, but Griffin kept his powder dry, in case he needed it one day.

When Jamie asked, Griffin considered whether this was worth his while. There were only so many favours to be had. But by helping out Jamie it meant the new DS was now in his debt. And this guy was getting stale anyway.

'A name, that's all,' Griffin says now. 'Someone's made a

formal complaint about the serial murder last year.'

'The one Bishop was SIO on? I heard someone was looking into that.' A long pause. 'A name? That's it? And it won't come back to me?'

'Have I said anything in fifteen years?'

Another beat. 'I'll message you the details. Then delete my number off your phone, Griffin. We're quits.'

'I'll decide when we're quits,' Griffin retorts, but the man's already gone.

He looks over to Brody waiting in the truck and pulls his packet of cigarettes out of his pocket, lighting one. He takes a long inhale, then strides towards the Land Rover.

'Finish that outside,' Brody says when he opens the door.

'It's my car,' he replies, but he stays in the cool air, the drizzle settling in his hair, taking a few drags.

'Your call,' he says to Brody through the open door. 'What would you do next?'

'Wait for the PM. Get his medical records. Then draw a big black line under the whole sorry mess.'

He nods, stubbing the cigarette out on the concrete and climbing in the truck. 'I'm starting to agree with you. Want to go for something to eat?'

He says it casually, fancying the company, but the look on her face is so full of disgust he regrets it immediately.

'Nothing in it,' he quickly adds. 'Just as colleagues.'

'No. Thank you. Drop me back at the nick.'

Griffin does as he's told.

Chapter 32

Brody calls Cara on the journey back to the nick; Griffin's glad he doesn't have to make conversation. Is going to the pub with him such an unpleasant proposition? She didn't have to be that abrupt.

Cara tells them to call it a night so Griffin drops Brody in the car park and heads to the pub – with or without company, he's in no rush to go home and risk another confrontation with Ron. The stolen notebook from the document store burns a hole in his pocket; the photos on his phone demand to be examined.

His local is a massive Wetherspoons, perfect for its anonymity. He orders a pint of Coke and a pie and chips and takes a seat at the far end of the pub, back to the wall.

When he's sure he's not being overlooked, he takes the small notebook out of his pocket. It's the same as the ones he's used for years. The Hampshire Constabulary crest at the top, *Pocket Notebook* below in blue block capitals. He flicks through.

Luckily, this particular PC seems to be female, with handwriting that's actually legible. She's a detailed notetaker, probably at the beginning of her career. Times, places, names, and a brief description of what she was doing and why. He riffles through to the right time – etched on his memory. February 24, 1999. The day his dad died.

And there it is.

She wasn't the first on the scene but was called out later to gather evidence and do preliminary interviews. She writes in a scratchy black biro, the pages now water damaged and dried, wrinkly to the touch. The words are brief but paint a picture more compelling than any essay.

24/02/99. 23.46. Visit to NOK. Wife – Angela. No answer at door. Left card.

Griffin remembers both he and Cara were out that night. In town, drinking. Underage, in his case, but who cared about that? Cara arrived home at one in the morning to find their mother, crying. This was before they had mobile phones, no way of contacting them in an emergency, and it resulted in Cara phoning around his mates' parents, trying to track him down. In the end, she drove out to the local park. Found him lying in the grass, drunk out of his skull, stoned. Somehow dragged him home.

He woke that morning in his own bed, fully clothed and confused, the inside of his mouth feeling like someone had poured turps down it. And Cara, sitting by his feet, her face red and blotchy.

'Is it Dad?' he'd asked, instinctively knowing. And she'd nodded.

What followed was a mixture of feelings. Sorrow, yes, because he was his father and he loved him. But also, relief. The family was nicer without him in it. The unpredictable, chaotic presence had gone. His mum was more relaxed. She went back to work and made friends, and he and Cara could have mates around again, safe in the knowledge their father wouldn't turn up and make a scene.

Griffin flicks through the photos on his phone, squinting at the tiny images. The car, almost sideways. Skid marks on the tarmac – the wheels had locked at some point; he had tried to brake. A last-minute regret, or something else? Car crashes are not Griffin's area of expertise, so he puts a call in, to his mate at the Serious Collision Investigation Unit. Sergeant Danny Cohen doesn't answer, so Griffin leaves him a message, details sparse. *Cold case: would value your opinion.* Enough to elicit some interest.

He goes back to the notebook. A later page.

00.34. Call from NOK. Return to 45 Summersdale Road. Death notice to NOK.

A few simple words to convey the news that would destroy them. But Griffin frowns. He looks to the previous page. Where had his mother been that night? She never went out. They would leave for the pub and she'd be on the sofa. Return and she'd be in bed, food in the fridge under a clingfilmed plate.

His dinner arrives. Dried-up offerings, the pastry burned, the gravy salty, but better than anything he'll get at home. He coats it in tomato ketchup then eats it, one eye on his phone as he reads the reports taken that night. An interview with his mother, simple questions. *How had Mark been acting lately? When did you last see your husband?* And, *Where were you that night?*

At home, she had replied. *I fell asleep on the sofa. Didn't hear the bell.* It sounds plausible enough; the interviewer didn't ask any follow-up questions. And why would they? She wasn't a suspect. This wasn't a suspicious death.

178

But it's Neil Lowe's replies that give him pause. *I was at home. Fell asleep on the sofa.*

Griffin leaves his soggy vegetables and goes outside for a smoke. While he drags on his cigarette he ponders those identical replies. Both of them? Asleep? The same exact wording again. A sign of collaboration, a lie.

Griffin smokes quickly, his anxiety making him inhale and exhale almost immediately. Maybe it's time to find out why.

Griffin returns to his table, pushes the remainder of his dinner aside and gathers up his belongings. He heads home, a mess of knots churning his insides. What were his mum and Neil trying to hide? Was it a simple affair, or something more sinister?

He parks his Land Rover a few streets away in the hope of avoiding Ron Warner, and walks slowly to his flat. But as he draws closer, he notices a figure lingering in the forecourt. A man, with a plastic bag in his hand, something heavy inside. As Griffin watches, he glances towards the darkened windows of the Portakabin, then away again. Hesitating. Suspicious as hell.

Griffin approaches, softening his tread, until he can make out the man's face. But he drops his wary approach when he realises who it is. It's Dougie. Isabel's best friend. He speeds up again, no longer worrying about being seen, and shouts a hello when he's closer. Dougie turns sharply, the look on his face vacillating between fear and eagerness. He tentatively lifts a hand.

'What are you doing here?' Griffin asks. 'Your house is miles away.'

'I ... I don't know.' Dougie bites his lip. 'I didn't expect to see you.'

'I live in the area,' Griffin says, vaguely. He feels like he needs to hide his association with Isabel, shame re-emerging. 'You wanted to see where Issy died,' he says.

Dougie pauses. He looks over at the Portakabin again. 'I just ... miss her.' Griffin knows a bit about grief, and stays quiet, waiting for the guy to talk. Dougie continues: 'We had good nights in there. Talking. Drinking. Doing—' Guilt flashes. Griffin chooses to ignore it. 'Getting ready to go out. Then dancing all night, until we'd come back here, fall asleep, and wake, panic that her dad would arrive for work and find us.'

He looks to Griffin now, understanding.

'You work here, don't you? I thought I recognised you, when you came around. You're the security guard. So, what? You're a cop but you do this on the side?'

'On and off,' Griffin says, unsure whether he's referring to the policing or security.

'You'd wake us, rattling around. You knew we were here?'

Griffin nods. 'Always. I didn't realise it was you, but I knew Issy stayed the night here sometimes. And so did her dad. He didn't mind.'

'Issy always had good things to say about her dad. She felt rotten, she said, for being such a screw-up and giving him a hard time.' Dougie peers at Griffin. 'Did you sleep with her?'

'No,' he says. 'But she tried.'

'Don't feel bad. She came on to everyone. Even me. Did she ... Did she ask you to ...'

Griffin knows what he's referring to. 'Yes.'

180

'Did you—'

'No.'

Dougie looks to the concrete, scuffing his toe in the dirt. 'Some guys did. I'd see her, face all smashed up, bruises. She said she deserved it. Poor Issy. I hope she's happier, where she is now.'

Griffin doesn't believe in heaven or hell, only the sort that humans inflict on each other in their time on earth, but Dougie doesn't need a lecture.

'Go home, Dougie,' he says.

Dougie stares at the Portakabin for a moment then down to the plastic bag in his hand. He holds it out to Griffin. 'Here. I don't want them.' Griffin takes the bag before realising at the last moment that it's a four-pack of beer.

'I can't—' Griffin begins.

'Please?' Dougie's face is stricken. 'I can't drink tonight. I thought I wanted to … but … it doesn't help, you know? Don't let me drink.'

And without waiting for a reply, he shuffles away.

Griffin opens the plastic bag of beer in his hand. Heineken. Not the best, not the worst. Not what he should be drinking, in any case.

He stands there for a moment, knowing that he should walk across to the bins and drop the alcohol inside. But instead, he reaches down and takes one of the cans out. Placing the others at his feet, he tugs the ring pull. A flood of froth emerges and without thinking he places his mouth against the top to stem the flow. And the taste. The bubbles. The smell. Everything about it is irresistible.

He can't help himself; he opens it fully then takes a swig. And another. Blissful, instant relief. The bitter hops on his tongue, the sweetness. The buzz as the alcohol goes straight to his head after three, four months of not drinking.

The rest of the beer goes in long, deep swallows and he crushes the can in his hand, looking at it. He feels better. For a few short moments he's forgotten about his father and the secret between Neil and his mum. He's forgotten about how he failed Isabel, how everything had gone wrong with Jess. Who cares that he shouldn't be doing this? He's better now, he can control it.

He glances around the car lot then hurries to his door, down the stairs to his flat, where he opens the next can, then the next, and the next. And by the time all four have gone he lies on his bed, and watches the shadows move across the ceiling, a pleasing numbness taking over.

He burps. The alcohol has flooded his head, he regrets nothing. And the room swims as he falls into a deep, drunken sleep.

DAY 5

FRIDAY

Chapter 33

The care home hasn't changed. Nearly two years since he was last here, Griffin realises as he rings the doorbell, that's how much of a shitty son he is. Even the assistant is the same: Miles, in his mustard yellow jumper.

'Hello, Griffin,' he says. 'Long time no see.'

Griffin doesn't bother with pleasantries. 'Same room?'

'Yes. But you should have phoned. She's not great today.'

'I'll cope.'

Miles shrugs. 'Sign in first,' Griffin hears as Miles walks away.

'Sarcastic bastard,' Griffin mutters as he bends down to the visitors' book. Even if he does have a point.

Griffin's hangover is making him grumpy; he'd woken that morning with a cat on his chest, a thumping headache, and a dry mouth. A familiar foe. He'd downed a pint of water then stood in the shower, letting the jets pummel his face, trying to wash away the regret and self-loathing. Frank yowled; he threw away the rejected dried food then retched as he chopped up some leftover chicken. No more, he told himself, sweeping the empty cans into the bin. Day one. Start again.

He scribbles his name in the visitors' book, then flicks back to previous pages. Cara usually visits on a Wednesday, although not this week, he sees. And another visitor – *Andrew Elliott*, then, next to it in a childish scrawl: *Tilly* and *Josh*. Roo bringing the kids to visit their grandma. So that cheating bastard does have a good side.

He closes the visitors' book and pushes through the double doors, following the corridor to his mother's room at the end. The same watercolour prints are on the wall, faded to yellow over the years. One has tilted, and Griffin corrects it as he walks. The place smells of disinfectant, of bleach. The socially acceptable alternative to the piss and sweat that Griffin can detect underneath.

He knocks on his mother's door but doesn't wait for an answer. He calls out as he enters.

'Mum?'

It's one room, with a bathroom off to the right. His mother is propped up in a hospital bed, rails either side, facing towards a large window overlooking the garden. Her eyes are closed; she has a small smile on her face. She looks beatific.

'Hello,' he begins. He places his hand gently on her arm. 'How are you?'

She opens her eyes slowly and the smile evolves. She reaches a papery hand towards his face, veins and bones visible below the thin skin. He notices her nails are neatly trimmed and filed, her clothes worn but clean. She smells of lavender talcum powder.

'I wasn't expecting you today,' she says. 'They said you weren't coming.'

'You know me, Mum. Never good at planning.'

She frowns. 'Well, you're here now. Make me a cup of

184

tea. Tell me about work.'

Griffin heads to her tiny kitchenette in the corner and puts the kettle on. There are two mugs in the sink; he washes them up while he waits.

'I've gone back to the nick,' he says, shouting over the fizz of the kettle. 'I'm working with Cara again.'

He's not sure his mum has heard, but his phone rings, distracting him. It's Rick from the IOPC.

'Two names,' Rick says, getting straight to the point. 'A married couple: Jennifer and Gordon Blake. Does that mean anything to you?'

'No. Does it say who they are?'

'Didn't look that far. All you wanted were the names, you said.' And he hangs up. Jennifer and Gordon Blake, Griffin thinks, making a note on his phone. He won't send it to Jamie yet – he wants to see his face when he tells him. Make sure he's not going to do anything stupid and get them both into trouble.

The kettle clicks off. He pours the water, takes milk out of the otherwise empty fridge and dumps the teabags in the bin. Before he carries them back to his mother's bedside, he has a quick look in the kitchen cupboard. Nothing but aged crockery; what does he expect to find?

'The nick?' his mum echoes as he puts the tea in front of her. 'And who's Cara?'

He frowns. This is obviously what Miles meant about a bad day. 'Your daughter, Cara?'

He's met by a blank look. 'Are you cold?' he continues, starting to scour the cupboards. 'I'll look for a blanket.'

While he searches, he thinks back to when he last saw his mum. At that point she could remember who he was, who Cara was, but certain pieces of information had already been lost. That Cara had got married. That Griffin's wife had died. That she had grandchildren at all. Today it seems that deterioration has worsened.

His search is quick and pointless. Neat piles of her clothing; old paperbacks; belongings stashed away for who knows when. Nothing that might give any indication of what happened to his father.

But maybe she can remember something of the past.

'Mum,' he says, and her brow furrows again, seemingly unable to reconcile the label. 'Angela,' he tries instead. 'Do you remember Neil Lowe? From the office?'

'Yes, of course. He's your best friend. Why would I forget Neil?'

Griffin pauses. She thinks he's his father, lost in a world over thirty years ago. He shouldn't … But he needs to know.

'What's going on with Neil, Angela,' he asks softly.

For a moment, she's frozen. Her watery eyes lock onto him and she reaches forward with her hand and touches his cheek. 'Mark …' she says, no more than a croak, then a tear rolls down her face.

Griffin tries again. 'Is something going on with Neil?'

'No, no …' She shakes her head, trying to pull a memory loose. 'It's a secret. How do you know?'

'I found out—'

'I knew you wouldn't understand!' It emerges as a shriek, her normally tremulous voice finding force. 'You've never been there for me. Ever. And Neil … Neil helps me. He understands.'

Griffin reels backwards. Not at the words – which in some part he already knew – but at the force of her anger.

'He works alongside you every day. He knows what a nightmare you are. Your moods. Your selfishness. How can

186

you blame me for what we've done?'

'I don't blame you—'

'You do. I can see it on your face. You blame me. When all I wanted was a few moments of human connection. With a real man. Someone who can look after me – and the kids. Did you ever think of them?'

She's shaking now. A full body tremor that worries Griffin. She's a frail old woman, what has he done? He reaches forward, but she bats him away; just the force of that contact makes a red bruise rise on her arm.

'Please, calm down. We can sort this out.'

'There's nothing to sort out, Mark. I'm leaving you. I made that clear. You're only here for the files. Those damn files. Go.' She points towards the door. 'Get out!'

Griffin backs away, reversing into Miles as he appears in the doorway.

His mum starts sobbing and Miles looks at him, angrily.

'What did you say?'

'I … I …'

'I told you she wasn't having a good day, and now look at her. It'll take us hours to calm her down.'

'I didn't—'

'Leave. Please.' And Miles closes the door in Griffin's face, blocking out his mother's sobs.

Griffin stands in the corridor, feeling like an absolute shit. He starts to leave, until his gaze catches on the cupboard doors lining the corridor. Storage. Maybe … He picks the one closest to his mother's room and pulls it open. A hoover and a box of cleaning products. He tries the one on the other side, and this time finds her belongings: old clothes pile messily on top of blankets and spare pillows and books. And at the bottom: a cardboard box, files stacked inside.

187

He pulls it out, the other bits and pieces collapsing to fill the space, and looks at one of the labels. *Griffin and Lowe, 1996–1998.* They must be important for his mum to have kept them all these years.

He carries the box towards the exit, and as he does, two more orderlies come barrelling towards him and into the room. One of them has a syringe in his hand and as they open the door Griffin can hear his mother's crying has escalated to a hysterical scream.

Griffin stands in the darkened corridor, reeling, the box balanced in his hands. He's got his answer, but at what cost?

Chapter 34

Ollie's technical vernacular is driving Cara nuts. The analyst is explaining to the team what he's been doing, talking about scraping, parsing and something to do with snakes. She's already annoyed – Griffin is AWOL; her calls have all gone unanswered – and the indecipherable jargon is making matters worse.

'In English, please, Ollie?' she interrupts.

He looks up, a broad smile spreading across his face. 'Basically, I've set up an application, or a bot, that will visit a website, grab relevant pages and extract information. This is then saved and searched.'

'And you've done this for all our victims?'

'Yes. Everything about them I could find. We already have their bank statements and, as I mentioned before, none of them except Isabel Warner used social media, but that's not to say there isn't information out there. Shopping habits, posting on chat boards, mentions in the local newspaper. I'm always surprised how stupid people are when it comes to their internet security. Intensely private information can be accessed in seconds. For example, did you know that

Griffin's a Gemini, which explains a lot, and Brody here won Little Miss Wiltshire at the age of ten.'

All eyes turn to Brody. 'In a beauty pageant?' Shenton asks, disbelieving.

'Yes, now piss off,' Brody snaps.

'Get to the point, Oliver,' Cara says. Ollie gives her a look which tells her he knows more about her than she would wish, but turns back to his notes.

'This scraping,' he says, 'combined with data from witness statements and what we already know from our own investigation has given us a few points of commonality. They all live within seven miles of each other.'

'We knew this already.'

Ollie continues, unperturbed at Cara's tone. 'They all shop at a small Tesco Express in Chandler's Ford. They're all part of a Facebook group called *Mental Health Matters*, but, as I mentioned before, none of them have been on it for a while.'

'Could they have met someone on there?' Brody says. 'And been targeted as a result?'

'Possibly. But the group has twenty thousand members. So it wouldn't be an easy search.'

'Can we have the data on anyone they've interacted with?'

Before Oliver replies, Cara's phone vibrates in her pocket; she surreptitiously pulls it out.

It's Charlie. *I know you're busy but you have to eat. 7.30 p.m. I'll pick you up?*

This date couldn't have come at a worse time. But he's right, she will need dinner. She could eat, go home early. Do some work later if needs be. And she wants to see him; a spark of a silly grin has taken hold of her face.

Yes, okay, she replies, then her address. And, realising she sounds a bit blunt: *Looking forward to it.*

She turns her attention back to the team, who are now discussing the interviews with friends of Kate Avery that Jamie has retrieved from Response and Patrol.

'Acquaintances would be more accurate,' Jamie says. 'The closest neighbour is the next farm, a few fields away. She said she used to speak to Eileen regularly, but nothing for a good year. Nobody had spoken to Kate in months. Not even the postman.'

'All the victims were served by the same Royal Mail Delivery Office,' Oliver offers.

'Did they all have the same postie?'

'In this day and age? When was the last time you had the same postman two days in a row?'

Cara senses the discussion is heading down a rabbit hole. 'Write it down,' she says, interrupting them. 'Move on.'

Shenton adds it to the board, along with the other points of commonality. Cara notices he's added the wording from Jessop's suicide note. *You can't save me.* It's galling that nobody could.

Back to reality. 'What else?' she asks Ollie.

'They've all tried to sell furniture on Southampton FreeAds. And they all bought Taylor Swift's latest album.' Oliver sits back and crosses his arms with finality.

'Along with millions of other people,' Brody says.

'That's it?' Cara replies, unable to keep the annoyance out of her voice.

Oliver looks cowed. 'So far. I'm waiting for the data from the medical reports from Dr Ross, and I need to input everything we've got from the interviews and enquiries we've followed up on. But that all needs to be entered by hand and—'

191

Cara cuts him off. 'Shenton, help him …' Her mobile starts ringing and she glances at the number. Her mother's care home. 'I've got to take this.'

The team know what they're doing; she leaves them and goes into her office, closing the door. She answers the phone and the man on the other end talks at her for a moment. Cara listens intently, struggling to catch up.

She slumps behind her desk. 'I'm sorry,' she says to Miles, her voice rising in exasperation. 'But my brother's done what?'

Chapter 35

Jamie's listening to Oliver, but all through the briefing his gaze flicks to the door, waiting for Griffin. He messaged him last night but got the one line answer: *I'll speak to you tomorrow.*

Jamie's jittery, nervous about the chain of events he's put into action. He's always been law-abiding. Following procedure, never cutting corners. But lately it's felt like nobody else is following the rules, so why should he?

As Cara's called away, the door opens and Griffin arrives. He looks pale, weary, but they all do. He can't imagine anyone is sleeping well.

The group disperses. Griffin sees him staring and nods in acknowledgement, then inclines his head towards Cara's office. He needs to speak to the boss first, understandable.

Jamie busies himself looking at the Facebook group Oliver mentioned until raised voices attract his attention. Behind the glass wall, Cara is gesturing wildly, her face contorted with anger. Griffin is straight-backed, but quiet. Jamie gets the feeling it's nothing to do with work; everything Cara does as a DCI is measured and steady and this is definitely not that. Only family can provoke fury of this magnitude.

After a moment, the shouting stops and Griffin leaves. Everyone, Jamie included, innocently turns back to their screens. Jamie feels a tap on his shoulder.

'Outside,' Griffin says.

Jamie follows him from the incident room, guessing correctly that they're heading towards the smoking shelter. Griffin's cigarettes are already in his hand by the time he arrives, lighter in flame in seconds.

He takes a long inhale and blows the smoke into the rain.

'What happened?' Jamie asks.

Griffin shakes his head, head bowed to the ground. He takes another few short, hungry drags.

'Listen, I got the information.' He looks up, meets Jamie's gaze. 'Are you sure you want it?'

'Yes.'

Another inhale, smoke coming out of his nose in two long plumes, then the rest in a gust from his lips as he talks. 'You're a good bloke, Jamie. A good cop. A trustworthy one, and that's a rare thing, these days. You need to be sure. Because once the evils are unleashed it's impossible to go back.'

'Tell me.'

'Jennifer and Gordon Blake.'

The names stab Jamie like knives to the chest.

'You know them?' Griffin asks.

Jamie nods. He turns away from Griffin, not wanting his colleague to see how much it's affected him. 'Can you hold the fort for me? Tell Elliott I need to go out for a bit?'

'Sure. But Hoxton—'

'I'll be back in a few hours.'

And before Griffin can say any more he's striding away, towards the car park.

Once he gets in his car he takes deep breaths. In for ten, out for ten. It doesn't calm him. He wishes he smoked. He wishes he drank, any vice he could use to anaesthetise the deep ache in the middle of his body. A thousand questions whirr in his head – and only two people know the answers.

He starts the car, and drives.

Half an hour takes him out of the city. Jamie switches the radio on, then off again, the additional noise not helping his addled brain. He knows the route by heart, barely having to think as he makes the twists and turns into the pretty village with its post office and town hall and picture-perfect church.

He takes the last junction and pulls into a gravel driveway. There are two cars parked but that's no guarantee of someone being home, knowing how sociable the Blakes can be. He gets out and walks to the front door, ringing the bell.

'Jamie! How lovely to see you!' The greeting is enthusiastic with open arms. Jamie reluctantly accepts a hug. 'How are you?'

'I'm fine,' he says flatly. 'Jen, can we talk? Is Gordon here?'

'No, he's at bridge club.' Her expression turns to concern. 'Is it about Pippa? Has something new come up?'

'You could say that.'

He's ushered into the lounge. To sit on the Chesterfield sofa, in front of the bookcases with tomes on photography and art, the room where his wife had grown up.

Jennifer and Gordon Blake. His in-laws.

His mother-in-law sits opposite him. She has aged since

Jamie saw her last. Nearly a year ago – at Pippa's funeral. Standing next to Jen and Gordon as her coffin was lowered into the earth, feeling stiff and awkward, knowing that he was the reason for their sobs. His failure to save her. And the knowledge now that they thought the same, makes matters so much worse.

He examines her face, looking for any trace of guilt, but all he can see are the sorrow lines, scored into her forehead. She's lost weight, her body has withered and sagged, torn apart by the grief of losing their only child in such a brutal and violent way. Jen looks worried now, apprehensive. That something he tells them is going to destroy them again.

'You put in a complaint,' he says. Matter-of-fact. 'To the IOPC.'

Her face falls. She looks as if she's going to cry. She stands up and walks across to the side table, picking up the phone and dialling.

'Gordon,' she says. 'You need to come home.' Then a pause. 'Jamie's here.'

She replaces the phone. Sits down again, clenching her hands in her lap. Then she jumps up. 'Do you want a cup of tea, dear,' she says. 'I'll get you a cup of tea.'

He lets her go. She doesn't want to sit in front of him, in this quiet living room, with only the tick of the grandfather clock to distract them. He waits, listening to the sound of the kettle, the chink of a teaspoon in fine china. Outside the window, blue tits and sparrows flutter around a feeder in the garden.

Jamie hears the front door opening, hurried footsteps and whispers. Then Gordon arrives in the room.

When Jamie first met him, he was in awe of his future wife's father. Terrified to ask for her hand in marriage, scared to broach a conversation about anything other than England rugby. Nearly as tall as Jamie, haughty, short grey hair trimmed around his balding pate, he greets Jamie now with a firm handshake. Like Jen, grief has stripped him of the padding; his jumper is baggy, his cheeks hollow. He gestures for Jamie to sit down again, and Jen appears with a tray of cups.

'They assured us it was confidential,' Gordon begins, as if that is the problem at hand. He declines the offer of tea from his wife, who perches on the chair next to him.

'Police know police,' Jamie offers as an explanation. 'So, it's true? You've put in a complaint against me.'

'Not against you. Against the investigation.'

'Same thing. I was the DS on that case.'

'But you weren't the man in charge.' Gordon sighs. 'This isn't personal.'

'It feels personal—'

'Oh, grow up,' the older man snaps. 'This wasn't an error in paperwork. This was a huge screw-up in a murder investigation, where people died. My daughter. Your wife,' he says pointedly. 'I would have thought you wanted justice.'

'We got justice,' Jamie replies. 'Going after Adam Bishop doesn't change that. Nobody on that investigation worked harder than him. He wanted to catch that killer. Don't you think he knows he screwed up? He was stabbed!'

'We understand,' Jen says gently. 'But …'

'Mistakes were made,' Gordon repeats. 'We want to make sure it doesn't happen again.'

How can Jamie explain to these people? That killers like the one they experienced last year are a one-off. An aberration that can't be planned for. No amount of policy or procedure could have predicted the events of last February, and Jamie knows that every bone in Adam's body wishes things could have gone differently.

'Why now?' he says instead. 'Pippa died eleven months ago. The inquest has been closed. Why complain now?'

Jen looks nervously to Gordon. 'We had a phone call,' the man says.

'From whom?'

'We don't know. Unknown number. Phoned, one evening, a few weeks ago. Said he was a journalist and how could we stand by and let this go.'

Jamie's incredulous. 'Let what go?'

'Pippa's death. She was abducted from the home of one of the lead detectives in the middle of a major murder investigation and nobody thought to offer any protection.'

'We had no reason to believe she was in danger. Don't you think that if we had even the slightest inkling that I would have left her that evening? That I would have …' He chokes back the emotion.

Jen reaches forward, touching his hand. 'We know that, love. But the police should have been more careful. With you all.'

'And that man, whoever it was, was right,' Gordon says. 'And the IOPC obviously think there's reason to investigate. It's out of our hands now,' he concludes, stubbornly.

'Who was this man?'

'He didn't give his name. Said he shouldn't have been calling, didn't want to risk the integrity of his job.'

'How noble of him,' Jamie says sarcastically. 'And you listened to the opinion of a man you've never met. Over me?'

'We haven't seen you for months, Jamie,' Jen says softly.

'I know, I've—'

'Been busy. You said,' Gordon says, his voice hard. 'Doing the same thing you were when Pippa died. Or maybe you've been at the pub.'

Jamie freezes. This *is* about him. About his failings as a husband. He's never forgiven himself for that fact: that he was out drinking when he should have been at home, protecting his wife. But before he can say anything, his phone beeps. He looks at it. It's Griffin.

Where are you? Elliott's getting suspicious.

That's the last thing he needs: a pissed-off boss. He has a job to do. The same job he was doing when Pippa died.

'I loved her,' he says.

And he stands up, walking out of the house. Heading to yet another place of death and misery. He leaves the undrunk tea growing cold in the stale living room, the knowledge that people who once loved him blame him for his wife's death.

There are no arguments.

Especially when he feels the same way himself. It was his fault. He was wrong to ever believe otherwise.

Chapter 36

Hours later, Cara is still fuming from Griffin's trip to the care home. The first time in nearly two years and he upsets their mother so much they have to sedate her.

'What did you say?' Cara hissed, trying – and failing – to keep her anger under wraps. 'She thought you were Dad.'

'She assumed and—'

'And you asked her about Neil? She's a frail old lady, Nate. Your mother! Not a murder suspect.'

'Did you know? About her and Neil?' Griffin snapped.

'I guessed. Years ago.'

'And you didn't tell me?'

'No, I didn't. And why does it matter? I understood, then. Same as I understand now. Dad was a nightmare. She spent a lot of time with Neil, trying to get to grips with his bipolar. It was inevitable things would go that way.'

'But what if—'

Cara cut him off, knowing where his mind was going. 'No, Griffin,' she said sternly. 'She did not collude with Neil to have Dad killed.'

And that was the end of the conversation. He'd stormed

out of there; Jamie hurrying after him. Then Griffin came back, but Jamie disappeared, not returning until hours later, looking like death warmed up. Fucking hell, this team, she thinks. What a collection of misfits.

She's been out to the incident room a few times, assigning tasks and reviewing lines of enquiry as they conclude at inevitable dead ends. Jamie's discovered that Kate Avery bought a book from the Dog's Trust charity shop next door to the Tesco, and Brody's looking into the mental health Facebook group, with some help from Shenton.

She's in her office working through reports when something tells her to look up. The normal typing and chatter has paused; a silence that means someone important has walked in.

But it's not Halstead or even the chief constable that's now standing in her doorway. Even stranger than that – it's the pathologist.

Dr Ross knocks once against her door frame.

'I'm sorry to disturb you,' he says.

An apology, even more out of character.

'You're more than welcome, Greg,' Cara says. 'Anytime.' She decides candour is the way forward. 'What's up? This is hardly your normal commute.'

'No.' He pauses. 'So, it's true, what they're saying?'

Cara cocks her head to one side. 'What are they saying?'

'That it's a multiple. You're treating these suicides as a serial killer.'

Cara's hesitant. Halstead told her to keep it quiet; she wonders who's been talking. But Ross is a trusted colleague and an integral part of their investigation. He's seen it all, and worse. He deserves to know the truth.

'We are. Yes.'

Ross nods slowly.

'What are your views on that?' Cara asks.

The pathologist tightens his brows; his long thin fingers lace together, then release. 'I don't like it,' he says at last, standing in the doorway.

'But could we be right?'

'I've just finished the PM on Peter Jessop. Your bridge jumper. And my official cause of death is major polytrauma consistent with a fall from height. Death resulting from injuries to multiple body parts and organ failure with a massively high injury severity score. Unsurvivable, in other words.'

'Suicide?'

'Same as Kate Avery and Colin Jefferies. Not that there was much left of Jefferies to post-mortem,' he finishes bluntly.

'But your unofficial thoughts?'

'I'm a man of science.' He looks Cara right in the eye; in the dim light of her office his blue eyes look almost violet. 'I don't put stock in speculation or conspiracy theories. I look at what I'm seeing in front of me and make a decision.'

'And?'

'And I can't help but think something weird is going on.'

Shutting the door behind him, he takes two steps towards her and sits down in the chair.

'Peter Jessop had been diagnosed with schizophrenia, only just started his treatment, on a variety of medication. He was on olanzapine and sertraline. An antipsychotic, and an antidepressant. But I found no trace of atypical antipsychotics or SSRIs in his system when he died.'

Cara stares at him. 'We found both those drugs in his bag left at the scene.'

'Well, he wasn't taking them.'

'Could that have been why he killed himself?'

'I'm not a psychiatrist or a psychologist, Elliott. My job is to give a medical cause of death. Not theorise what brought him to the bridge in the first place.'

'But—'

'But yes.' Ross sighs. 'My hypothesis would be that Peter Jessop stopped taking his medication, and that could have …' He stresses the words. '*Could have* made him high risk for suicide.'

Cara's head spins. 'Was there anything from the other post-mortems that seemed odd?'

'Nothing medical.' Ross senses what Cara's about to ask. 'Behavioural, if you must know. Colin Jefferies. Your train jumper. Looking at his medical notes, it was clear he was severely agoraphobic. To get him out of the house would have been a huge feat. Let alone persuade him into a car and to a train station. In rush hour.'

A thought occurs to Cara. She stands up and opens the door, shouting into the incident room at Brody.

'Alana – has the lab come back on the sample and glass found in Colin Jefferies' sink?'

Brody frowns. 'Yes. I think …' She stares at her computer screen for a moment. 'Yes, here. There were traces of a geminal diol in the leftover orange juice. More than likely chloral hydrate?'

Cara looks at Ross.

'It's a sedative,' he says. 'Old school. Doctors prefer to use other benzos nowadays, but it would have rendered him adequately dopey. Someone could have slipped it in his orange juice and half an hour later he'd be compliant.'

'Compliant enough to get him to a train track in rush hour?'

Ross nods. He stands up. 'I'll head back to my office. Go through all the notes again. See if I can find anything else that might help.'

'Thank you.'

Cara hasn't moved, standing in the doorway of her office, her head spinning. She's right. Something weird is going on.

She watches Dr Ross as he makes his way through the incident room, until his attention is caught by the whiteboard. She can see him scanning the faces of their five victims. Smiling photographs, and all the information – what little they have – written below.

She sees him lean forward and run a finger under the black block capitals she's written there. *WHAT DO THESE VICTIMS HAVE IN COMMON?*

He turns back to her.

'You do realise,' he says, slowly. 'You must know …'

'What?' she snaps from the doorway. She hurries to his side.

Ross's face is serious, his shoulders hunched.

'All of your victims. They're registered to the same GP.'

Cara doesn't move, and in her stunned silence, Ross repeats himself.

'They were all treated by the same doctor.'

Chapter 37

Nothing sours a GP receptionist's expression more than a queue jumper – especially one displaying a police warrant card. Griffin steams past the row of grey-haired patients, leaving the posters for flu jabs and mental health helplines flapping. Brody follows behind him, arm outstretched.

'DS Griffin and DC Brody to see Dr Hammond.'

The receptionist sucks on her teeth; she looks at the ID impassively. She rolls her eyes at the old woman at the front of the queue.

'I'm assuming this is important?' she says, glacially paced and just as cold. 'He's with a patient.'

'Now. Please,' Griffin adds with a patronising smile.

She gets up slowly; he follows her to the entrance of the reception area then down a long corridor. She pauses outside a door, fist raised to knock.

'I'll need to go in first,' she says. 'His patient might be in a state of undress.'

'Then please. After you.'

She knocks. The reply comes back after a brief pause. A male voice, tetchy. 'Yes?'

She pokes her head around the door. 'Police to see you, David. Detectives.'

'Police? What?'

Griffin's had enough of the dawdling. He gently pushes the receptionist aside and shoves the door open. Contrary to expectations, the doctor is alone, seated in front of his computer. He looks up, surprised, as Griffin enters, Brody behind him.

'Dr David Hammond?' Griffin begins. The doctor nods. 'DS Griffin and DC Brody, from Major Crimes. We'd like you to come with us, please.'

The doctor's mouth drops open. He looks past Griffin to the receptionist, her head poking around, nosey. Brody pushes the door closed in her face.

'I can't just leave,' the doctor stutters. 'I have patients.'

'They'll have to wait. Dr David Hammond, we are arresting you on suspicion of encouraging suicide—'

'Suicide … What—'

'—you do not have to say anything, but it may harm your defence if you do not mention, when questioned, something which you later rely on in court. Anything that you do say may be given in evidence.'

The doctor's mouth opens and closes like a dying fish. Brody takes the cuffs from her belt and pulls him to a stand, securing his hands behind him.

'Suicide …' he repeats. 'But who? When?'

'We'll deal with your questions back at the station.' Griffin places one hand on the door.

'Please. Can we go out the back?' His voice is desperate. 'If my patients see me in handcuffs my career is over.' Griffin glances to Brody. She shrugs.

'Fine. Don't try anything stupid.'

'I won't. Thank you. Oh God. Who?'

Dr Hammond repeats this annoying refrain as Griffin guides him out the back of the GP's surgery to the car park. Brody brings the car around and they load the doctor inside, still chanting in monotone.

'It can't be a patient,' he's saying. 'But who's dead? Nobody's died. Is this about ... about that man? Was it you who spoke to me?' He directs this last question to Brody, who doesn't reply. 'The suicide. But I haven't killed anyone.' He looks over to Griffin, next to him in the back seat. His eyes are darting and frantic. 'I haven't. I swear.'

'Let's get you sorted at the station, and then we can have a nice chat.'

He retreats into silence, his shoulders bent as the car continues its way to the nick.

Normally they'd send uniforms to make the arrest, but Griffin wanted to see first-hand how he reacts. He doesn't look like a killer. But Griffin's learned over the years that appearance is rarely reflective of the person within. He looks like a middle-class, middle-aged GP. He's wearing smart trousers, black shoes; shirt and a sweater vest over the top. He's clean-shaven with bushy eyebrows and neatly trimmed hair. But Shipman seemed like a nice old man; everyone fancied Bundy. You never know.

They drive to the back door, to custody, and guide him out of the car. He's quiet now, mumbling a thank you or a please when questions are directed his way. He seems confused – a man lost in a world he knows nothing about. He's polite, does as he's told. Rejects the offer of a drink. Says he would like a lawyer, and could they call him one, please?

Griffin and Brody provide the requisite information,

then leave the custody sergeant to it, heading back up to the incident room to plan their approach.

The clock starts ticking. It's 3.46 p.m.

They have twenty-four hours.

Chapter 38

Five photographs are laid out in front of Dr David Hammond. The warnings have been completed; paperwork signed. Here they are.

Griffin works from left to right, his finger tapping below each one.

'Colin Jefferies, Isabel Warner, Eileen Avery, Kate Avery, Peter Jessop.'

Hammond's gaze flicks between the photographs and Griffin's face, his mouth open.

Griffin lets the silence hang.

The solicitor sighs. 'You need to ask a question, DS Griffin.'

Griffin gives him a disparaging look, then turns to Hammond.

'Do you recognise these people?'

'Do I …? Um …' He scans the photos, then glances to his solicitor. 'No comment,' he mumbles.

'I'll help you out. They're all patients registered to you at your surgery. Or at least, they were.'

'They were …?'

A nervous tic, Hammond's habit of repeating the beginning of the question. It's getting on Griffin's nerves. 'Do you know them?'

At last Hammond gets a full sentence out. 'They're all dead?'

A third time: 'Do you know them?'

'I …' He points to the photo of Eileen Avery, the old woman with dementia. 'This is Eileen. I spoke to the police on Wednesday. A male detective. He said that she'd died. But I was told her daughter killed her.' He points to Kate Avery. 'Her.'

Griffin ignores the question. 'So … yes? You do know them?'

A cleared throat from the solicitor.

'No comment,' Hammond says again weakly. 'But …' He turns to the solicitor. 'I want to know.' Back to Griffin. 'Is what you're saying true? You're not allowed to lie to me, right?'

'No, we're not allowed to lie.'

'These people are all dead?'

'Yes. All over the last week.' Griffin works along, his finger pointing under each photo in turn. 'Train, overdose, suffocated, gunshot, fall from height.'

The solicitor tilts his head to one side, interested.

The GP speaks: 'That's how they all died? But those are … They're suicides. With the exception of the woman murdered by her daughter.'

'People who killed themselves at your instigation. Isn't that right, Dr Hammond?'

'What? What! No!'

'Dr Hammond …' the solicitor warns. 'What proof do you have of this?' he directs to Griffin. 'Given you've refused to share anything with me in discovery.'

'For starters, all five were patients of Dr Hammond, here. All of whom had appointments over the last month. What are the chances of that?'

'They … I … No.' Hammond points to the photo of Isabel Warner. 'Not her. She's not my patient.'

'She was registered to you at the surgery.' Griffin takes a long printout out of his file, the names all highlighted. 'See here?'

'Okay, but I don't remember her.'

'Nineteen. Abused as a child by her stepdad. Diagnosed with depression, anxiety and PTSD. Isabel Warner,' Griffin repeats. 'Nice that you have such a personal relationship with your patients.'

'I have hundreds of patients registered to me at the practice. I see dozens a week. It would be impossible for me to remember every single one.'

'Except this one came to see you just after New Year. On the third of January.'

'I … No.' Then he jumps. 'It must have been Fran. She's my trainee – a junior doctor at the surgery. She takes loads of my appointments and runs them past me if she has any problems.'

'So you're saying you never met Isabel Warner?'

'No!'

'And that when we've finished the search on your house and office we're not going to find a computer or phone from which you messaged Isabel on social media?'

'You're doing what?' But he shakes his head with confusion. 'No. I've never messaged anyone on social media in my entire life. I don't even know how to do it.'

'*Have* you found a computer?' the solicitor asks.

'Not yet. But we will.'

211

'And what other so-called evidence do you have, detective?' the solicitor challenges.

Griffin stays silent, knowing they have nothing.

'Have these people had a post-mortem?' the doctor asks. But without waiting for an answer, he turns to the solicitor. 'Ask for the results from the PMs. What did they die of?'

'What do you know about chloral hydrate, Dr Hammond?'

'Chloral … It's a sedative. But nobody prescribes that any more.'

'Do you?'

A glance to the solicitor. 'No comment.'

'My colleague here, DC Brody, spoke to you on Tuesday about a patient of yours called Colin Jefferies. Do you remember that?'

Another glance; a small nod in reply. 'Yes. He was the man who killed himself on the train tracks.'

'Do you remember what you were treating him for?'

'Off the top of my head? I don't remember.'

'We were talking to you about him three days ago. You've forgotten him already?'

'Okay, yes. Agoraphobia and anxiety.'

'And what do you think would happen if you took someone with agoraphobia and anxiety to a train station in rush hour, dosed up to his eyeballs on chloral hydrate?'

Hammond's mouth drops open as he looks between his solicitor and Griffin. 'You can't think … That's not … I didn't …'

'Someone did. Where were you on the morning on Monday the fourteenth of January?' Griffin asks.

'This Monday? I was at my surgery.'

'At six-thirty a.m.?'

'At six-thirty I was at home. With my wife, and my two children.' He's defiant now, confident in his assertion. 'Then I drove to work, with my wife, dropping her at the school where she works on the way.' He sits back, triumphant. 'Any other dates you want to know about?'

'When did you last see Kate Avery?'

The doctor throws his hands into the air. 'I don't know. I'd have to check my records. Again.' He turns to his solicitor. 'This is ridiculous. These people killed themselves. And I bet that whatever time they did it I was with someone. For the last few weeks I've either been at the surgery, or with my family. I literally don't go anywhere else. Ever.'

Griffin glances across to Brody – she looks defeated. Their case is falling apart.

He stacks the notes into a pile. 'Interview concluded seventeen thirty-five. We'll pick this up again in the morning.'

'In the morning! You're going to keep me here overnight?'

'You'll be quite comfortable, Dr Hammond,' Griffin says, not being able to resist a quick smirk.

'Good God. All this for some suicides!' the man explodes. 'Why can't you investigate some actual murders? Like the one I told you about. I even gave you the guy that killed her.'

'Sorry?'

'Oh, now you're interested.' The doctor sits back in his seat, glaring. 'I phoned the police a few months ago. About one of my patients. She'd been terminally ill and had died.'

'And?'

'And her husband killed her. If you'd bothered investigating properly at the time, if you'd bothered to follow up on the post-mortem results, you would have discovered that for yourself. Gillian Randall. Look it up.'

'I will. Thank you for your help,' Griffin concludes and

213

switches off the tape.

Uniforms lead Hammond back to his cell; the solicitor departs with a sarcastic look backwards, disgruntled that his afternoon had been ruined.

'Anything?' Cara asks, the moment they set foot in the incident room.

'Nothing,' Griffin says, and Cara's face drops. 'Alibi for Southampton station on Monday morning. Says he's never met Isabel Warner, that his trainee GP saw her. I assume we haven't found anything new?'

'Not yet. We've seized his computer from his office. SOCO are at his house now.'

'We need something. All we have is circumstantial based on the fact all his patients are registered to him and he has the know-how.' Griffin pauses. 'Have you heard of someone called Gillian Randall? He says he called it in as a suspicious death.'

'Was that the euthanasia case?' Shenton chips in. Griffin jumps. He wasn't even aware he'd been listening. 'Yes, here it is.'

Griffin looks across; Shenton has her record up on the PNC.

'Sixty-five. Stage four pancreatic cancer. Husband called 999 on the twenty-ninth of November because she was unresponsive. Declared dead at scene.'

'And the doctor said it was murder?' Griffin asks, looking over his shoulder.

'Yeah. His statement ...' A few clicks. 'Patient was terminally ill but up until that time had been stable. Type three diabetes from the cancer, on an insulin pump. GP was concerned about the husband assisting her death.'

'And did he? Was a PM completed?'

'Yes. There was nothing to indicate a suspicious death and cause was attributed to the cancer. There were high levels of morphine in her system, but that wasn't out of the ordinary. She was an ill woman.'

'What did the husband say?'

'What you would expect. Devastated. They didn't push him too hard.'

'No?' Griffin glances across at Cara. 'Seems a bit of an oversight?'

'Don't blame me, it didn't even reach my desk. See, here?' Cara points to the screen. 'CCTV shows both the father and son visiting the local Tesco superstore at the time of her death. Case closed by PS Green. It was dealt with locally.'

'The doctor's deflecting?' Griffin slumps in a seat behind Shenton. 'We have nothing on this guy and the solicitor knows it.'

'That computer might show something.'

'Ten quid says it doesn't.'

Cara shrugs. 'Well, we're not going to get anything done tonight. Go home, everyone. We'll pick it up in the morning. Give Dr Hammond another go after SOCO have finished and he's had a night in the cells.'

Brody nods; Cara heads back to her office. Shenton reaches out to shut down his computer, but Griffin stops him.

'Jot down that address, will you? For the Randalls.' Shenton looks confused but does as he's asked on a Post-it. 'No harm in dotting the i's on this one,' he says, pocketing the note.

But before he heads out, he notices Brody give him an inquisitive look.

'Do you want to come?' he asks, out of politeness.

She picks up her bag and follows him out of the door.

215

Chapter 39

Griffin and Brody find the house easily – a neat mid-terrace with two small evergreen trees in pots either side of the door. They ring the bell.

After a moment, Griffin hears shuffling footsteps and it opens. A tall, slender man stands there, his face grave.

'Yes?' he says.

'DS Griffin. DC Brody. From Hampshire Police.' The door starts to close. 'Please. A quick conversation.'

'I've said all I want to you people. My lawyer told me the CPS weren't pressing charges.'

'They're not,' Griffin says to a nearly closed door. 'But we've had some similar cases recently. Ones that might link to your wife's death.'

The man hesitates. 'You have?'

'Yes. Can we talk? It won't take long. I promise.'

There's a pause, then the door opens. 'Ten minutes.'

The man turns and walks into his house. Like the front garden, it's tidy and ordered – letters to be posted lined up next to the front door, the addresses written in a neat hand. Shoes carefully put away in cubby holes. Two coats on two pegs. Griffin follows the man through the house into a clean, neat kitchen, Brody lagging behind. She's been quiet the whole journey over; he wonders why she even agreed to come.

'Would you like anything to drink?' Randall asks. 'Tea, coffee?'

'Coffee, thank you.'

Brody declines.

The man gestures to the dining table and Griffin and Brody wait while he puts the kettle on.

The room has the flourishes of a woman's touch. Nick-nacks on the windowsill – an assortment of small china birds, posed in flight. A stained-glass robin hangs against the window.

The man catches Griffin looking at them.

'They were Gilly's. She loved the birds on the feeder. By the end it was all she could do.'

'I'm sorry for your loss, Mr Randall.'

'Please, call me George.' He places a mug of milky coffee in front of Griffin and sits down next to him. 'What would you like to know?'

'Can you tell us the circumstances of your wife's death? Sorry to put you through this again.'

George waves Griffin's apology away. 'It's fine. There's not much to say. She had stage four pancreatic cancer. It's terrible. Watching your loved one waste away, in front of your eyes. She tried to be optimistic, and we did as much as we could together, but in the end she was just too weak.'

'Had her consultant discussed how long she had left to live?'

'He had, yes – a few months, no more. But we didn't

think … It all happened so fast. We thought we had longer …' He pauses, lost in thought. 'On reflection, maybe I should have known. But there's nothing to be gained from regret, is there?' He laughs ruefully.

His words hit home to Griffin. 'There's always a thousand things you could have done differently. When the reality is there's nothing good in an impossible situation.'

George gives him a long look. 'You've lost someone?'

'My wife.' Griffin feels Brody's eyes on him, not enjoying discussing the personal in front of a work colleague.

'I'm so sorry.'

Their mutual grief stops their conversation, until Griffin moves it on. 'And you were the one that found her? That afternoon?'

'Yes. I'd got back from Tesco, and she was in bed, as normal, but her eyes were open, just staring.'

'One of the points the investigating officer picked up on was why didn't you attempt CPR? You had First Aid training?'

'Yes.' He shrugs. 'What would have been the point? I could tell she was dead, so why haul her out of her warm bed, onto the floor. Probably cracking a few ribs in the process. Doing something I know she wouldn't have wanted?' He looks at Griffin, his eyes watery. 'Just to satisfy some box-ticking policemen?'

'She didn't have a DNR order?'

'We'd discussed it. Never got around to putting it formally into place. You think you have all the time in the world, don't you, DS Griffin? It's a shock when you discover you don't. All the things left unsaid. All the times I was short with her.'

'I'm sure she knew how much you loved her.' Griffin

pauses, uncertain how to ask the next question. 'And you didn't suspect anything … untoward?'

George frowns. 'What do you mean?'

'Had anyone been talking to her? Online, maybe?'

'No. Only me. She had a phone, but she rarely bothered with it, except to talk to my son.'

'You have kids?'

'Just one,' he answers quickly. 'He … It was a huge loss. For both of us.' He looks at Griffin, curiously. 'Why? What other cases are you thinking this connects to?'

'I don't think it does, now you've told me more about it. We've had a series of deaths throughout the city. Ones where cause isn't clear.'

'But Gilly had a post-mortem. You people insisted on it. Cutting her open …' His voice is hard now. 'For what? So you could prove how a dying woman spent her last moments?' His voice trails off. He shakes his head, sadly. 'Are we done here?' he concludes. 'I get tired quickly nowadays.'

Griffin understands. There were days after Mia's death, even once the physical wounds had healed, when he felt so exhausted his bones ached.

'Thank you for your time, Mr Randall.'

They both stand, George showing Griffin to the door. But he pauses, thinking.

'What did you find helped?' George asks, as Griffin steps out into the street. 'After.'

Griffin frowns. What advice could he possibly give? 'Keep busy,' he says. 'And spend time with the people who love you.'

George nods. 'I took a week off work. Went back as soon as I could. Only way I know how to make a difference. Take care, Detective Griffin.'

Griffin walks quickly away from the house, not caring if Brody is following or not.

'You were good with him,' Brody says once they're in the car. Her first words since they arrived at the house.

He turns to her, angry she had seen him so vulnerable.

'Why did you come, Brody?'

'Do you want a drink?' she asks, unperturbed by his fury. 'I know a place near here.'

Griffin pauses, surprised by the change. He glances back to the old man's house, feeling sadness for his loss, as well as his own. So many people, so much suffering. He's glad the old man feels he can make a difference, because right now Griffin's not achieving anything.

'Lead the way,' Griffin replies.

Chapter 40

'What am I doing? What am I thinking?'

Cara stands in front of the full-length mirror, talking out loud to her reflection. She pulls at the dress as it bunches around her middle. It looks awful. She *feels* awful. Why the hell is she going on a date?

She glances at the clock. Fifteen minutes until he's here. She quickly tugs the dress over her head then puts on black jeans and a smart jumper. That'll have to do. She's done her hair; she has make-up on. Charlie's used to seeing her at work, dog-tired, hair scragged back – surely anything is an improvement on that?

The bell rings. Shit. She hurries down the stairs and opens the door. He smiles apologetically.

'I'm early, I'm sorry. It's so rude. But I couldn't wait in the car any longer.' He thrusts a bunch of peonies at her. 'These are for you.'

She takes them; she can't help but return his smile. 'Thank you. How long were you waiting?'

'Twenty minutes, give or take. But around the corner, so you couldn't see me. Your neighbours probably reported

221

a stalker.'

His words remind her of the shadowy figure she thought she saw outside her house at the beginning of the week, and the prickly unease returns. Could that have been Charlie? But that's ridiculous, insane. And besides, she hasn't noticed anything for a few days, not since Griffin barged his way in on Wednesday.

She needs to stop imagining bad guys around every corner. Ulterior motives behind innocent smiles. Look for the positive: Charlie's just keen. And it's endearing, his honesty.

'Well ... I ...' She gestures to the flowers, and ducks back into the house. She thinks about leaving them on the work surface, but fills a pint glass with water, plonking them inside.

He's waiting on her doorstep. He looks nice. Dark jeans, a blue checked shirt. Not too smart, and she's glad; she doesn't think she can cope with anywhere posh. She realises she should have invited him in, but the empty rooms, the packing boxes ... The *For Sale* sign is bad enough.

'Shall we go?' she says, forcing a smile, despite the butterflies. She's nervous. Where did that come from?

'Your chariot awaits,' Charlie says grandly, gesturing to an aged Ford Fiesta at the kerb.

She climbs into the front seat, fastens her seat belt. He does the same and starts the engine, quickly turning the music down as a song she remembers from her early twenties blasts out at full volume.

'Sorry about that ...'

'"My Chemical Romance", eh?' she says. She does the maths, worried he may be younger than she thought.

'Ex-emo kid.'

He smiles, dimples appearing on his cheeks. She feels herself relaxing. 'Where are we going?'

'Well … since I wasn't sure what food you liked, and you weren't much help …' – he had asked, she had replied 'anything' – 'I thought my local pub might be the way forward.' He glances again, trying to gauge her reaction. 'Is that okay?'

'Perfect.'

She's relieved. Local pubs serve alcohol, and usually steak, so she's on easy ground.

He puts the car into gear and they drive. Cara wishes he would turn the music back on; anything to get rid of the awkward silence.

'How's the case? You made an arrest?'

'Dead end,' she says. 'Unless you can tell me otherwise?'

He winces. 'Sorry. Nothing yet. The SOCOs brought in the home computer a few hours ago. The team are working on it now.'

'And you're out with me?'

He grins. 'Some things are more important. And you can hardly criticise.'

She smiles back, the uncomfortable moment gone as he indicates into the car park of a pub. The Rising Sun Inn. He parks up. A line of spotlights points the way to the welcoming wood-panelled entrance; a woman in black with an artisan-looking apron greets them.

'Table for two?' she asks.

'Name of Mills.'

She nods. 'Come this way.'

Cara follows Charlie into the main restaurant of the pub. It's not as she expected. She thought a local would have a gawdy patterned carpet, maybe a few football shirts on the wall, Sky Sports playing on a distant TV. Not this place. This pub is traditional, minimal, classy. White walls, pine tables, colourful artwork that she actually likes. The tables have bright cutlery, shining glassware. A spray of blue flowers in the centre. She touches one as she sits down. It's real. No artificial hyacinths for this place.

A crisp white napkin is placed in her lap, a cream card menu handed to her. As the waitress departs, she whispers to Charlie.

'This is your local?' This is a nice area. Expensive houses. Low crime statistics. 'Where do you live?'

He looks awkward. 'Okay. Not my local. I wouldn't bring someone like you to my neighbourhood pub. You'd probably get mugged walking through the door.'

Cara laughs. 'Someone like me?'

'Someone I'm trying to impress.'

'You're trying to impress me?'

'Of course!' The two red spots appear on his cheeks again. 'Is it working?' he says, quieter.

'So far. You've got a long way to go yet.'

'I like a challenge,' he replies.

Their eyes sink to their menus. It's standard pub fare, but a hundred per cent nicer. She opts for the steak as predicted, then turns over to the wine list.

'The merlot is good,' Charlie says. 'Shall we get a bottle?'

She raises an eyebrow. 'Drinking and driving?'

'I'll leave the car here. As long as you don't mind getting a taxi back?'

The waitress comes over; they order. The same – steak, medium rare. But peppercorn sauce for Charlie, mushroom for her. They retreat into silence as she comes back with the bottle of wine. It's opened, Charlie tries it. A generous glass is poured for them both.

Charlie holds his up. 'Cheers.'

She clinks. 'What are we celebrating?'

'That you agreed to come out with me?'

'That'll do. Not much else to write home about at the moment.'

'You'll find something.'

'It's a shit show,' she blurts out. She takes a long sip of her wine. He's right, it's delicious.

'That bad?'

'Worse. Everything we have on our suspect is circumstantial. We'll have to release him first thing unless something comes up. And who else do we have? No leads. No other suspects. Sometimes I'm not even convinced we're looking at a crime. What if I have it all wrong? What if these people did just kill themselves?'

'You know they didn't. We have the digital trace to prove it for Isabel Warner. And you're right. Your instincts are spot on.'

'Not always.'

He opens his mouth to say something. Then shuts it again.

'What?' she pushes.

He shakes his head.

'Go on?'

He winces. 'Do you hear from him?'

Charlie doesn't need to say a name. Cara knows who he means. *Noah Deakin. The Echo Man.*

'No. Never. Sometimes I wonder what I would do if he called. If he wrote from the prison. Would I listen to what he had to say?'

'What conclusion did you come to?'

225

'Nothing can excuse what he did. Nothing. But ...' She grasps at the wine again. Takes a long gulp. 'He was my friend. My best friend.'

'You miss him.'

'I do.' She forces a laugh. 'Sorry. I didn't mean to get so serious, so quickly. Here we are. Supposed to be having a good time.'

'It's fine, Cara. I get it.'

She looks up. Behind his glasses his dark brown eyes are sympathetic. She clears her throat.

'Anyway. Tell me something about you. You run the digital department. How did you get there?'

Charlie offers one last gentle smile, then takes the hint and moves on. 'I'm good with computers. I have a logical mind.'

'So why not go into tech? Earn some proper money?'

'Same reason you're not running some multinational company somewhere. I wanted to be at the coalface. And unlike some of my colleagues, it seems I am able to translate the gobbledegook into something that makes sense. The important people like that.'

'So they promoted you.'

'A few times.' He laughs. 'I know how the digital guys think. But I also know how to manage the top brass. And that matters.'

'Well, Griffin likes you. And that's saying something. He doesn't like anyone.'

'I'll take the compliment. How is he doing?'

Cara shrugs. 'Fine. As good as he'll ever be. I worry, but I'd rather he was here, getting on my nerves, than doing who knows what in that basement flat.'

'Can I ask ...' He pauses, and Cara wonders what he's

going to say. 'Nobody calls him anything else, ever. Why do *you* call him Griffin? That must be your name too?'

She laughs, relieved. 'It is. It was. Oh, I don't know. He's always been Griffin. At school, that was what his mates called him. Only Mum and Dad called him Nate. I was always just Cara – Griffin's sister. So it was easy to get married and change my name to Elliott. Made more sense at work, too. When he started out he wasn't the sort of Griffin you wanted to be associated with.'

'Even I'd heard of him. Back then. Around the nick. He was legendary.' He chuckles. 'Still is.'

The food arrives; it looks delicious. Cara tucks in with zeal, realising it's been a while since she's had a decent meal.

'So, you and your husband … you're separated?' he asks after a few mouthfuls.

'No, Roo's sitting on the sofa waiting for me to come home.' She laughs at his sudden confusion. 'Of course we're separated. Would I be out with you if not?'

'Just checking. And your kids? You have two, right?'

'Yes. Tilly and Josh. They're living with Roo at the moment. It's easier, with the hours I keep.'

She stops. He nods. She feels defensive, for having to explain why her kids aren't living with their mother. But why should they be? In this day and age.

The waitress comes over and pours more wine. 'Another bottle?' she asks. Cara's surprised to see it empty.

Charlie looks to her and she nods. 'In for a penny.'

'And you? Since we're getting personal?' Cara says. 'Why are you single?'

'What's wrong with me, you mean? Thirty-five-year-old single bloke.'

'You're thirty-five? Fuck! I have six years on you. But

227

that's not the point. What's wrong with you?' She echoes his words with a smile.

He shrugs. 'I've had girlfriends. I was even engaged once. But it didn't work out.'

'How come?'

'Is this an interrogation?' He grins. 'I would hate to be up against you in an interview room.'

'You're deflecting, Mr Mills. Answer the question.'

'Okay, so … The woman I was engaged to was offered a job in San Francisco and I didn't want to move to the States. Another decided, after a year, that she didn't want children—'

'And you do?'

'Maybe. Don't have to be mine.' He smiles. 'Happy now?'

'That you're not a gaslighting sociopath?'

'Not as far as I know. Do you want more wine?'

'Yes. Please.'

He pours and they grin at each other. This is going better than she predicted. She's relaxed, full of good food and wine, in the company of a lovely man. And he is lovely. The candlelight twinkles across his face. Nice features, nice eyes. For the first time she wonders what he looks like under that shirt … She feels her face blush.

'All done here?' the waitress asks, saving her from her thoughts. 'Would you like dessert?'

Charlie defers to her.

'We'll take a look,' Cara replies. 'Thank you.'

The waitress passes the menu across. Cara peruses it in silence for a moment then casts a glance upwards at Charlie. His attention is fully on her, not even looking at the options.

'Do you want anything?' he asks.

'Do you?'

'Coffee?'

'Back at yours?'

He raises an eyebrow. 'If you'd like to?'

'Yes, I would.'

He glances behind him and raises his hand for the bill. The waitress comes over.

'Was everything okay?' she says as Charlie touches his card to the machine.

'All good, thank you,' he replies. He looks back to Cara. 'Just nipping to the loo.'

He gets up, Cara's eyes following him.

'You guys calling it a night?' the waitress asks.

'Not yet,' Cara replies with a grin. The waitress gives her a cheeky look.

'Good for you. He's hot,' she adds. 'I like that nerdy thing he's got going on.'

'Me too,' Cara replies. She grabs her coat as Charlie heads back towards her.

'Taxi'll be five minutes.'

She nods. She follows him to the entrance; he holds the door open; they wait, out in the cold, for the taxi to arrive.

They stand in silence, side by side. Now she's committed to going back to his, the nerves have returned. It's the first time she's been with a man since Roo – she mentally does the calculation. Over fifteen years. She wasn't expecting this. Is it the wine talking? Should she …? Too late now. Perhaps this is too much. Dating someone from work. She could back out?

They see the taxi in the distance and Charlie raises his hand. Then he faces her.

'Are you sure?' he asks. 'You don't have to—'

'I want to.'

She really does.

They get into the taxi; Charlie gives his address. It's not far. She's hyper aware of him next to her. The warmth of his hand, resting gently on her knee. The rustle of his coat as he shifts position. The taxi smells of something artificial – air freshener, and she doesn't like it. She leans closer to Charlie; gets the scent of his aftershave. Much better.

The taxi stops. Charlie pays. He opens the door and gets out; she does the same. He doesn't say anything as they walk up to the front door. Maybe he's as tense as she is. She can't tell what he's thinking as he puts his key in the lock. It's a nice place. Small. But tidy.

'Sorry about the mess,' he says as he switches the light on in the living room. 'I wasn't expecting …' His voice trails off.

'Nor was I,' Cara replies.

He grins, his face is flushed. He *is* nervous. It makes her like him all the more.

'Do you want a drink? Coffee, maybe, or …'

'We both know I didn't come back here for coffee.'

Her voice falters as she says it, but it's the impetus for Charlie. In two quick steps he's in front of her. He takes her face gently in his hands and he kisses her. It's nice. Different, but nice. She kisses him back. She's enjoying herself, enjoying him.

He shrugs off his coat, she does the same. His hands run through her hair; she lowers hers, pushing under his shirt. He jumps. Laughs.

'Your hands are cold.'

'Sorry,' she murmurs, but her mouth is against his as she kisses him again. He gropes for her hands and replaces them under his shirt where his skin is soft and warm. She pulls it

230

over his head; he does the same with her jumper.

The living-room light is bright and unflattering. He pulls away.

'Do you want …?' He points upstairs. To the bedroom. She nods.

He leads the way, her hand in his. He pushes into a small room – double bed, chest of drawers, not much else. He doesn't turn the light on but there's a street light outside, behind the curtains. She can see him just fine.

They kiss again. More urgency. She feels that desire herself, wanting to be with this man, this *new* man. This man who seems normal, who she actually likes, who hasn't got ten years' worth of baggage. Who doesn't think about serial killers last thing at night. And before she knows it his face comes into her head. Not Roo, but *him*. Noah. Those strange dark brown eyes: the way he used to look at her, as if he could see inside her soul. She pulls away, her eyes snapping open.

Charlie looks at her strangely. 'Are you okay?' he asks.

'Yes. I'm sorry. It's … it's a lot.'

'We don't have to?'

She nods. 'I'm sorry.'

'Don't apologise,' he replies, although his face is downcast. He steps backwards, away from her; she feels that distance. The rejection. 'Do you want me to call you a taxi?'

'No, no, I'll walk—'

'You can't walk—'

'I'll be fine.'

She turns away feeling foolish, and hurries out of his bedroom, down to the front door, picking up her coat and jumper on the way. She hears his footsteps follow.

'Cara,' he says, and she pauses, one hand on the latch. She turns. He's standing on the stairs, clearly uncomfortable. She's done that to him. Her indecisiveness and mixed messages.

'Have I done something wrong?' he asks.

'You— No. Absolutely not.' She shakes her head and pulls the door open, stepping out into the dark, rainy night. 'It's me,' she says as she pulls the door closed behind her. 'All me.'

Chapter 41

Two drinks in and Griffin has to acknowledge that whatever good intentions he had at the beginning have all gone downhill.

One drink, he told himself as he walked into the pub. I'm not an alcoholic; prescription painkillers are my problem. One beer. Brody ordered a large G and T. Griffin paid.

It's a place he knows well. Shabby, but not so dirty you worry about health and safety infractions. Proper beer mats. Stained wooden tables, wobbly chairs. They take a seat on the far side. The first drinks go down with little conversation. Griffin leaves her to her thoughts; there's obviously something she's working through. By the second, his patience pays off.

'What have you heard about me?' she asks.

'You came from the Met. Asked to be transferred.'

'And that's it?'

'Seems like a strange request. But yes, that's all Cara said.'

She pauses, staring at the glass as she turns it around in her hand. 'Can I trust you?' she asks after another beat.

'Up to you. Can you?'

'My gut says yes.'

He shrugs. 'I've spent a lifetime being judged. I try not to do it to others.'

'It's true, I was at the Met. But it was an ultimatum. Transfer or be fired.'

Griffin watches her, she's clearly uncomfortable and he wonders why she's telling him this. He stays quiet, knowing there must be more to the story.

'I worked in child protection. Online Child Sexual Exploitation, to be precise.'

She pauses again.

'That's a hard place to work,' Griffin says tentatively.

'It was. Day after day, seeing … that. It gets to you. What some of these men do to these kids. Some of them no older than toddlers. And … And I fucked up.'

She takes a long gulp of her drink before she continues, her eyes down, focused on the glass.

'There was this one guy. We thought he was part of a group, but he was the one we caught. He had thousands of images, tens of thousands, and was selling them. But not only that. He'd get orders, and he'd farm them out to men who would be only too obliging to film for him.' Brody looks at Griffin, her eyes raw. 'He was procuring child abuse. Buying it.'

Griffin feels sick. But he stays quiet, letting Brody tell her story.

Her eyes drop back to her glass; she runs a finger down the condensation on the side. 'We knew we had him. That bastard was going to be inside for the rest of his life, but we wanted these men. The abusers. You know how much the prisoner population loves a nonce – he'd have spent the rest of his days having the shit kicked out of him, so we offered protection inside. Solitary, whatever. But he refused. Hours, days like this. Nobody had slept for months. None of us could, given what we'd seen. And then ...'

Griffin sits forward. He wipes his sweaty palms on his trousers.

'Then one day I was alone with him. My sergeant had stepped out to talk to his solicitor, the tape was off. They were trying to hash out another deal, whatever, but this man, this absolute arsehole of a man, leaned forward towards me and whispered, "Do you have kids?" I froze. Didn't know what to say. But he took it as a yes, and he ... he said ...' Brody's voice cracks. She clears her throat. 'He said, "Because if you do, we'll get to them. Anywhere. Anyhow. My clients are always looking for fresh merchandise. Once broken never the same. Those fresh ones. Like fucking a paper cut."' She looks at Griffin, his horror reflected in her eyes. 'Precisely those words. I remember as if it were yesterday. So I picked up the thing closest to me, and I stabbed him with it.'

Griffin blinks. 'What was it?'

'A biro. I don't remember much after that, I was so ... out of my mind. But my sergeant said I rammed that pen right through his hand. They came in once the screaming started, dragged me out of there.' She stops and meets Griffin's shocked stare. 'I don't even have kids.'

'What would you have done if you had?' he replies, and Brody laughs. A sharp bark, followed by a peal of near hysteria.

'Fuck, who knows?' she cackles, then her mirth fades as quickly as it arrived. 'Probably killed him,' she says, 'then I would have been sitting in a jail cell rather than in this pub with you. They suspended me for six months. My rep managed to argue extenuating circumstances, PTSD induced

235

by months of watching that shit. Threatened to sue the Met. They eventually agreed I could transfer.' She sits back and cradles her drink in both hands. 'So here I am.'

'Fuck,' Griffin replies.

'Quite. Are you …' she starts. 'Do you get help? With what happened?'

'Some.' He takes a long gulp from his beer. 'Therapy. Counselling.'

'Does it work?'

'Fuck, no.' He laughs. 'But it makes those in the top offices happy. And that's good enough for me. I go along to my mandated sessions. I regurgitate a whole load of shit that ticks the boxes, and they leave me alone for another six months. The rest of the time, I work out, don't get enough sleep, and now I'm back at work I do all I can to nail these bastards to the wall. What do you do to let off steam then? Please don't say you play golf now, or some other well-adjusted activity?'

She chuckles. 'No. Hell, no. I run. A lot. I self-medicate with alcohol to fall asleep, and down coffee in the morning to wake myself up.'

'Do you have a husband? You said you don't have kids.'

'No, and no. You?'

'Nobody but Frank.'

He enjoys the look on her face. A moment of panic, of incomprehension.

'My cat,' he adds.

'Your …' She snorts, then shakes her head with disbelief. 'You don't seem like the cat type.'

'I don't think I am,' he replies. And she gives him a look he can't fathom. He tips the last dregs of beer into his mouth.

'Another?'

'Please. Same again.'

Griffin gets up and makes his way to the bar. He orders quickly and, while their drinks are being poured, he looks back to Brody. She's staring into space, lost in her own thoughts, and stays that way until he puts the glass in front of her. She snaps herself out of it with a smile.

They move on to easier topics. Gossip from around the station; what Brody thinks about Southampton; what Cara's been up to – Griffin trying to find out more about his sister without actually asking her. Brody gets another round, followed quickly by Griffin, and before they know it it's last orders.

Griffin glances at his phone, the digits distorted.

'Well, I'm not driving anywhere,' he slurs. She tips back the last of her drink, looks surprised to find it already empty.

'I'm not far away from here. Walk me home?'

Griffin agrees, and together they set out down the rain-drenched pavements. The weather's been on and off all day, but Griffin is relieved to see it's holding for the moment. There's a thick feeling in the air, as if a storm is gathering. They walk in silence, Griffin taking Brody's lead as they meander through the residential streets. And then, in a matter of seconds, the heavens open. The sort of rain that pours from the sky, drenching them. Brody squeals and grabs Griffin's hand, pulling him into a run, around a corner and then up to the doorway of a small, terraced house. It still has the *Sold* sign up, and she struggles with the keys, finally getting in. They throw themselves through the doorway and stand in the tiny hall dripping and laughing.

And then her mouth is on his, or maybe his on hers, he's not sure who made the first move. Hands tugging at soaking wet clothes, fabric sticking to skin, peeled off in a slop of sodden outer garments. At one point Griffin pauses, about to ask, are you sure, but one look from her tells him that yes, she is. That and her hands, pulling his shirt up, unbuckling his belt. They make it up the stairs, removing shirts, trousers, jeans, underwear. Fall into the bedroom, onto the bed. She pulls him on top of her and that's it, no discussion, she hands him a condom and they're fucking.

It doesn't last long. *He* doesn't last long, how could he? Her legs around his waist, pulling him in; her hips rising in time with his. She made no effort to slow things down, it was a hundred miles an hour from the moment they walked into her house. After, they lie, naked, on top of the bedcovers. The room spins. He's drunk, as is she as she staggers to the toilet, sitting down and having a wee without closing the door. He feels exposed now, here; he gropes around for his clothes, remembers they're scattered outside the bedroom door and accepts defeat. He pulls the duvet over the top of himself and settles back on the pillow.

Brody's bed is soft. It smells nice, of washing powder and perfume. And before he knows it, he's asleep.

Chapter 42

Griffin wakes to muffled buzzing. A phone, close to his head. He ignores it, swallowed by the comfort of the bed, by the warmth and bliss of sleep. It stops, but another sound starts up. A ringtone. His, this time.

Slowly his consciousness comes around. Where he is. Who he's with. He glances across. Brody is sleeping, her back to him, her hair in fluffy peaks on the pillow. Still early, that dim glow of morning.

His phone stops, then starts again. This time he pulls himself out of bed and, naked, locates his phone from where it's been left in the pocket of his jeans, dumped in a damp pile by the bedroom door. He answers it in a whisper, then groans as the hangover kicks in. He crawls back into bed.

'Griffin? Get up. We've got a problem.'

It's Cara. 'What?'

'A new body.' There's a muffled conversation at the other end of the phone, followed by a volley of swearing. Griffin's awake now and he waits while his sister gets control of her emotions. 'Just come. I'll send the location. You'll see.'

'On my way, boss.'

'And can you call Brody? I've been ringing, but she's not picking up. I've got to go.'

She hangs up and he looks across to Brody. She's lying on her front, looking at him, warily. He relays the message but before he's even finished she's out of bed, pulling clothes from the wardrobe.

He does the same, enduring his soaking jeans, shivering when he puts on his cold shirt. She has her back to him as she gets dressed; he tries not to look. The dance of social niceties and embarrassment that he knows too well.

'You can't wear that. I have something that'll fit you. As long as you're not too fussy.' She opens a drawer. Throws a black T-shirt at him. He looks at it – a Metallica logo in silver across the front. He raises an eyebrow.

'Not mine. Belonged to an ex.' She smooths her hair down in front of the mirror.

'We'll have to take your car,' he says as he pulls it on. Fits perfectly; she must have a type, he thinks ruefully. 'Mine's at the pub.'

'I'll drop you off there,' she replies. 'We can't arrive together.' She pauses, looks at him sideways. 'I'm sorry. I shouldn't have done that.'

'I was there too. I had a say in the matter.'

'But you wouldn't have … We wouldn't have if it wasn't for me. Forget it happened.'

And with that she hurries out of the bedroom.

He follows her, gathering clothing, putting his wet coat on. They go out to her car – a sensible Nissan Micra that starts in one go and is clean and doesn't have rubbish littering the footwell. It even has heated seats.

Griffin presses the button and a warm fug fills the air as his clothes dry on his body. They don't talk. She drives to

240

the pub, to where his Land Rover is sitting alone and sad in the car park.

He gets out and closes the door. But before he can even wave, she drives off.

He gets in his truck. Okay, he thinks. Back to work.

Griffin is not a fan of nature. He was never at home roaming in the woods, not before, and certainly not now.

There is a body. Hanging from a low branch, the rope pulling the neck taut, head at an angle, face red and bloated. His feet are barely off the ground; if he'd been any heavier the noose wouldn't have done its job.

But as it is, this man is dead. Griffin risks looking closer. The rope is thin, cutting into the skin, rising to a point. A ligature mark, a common pattern in suicidal hangings. His eyes are open and bulging. Griffin takes a step back and sighs.

'Bugger,' he mutters.

'He's not been here long,' comes the voice behind him. He turns, it's Ross, his phone against his ear. 'If that's what you're wondering.'

'How long?' Griffin asks, as Ross finishes his call and hangs up. 'No more than a few hours?'

'Correct. Body's still warm, rigor's kicking in – so some time around four a.m.' His phone rings again and he backs away, but not before he gestures with a gloved hand towards the man's shirt pocket. There's a piece of paper sticking out of the top.

Griffin pulls it out gently.

It's a sheet of lined A4, ripped from an exercise book, folded in eight. He opens it. There are a few words written in a spidery scrawl.

I'm sorry. I did it. Forgive me.

Brody joins Griffin at the body. She takes one look at the man's face and gawps at Griffin.

'Fuck,' she says. 'How?'

He shows Brody the piece of paper.

'A confession?'

'Looks like it.'

Ross returns. He takes in Griffin and Brody's shocked expressions, registering their confusion. He gives them a look. 'What are you not telling me?'

Griffin points up at the hanging body. 'We arrested this man yesterday,' Griffin says, grimly. 'We thought he was in custody. This is Dr David Hammond.'

Chapter 43

'You let him go?' Cara snaps.

She's been trying hard to keep her voice level but as she's currently staring up at the corpse of their prime suspect – a man she believed was locked up safe and sound in custody – the anger and frustration and annoyance can't help but bubble to the surface.

'Watch your tone, DCI Elliott,' Halstead says at the other end of the phone. 'You had no reason – no evidence – to hold him. Something his lawyer made abundantly clear.'

Cara opens and closes her mouth again, shutting out a response that would get her suspended.

'What you need to be focusing on right now,' Halstead continues, 'is why you didn't realise he was a suicide risk. Did you do a risk assessment?'

Cara can hardly believe it. Her boss is trying to lay this on her.

'Dr Hammond had no mental health problems. No red flags in his file. When I left him, yesterday evening, he was rational and stable.'

'Even though you'd arrested him? For no reason?'

Cara grits her teeth so hard her jaw aches. A swell of anger creeps around her body. She takes the phone away from her ear and presses the red button.

'Did you hang up on your boss?' Griffin asks, a trace of amusement showing on his face.

'The reception was bad,' Cara replies. 'What can you tell me?'

'Not much.' Griffin points back to Ross, bent over the dead doctor now lying on a black bag in the leaves. 'They've only just cut the body down. Brody's speaking to the dog walker who found him. What do you make of the confession?'

Cara gestures to Griffin, who shows her the suicide note, now in its own evidence bag. 'It seems ...'

'Convenient?' Griffin finishes for her. Cara nods. 'I thought that too. I believed him. I honestly did. I was convinced we were going to be letting him go this morning.'

'Well, Halstead beat us to it.'

Her phone beeps. She looks at the message and feels overwhelming dread.

I'll be around with the kids in half an hour.

Shit. *Shit.* There's no way she can look after Tilly and Josh this weekend.

'Give me a sec,' she directs to Griffin.

She walks to a quieter part of the forest and dials, already dreading Roo's fury. But her explanation is met with silence.

'It's another body. I have to work this weekend, Roo. I'm sorry.' More dead air. 'I'm the SIO. This is important.'

'Your kids are important.' Flat. Impassive.

'I know. I know. Do you think I want to do this?'

'I don't know, Cara. I don't understand you any more.'

And he hangs up, leaving her staring at the dead phone.

244

She lets out a frustrated groan. She couldn't feel any worse. She's a terrible mother, she thinks, letting a well-worn guilt wash around her body. She'll make it up to Tilly and Josh. Somehow. When all this is over. *But when will that be?* her psyche throws back. *When?*

She rakes her hands through her hair then pushes her phone into her pocket, heading back over to Ross. She stares at the other part of her life that's failing: the body of the man who was under her care barely eight hours ago.

Ross looks up at her.

'What do you make of this, Elliott?' he asks.

Cara bends down and peers closely where Ross is pointing. The eyes are surrounded by tiny pinpricks of red.

'Petechiae. Commonly seen in strangulation.'

'Correct. Same here,' he says, using his forefinger and thumb to open the eye. Cara can see red blotches in the whites. 'And these marks, on his neck, below the rope?'

'Bruising and scratching.'

The pathologist's face is grim. He raises the GP's hands by the wrist; the nails are broken, one ripped away. 'Wounds consistent with someone scrabbling at their neck, trying to get purchase on whatever was strangling him.'

'Did he have second thoughts?' Cara says. 'Try to save himself?'

'Maybe. But take a look at this. Multiple grooves as the rope shifted position, here and here.' He points with a gloved finger at the deep red gouges in the flesh of his neck. 'A free-swinging hanging, like this one, wouldn't normally show the classical signs of asphyxia, like congestion of the face and petechial haemorrhaging. Death would usually occur almost instantaneously from vagal inhibition. From sudden pressure on the neck. But this ...' Ross looks back

245

to the dead man, something close to sympathy on the normally stoic pathologist's face. 'This went on for a while. Long enough for him to evacuate his bladder, possibly even have experienced convulsions. Once I get him back to the mortuary I'll be able to confirm, but I'm sure I'll find sustained damage to the larynx, the thyroid cartilage and the hyoid bone.'

'What are you saying, Greg?'

The pathologist stands up, removing his gloves. 'This suicide has been staged. And not well.'

Cara stares at him, then back to the body as Ross finishes his sentence.

'Your hunch was correct. Something odd is going on. And this guy …' Ross pauses, looking grimly at the corpse of Dr David Hammond. 'This guy was murdered.'

David

He's left the house. He's drained but he can't stand the questions from his wife; the fussing, her obvious worry. His solicitor was reassuring – getting him released was the first step, he would make sure no charges were brought. 'A spurious accusation,' he had said as he walked David out of the police station. 'We might even put in a complaint.'

David thinks of this happily as he strides away from his car. It's early, the sun isn't even up, but he enjoys the cold, crisp air in his lungs after the stale stench of that police cell. He walks fast, his arms swinging. Away from the traffic and concrete, towards the cool liberation of silence.

When he's further into the woods he turns his torch on, lighting the footpath with a narrow beam. It's a route he's trodden many times and resolves that this year he will get that dog. Something to keep him company on these lonely strolls; that will enjoy the peace and quiet as much as he does.

His feet kick through the undergrowth; all he can hear is the crunch of leaves underfoot, the repetitive in and out of his lungs, heavy with exertion. Except … there. Another set of footsteps, echoing his own. He stops, turns. He swings his torch down the path. Nothing.

He chuckles to himself. All this talk of murderers is making him paranoid. But the next thing he feels is something hard around his neck.

At first, he freezes. The shock, the unexpected squeeze at his throat. Then reactions kick in. His hands go up and scrabble at the rough rope. A sting as his nails scrape at skin, sticky fingers as he draws blood. A constriction; he wants to cough but he can't. He can't breathe. He tries to turn but something knocks his legs out from under him and he falls. Down. To the soft leaves, the mud.

The rope is tighter now, biting into his flesh. He claws at it but can't get purchase; his legs kick but he can't grip in the wet mulch. He feels himself being pulled, dragged, and all he can think is *I can't breathe, I can't breathe, I can't.*

He flails. It's useless. With every exertion his energy fades. He sees flashes of black sky, of shadows. Of branches silhouetted against stars. He hears his own gasps, his heartbeat booming in his ears, fast, repetitive, fading, as he's hauled across the ground.

And then, respite. A slight loosening, and a gust of cool air makes its way into his lungs. He coughs. He sucks in wonderful, beautiful oxygen. But not for long. Tight, pain, choking. It starts again.

And this time it's worse.

He's pulled vertical, heavenwards, his legs wobbly against the now tilting ground. One shoe has gone, lost in the struggle, and he feels damp, twigs, mud underfoot. In his panicked state he slips, he falls. The noose tightens leaving him choking. His mouth is open, desperate. He flails again, gets himself upright, but any slack on the rope has gone as

248

it continues to pull. On tiptoes now, nails abrading his neck, the sting of raw bleeding flesh. To no avail.

And then there's no ground. He is in mid-air. The pressure on his neck is excruciating, agony in his throat, his head, his lungs. His legs jerk, his eyes bulge. He thrashes and whirls. He loses control, a gush of warm urine soaks his legs. His arms feel heavy now, they drop to his sides. His vision is dull, he sees only flickers, the last semblance of shadows searing the night.

His eyes roll upwards. They're wild as he mouths a silent plead. *Please.*

He's aware of someone standing below him. He feels a touch on his leg then the sensation of his body spinning, rotating on the rope.

And a voice.

'It's your fault she died,' it hisses.

And the world turns black.

Chapter 44

When Jamie arrives at the crime scene the SOCOs have started to work, pulling on white suits and overshoes and gloves as a blue and white cordon is constructed around the area.

A low murmur of dread drags at his insides, only adding to the burn of guilt and self-hatred that's been growing since his conversation with the Blakes.

Pippa has been in his head more this past week. The complaint, coupled with the break-in at his old house hasn't helped, but he's started seeing her everywhere. Every woman with long blonde hair is her. Even her perfume follows him. He was sure he detected it in the house this morning, in his car. Places where it shouldn't have been, or where fresh air and time should have long dissipated it from the ether.

He signs in with the scene guard, suits up and joins Griffin and Cara as the body is being zipped into the black bag to be taken away. Griffin's gaze lingers a moment too long on his face; he gives a small nod in return. An unspoken message to confirm that no, he hasn't done anything stupid with the information Griffin had given him.

But maybe he had. Maybe Jennifer and Gordon Blake would tell the IOPC, start an internal investigation in their own ranks as to where the leak had originated. Or maybe they'll leave him alone, content with the damage they've already inflicted.

Cara's words pull Jamie back to the here and now.

'Uniforms have confirmed Hammond's car is parked on the far side of the woods, down there.' She gestures to a snaking leafy trail behind them. 'There are multiple paths into these woods. We have no way of knowing where our killer came from, and don't have the resource to search every one.'

'What about the forensics on the body and the rope?' Jamie asks.

'Rope's packed up for evidence. Ross will handle the fingernail scrapings and other trace from the body. Let's hope we get a hit.'

'Assuming they're in the system,' Jamie comments, and gets a sharp look from Cara.

'Have you got any better ideas?' she snaps.

'No, boss.'

'Good. Griffin, take Brody and go to Hammond's house. Uniforms have done the initial death notice but we need a follow-up. See if the wife noticed anything suspicious over the last few days. And go easy. Chances are we're not her favourite people right now. If in doubt, back off. Jamie, search the car.' She hands him a set of keys in an evidence bag. 'Call SOCO if you think there's anything useful. We'll meet back at the nick when you're done.'

They nod and go their separate ways. Jamie plods down the path, out of the back of the cordoned area, discarding his suit as he goes. His tread is slow, his mind full.

A man is dead. Someone else's husband, son. He had two young boys. Kids that will grow up without a father. Jamie is stunned by the onslaught of deaths this week. Lethargy would be better, but he feels heavy. Tired and worn out, finding no comfort in the routines of work. An ache gnaws in the pit of his stomach. He should be hungry – he hasn't eaten anything since lunch yesterday – but the thought of food makes him feel sick. He'll do the job. Go back to the nick. Go to bed. And maybe never emerge.

He sees the car on the edge of the forest. It's an Audi Q5, an SUV. Nice, barely a few years old. He clicks the fob through the bag and the indicators flash. He starts with the boot. It goes up smoothly, revealing a set of golf clubs. Does he keep them here? Always ready for a round when he has the time? Jamie puts gloves on then shifts them out of the way, filtering through the other belongings in the back. A few pens drop from the doctor's bag; brightly coloured, with drug names on the side. He picks one up – Prozac, emblazoned in large green lettering. Briefly he wonders about the drug. Would it help? Shift him out of this low mood he's found himself in for the last few months.

He pulls his phone out of his pocket and finds the number for his local doctor. He dials before he can talk himself out of it. Rare for a GP's surgery to be open Saturday morning, but it connects, and an automated message guides him through the options before putting him on hold, the muzak making his headache worse.

He places the phone on speaker and leaves it playing on the roof of the car while he continues his search. Car manuals in the glove box, a pair of sunglasses. In the centre console there's loose change, a charger cable, and a small toy car. Jamie rolls the wheels against the palm of his hand, picturing Hammond's sons. He knows from the file that one of them is six, young – too young – to have lost his father, and he hopes that Griffin and Brody are going easy on the wife, who will have nothing but sorrow and fear, and the horrors of paperwork in her future.

A voice blasts into the quiet of the forest and Jamie snatches the phone up. The receptionist asks for his name and date of birth, then meets his request for an appointment with a GP with a stony silence, then a question.

'And what is it concerning?'

'I … Umm.' Jamie feels stupid, a time waster. 'My wife died last year and I haven't been sleeping. I'm down all the time and …' His voice trails off. 'I was hoping the doctor could help.'

'You're depressed?' she says.

Jamie doesn't feel like it's up to the receptionist to diagnose him, but it's as good a description as any. 'Yes, I suppose so.'

There's an answering pause, and the clicking of long nails on keys.

'Someone's just cancelled, you're in luck. There's an appointment Monday morning at nine. Will that work for you?'

Probably not, Jamie thinks. What with a major murder investigation and a serial killer on the loose, but it's that or nothing. He thanks her and hangs up.

He should feel better, shouldn't he? The first step towards speaking about this shitty mood that's only getting worse, but all he feels is a sense of dread. That he'll have to speak to someone, articulate what's been going on in his head. The thoughts he's barely dared to acknowledge, even to himself. That, to a degree, he feels everyone would be better

253

off without him, and that any world that expects him to live without Pippa isn't one he wants to be a part of.

He hears the crack of a branch to his right and spins around. His eyes search the undergrowth but there's only brambles and leaves. An animal, a deer or a rabbit at most. He sighs. Paranoia is getting the better of him; he *is* going crazy.

He shuts the car door and moves around to the driver's side. There's nothing here. It's just the grubby but well-maintained Audi belonging to the man who's dead and hanging from a tree. He holds on to the steering wheel and lowers his head into the footwell, checking under the seat.

And that's when he sees it. A small green plastic square. He photographs it in situ, then picks it up with a gloved hand. It's a different colour, different size, but he recognises it immediately.

A GPS tracker. Same as the one they found in Kate Avery's handbag. And straight away, Jamie knows. He's been following his victims. And this is how.

Chapter 45

Cara couldn't wait to get away. From the woodland, the wet leaves underfoot, the latex of crime-scene gloves on her hands. The smell only a corpse can leave behind.

She's always noticed a shift in the air when a dead body is near. A charge, like a disruption has been made to the cosmic order of things. Ridiculous when she's never believed in God, but she feels those ghosts, that's for sure.

Back at the nick, she washes her hands in the bathroom, sweeps her hair back and stares at her face in the mirror. Her skin is grey, the bags under her eyes almost black. She feels clammy, a layer of sweat cold on her skin, and walks back to her office, quickly changing her jumper and top into the clean clothes she keeps there.

It helps. The coffee even more so.

She holds the hot mug in her hands as she stands in front of the whiteboard. Now, they wait. For the evidence from Hammond to come back from the post-mortem, hoping for skin cells or DNA from the rope being processed by the lab.

She starts updating the board from this morning and glances to the pile of textbooks and notes on Shenton's desk. She wonders how Hammond's death has influenced their killer. She doesn't need Shenton's PhD to know one thing: he can't be happy.

Up to now he's watched from afar, a puppet master, guiding his victims to their death. Elaborately planned set-ups: driving Colin Jefferies to his apogee of his terror; stealing Kate Avery's car, leading her to believe she had the Alzheimer's she feared. And the bombardment of text messages and social media trolling that pushed Isabel Warner to her overdose. No, this murder wasn't meticulously planned. It was hasty, in reaction to Hammond's release, to the possibility of him talking to the police. Up close and personal. There would be evidence left behind, scratches, maybe even skin cells under the victim's nails where he'd fought with his assailant.

This change in MO is odd. He must be worried. Desperate. And desperate men make mistakes. Ones that make them easier to find.

Cara hears footsteps behind her as Griffin and Brody come into the room. Griffin walks straight towards her while Brody heads to her desk.

'Anything?' she asks.

'You were right,' Griffin says. 'She hates us. But no, Hammond's wife didn't have anything helpful to add. Bar threatening to put in a complaint.'

'That was to be expected,' Cara replies.

'She wouldn't stop talking about his charity work,' Brody says from behind them. 'Some helpline he worked on. As if this made it impossible that he could have been a killer. *GetHelpNow*, it's called. All one word. Bundy worked at a rape crisis centre, didn't he? And we all know what he got up to.'

'But Hammond wasn't a killer,' Griffin says. 'We know

that now. We checked in with the SOCOs on the way back,' he adds, turning to Cara. 'Two sets of footwear marks leading down the path. Only one going back. They're taking casts.'

'Good. It's something. They'll have to believe us now. Definitive evidence of the involvement of a second party in the death.'

'What does Halstead say?'

Cara winces. 'Haven't called her. I was putting it off.'

Griffin snorts with amusement. 'Good luck. Boss,' he adds, the emphasis stressing that she's in charge, in the position he doesn't, and never has, envied.

He leaves her to it, and she heads to her office to make the dreaded call to her detective chief superintendent. She sits down at her desk and picks up the phone, but before she calls she notices Griffin lean in to speak to Brody. And something about their body language catches her eye.

Griffin's talking, but as he does so, one hand reaches towards her waist. It's a recognisable gesture, more personal than she would expect between colleagues, but before he makes contact Brody shakes her head and he quickly pulls back. Griffin's not one of *those* guys – never been the sort to wolf whistle or hassle – but even so Brody's response wasn't one of anger or retaliation. It was a rebuff.

Interesting, she thinks. But she hasn't got the time to worry about that now. Turning away, she dials Halstead's number.

Reports and evidence and lines of enquiry are more important to Cara than the disapproval of her boss. Halstead's response was abrupt when Cara updated her on Ross's assessment: 'You're the *expert*. I trust my detectives. The responsibility for this investigation lies on your head, Elliott.'

Cara imagined the sneer. The implication was clear: succeed and I'll take the credit. Fail, and I'll throw you under the bus.

It's hardly a supportive working relationship.

She busies herself with updates on the case. The tracker Jamie found in Hammond's car has been sent down to digital and Cara wonders who was there to receive it. Charlie, or one of his team?

Shenton pokes his head around the door of her office. He's shadow-eyed but pink-cheeked, which Cara has come to understand means only one thing.

'And?' she asks.

'I'm finished.'

'Tomorrow morning,' she confirms, and he nods. 'Be ready.'

He starts to leave. 'And the CCTV, Toby?' she asks. 'Hammond?'

'Nothing yet, boss. The country roads don't have coverage and we're waiting for Hants County Council to come back on the others. It's Saturday,' he concludes.

'Chase them,' she replies. Then she glances up at the clock. Gone six. 'Then go home. Tell the others.'

Cara watches as the message is passed on to the team. Griffin gets up and leaves without a backward glance to Brody, so perhaps Cara was imagining something between them. Brody follows, Oliver too. Jamie is slower to leave, his head down as he picks up his coat, his shoulders stooped.

She gets up and shouts from the doorway of her office.

'Jamie?' He looks over. 'You okay?' He nods. 'Good work today.'

He holds his hand up as he leaves.

It's late. Late enough? She's been deliberately idling, but

258

now takes the risk and grabs her coat and bag, turning lights off in the empty office as she goes, casting an eye over the whiteboard before the switch plunges it into darkness.

Six victims. And they have nothing.

She's still thinking about possible lines of enquiry as she rounds the corner into the car park and walks straight into Charlie. The man she's been trying to avoid.

She jumps, steps back a pace. He apologises automatically, then colours when he sees who it is.

'Sorry, sorry,' he repeats. 'You okay?'

'Yes. I was … thinking.'

'I heard about Hammond.'

She frowns. 'Not ideal.'

'Understatement,' he replies. His tone is cutting; he thinks her unfeeling, a lead detective who doesn't give a shit that her prime suspect is dead.

'Did you get anything from the tracker?' she asks.

'I emailed the results to Jamie.' He pauses; she waits for the summary and eventually he sighs. 'Nothing. Generic branded GPS tile. The serial number isn't registered. There's nothing to help your investigation.'

'Thank you.'

Charlie stares at her for a moment, expecting her to say something else. Then his face falls. 'Okay. Goodnight.'

He starts to leave, his head down.

'Charlie?'

He turns, eyes questioning.

'I'm sorry,' she says. He nods slowly. 'I am. It wasn't you.'

He gives her a small half-smile. 'So you said,' he replies, and walks away.

She hates that she's done this. That once again she's turned something good to shit.

259

Chapter 46

Griffin strides away from work, a prearranged meet in the forefront of his mind. Plus, he's keen to avoid another awkward conversation with Brody – he can only take so much rejection in one day.

All through the car journey to the Hammonds' and the interview with the wife, Brody had been reticent but professional. Calm but cold. The friendship they had shared at the pub last night disappeared the same time they discarded their clothes on Brody's bedroom floor.

Griffin's used to one-night stands, perhaps this is new territory for her. Maybe she's embarrassed, or worse – ashamed. He tries to put her out of his mind.

He gets home, a shower and food in his future, but as he gets out of the Land Rover he sees the box of files he picked up from his mum's house the day before, resting in the footwell. He carries it down to his flat, placing it on the table and looking at it, his hands on his hips. But neither this box nor Brody were his reason for wanting to get away tonight.

Sergeant Cohen from the serious collision unit has been

in touch. And he wants to meet.

Griffin has opted to message his home address to Cohen – convenience, quiet and secrecy overcoming any embarrassment over his pathetic living situation – and after half an hour the knock comes loud and clear on the top metal door. Griffin bounds up to answer it and claps his old friend in a solid embrace.

Danny Cohen and Griffin were on duty together, back in the day. Griffin fresh from policing college and Cohen only a few years out himself, both young and stupid and desperate to see some action. They were heavy with the right foot and enjoyed nothing more than sticking the siren on, the love of the road a precursor to where Cohen has ended up today.

Fifteen years on, Cohen has the same wiry black curls he had back then, now accompanied by a bushy beard. Time has thickened him out, turned his old jaunty run into a slow stroll.

'All that time behind a desk getting the better of you,' Griffin jokes as Cohen greets the cat then installs himself at the kitchen table with a sigh. Frank joins him, leaping up to his lap and winding himself around in his hands.

'Watch your mouth, probie,' Cohen replies with a grin. 'Get me some coffee.'

Griffin does as he's told, placing a mug of strong instant, two sugars, in front of his former partner.

'I'm doing this as a favour,' Cohen says, his eyebrows low and serious. 'Nothing is to leave this room.'

'Agreed,' Griffin says, sitting opposite him. 'But you've taken a look?'

'I have.' Cohen gently encourages the cat back to the floor and pulls his rucksack onto his lap. He takes out a wedge of

261

paper, the file Griffin recognises from the warehouse a few days ago. 'I don't know why you need me. You've seen these for yourself.'

'I don't have your experience. You see things I can't.'

Cohen eyes him warily, looking for signs of a piss-take. Seeing none, he opens the file. 'I'm assuming there's no need for me to be delicate.'

'Crack on.'

'In that case …' He lays the paperwork out on the table, photos face up, and already there are shots Griffin hasn't seen before. He pulls one of them across. His father, lying on a black body bag in the middle of the road, the blue flashing lights of a police car in the background. 'What do you want to know?'

'Did he kill himself?'

Cohen takes a swig of the coffee, stalling for time. 'You and I both know that if someone wants to kill themselves, rational thought doesn't come into it. We've all encountered people at the top of a bridge, idiots running into the road. And we have a sixth sense for these things. Cry for help, versus the more serious guys.' He taps on the photograph. 'And whatever this accident was, it wasn't a cry for help.'

Cohen looks up at Griffin, assessing if he should continue. Griffin nods. 'And?'

'And in 1999, there were no airbags, at least not in a Ford Focus like this one. No ANPR or traffic cams. No forensic collision investigators, or if there were, they weren't as advanced. Photography was all film, assessments made by hand with a tape measure and pencil. But the investigators did manage to come to a few conclusions.'

He points to a photo of the road, a line marked down

262

the outside. 'It was raining that night. This line shows how the water was running down the road, and there were puddles. Your father's tyres were worn, not great in weather conditions like this one. It would have made braking impossible, even if he had tried.'

'There were skid marks,' Griffin interjects.

'Only a few.' Cohen finds the photo Griffin is referring to and pushes it across. 'Not as many as I'd expect if he simply lost control and tried to stop. This pattern shows the brakes weren't applied until the last minute.'

'Meaning?'

'My guess? That either his reaction times were so dulled by the medication and alcohol that he didn't realise what was happening until too late, or he had last minute doubts about what he was doing. If – and I mean *if* – he was planning on driving straight into the tree. As you know, he wasn't wearing a seat belt. And that could show either intention, or intoxication. The car didn't have the seat-belt sensors that modern ones do, so it could have been oversight. There were no pre-collision defects, nothing wrong with the mechanical set-up of the car. Lucky for us, when the car lost power the speedometer stayed where it was, at sixty-three miles per hour. Doesn't always work, did here. His lights were on. We know this because the filament in the bulb is distorted, with debris stuck to it. See?' Another photograph is pushed Griffin's way; he can see the wiggly lines of the filament inside the smashed bulb. 'There was no evidence anyone else was in the car with your father, and no witnesses came forward that saw or heard the crash.'

'So?'

'So, it leaves us in the dark.'

'The death wasn't declared a suicide,' Griffin says.

263

'It rarely is, in the absence of a note,' Cohen replies. 'Even now.'

Griffin looks at another photograph. The right-hand side of the front is embedded in the trunk of the tree.

'He didn't hit it straight on.'

'No. Whether it was an instinctive reaction, or a genuine desire to avoid the tree, I don't know. But what I do know is your father went through that windscreen at a high speed. Cause of death was blunt force trauma, mainly to his head and skull as he came through the windscreen.'

Griffin picks up the photograph and holds it to the light, looking closer. 'What's this bump here?'

Cohen gestures for the photo and Griffin passes it across. The other man squints at it. 'The damage to the passenger side, back?' He frowns. 'I don't know.' He rummages in the other pieces of paper in the file, finds another photo and compares the two. 'Here it is again. Wait ...' More scrabbling, the technical report this time. 'Yes, here it is. "Damage to off-side rear. Grey paint samples taken. Indicates collision with secondary vehicle."'

'He was hit by another car?'

'Yes, but it could have been at any time. There's nothing to say it was involved in the crash.'

'But it could have been. Here ...'

Griffin takes a piece of paper and a pen and draws a rudimentary outline of the shape of the road. He marks the tree with an X. 'Dad could have been driving like this. Fast. Rain. Alcohol. Another car hits him from behind on the left-hand side, causing him to lose control and hit the tree.' He guides his pack of cigarettes down the makeshift road, demonstrating how it could have happened.

Cohen clicks his tongue, thinking. 'It's possible. But

it's also possible your father reversed into a grey car, then headed off to kill himself, changing his mind at the last moment and steering away, resulting in the car hitting the tree at the slight angle.'

'I don't remember seeing that damage.'

'Did you check your father's car every day?' Griffin has to admit no. 'Could be something or nothing.' Cohen leans back in the seat and sips at the coffee. 'I hate to ask this – but why does it matter? Your father is dead. We know what killed him – this tree. What's the difference?'

'There's a difference,' Griffin replies.

It's impossible to explain to someone who hasn't lived it. Griffin feels the distinction deep inside.

For twenty-four years he believed that his father hated his life so much there was no way out – and no reason for living. That his daughter, his wife, his son – *him* – weren't enough. Griffin's always felt that acute sense of failure. That something about him wasn't worth loving, wasn't worth trying for. Or that he'd done something so wrong he had caused his father's death. If there was a chance that that might not be true, wasn't it worth digging for?

'What if it was your case?' Griffin asks. 'What would you say?'

'I don't know, mate,' Cohen replies. He starts to gather up some of the photographs and notes, putting them back in the file. 'My job is to try to ascertain whether a crash caused someone's death, and how. All I can say for certain is your father was driving at over sixty miles an hour, down a country road, with a large amount of alcohol in his bloodstream. He didn't have his seat belt on, he didn't brake until the last moment. All of that combined meant that when your dad lost control and hit the tree, there was no going back. Did he mean to kill himself? I'm sorry. I don't know.' He pauses. 'What does your sister say? Elliott? Isn't she a DCI now?'

'Yes. And she says I should leave it alone.'

Cohen nods slowly. 'She was always smart, your big sister.'

Griffin thanks his friend and, with reassurances that they'll meet soon for a proper drink and catch-up that neither of them mean, Cohen departs, leaving Griffin alone with nothing but his thoughts and a silent cat for company.

The theory is ridiculous. But the idea stirred up by that damage to the back bumper nags. Someone *might* have been out there that night. They *might* have run his father off the road. But who? His mother wasn't a murderer, any more than Neil was. It just seems that bit too convenient that things have turned out so well for Neil as a result.

The box from his mother's flat was moved to the floor when Cohen arrived, but now Griffin picks it up and removes the first box file, resting it on the table. He opens it; a photograph greets him. His dad and Neil standing, puff-chested, outside the first ramshackle office. Sepia toned edges, faded colour; Griffin squints at the image, seeing traces of himself in his dad's face. The same dark brown hair, the same height, his dad towering over Neil. Tight jeans, flaring at the ankles. Wide lapels. Silly proud grin.

He turns it over. *Mark and Neil, 1977* is written on the back in his mum's handwriting. He lays it gently on the table, then pulls out the next few documents. Newspaper clippings, adverts in their local rag for the law firm. Formal certificates – a law degree from Oxford, the follow-up postgrad qualification. This box is no more than mementos, souvenirs of his father's life and career.

It stirs up memories in Griffin. Feelings he's not used to controlling about a man whose face he can't remember, not clearly. He looks to the fridge, even though he knows what he wants isn't in there.

The drinking for the past few nights has resurrected old urges. He's enjoyed the release; alcohol easing the stiffness, smudging the edges. He won't go back to the oxy, no way, but how could a few beers hurt?

He gets up, grabbing his keys and wallet and leaving the flat. It's a short walk to the off-licence, telling himself that he'll get a six-pack, drink two. Nothing to worry about. He grabs the beer, pays while a voice nags in the back of his mind: *Remember what you did last night? You lost control!*

He got drunk and slept with Brody. So what? It wasn't a bad thing; she had wanted it as much as he did. Even if work was awkward today. He found himself lingering on her face while she was talking to Hammond's wife, remembering her soft, lithe body under those clothes, but so what? What's wrong with a one-night stand, even with a co-worker? It won't happen again.

He gets home, cracks open the first beer. It goes down smoothly while he looks through the box file. Finding nothing of interest, he turns his attention to the next. A lever arch, more formal this time.

Frank watches him from the sofa. He's sitting on the arm, formal and neat, front paws resting together. Griffin glares at his imagined judgement; the cat looks away, his tail flicking from side to side, before he jumps off and makes a swift exit through the open window.

'Fine. Be like that,' Griffin mutters, refocusing on the folder.

The second beer. A nice buzz taking hold. He needs it for this stuff. Rows of numbers, spreadsheets, accounts. The early ones written in pencil, pound signs and amounts carefully entered in rows, brief descriptions next to them – case numbers, Griffin assumes. But accountancy isn't his forte, analytics and stats have always been a mystery to him.

He thinks about Ollie Maddox at work. He's got that sort of brain; he'll get him to take a look. Pleased, he puts the files away, and reaches for another beer. It's the last one – shit, he's got through all six while he's been sitting here.

No point in keeping one, Griffin thinks as he flips the ring pull. He leans back contentedly in his chair. He'll get Ollie's opinion on the files, and that'll be it. He can stop thinking about his dad. That's one benefit to the beer – the worries about his father now feel far away, just out of reach, the alcohol conveniently dulling his senses.

He puts the last beer to his lips releasing a sigh of satisfaction.

One more day, then he can officially put this whole business behind him.

Chapter 47

He's waiting for Cara as she arrives home. That ridiculous red Merc, lurking in the drive where it always used to be.

She parks up; there's nobody in the driver's seat. He must be inside, waiting, a fact that annoys her even though it's officially his house.

He will have heard her arrive and she gets out, steeling herself for the inevitable argument. He opens the front door before she can get to it, his face stern as she pushes past him.

'Sarah's with the kids,' he says.

The twitch of irritation grows but she says nothing as she sees the half-filled mug left on the dining table, the chair pulled out where he had been sitting.

'You could have called,' she says.

'You would have avoided me.'

Cara doesn't deny it. 'How long have you been here?'

'Not long.'

She touches the kettle – it's warm and she clicks it on. She gets one mug out of the cupboard, one teabag.

'I won't stay long,' he says, responding to her unsubtle message. 'We need to talk.'

'So, talk.'

She makes the tea. She doesn't want it, she'd prefer wine, but she won't give him the satisfaction of lecturing her on that, too. He stays quiet while she dunks the teabag, adds milk.

She turns to him, cradling the scalding mug in both hands. She stays standing, one hip leaning on the work surface.

Roo sits down again at the dining table. 'I'm applying for sole custody of the kids,' he says. His face is defiant, and she wonders how she ever loved him, this cruel man who doesn't understand her, who can't offer any empathy to what she's going through. She grits her teeth, glares.

'You'll have visitation rights. You'll see them, but this, Cara. This. It isn't working.'

'I told you the house is on the market. I'll get somewhere suitable. And work ...' She trails off. Even to her own ears her excuses are pathetic.

'Work will always take over. You know that as well as I do. The kids need stability. Somewhere permanent to live.'

'And that's with you, is it? A head chef who works all hours.'

'I'm getting a new job. A position has come up at Rochefort. I'm going to take it.'

'But you hate Rochefort. The food's shit. Franco-anglaise garbage, you said.'

'It won't be once I'm in charge.' A glimmer of a smile. The old joke between them. Then serious again. 'They're prepared to offer me steady hours. I need to take it. For the kids. And Sarah will fill in the gaps.'

Bloody Sarah again. 'I bet she's loving this. She was always waiting in the wings. For me to fuck up.'

His jaw tenses. 'Well, you're certainly doing that now.' His upper body swells, gathering his anger and storing it in his chest, deep inside. 'You need to decide what your priorities are. If it's work, whatever case is taking precedence right now, then fair enough. But these are the consequences.' He stops, about to say something else.

'Go on then,' Cara prompts. 'What?'

'I was only going to say …' He shakes his head. 'You've changed, Cara. Your humanity. Your love. It's gone.' He stands and walks away, turning back for a second in the doorway. 'I wanted to tell you face to face. Rather than you finding out in a letter from our lawyers. I didn't want you showing up, screaming and shouting on my doorstep.'

'How fucking decent of you,' she snaps, but she's sniping at empty space – the front door has closed, his Mercedes already growling in the driveway.

She listens to it rev, then fade as he heads off into the distance. She looks down at the mug of tea. She's been holding it so tightly it's burned the palms of her hands. They're red, inflamed.

She releases her fingers, prising the strained joints away from the ceramic and pouring the tea down the sink. Then, with shaking hands, she reaches for the gin in the cupboard.

Ken

His breath is sour; his mouth as dry as his sandpaper skin. He licks his lips, but the sores at the edge of his mouth crack, stinging.

He feels the cold, and standing out here, in the middle of January, isn't helping. He swigs vodka direct from the litre bottle, relishing the burn at the back of his throat. Cheap stuff, necessary. The small tremors he's used to have grown into a full body shake. He's not sure he can go through with this. Not sure he's capable.

But he must. He's been promised marvellous things. The only gift he's wanted for a while now. Blessed relief. Blessed darkness. If he does this one job.

If.

It's taken a tremendous effort, to get himself here today. But it'll be worth it. He takes another few steps towards the grand block of flats, towards the security cameras and the access codes and the keyless entry.

He's been told what to do.

He wears no mask. Has no gloves as he presses the fob against the sensor. It buzzes. He's in. As he pushes the door open he looks up to the camera. It stares back, impassively. If it all goes to plan tonight, this will be the last known sighting of him. Vanished, off the face of the earth, to wherever people go.

He's always believed in that crap. An almighty God. Heaven, hell. Especially now he's experienced it first-hand. Hell has been his life for the last two years. Hell has been an ever-constant agony, all prayers to end this shitty existence going unanswered. He has no family, no friends. Until him.

His guardian angel. An offering, contained in a crackly white paper parcel. There will be more of this, he promised. But everything comes at a cost.

He walks on creaking legs towards the lift. It's nice, this place. Must cost her a fortune. Better than his one-room shithole. His threadbare armchair, the television. Spending precious days of his meagre existence staring at bare walls, out of the window to the rain beyond.

This is the furthest he's ventured for weeks – trips to Asda notwithstanding. To buy the basics. A bit of bread, butter. Anything he can stomach without vomiting. That's not much nowadays. His body is no more than a withered skeleton. Shifting bones, barely a life.

The lift arrives with a ping; he presses the button. Ten floors up. No way anyone could get through a window. No way anyone would get in, full stop, if it weren't for the fob, and the keys he feels, heavy and solid, in his pocket.

He gets out. He counts the doors, stopping when he reaches 10–14. He pauses. Will this even work? Nothing has stirred down there for years, although he's been assured that with the right drugs, everything will come to life. For hours, he's been told. Imagine that. He laughs sardonically to himself. One last hurrah, and this is what he does with it?

The key slides smoothly into the lock. It turns with an almost inaudible click. Now the second, the bolt. The same. Nicely oiled. Like he's going to be.

He takes another gulp of vodka, then pushes the handle. Slowly the door opens.

Inside, the flat is quiet. It smells different to his own – clean, feminine. Of scented candles and citrus bubble baths. Not of faeces and sweat, of rotting flesh, barely alive on the walking corpse.

All the lights are off and he gropes his way through. She'll be out of it, he's been told. Sleeping pills, takes them every night. For her anxiety. For her PTSD. To wipe her past so she can get some rest.

Act quickly, and you should have enough time. Don't dawdle, or she'll wake up properly, and then you'll be in trouble.

'I don't care about trouble,' he had said.

'But you care about what I can give you, don't you?' the man replied, with a grin. 'Everything you've ever wanted.'

He takes the cable ties out of his pocket. He holds them in one hand with the vodka, the third key unlocking the bedroom door and pushing it open.

And there she is. He pauses, watching her. Sound asleep on her back, her mouth open, defenceless, unaware. She is as beautiful as he promised. My gift to you, he had said.

He wonders how he will be judged, in the next life. When he's gone and he's faced with his maker. Will He understand? What lengths he had to go to, to get what he needed. A final, selfish act. More than selfish – evil. It's immoral what he's about to do. He knows that, but he's never cared. Love, respect, kindness – noble gestures of a world where none have been offered to him.

It's been a while since he's been with a woman. In his past he had whoever he wanted. He didn't mind the tears, the cries for help. They were his to take. Until this illness got the better of him. Retribution? If so, it was from a lesser God than the one helping him now.

He steps into the bedroom. Closes the door behind him and locks it again, pocketing the key. He shuffles towards her; his heart thumps hard – he wonders if he'll have a heart attack before this is even done. He puts the vodka on the bedside table next to the spare ties; he holds one in his hand. Tentative, but prepared.

And in one move, he's there. No more thought, just action. He didn't realise he had it in him, but when the motivation kicks in, even he can achieve miracles. He snaps the tie around one wrist, zips it up as far as it can go, pinching the flesh. She jerks, her eyes open. But the second hand is grabbed, two attempts and it's threaded through the first. Done. She's caught, her hands behind her back, twisted skin, but secure.

She's fully awake now, bucking against her fastenings. Her legs kick out; she screams, until he shoves a dirty cloth into her gaping mouth. He brought that especially, the instructions were specific. A rag, stinking of petrol and grease. Cable ties. Her flat, while she is sleeping.

Her legs next. She's still kicking, her duvet and sheets rucked up in the mess. He reaches to grab her ankle and gets one in the face for his efforts. Blood in his mouth. A tooth wobbly. He's loses his temper now, and takes the knife out of his pocket. A switchblade, like he was told. He leans down to her face, her eyes panicking as he holds it against her neck. He knows what he has to say.

'Don't move, you little bitch, or I'll slit you from ear to ear.'

The words act like magic, she stills instantly. She starts crying then, snot, tears, streaming down her face. She swings her head from side to side, moaning quietly.

He backs away from the bed, gawping at the miracle in front of him. He rubs his hands together; papery skin falls like dandruff.

It's like he said it would be. He reaches into his pocket and takes out the last piece of the puzzle. Two small blue pills. He pushes them out of their blister and swallows them dry. How long, he wonders, but he can already feel things stirring. Whether it's watching her – her smooth, soft skin, her white cotton knickers, already askew. Or whether it's the pharmaceuticals, who cares. But he's going to enjoy this.

Who knew he was this much of a bastard? It's a side of him he finds interesting. His wife was right, all those years ago – he is an evil cunt. He'd hit her. The back of his hand against her cheek. A slap. A painful pinch. For whatever infraction annoyed him that day.

This girl? She's done nothing. But she is his gateway. And he'll get his fuck in first.

He kicks his boots off, lowers his trousers, his stained pants. She sees him and lets out a low howl, squirming on the bed. He raises the knife again, and she stops.

She's on her side, watching him, her eyes wide. She's making no attempt to get away, although it's only her hands that are tied. He said it would be like this. That she would be frozen with fear, her worst nightmares coming to the fore, but he didn't believe it.

He clambers on the bed, pushing her onto her front.

She resists, but it's futile, he's on her now and he grabs her wrists, pulling her arms up behind her back. She squeals, her shoulders and arms at awkward angles, but it's an automatic exclamation of pain, rather than resistance. She knows she is beaten. What will happen next. Her halting exhalations confirm it.

He pushes her legs apart. He pauses, almost salivating, looking at the two perfect globes of her ass, knowing what treats lie within. This isn't his thing, but the man was specific. And who is he to say no? He savours the moment, looking at her face. It looks like she's trying to say something, and he reaches up and pulls the gag out of her mouth.

She stutters words between her sobs.

'Kill me,' she says. 'Please. Kill me.'

He smiles. 'No,' he replies. 'That's your job.'

DAY 7

SUNDAY

Chapter 48

The whole team are in; Cara has been waiting, but now gets up from her desk and walks out to the centre of the office. Shenton watches her, fingers fidgeting at the collar of his shirt.

'Everyone?' She claps her hands together and faces turn. Brody, Jamie, Ollie, Griffin. A small but dedicated group. 'Shenton has the floor.'

Cara pulls up a chair with the others and waits while they gather around. Brody and Jamie seem intrigued; a smirk hovers on the edge of Griffin's mouth – he knows what's coming. She gives him a nudge with her elbow, warning him to behave; he mouths *What?* at her, his face a mask of mock innocence.

'You know what,' she whispers back.

Shenton opens his notebook; his hands are shaking as he turns to the right page, paper fluttering. He glances up, once, then his eyes lock on his notes. He looks like a small child about to do a show and tell, but Cara knows that once he starts talking – about this, his specialist subject – that his confidence will grow.

'We know a few things about our killer,' Shenton begins. His voice has a slight tremor, he clears his throat. 'He's meticulous. The way he gaslights these people to kill themselves – it's clear he's a man who knows what he's doing.

'He's educated, although he may be an autodidact. Self-taught,' he adds with a glance to Griffin. 'And he's smart – intelligent enough to learn skills such as the software coding he needed to target Isabel Warner. But I don't think he has a job – at least not a steady nine to five. He's able to follow his victims all hours of the day – and he can drive and has access to a car. All of this together points to an organised offender. Planned, and in control. He's competent, and will, to all intents and purposes, appear normal. He leaves nothing behind – no forensics or fingerprints – which makes him significantly harder to catch.'

'But he did,' Brody says. 'With Hammond.'

'That's an interesting one. He broke his routine – went hands on to kill him. Which makes me think there was something particular about Hammond that our offender couldn't risk.'

'We were too close?' Griffin suggests.

'Yes. Or Hammond was too close to him. Somehow, he knows what's going on in our investigation: it's likely he's following reports of the deaths in the media and might have already inserted himself into the case.'

'And you think he's a man?' Jamie interrupts.

'Almost, without exception, British serial killers are white men.'

'Rose West, Myra Hindley?'

'All who killed in conjunction with men. The exception to these are so-called Angels of Death, like Beverley Allitt.

279

Nurses or doctors who intentionally kill people under their care. So yes, I think this is a man. Plus, we have Colin Jefferies' neighbour who says she heard a male voice, and the CCTV from the Tesco where Kate Avery's car was stolen.'

He looks to Cara, unsure. She gives him a reassuring smile.

'We all know the main types of serial killer, right?' Shenton says, moving on. Everyone nods. 'Visionary, mission, hedonistic, and power and control. Ruling out visionary, as most are in the grip of some sort of delusion, and therefore disorganised, my assumption is our man has a piece of each of these. He is enjoying himself, no doubt, but we haven't seen a sexual element to the crimes, no sadistic desire to watch these people die. No, my assertion is that something links these victims, beyond age, gender, background – something that drives him to kill them. And that says to me that he's predominantly a mission killer.'

'What about power?' Cara asks.

'I believe that all serial killers have this in some respect. The common component to all is they will have experienced some sort of abuse in their past – whether it's emotional, physical, sexual – and specifically, that our killer has lived through a significant event where he was helpless and totally at the whim of something outside his control. This was, in all likelihood, his escalating incident. And, given the timeline of his killings, probably took place in the last few months.'

'But what?' Brody asks. Shenton shrugs and Brody scoffs. 'This is all well and good, but we need to catch him. We can't arrest a theory.'

Brody's doubt throws Shenton for a moment and he pauses, his cheeks going red. Cara catches Brody rolling her eyes at Griffin and gives them both a hard stare.

'Can you give us any indication of his age or demographic?' Cara says.

'The specific geography of our victims suggests he knows this area well, so I would predict he's local, or close by. White – as I said before – and young. He would have needed considerable strength to overpower Hammond and hang him from that tree. Something else I'm sure of – if we find this guy, he's going to talk. Traditionally, serial killers either "lay out" or "cover up" and this applies to their arrests too. Fred West buried his victims and killed himself before he talked about his crimes. Same with Shipman. Bundy and Dahmer were the opposite – while they weren't necessarily coherent or truthful, they talked at length about what they'd done. We catch this guy and we're not going to be able to shut him up. He's proud. A man on a mission.'

'So, assuming this is, as you say, a mission killer,' Cara asks, 'what's he trying to achieve?'

'Mission killers have one goal: to eliminate a certain group of people. He is using their deaths to try to reorder a world in which he feels powerless and ignored.'

'Like the Unabomber?' Oliver suggests.

'Exactly like him. Ted Kaczynski's manifesto argued that the industrial revolution had been a disaster to the human race, and therefore targeted people he believed to be advancing modern technology. Like our killer, he murdered from a distance, and like our killer, he wasn't insane. He was smart – a former professor of mathematics.'

'But a psychopath,' Brody says.

Shenton nods. 'It's likely he'd score highly on lack of remorse and lack of empathy. We know he's manipulative and probably has some level of superficial charm. He won't believe what he's doing is wrong, and as this progresses, we'll see a greater level of risk-taking and impulsivity, as we have with Hammond.'

'When will he stop?' Cara asks.

Shenton pauses. He lowers his notepad slowly, his pale blue eyes locked on Cara. 'Our offender has created a fantasy in his head. Not dissimilar to those of sexual sadists – an image of the perfect act of his kill. Ridding the world of these people one at a time. But the act of killing leaves him wanting more. Because it's not perfect, there are always ways he can improve. And so he thinks about the next. And the next. He won't stop until we make him.'

'And how do we do that?'

'We work out what his mission is.'

The whole room stills. Nobody wants to meet each other's gaze, everyone unwilling to throw a theory into the mix and risk it being wrong.

Cara stands up and writes a heading on one side of the board. *MISSION?* She underlines it twice.

'Write your thoughts here. Anything. Everything. I'll start.'

She writes *MENTAL ILLNESS* in small black capitals.

'All our victims were ill enough to kill themselves. That's one thing we know for sure.'

'Was that there all along?' Griffin says. 'Or did our killer exacerbate it?'

But before Cara can answer, her mobile starts to ring. She's not sure whether it's Shenton's words or a Pavlovian response, but the sense of foreboding is immediate. She raises her phone to her ear.

And her worst fears are realised.

'DCI Elliott,' the voice from Control says. 'It's one of yours.'

Chapter 49

The room is in shadows, blinds drawn. A perfect triangle of light shines through a small gap onto the bath, where the woman is lying.

Griffin's wearing a full crime-scene suit, boots, gloves – but even through the mask he can detect the iron tang of blood. Dilute but prevalent.

'Downstairs flat called the landlord,' Brody says from the door to the bathroom. 'Water coming through their ceiling. Demanded he get access. He let himself in and found this, called 999 straight away.'

'Did he touch anything?'

'He turned the water off.'

Griffin gives a questioning look to the SOCOs, they nod, so he pulls on the cord and the blind opens. He wishes he hadn't.

The woman lies on her back in the now cold bath. The water is pink. Two long slash marks run the length of both arms, the second – on the right – is jagged and shorter than the other, the effects of the first wound dulling her ability to inflict the next. She's fully clothed, in baggy blue tracksuit bottoms and a black T-shirt. The material hangs in the water, shifting. The water is up to the top and has sloshed over, creating a lake in the bathroom and the hallway beyond.

'She didn't want to lie here dead for days,' Brody says. 'She knew the flood would alert someone.'

'Or she wanted to be found?' Griffin asks. 'Maybe it was a cry for help?'

'I don't think so.'

Brody tilts her head and Griffin follows her, his overshoes squelching from the bath water as he walks to the bedroom. It's in darkness, the curtains closed, and Griffin turns the light on. He stops dead in the doorway.

The bedclothes are in disarray, duvet and pillows discarded on the floor. The bottom sheet is creased and rucked, but it's what's across it that gives Griffin pause. Blood. And a lot of it. Pools, spatters, smudges, across the bed and the headboard.

A bloodied vodka bottle lies on the carpet.

'And that's not all,' a SOCO says, before plunging the room back into darkness and switching a black light on. Instantly a whole new world comes into stark focus: bright blue droplets and smears across the sheet.

'Semen?' Griffin says, with disbelief.

'We've already taken samples, but we'll package it all up for the lab for further analysis,' the SOCO says, switching the light back on.

'Griffin?' Brody's standing by the side of the bed. She gestures with a gloved hand.

It's a piece of writing paper, light blue, decent quality. Words are scrawled in wobbly biro.

This is my only escape.

Griffin frowns. 'Escape from what?'

Brody shrugs. The gesture is apathetic but she turns quickly away from Griffin, her head tilted down, her shoulders slumped.

'We found these,' a SOCO says from behind them. She holds up two evidence bags.

Griffin leaves Brody and peers at them. One contains a piece of material, dirty, torn. Wet. The other some snipped cable ties.

'She was restrained?' he asks, but without waiting for an answer he heads back to the bathroom.

Inside, Ross has arrived. The body is being photographed so has been left in situ for the time being. Ross is crouched next to her, examining her in the water.

He repeats his question to Ross, who picks up her wrist and holds it out to Griffin. While the slashes had been his main focus before, he now sees the telltale lines of bruising and abrasions, consistent with the cable ties.

'Signs of sexual assault in the bedroom,' Griffin comments.

'I heard,' Ross says. 'And a note? Bag it up. I'll want to see it later.' He stands up straight. 'I'll look her over more closely at the mortuary, give you proper COD. I wouldn't want to speculate now.'

'Time of death?'

'Impossible to say. The temperature of the bath water complicates matters. Interferes with the normal timeline of cooling. Your best bet is to piece together your TOD from witness reports. What's her name?'

'Lisa Hobbs.'

Ross's head snaps up. 'Hobbs?' He looks back to the victim and his face falls.

'You know her?'

285

'Know of her,' Ross replies. 'I'm surprised you don't.' He studies the woman carefully. 'I'll prioritise the case. Come by later today. You'll have your answers.'

He gathers his stuff and leaves; the SOCOs move in to finish their photography, their samples. Brody join Griffin in the bathroom.

'Is that normal?' she asks. 'For Dr Ross to be that obliging?'

'Hell, no,' Griffin replies, but is interrupted by shouting from the doorway. A female voice, hysterical, demanding to be let in. He gestures to the front door. 'Looks like we'd better see to that.'

Chapter 50

The woman quietens as Griffin walks towards her, her entry blocked by the scene guard.

'Please, will someone tell me something. She's dead, isn't she?'

Brody introduces herself and Griffin, then moves the woman to the far side of the corridor.

'I'm sorry, but Lisa is dead, yes.'

The woman lets out a wail, and slumps against the wall. She covers her face and sobs quietly for a moment. Brody places a hand on her shoulder; after a moment, she stops and looks at Brody with red-rimmed eyes.

'Did it happen again?'

Brody tips her head to one side. 'Did what happen?'

'The … The attack.'

Griffin catches Brody's glance. He's as much in the dark as she is. 'Attack?' Brody attempts to clarify. 'I'm sorry, Ms …'

'Carter. Dannie Carter. Lisa was attacked.' She pauses, swallows. 'Raped,' she adds, her voice hushed. 'Last year. In the middle of the night. Someone broke in. Did they … Did they do it again? Did he kill her this time?'

'It's still early days, but our investigations don't show forced entry. Might she have let someone in?'

'No. No way.' Dannie shakes her head emphatically. 'Whenever we come around, we have to call first. If she isn't expecting anyone, she doesn't open the door. She's safety conscious. Paranoid, even. And rightly so, given what's she been through. But here. Here she thought she was safe.'

'She was new to the building?'

'Moved in six months ago. Top floor. Brand new place, all the security and cameras. That's why she liked it.' She glances towards the flat, picking at her lip. 'Did she kill herself?' she asks quietly.

'Why do you ask that?' Griffin replies, avoiding the question.

'She'd tried it before. Once. But she regretted it straight away, called an ambulance. They pumped her stomach, she was fine. Well. Not fine. But better. I thought … I thought she was over the worst of it. She'd been speaking to someone.'

'Do you know who?'

'No, sorry. I assumed it was a shrink.'

'And what did she take? Last time she tried to kill herself?'

'Oh, Christ. I don't know. Everything. All her prescription meds, all at once. And there were a lot of them. Enough to run her own pharmacy, she said.' She laughs then, it turns into a sob. 'I knew it. When she didn't answer her phone this morning. I knew she was dead.'

Griffin and Brody take her details and persuade Dannie to go home, promising to share more information as soon as they have it. They leave the crime scene, walking down the stairs and back to the car.

'She might have killed herself,' Brody says. 'Depressive symptoms, acute emotional distress, history of trauma, lived alone, lack of social support. She'd be a prime candidate for suicide.'

'On that basis, so am I,' Griffin comments bleakly. 'Let's be sure.'

The moment they get back to the office, Brody updates Cara while Griffin pulls up the PNC. He types in *Hobbs, Lisa*, Cara hovering behind them. Her best mate was right – rape, false imprisonment, GBH. Griffin reads the details, horror and disgust growing with every word of her account.

A man broke into her ground-floor flat in the middle of the night. Tied her hands behind her back with cable ties. Threatened her with a knife, stripped her naked, then violently raped her. Help was only called when he left and she managed to stagger to the phone. The attack had gone on for eleven hours. She'd been left beaten, bleeding and traumatised. Hospitalised for a week. And the man was never caught.

They had plenty of leads – except the most important. He'd left no DNA. No fingerprints, no seminal fluid. She'd been blindfolded, but she'd remembered the smell of the rag he pushed into her mouth, the scent of his aftershave. CK One. Grease. Oil. Griffin can see that one of the working theories was he was a mechanic, but the trail had gone cold. A stranger rape with no leads. No cameras. No evidence. The poor woman had been left with nothing.

Brody wordlessly sits next to him, reading the notes on the screen. She sinks lower, her chin resting on her hands, her frown deepening as they digest the information.

Cara paces behind them as Griffin reads the salient points aloud. 'And that's it?' she says, when Griffin sits back.

'That's it. On the system, at least. We could dig out the files, but I'm not sure it would help us.'

'Nor her. Not now,' Cara says, and Brody lets out a shout of frustration.

'Why wasn't this guy caught? Why didn't they exhaust every avenue?'

'Perhaps they did,' Griffin says. Brody gives him a dubious look. 'Where's Jamie?' he directs to Cara.

'With the landlord, getting the CCTV,' she says. 'So the rapist before left nothing behind, in direct contrast to the guy who was there last night. If there was a rape, or forced coercion to suicide, we should know who soon enough. Go and see Ross. See what else he can tell you.'

Griffin nods; Brody picks up her coat. Griffin's used to being a one-man show, but clearly they work together now. Griffin's surprised to realise he doesn't mind.

Chapter 51

Jamie's glad of work to distract him, of the unrelenting barrage of misery and pain that doesn't belong to him. He helps coordinate the house-to-house, the door knocking on every number in the block in the hope someone was listening.

Another woman is dead. He speaks to the landlord, who assures him that the CCTV footage will be sent over in the next hour. But Jamie's senses are twitching – he seems shifty. And not just because someone's killed themselves in one of his flats.

'Mr Pappas,' he says, pulling the man to one side in the large entrance hall. 'What aren't you telling me?'

'It's not a crime, is it?' the man blurts out. 'It's not my fault.'

'Did you do something to Lisa Hobbs?' Jamie asks slowly, the caution at the tip of his tongue.

'No. No! But ...' He glances around. 'My house was broken into, and I didn't report it.'

Jamie frowns. 'Okay. And?'

'And ... They might have taken a fob for the entrance. And the spare keys.'

Bloody hell, Jamie thinks. 'When was this?'

'Last week. I didn't mention it because … Well. It would have cost me a fortune to replace all the locks in this place. Ten floors, twenty flats on each floor. Do you know how many that is?'

'Yes, and I can guess how much you're making a month in rent, *Sir*.' He says this last word with disgust. 'And you'll be replacing them all now? Or maybe I need to take you in for gross negligence manslaughter.'

He backtracks quickly. 'Today. And I'll get that CCTV to you straight away.'

The landlord hurries off, glancing back to Jamie before he rounds the corner. Jamie frowns. It all adds up to a calculating and determined offender. As if they didn't know that already.

The landlord is true to his word – on the matter of the CCTV at least. Jamie logs on to the police network and the files have already been uploaded. He finds the one for the main door to the building and scrolls until the right timestamp appears for last night. A series of people cycle past – all confident, casual – until one guy catches Jamie's eye. He's small and squirrelly, shabbily dressed. He glances upwards to the camera and Jamie gets a good view of his face.

He calls Charlie straight away.

'If I send you some video can you pull an image of our guy and run it through facial recognition? As priority?'

'Absolutely. Send it now.'

Jamie puts down the phone as Cara appears at his elbow.

'That was Charlie,' he says. 'He's going to run facial rec for us.'

292

Jamie's paused the video on the man's face. Cara shudders. 'And you think he's our man?'

'He's a likely candidate.'

'Good.' Cara pauses, then sits down next to Jamie. She lowers her head towards his so only the two of them can hear. 'Listen, Jamie. Halstead told me about your promotion, about the complaint, and it's bullshit.'

'Thanks, boss.' Jamie feels a prickling and hates himself for the way he is now. Always so emotional, so close to tears.

'We'll sort it out. I won't let them suspend you.'

'Suspend me?'

Cara colours. 'It's been discussed. But it's not going to happen,' she says quickly.

'I need this job. I need to work,' Jamie says, desperation creeping into his voice. The idea that he could be stuck at home with nothing but his thoughts? It's horrifying.

'I know.' She places a reassuring hand on his arm. 'We'll sort this out,' she repeats. 'And I'll make sure you get that promotion.'

She pats him on the shoulder and leaves him to it. He's grateful. His loathing and self-hate are the only thing keeping him afloat. Any more nice words and he might lose it completely.

Chapter 52

The post-mortem has just started as Griffin and Brody arrive at the mortuary. The body of Lisa Hobbs has been laid out on the slab and a technician is carefully combing through her hair, capturing vital evidence.

Ross is head to toe in PPE, doing his preliminary assessment of the body. He shouts across as soon as they arrive: 'Get suited up. You need to see this.'

They do as they're told; Griffin heads across, Brody following.

Ross doesn't wait, but stands back, allowing Griffin to take a look.

'What do you see?'

Griffin casts his eye over the body, Ross's intimation obvious. Ridges cut into both her wrists, the red band chafed and scabbed.

'We already knew she was tied up,' Griffin says. 'And tight, by the looks of it.'

'That's not all,' Ross replies. He indicates to his technician for help and the two of them carefully roll the body. Griffin hears a quick intake of surprise from Brody, but he can't look away.

A network of bruises cover the white skin of her back. Handprints, finger marks, abrasions, where her attacker held her down. Thin red cuts litter her neck – a knife held, threatening, not caring whether he broke the skin. And that's not the worst. The bruises continue across her buttocks, down her legs, the inside of her thighs. Marks where his fingers pressed hard into her skin, forcing her legs apart.

Ross leans forward and does it tenderly now, moving her limbs so they can see. Brody makes a small moan and steps away; Griffin tenses his jaw, disgust and anger coursing in his veins.

'Extensive damage to her vagina and anus. The semen found at the scene indicated she was raped, but first, judging from the damage inflicted here, then abused with something else, most likely a large bottle. It wasn't quick. We're talking sustained violence.'

'Posthumous?' Griffin says, reaching for even the slightest bit of hope.

But Ross shakes his head. 'All while she was alive and very much kicking. Damage to her toenails and feet show extensive defensive wounds, not that it did much good. Abrasions to her tongue, gums and lips, probably from her face being pushed into the bed, and from the pain she must have endured.'

'Turn her back over,' Brody says quietly.

Ross does as he's asked, gently laying her on the stainless-steel table and covering her with a blue drape.

'Did this contribute to cause of death?' Griffin asks.

'It didn't help,' Ross says grimly. 'Blood loss, psychological distress, yes. But she was alive for at least a few hours after this happened. All abrasions and bruising show some clotting and scabbing. She would have been in a huge amount of pain. She didn't call 999?'

'There's nothing on the system.'

'Poor girl.' Ross looks back to the body. 'I need to complete the PM but my assumption is cause of death was from exsanguination – massive blood loss from the knife wounds to both arms, severing the radial artery and the cephalic vein. I believe she killed herself. But only after she was put through this torture.'

'Could it have been the same man as before?'

Ross sighs. 'If it wasn't, it's someone who had a good knowledge of what happened. I knew about the case; I worked on the original investigation as a medical advisor. And this is what happened last time.'

'Sorry?'

'The cable ties, the rag in her mouth. Turning her over to her front. The damage wasn't as extensive, but he did the same. Anal rape, then the vaginal rape with the bottle. Her witness report was …' His voice trails off; he swallows. 'She was an incredibly brave and determined young woman. I'm sorry things ended this way.'

'What leads did you have last time?'

'You've read the file?' Griffin nods. 'As I said, I was only the medical advisor. But I remember they didn't have much. That's what makes this different. The semen on the bedsheets, inside her. We've taken swabs, we'll get them sent to the lab asap. We've also taken scrapings from under her fingernails and I wouldn't be surprised if you have skin cells there, too. SOCO are still at the flat, but you should expect prints, footwear marks, the whole trifactor. He was not being careful.' Ross looks back to the body. 'I'll complete the PM. Let you know if I find anything that contradicts my original hypothesis.'

They stumble out of the mortuary in silence. A mixture of disgust, anger and horror pummels Griffin's brain. He needs a break; he needs a drink. He needs some release from the turmoil in his head.

He looks down at Brody. She has tears in her eyes. And then she reaches up and kisses him. Hard.

Chapter 53

Maybe if they hadn't done it before. Maybe if the Land Rover hadn't been parked in a dark secluded alleyway. Maybe if he had a bit more willpower. Maybe if one of those things had been in place, Griffin wouldn't have ended up here. Brody, both hands on his face, pushing him up against a rough brick wall.

'Alana … I …' he says, making some effort to resist.

'What?' She stands back for a moment.

'You said last time was a mistake.'

'I changed my mind.' She pauses. 'Do you want to?'

'Yes. But—'

'So shut the fuck up.'

There is no one around. No cameras, no passers-by. It's dark. Their only witness here might be a lone fox, as Brody takes the car keys out of his hand and unlocks the passenger side door.

'Get in,' she instructs. He does, then waits, obediently, as she pulls her skirt around her waist, removes her knickers then straddles him.

He takes her advice. Shuts the fuck up and kisses her,

his hands awkwardly pulling his trousers down, groping for a condom. She must be uncomfortable, her knees jammed against the door on one side, the gear stick on the other, neck bent against the top of the roof, but she guides him inside her and he is lost. In the sensation of being fucked by a beautiful woman in the front seat of his Land Rover, the smell of diesel, old dog, contrasting with her perfume, her skin. Her.

The space is cramped, so he lets her do the work. Her mouth on his, their lips together, more sharing breath than kissing as she grinds her pelvis against his. Her eyes are closed; she's completely lost, enjoying the moment. He tries to shift position but she places her hand, fingers spread, on his chest, pushing him back.

'Don't move,' she says, her voice husky.

One hand still resting on his chest, she places the other between her legs, fingering herself. The act is so confident, so brazen, here in the middle of this alleyway that he has to force himself to hold back. Staying still is almost an impossible feat, his body with a mind of its own as he moves as little as he can, in rhythm with Brody as her thighs move her up and down his cock. She's barely acknowledging him, her body shaking, her eyes screwed shut as – her mouth open, her cheeks flushed – she comes with a cry and a shudder.

He figures that's his cue to do whatever the hell he wants and grabs her firmly by the hips, thrusting upwards in his own rhythm until he comes.

She slumps onto his chest, him still inside her.

'Fucking hell, Alana,' he mutters.

She laughs into his neck. 'I feel better now.'

'Glad to be of service.'

'Don't you?' She looks up at his tone, her face close to his, restricted by the roof. 'Are you offended?'

He considers her question as she moves off his lap, pulling her skirt down and sitting in the driver's seat. He awkwardly removes the condom and does up his trousers, picking up a takeaway cup from the footwell and dumping it inside.

'Not as such,' he replies. 'A bit of warning would be nice.'

'Shall I schedule it in your diary next time?'

'Send me a memo. But seriously, what is this? A casual arrangement? Stress release?'

'A bit of both.' Brody looks at him sideways. 'What would you like it to be?'

'I've just got out of a relationship. I'm not sure I have the ...'

'Emotional capacity?' she suggests.

He looks at her, trying to gauge if she's taking the piss. She seems serious.

'Yes, that. To have a proper relationship.'

'Then fuck buddy it is.' She smiles again, but softer this time. 'Look, Griffin. I like you. I think you're hot. I wanted to have some fun with you, and you didn't protest, so we did. Our job is full on and messed up, and sometimes it's good to let off steam.' She leans over and kisses him gently on the lips. 'If you're not comfortable with it, then tell me, and we'll stop.'

'It's fine,' he says quickly. She raises an eyebrow. 'Better than fine,' he adds. 'But next time ...' He stretches and a bolt of pain runs up his spine. 'Can we go somewhere more comfortable. The last thing either of us needs is an arrest for outraging public decency.'

'Deal.' She opens the driver's door and climbs out. He

300

does the same, and they swap places, him climbing behind the steering wheel.

He starts the engine. 'Shall I drop you home?'

She nods, and he pulls out of the alleyway, starting to drive. She's retreated into silence again and he glances across. She catches his look.

'What?' she snaps.

'Are you okay?'

She chews on her lip for a moment. 'How do you deal with this?' she says at last. 'The death, the murder I was used to at the Met. At least, as accustomed to that as anyone can get. But the deliberate, calculating act of this. It terrifies me.'

'The only way detectives know how. Alcohol, and catching the bastard.'

'It makes me so fucking angry,' she continues, barely acknowledging Griffin's response, 'that it's always women. Kate, Isabel, Eileen. Now Lisa today. Always women that get killed. That get tortured and traumatised and tied up by men who think it's their right. Their God-given fucking right – to attack us and follow us and make fucking wolf whistles because, you know, it's *banter*.' She says this last word in a mocking tone. 'And we're expected to stand by and smile sweetly and put up with this bollocks.' She jabs a finger out of the windscreen into the cold dark night. 'Nothing's changed. The only thing I have faith in nowadays is the younger generation. People call them snowflakes, or woke, or whatever insult is trending that day, but in reality they've decided they're not going to tolerate this bullshit any more. And the gammon-faced white middle-aged men don't like it. Lock them up,' she says, losing steam. 'Lock up the bastards.'

Griffin stays silent. He doesn't disagree, but neither does

he want to add his view to something that is not his area of expertise.

'You have no idea,' Brody says, quieter now. 'What it's like being a woman. Growing up in this world and knowing that fifty per cent of the population could kill you with their bare hands.' She pokes Griffin on the arm as he pauses at traffic lights. 'Look at you. Six feet. Built like a fortress. I bet you don't have to worry about anything.'

Her words take Griffin back in an instant. Hog-tied, defenceless, on his own bedroom floor while his wife was killed in the room next door. He grips the steering wheel hard, aware of the cars behind beeping as the lights turn green.

He jerks back into life, pulling away from the junction. He feels a hand gently touch his arm.

'I'm sorry,' Brody says. 'I didn't think …'

He shakes his head, staring out of the windscreen. 'I know what you mean. And you're right. I'd never felt even the slightest bit vulnerable until that night. And the truth is that I probably could have overpowered him. If I hadn't been worried about the gun, and him shooting Mia … That's the guilt I live with every day.'

'That was your wife's name? Mia?' He nods. 'What was she like?'

Griffin thinks for a moment. It's impossible to describe someone like Mia adequately. 'She was bright, funny. She had this laugh – this awful laugh – that you could hear a mile off. But I couldn't resist it. She was kind, when she wanted to be. But she had no tolerance or patience.'

'She must have, if she was married to you,' Brody says with a hint of a smile.

'That was the strange thing. I was the king of lost causes.

302

I never did work out why she was with me.'

'She was in love.'

Griffin glances at Brody in surprise. He hadn't thought of her as being sentimental. He shrugs, feeling awkward to have shared so much with someone he hardly knows. Despite the fact he's had sex with her twice.

He's glad when they pull up outside her house. She gets out, and he watches her in the rear-view mirror as she makes her way inside. She knows he's watching her – she wiggles her fingers in a sarcastic goodbye and he shakes his head in disbelief. He had wondered whether she'd invite him inside. Offer a drink, anything to make him feel less of a … He struggles for the word. Transaction. That he's there to serve a purpose rather than she actually likes being with him. It's an odd feeling for Griffin, that he's being used, and as he puts the truck into gear he realises he doesn't want to go home. To sit alone in his flat, and mull over the events of the last week. The thoughts of his dead wife that Brody has stirred up.

He picks up his mobile and wonders who he should call. Not Cara. He wants a drink and she will only judge. So he phones the only person who he knows will understand.

Another man, widowed before he was forty.

Chapter 54

Jamie only said yes on the spur of the moment, thinking there was no chance Griffin would turn up. They have nothing in common, except for dead, murdered wives, and even Jamie has to admit that's a tenuous start for a friendship.

He arrives at the bar and Griffin's already there, a pint of beer in front of him.

'What would you like?'

Jamie scans the pumps, spots his usual, and realises that this is the first time he's been in a pub since that fateful night when Pippa disappeared.

'Peroni,' Jamie directs to the barman. 'Thank you.'

The two men wait, mute, as the lager is poured. Griffin pays, then gestures to a small table on the far side. They sit down wordlessly and gulp at their drinks.

'How're you finding being back?' Jamie says when he can't stand the yawning silence any longer.

'S'okay. Work. You know? Better than sitting at home, watching shitty cars on the lot all night.'

'Anybody ever try to steal them?'

Griffin sips at his pint and shakes his head. 'Never.'

They sink back into staring at their drinks. Griffin picks at a beer mat, shelling pieces of grey cardboard onto the table. He seems uncharacteristically sombre.

'You okay?' Jamie asks. Griffin looks up, confused. 'Just wondered. You inviting me out tonight. I didn't think I'd ever see that happening.'

Griffin smiles weakly. 'Thinking about that poor girl again. Lisa Hobbs. What she must have gone through. Once – that's torture. But to put her through it again, knowing it would be the thing to tip her over the edge. What sort of sadist does that?'

'The sort of person Shenton was talking about.'

'And you put stock in what he said?'

'Don't you?' Jamie asks.

Griffin shrugs. 'He was right about the Echo Man. We just didn't put it together fast enough.'

'I heard about that at the time. Everyone did. It was impossible to be in the police force and not follow it.'

'You all thought we were incompetent, right?'

Jamie gives him a sympathetic look. 'It was an impossible case.'

'What were you doing?'

'Picking up all your shit.' Griffin barks a laugh as Jamie explains: 'All the other investigations – the ones you couldn't deal with because of the Echo Man case – that fell to Adam and me. We had a few DCs and that was it, watching you guys from afar, desperate to be involved.' Jamie sips at his lager pensively. 'Be careful what you wish for, eh?' He tries to smile but it feels forced and he turns away. 'If you can believe it, I moved down from Basingstoke to your Major Crimes team for some peace and quiet. My logic was that lightning couldn't possibly strike in the same place twice.'

'Or three times.'

'Yet here we are.'

Griffin lifts his glass and they grimly chink them together. Griffin stares at him, trying to read his mind. It's annoying.

'What?'

'How are you doing?' Griffin asks. 'Now your wife's dead?'

Jamie blinks in surprise. 'That's blunt.'

'I can't stand all the pussyfooting around. All the euphemisms. "Passing." "Left us." "With God."' He scoffs at the last one. 'It's such bollocks. Mia's dead. Some cunt killed her. I'm fucking angry, as well as a whole load of other shite.'

'Then, yes. I'm angry.'

'Good.'

'As well as feeling bloody awful most of the time. I don't sleep. I can't concentrate. I miss her so much it physically hurts. Throw in some self-loathing and regret and yes, it's good. I'm good, thank you very much. Thank you for asking.'

Griffin laughs and after a moment, Jamie joins in. It felt refreshing to say all that out loud. To articulate the shit that's been going around his head with someone who will understand.

'Seriously though,' Jamie adds, 'what do you say to all these people who ask? "How are you?" Do they want to know or are they asking so they can feel like they care?'

'Depends who it is. Mostly – the latter. Just smile weakly and nod. That's all they want.' He gestures to his pint. 'Another?'

'Yeah, but it's my round. Same?'

Jamie gathers the empties and heads to the bar. While

306

he's waiting for the pints, Griffin has gone out for a cigarette and he looks at him behind the window, his black coat a dark silhouette against the frosted glass as he bends down to the lighter. This apocryphal being, whose myths he'd heard around the nick, long before he became infamous for the serial killer who killed his wife.

Cops had a grudging respect for the way he did business. His patrols were single-crewed and in the worst areas; his car always came back covered in bumps and dents, sometimes even blood. In the end they left a specific one for him. It smelled of dirty protests and puke, and nobody wanted to be picked up in that car. He was on first-name terms with drug dealers, informal CIs who dropped him the nod, anything to keep him away from their turf. But when it came to obeying the rules of the law, he was always just the right side of the line. He wasn't dirty; he didn't take bribes. He was respectful to women. Faithful to his wife.

It's this side of Griffin he can see now. A fragile human, who lost the woman he loved in the most unimaginable of circumstances, who's alone and lonely, and fancied someone to have a quiet pint with. Jamie places the drinks on the table as Griffin emerges from outside, smelling of cigarettes.

'Still pissing it down out there,' he grumbles, running his hand through his hair, dispelling the worst of the rain like a wet dog.

Jamie drums his fingers, bizarrely nervous in anticipation of what he's about to ask. Breaching the final barrier of unspoken vulnerability he's about to lay bare.

'Nate,' he begins. And Griffin looks at him, intrigued with the use of his proper name. 'Does it get easier?'

Griffin takes a sip of his beer, taking the question seriously. 'Yes and no,' he replies. 'No, because Mia's gone. And she isn't coming back. And that's partly my fault, however you look at it. You're always going to wake up in the morning and she won't be there. Sometimes, even worse, you'll smell her, and you'll forget, and have to remember all over again.'

Jamie nods. 'I notice her perfume everywhere.'

'Yeah. That shit doesn't go away. But also yes, it does get easier, because you get used to it. You'll pass her birthday, and Christmas, and your birthday, and you'll know, it's okay. You got through it once, you'll manage it again. And you pick yourself up, day after day. Sometimes you might even laugh, and your body will remember how it is to be happy again. And you'll feel guilty for that. For being happy without her.' Griffin frowns into his beer, eyebrows lowered. 'And other days you'll struggle to even get out of bed. Drugs help. Get some of those from your doctor,' he continues quietly. Then he shakes himself, giving Jamie a suppressed smile. 'And try not to be a miserable cunt every now and again.'

Jamie laughs. 'Have I been a miserable cunt?'

'No more than anyone else on the team. Don't worry about that. But normal people, you know. They like happy stuff. Put on a face.' He turns serious again. 'Keep your drug stocks to a minimum. Put your knives away. Have the number for the Samaritans close to hand. Just saying, from personal experience. Don't make it too easy.'

'I wouldn't,' Jamie says quickly. 'I wouldn't kill myself.'

But Griffin looks him straight in the eye. 'You say that now. Sitting with me in this nice warm pub. But sometimes in the middle of the night, it doesn't seem like such a bad plan.'

Jamie swallows. 'Have you ever tried—'

'No. But I've thought about it. I'd do it like that woman

308

in the farmhouse. Big fuck off gun. No messing. Bang.' He thuds his palm flat on the table; their beer shakes. 'Job done.' That gaze again. Unflinching. 'Call me, if you ever feel like that. Promise?'

Jamie opens his mouth, but before he says anything Griffin's phone rings, jumping on the wood. Jamie can see who's calling. *Cara.* Griffin raises an eyebrow then answers it.

He listens, his gaze fixed on Jamie. 'Understood, boss. On our way.' He stands up, drains his pint. 'They've got a match. On the semen found on the rape victim. Ties with the image from the CCTV. We're going over there now for an arrest.' He looks at Jamie's second pint, practically untouched on the table. 'You're driving.'

Chapter 55

Griffin crams himself into Jamie's Vauxhall Corsa; it starts on the second try. They drive through deserted streets; Griffin knows where they're going – a run-down estate at the far edge of Southampton. A common site for late-night rucks between drug dealers, for prostitution and domestic violence.

But today, a different scene greets them. The pavements are empty, except for the weeds poking through the broken paving slabs, the rubbish bins burned to a slime of plastic and left to rot. A scrawny tabby sits on top of a fence post, licking its paws. It regards them haughtily as they drive past.

A riot van is leaving as they pull up. Griffin gets out, and instantly feels the vibe of an unsuccessful arrest. Disgruntled coppers. Missed sleep for nothing.

He walks to the group and spots Cara with Brody. In front of them the door to a ground-floor flat is open, the frame splintered and at an angle. He and Jamie join them.

'He's not here?' Griffin asks.

Cara turns. 'Oh, he's here all right.' And Griffin knows what they're facing.

'Mind if I take a look?'

She hands him a pile of PPE. 'Be my guest. Put the mask on. You're going to need it.'

He heads inside, but before he goes, he looks for Jamie. His new friend seems business as usual, friendly as he gives orders to the uniform next to him, no doubt coordinating the house-to-house. From appearances, you'd never guess about his wife, how he's feeling. About the conversation they'd had at the pub.

He hears a shout from inside the flat, and as he looks back, towards their new crime scene and whatever horrors lie inside, Griffin realises. The call came in, interrupting them. Jamie hadn't made that promise.

Griffin does as instructed and suits up. The flat is dark. A few lights are on but the bulbs are dim, grubby with dirt. There's a long hallway, wallpaper peeling. One room to the left; he peers in. Dated brown carpet surrounds a single armchair. Cigarette butts across the table and floor. Thin curtains hanging at an angle, the rail broken.

He continues his search. The next – a bathroom. Thick brown rings of dirt and unimaginable substances on the sink and toilet. A smell – enough to strip paint. But it's not just coming from here.

There's a group of people in the final room. White suits, crowding around, waiting for someone else – SOCOs knowing not to touch until the pathologist arrives.

Because in front of them is a dead body.

The man lies on the kitchen lino, curled into a ball, his mouth contorted into a final scream. His clawed hands are next to his face, his knees tight to his chest. And the place is stained with blood.

His teeth are black with it, his lips dyed a deep purple. His chin, his clothes, the carpet, his hair. Every available space is pocked with smears and spatters, prints and pools. Like he'd flailed around the room, distributing blood as he'd moved. SOCOs are photographing the mess and Griffin peers closer. A hypodermic needle and syringe lie on the table, the plunger suppressed. There's nothing else – no medical packaging, no small glass vial. No indicator of what the man might have been injecting. Also on the table are boxes of other medication: dexamethasone, oxycodone, domperidone. The piles of pills remind him of Isabel, and his stomach twists.

But that's where the similarity ends. If their timeline is correct – that this man was alive last night – then he can't have been dead for longer than twenty-four hours. And in that short time, something's gone to work on his body.

The face is half gone, flesh scored and flapping, eyes no more than bloody sockets. The clothes are dirty and soiled, his fingers are bones, chewed to stubs. There's a stench of something indescribable in the air – decaying body and animal shit. Griffin can see scratches on the back of the door, furniture clawed to shreds. Two empty bowls next to the kitchen counter, one for food, one for water.

He gives a questioning look to the SOCO standing next to him.

'Cats,' the man says. 'He had cats. And they were hungry.'

312

DAY 8

MONDAY

Chapter 56

Jamie wakes, confused, the edge of a dream hovering in the darkness. He subconsciously reaches out to his left then opens his eyes when he touches nothing but cold sheets.

Pippa had felt very real in this one. Her face, a warm smile. He'd even been able to touch her soft skin, his arm reaching out to enclose her in a hug.

Where have you been? he'd asked her.

I was here all along.

And now, the crushing reality. That he is alone and the bed is empty.

He scrunches his eyes shut, willing the dream to resurface, but it has gone, out of his grasp. Instead, all he gets are hot, bitter tears.

He hates this. The man he has become – this pathetic shell of a human who can barely function – but he also hates the world. For taking his wife away and imposing a life without Pippa. What he would give to take it all back. The trip to the pub the night when she had been abducted; the investigation that failed to find her before it was too late. He has nowhere to direct his anger. Not at Adam, around the other side of the world. Not at Pippa's parents, for putting in a complaint he now feels he deserves.

He forces himself to get out of bed. Puts one foot in front of the other and walks to the shower. He lets the scalding hot jets pummel his face and his back as some sort of penance. He can't stomach breakfast, and picks up his keys, resolving that maybe his doctor will help. A sympathetic ear, if nothing else.

It's cold as he puts the key in the ignition of his Vauxhall Corsa. The car chokes, the starter engine spluttering, petering out with a quiet wheeze. He tries again, but the car can't muster so much as a gasp.

He lets out a cry of frustration, banging his hands once, twice against the steering wheel, then gets out and slams the door shut with all his energy, causing the small car to rock on its suspension.

And it's then that he looks to the garage.

Adam's BMW has been shuttered up since he left five months ago. Adam had left the keys with Jamie, had insured him to drive the thing, saying, 'Keep the old girl running, won't you?' Jamie had ignored it, scared of the powerful beast.

But needs must.

He goes back into the house and retrieves the keys from the cupboard along with the fob to open the garage. A door in the kitchen leads directly inside and he stands waiting, watching the light trickle in as the electric roller door opens revealing Adam's pride and joy – a 1986, petrol, BMW 628.

Jamie doesn't know much about cars, but he's listened to Adam talk about this one at length. He opens the driver's door with some trepidation, puts the key in the ignition. She probably won't even start, he reassures himself, but as he turns the key it jumps into life with a snarl.

He revs the engine. A satisfying growl. A hint of a smile touches his lips – this could be fun after all.

Jamie makes it to the doctor's surgery without incident, allowing himself to put his foot down on the dual carriageway, enjoying the buck of the car as the acceleration kicked in. He parks in a secluded corner; makes sure he locks it up tight and heads inside.

He waits in the queue. Old ladies shuffling forward, the man in front of him with a hacking cough that makes Jamie keep his distance. At the front, the receptionist looks at him coolly.

'Your system can't find me,' Jamie says, gesturing to the automatic check-in screen to his left. 'James Hoxton. Appointment at nine with Dr Fowler.'

The receptionist's gaze drops to her screen. She stabs at the keyboard.

'Nothing here,' she says.

'Sorry? I made the appointment on Saturday.'

She clicks again without comment. 'Says here you cancelled that appointment this morning. Just after eight.'

'I …' Jamie's mouth opens in surprise. He feels a lump form at the back of his throat. 'No … I … I didn't.'

'Says here you did,' the receptionist repeats.

There's no point in arguing. 'Well, can I see the doctor?'

Her eyes slowly lower. 'Not today. You'll need to phone back tomorrow. See if any appointments have opened up.'

Jamie swallows. Frustrated tears prickle. 'Please,' he says, his voice choked. 'It's urgent.'

The receptionist stares at him for a moment. Jamie must

look as he feels because her eyes soften. 'I'll ask him to call you. Will that work?'

Jamie nods. He manages a strangled 'thank you' as the receptionist confirms his number before he stumbles out into the car park and sits in the front seat of the BMW. It smells of old cigarette smoke; of Adam's aftershave. Jamie's reminded of the numerous times he has sat in the passenger seat of this car with his best mate, and it's instantly reassuring.

He takes a few deep breaths. He hangs on desperately to the shred of hope that his GP will phone. That the doctor will say – or at least prescribe – something that will make things better.

Because right now, he couldn't feel any worse.

Chapter 57

'Couldn't have happened to a nicer chap,' Ross comments as he stands in the doorway, in full PPE, looking at the victim on the mortuary table. Next to him, Cara has to agree.

The results have come back already, confirming the body found chewed and covered in blood is the same man who raped and defiled Lisa Hobbs. Kenneth Laker, aged 69. Cara finds it hard to summon any sort of pity for the corpse lying before them. He's out of his body bag, but that's as far as the post-mortem has got. Clothed. Stinking of dried blood and faeces and vomit.

'I heard he wasn't nice to his cats,' Ross comments. 'Locked them in. Starved them.'

'That's what the RSPCA said when they came to pick them up,' Cara confirms. 'They had complaints on file.'

'Well, the moggies got their revenge,' he replies, and, looking at the body, Cara makes a mental note: remind Griffin to feed Frank.

'Why is his body like that?' she asks. 'The contortion. It looks like he's in pain.'

Ross takes a step forward towards the body. Rigor has

locked the man in place, his mouth open in agony, his limbs twisted into a ball. Ross forcefully strains at one of the arms, breaking the rigor; it releases with a crunch.

'Knowing your investigation as I do, I asked the lab to do some preliminary tests, as well as reviewing this guy's medical records. Kenneth Laker had stage four stomach cancer, spread to his bones. He can't have had more than weeks to live and would have been in a lot of pain. The syringe found next to his body?'

Cara nods.

'Heparin.'

'Blood thinner?'

'Yep.' They look to the emaciated body, at the brown-red crusts where blood has oozed from his mouth and nose. 'My guess is that when I open him up I'll find gastric ulcers and an upper GI bleed. The heparin would have massively exacerbated any internal bleeding caused by the cancer or ulcers. His last moments would have been in excruciating pain as he vomited huge amounts of blood.'

'So why did he inject it?'

'He thought it was something else? A painkiller? Twenty mils of morphine, even if it was diluted, would have made for a nice peaceful death. And twenty mils of heparin would have probably done ...' He casts his gaze up and down the body. 'This.'

Cara takes in the mess on the table as Ross continues to straighten out the limbs, cracking rigor mortis filling the air. It sickens her.

'He was that ill. And yet he managed to break in to a woman's flat and violently rape her,' Cara says. 'Do you think he had help?'

'He would have needed some strong motivation,' Ross

318

replies. 'Putting credence to my morphine theory. Your job to prove it.'

'So why give him heparin instead?' Cara says out loud, although she doesn't wait for Ross to answer. A swell of acid rises in her stomach and she takes the double doors at speed, throwing up in the nearest bin. She stands there for a moment, heaving, both hands clutching the top. The nausea subsides as quickly as it arrived and she stands straight, spitting a final glob of bile into the receptacle, then turns to leave the hospital. She should stay, but Ross will let her know any additional findings; her presence is needed elsewhere.

She can't take any more of this shit.

She'd barely slept last night. She'd stayed at the flat until the early hours, telling the rest of the team to go home while she coordinated the house-to-house, pointless though that was. Those that answered the door wouldn't talk to the police, and even if they had they would have told her nothing. A neighbourhood that keeps to itself, that ignores tortured screams late at night, even if they are coming from next door.

Not that there was anything to see. Their killer was back to his usual tricks, causing carnage from afar. No witnesses, just drugs. Swapping one thing for another. And that thought makes her grab her phone.

'Shenton?' she barks as soon as he answers. 'Get the drugs found on Jessop sent to the lab for analysis.'

'The olanzapine and sertraline?'

'Yes. Ask them to check that that's what they really are.'

'No problem. And boss? The lab came back on the rope used to kill Hammond. There are skin cells, DNA. And trace under his nails.'

Cara knows it's coming. 'But?'

'But there's no match on the system. Whoever it is hasn't encountered law enforcement before.'

Cara hangs up with a heavy heart. When they get him, they can prove murder. But they need to damn well find him first.

Twenty minutes later she's back at the nick, taking the stairs two at a time from the car park to the incident room. All the team are there – with the exception of Jamie.

She claps her hands to get their attention.

'Where's Hoxton?' she asks.

'Taking an urgent call,' Griffin replies.

Cara doesn't wait but relays what Ross had told her at the mortuary.

'We know he follows his victims,' Griffin says. 'Close enough to swap out medication?'

'Any news about the syringe?'

Brody pipes up: 'Lab confirmed the prints were Laker's. Nobody else handled it.'

'He injected himself. He must have known this guy. Trusted him enough to take whatever he was given.'

'Or was too desperate to care,' Griffin says.

Jamie comes back into the room, phone clutched in his hand. He looks pale. 'Sorry, boss.'

'No worries. Get one of the team to update you. What I don't understand is where did our killer get heparin? It's not something you can buy on the street.'

Griffin shrugs. 'You can buy most stuff on the street if you know the right people.'

'Fuck,' Cara snaps. 'What do we know for certain? Laker definitely raped Lisa Hobbs—'

'And Ken Laker is Isabel Warner's stepdad.'

All faces turn to stare at Oliver. 'You what?' Cara says.

'He's Isabel Warner's stepdad,' Oliver repeats, quieter. 'The shitbag who abused her when she was a kid.'

Cara gapes. 'That has to be significant,' she says. 'And the fact that he died in such an awful way.'

'Someone getting revenge?' Griffin suggests.

'Seems a weird way of doing it. Kill the girl one day, avenge her the next?'

'Are we looking at two people? Two killers?'

Cara suddenly feels hot. Suffocated. Standing in this incident room, as the team debate this surreal series of events. The photographs of the victims on the board stare down. She feels their silent judgement that she is failing to find their killer as bodies stack up around them. She has to get a grip.

'Right, enough,' she says, and the team quietens. 'Let's focus on what we can prove. Shenton, back to the CCTV. Trace Laker's movements from Lisa Hobbs' flat to his own house. Someone gave him that heparin – I want to know who. Jamie – follow up with the lab. See if they can tell us where that heparin came from.'

'I don't think—'

'Just try. Ask. Griffin, Brody – go back to the previous cases. What have we missed? There has to be something.'

And with that she turns on her heel and heads into her office. She shuts the door and slumps into her seat, pushing her fingers into her eyes and rubbing them, seeing colours. What are they missing? What. Is. She. Missing? Because Cara is the SIO. It's her responsibility and her responsibility alone to find this guy. Arrest him. Charge him.

Stop him.

Eight victims now, if you count Laker. Eight victims, all

321

ill, either mentally, physically or both. What do they have in common?

A flicker of something pulls at her consciousness and she stops, but it's gone. A wisp in the ether; she's spent, too distracted for it to make sense, and before she can grab at it again, her mobile phone rings.

No Caller ID. She picks it up, fearing Ross, or the control room. But when she answers it's not a voice she expects.

'Mrs Elliott?' the man says. 'This is Miles, from your mother's care home. We need you to come in immediately.'

'What is it, Miles?' She stands, grabbing for her coat and bag.

'You need to—'

'Fucking spit it out!' she shouts.

There's a long pause. 'I'm sorry to have to tell you this,' he stutters. 'It's not good news. Your mother died this morning.'

Chapter 58

Cara stands, frozen, in the middle of her office. The words swirl. Dead. Her mother. Dead.

She'd known it was coming. Her mother has been trickling away for years, a steady drip as the memories faded, but her actual death always seemed distant.

Until now.

Sounds from the incident room fade in. Ollie's laughter; the tap of Shenton's keyboard; Jamie talking to Brody. And, oh, shit. Griffin. She has to be the one to tell him. She's the older sibling, taking responsibility, yet again – the weight of it bears heavily on her shoulders. The practical side: organising a funeral, clearing out her room at the care home, sorting the paperwork and the will and the legal technicalities she has yet to discover. But also the emotional: informing Roo and the kids, managing Griffin's feelings, whatever they will be.

She takes a few steps now, slowly, her limbs heavy. She feels dazed, the loss and sadness not yet kicking in – a good thing, because she's here, in the office. She leans out of the door.

'Griffin?' His name comes out as a croak. She clears her throat and tries again. 'Nate.'

He turns. He must see something on her face because his forehead furrows. He gets up immediately, heading inside her office.

'Shut the door,' she instructs.

He does, but leans against it, his arms folded. 'What have I done now?'

'Nate, it's Mum.' But she can't get any more out. Her throat closes, her eyes brim over. She looks to the ceiling to stem the threatening tears, pushes her nails into her palms. It doesn't work. Griffin takes a step towards her, but he wraps his arms around his body, a stance that reminds her of him as a teenager, bracing himself for bad news. She pulls herself together enough to continue. 'Mum's dead. She died. This morning.'

'This morning? How?'

'They're not sure yet, but Miles said ...' She falters again; Griffin is next to her now, his arms pulling her into a hug. 'Miles said she died peacefully,' she continues into Griffin's chest. 'After breakfast. Yet another cup of tea she didn't finish.' Griffin makes a noise at her attempted joke. Not laughter, but an acknowledgement of her effort. She pulls away from him, wiping her eyes. 'We need to go down there. Give permission as next of kin for something. Oh, I don't know.'

'We'll go now.'

'We can't. The case.'

'Jamie can hold the fort. The case can wait.' He points to her coat and bag; she collects them obediently. She waits for Griffin by the door as he speaks to Hoxton. Jamie looks in her direction, his eyes sympathetic, then nods quickly, patting Griffin on the arm. She notices that gesture; she

324

likes that Jamie and Griffin seem to be getting on, maybe even becoming friends. Her brother needs some of those.

'Let's go,' Griffin says, and they leave, Cara aware of Shenton's eyes on them, questioning. Jamie will explain. Jamie will take over. Capable hands. He should be a DI, something else she needs to put right.

She silently follows Griffin to his Land Rover, letting him take over even though she hates this dirty truck, hates his driving. Her stomach feels empty, but she can't possibly eat. Her chest aches.

'This is how she would have wanted to go,' she says, dully. 'Warm and calm, in her bed.'

Griffin nods, but his jaw is set.

'She wouldn't have remembered, Nate,' she says softly. He stares at the road. 'Your last visit. She wouldn't have remembered.'

He nods stiffly.

'She always liked to talk about you, when I was there. What you were like as a kid. Always getting into scrapes. She loved you.'

She notices him swallow hard, his Adam's apple bobbing. He swipes at his eyes, annoyed.

'I was a terrible son.'

'That might be true' – he laughs, a bubble of sudden emotion – 'but she still loved you.'

He nods again, then turns away from her as they stop in the car park of the care home. He pulls the handbrake on, hard.

'You okay?' she asks.

'Fine. You?'

'Always.'

Griffin gives her a weak smile. 'Come on.'

325

Chapter 59

Miles greets them in the hallway wearing that same mustard-shit coloured jumper. A sympathetic smile, a head tilt. Expressions Griffin knows well from when Mia died; he hates them.

'She was a lovely lady, your mother,' Miles says. 'She will be missed.'

The words seem rehearsed, a standard script he trots out to all bereaved relatives, as he leads the way to the family room. Griffin follows Cara; her shoulders are stooped, her submission worn like a cape, pulling her down. So different to the usual straight-backed confidence at work. He worries that her resilience has finally met its match; wonders how much more she can take.

The three of them sit on scratchy blue sofas around a coffee table. In front of them is a leaflet titled *We're Sorry for your Loss: Next Steps*. So fucking insincere. But this is a business, like everything else. There's paperwork and bureaucracy. Money to be made.

'The undertaker is here,' Miles says. 'For when you're ready.'

Parked around the back, no doubt. No need to remind the current residents how all of them will depart this godforsaken place. He zones out as Miles talks Cara through the tick sheet in the leaflet. Death certificates, funeral arrangements, finances. He crosses through the line relating to post-mortem without mentioning it.

Griffin stops him, mid-sentence.

'Why isn't that required?' he asks.

'We would usually only ask for a post-mortem if the cause is unknown, or following a sudden, violent or suspicious death,' Miles replies. His patronising tone grates.

'A doctor's seen her?'

'Griffin—' Cara warns.

'Has a doctor seen her?'

'To pronounce cause of death, yes,' Miles says. 'And he had no reason to question putting anything other than old age.'

'She was ill, Nate,' Cara adds softly.

He nods; lets it go. For Cara's sake, more than anything else. Cara and Miles turn back to their paperwork and start talking again. Griffin's mind wanders.

He should have visited more often. He should have made the effort. He could have been patient with her on Friday, sat down and gently helped her remember that he was her son, not her husband. It could have been a nice morning, but no. He had to bulldoze in and ruin things. Again. He wonders whether that contributed to her death. Stress on a weakened heart, anti-anxiety drugs in a fragile body.

'Can I see her?' he blurts out.

They both turn. 'Yes,' Miles says. 'In due course—'

'Now?'

Miles blusters for a bit. 'Er … yes. I suppose so. We

haven't moved her.'

He stands; Cara gets up too. 'I want to go alone,' he says. 'Please.'

She pauses, then nods. 'I'll finish up here with Miles. We won't be long.'

Griffin trudges the corridors leading to his mother's room. The door is unlocked. The room is empty, except for that particular smell he's come to associate with illness and death. Sterile dressings, antiseptic, mixed with unwashed skin. A smell no number of scented candles or lavender talcum powder can cover up today. He tentatively steps forward.

His mother is lying in her bed. The guard rails are up; a futile gesture to health and safety when there is no one left to save. She's on her back, her eyes closed, her mouth gaping. Two half-empty cups of tea wait, unfinished, on the bedside table. A blue blanket has been pulled up to her chest, her arms laid out on top. She's wearing her old-fashioned Marks and Spencer's nightgown.

Her face is tinged yellow, her lips white. She doesn't look like she's sleeping, as he's heard many relatives say. She looks dead. So very dead.

Griffin has seen many corpses as a police officer – some peaceful, some not – and every time he's struck by how different a dead body looks to its living, breathing predecessor. If Griffin had the will to believe in a god, this would be his proof: the soul has departed, and the vessel has been left behind.

A sob forces its way through his chest. His vision blurs. This is the woman who taught him how to read, painstakingly sounding out words when the teachers at school had given up. Who stood next to him in his headmaster's office during yet another reprimand, but who would just say, 'Oh, Nate,' as they left, her disappointment leaving him feeling worse than any shouting match could. Who he saw crying through a crack in the door, unable to know how to console her when her husband had died.

He sags into a chair and puts his head in his hands. He gulps the fetid air, trying to control the flood of emotions threatening to derail him. He's lived without his mother for years, why does her death make any difference? Because that's it. It's just Cara now who knows where he's come from, how he's struggled. He has no parents, no wife. He is untethered to this earth.

He wipes at his eyes. He reaches out and touches her hand, to confirm to himself that she's gone and, sure enough, her skin is cool, rice-paper thin. He takes her hand in his. Her nails are neatly trimmed, but her fingers are little more than bone, marked with brown liver spots. And, creeping out of the sleeve of her nightdress, a vivid red bruise. He stands, pulling up the sleeve and taking a closer look. It seems new.

The image of Eileen Avery returns. Slowly, carefully, he leans over and looks inside her mouth, checking the inside of her lips, her gums. But there are none of the telltale signs of asphyxiation that were present on the old lady at the farm.

'Nate, what are you doing?'

He jumps back guiltily. Cara's standing in the doorway.

'She wasn't murdered,' Cara says. She takes two steps into the room, and as she sees her mother, her face collapses. 'Oh, Mum,' she whispers. She gently strokes a wisp of fine grey hair from her forehead, then turns to Griffin. 'Don't turn a bad situation into something worse, Nate,' she hisses.

'Please. There is nothing going on here. Nothing more than an old woman at the end of her life. Give Mum some peace.' Her voice cracks at the end and she starts to cry, but her gaze stays firm on Griffin. 'Leave it alone.'

He nods, and she turns back to their mother, taking her hand in both of her own as she quietly weeps, sitting by her bedside. Griffin lays a gentle hand on his sister's back, then retreats. But he can't help but look back to the bruise on her wrist. Wrapped around, as if someone had been trying to restrain her.

He walks decisively out of the room, almost straight into Miles.

'Who saw her this morning?' Griffin asks.

Miles frowns. 'Just me, I think. I'd have to check the rota. I woke her up first thing.'

'And after that?'

'I don't know. I was on breakfast duty. I didn't see anyone until I brought Angela her porridge and … found her.'

'Any visitors?'

'Maybe. As I said, I wasn't on the door. They would have signed in, if so. You could—'

But Griffin's already gone, striding down the corridor towards main reception. He doesn't stop to talk to the nurse on duty, just pulls the visitors' book towards him, the pen flying. Blank rows at the bottom; he runs a finger upwards. The doctor, the undertaker, *Janice Roper* to see Dennis Roper in 5B, and one other name.

Neil Lowe, it says. Sign in time 9.45 a.m. To see Angela Griffin.

Moments before she died.

Chapter 60

Griffin drives around for hours. Aimlessly smoking, until his throat hurts and his eyes sting. He ignores calls from Cara, knowing nothing she can say will make him feel better. Guilt churns in his gut, turning acid to anger. He wants to cry, but can't. All hate turns inwards.

Day turns into dusk. He finds himself on the motorway, on the M3 heading north. The fast lane is clear and he pushes the clattering Land Rover past seventy, eighty, further than it should possibly go. It feels cathartic, this release, and his thoughts turn to his father, driving at speed along that country road, and wonders again what was going through his mind. For the first time he considers it could have been suicide. His brain rotten with self-loathing and misery. How easy it could have been to miss that corner, to drive into that tree. Griffin imagines it now. Cars around him. The central reservation. Hard concrete. How simple.

The phone rings on the seat next to him and he scoops it up. But the name on the screen isn't his sister, it's Oliver. He answers it, breaking the law, shouting over the noise of the engine.

'Griffin,' the analyst says. 'I didn't want to call, but you told me to contact you as soon as I had a chance to look at them. Those files.'

His father's work records; he'd given them to Ollie yesterday. Griffin turns the volume on the phone up as high as it will go. 'It's fine, Ollie. What?'

'Well, they're company accounts, as you said. Mostly dull. But …'

'But what?'

'But your father's business was failing. Office rent, salaries, expenses. There was far more going out than in. Which seems odd, given the dividends that were being deducted.'

Griffin's patience is fading. 'What do you mean, Ollie?'

Oliver explains what those accounts show. And by the time he's finished, Griffin knows where he needs to go. Off at the next junction, heading back to Southampton.

Like the office, Neil Lowe has moved. His new house is a grand affair – the gateway is lit by spotlights, a parallel row leading to the front door. An address easily found on the police database. The gates open smoothly; Neil lets him in without objection and Griffin drives the clanking Land Rover over pristine tarmac to the entrance.

He parks alongside a sleek electric Jaguar F-PACE. The front door opens. He climbs out.

Neil is dressed in a woolly jumper and chinos, tweed slippers. Uniform of the off-duty professional.

'It's nice to see you, Nate,' he says, although his tone sounds like it's anything but. 'I've just got home, I was watching TV. I assume this won't take long.'

332

Griffin doesn't reply and follows him into the house. It's warm. Almost stiflingly so, and Griffin takes his coat off straight away. He doesn't want to show his admiration, but he can't help looking up through the full height hallway, a wooden staircase rising to intricately carved balustrades. He imagines four, maybe five bedrooms above.

'Do you want tea, coffee? Anything stronger?' Neil asks.

'Whatever you're having. Does anyone else live here?'

Neil walks through to the lounge. 'No.' He chuckles. 'Ridiculous, isn't it? I should sell up. Move somewhere smaller. But I had the cash, so ...' His voice trails off. He senses Griffin isn't in the mood for small talk. He busies himself at an oak sideboard, pouring a large glass of whisky from the decanter. Griffin takes it without comment. Neil raises his eyebrow but says nothing, pouring another for himself.

The silence hangs. Griffin gathers his thoughts, Neil getting more uneasy by the second. He shifts awkwardly, then sits down, crossing and recrossing his legs. Griffin perches on the chair opposite.

Neil gives him a long look. 'Why are you here?' he asks eventually.

'My mum died this morning.'

'I am sorry to hear that—'

'What happened between you and my mother?'

Neil blinks for a moment, then takes a sip of his whisky.

'It was a long time ago. Why are you digging this up now?'

'What happened?'

Neil sighs. 'We had an affair. Happy? It started about a year before your father died. You and Cara were teenagers, hardly at home. Mark was ... lost in his own head.'

'And you seduced my mother.'

'It wasn't like that! We would get together, talk about Mark. We were both worried. But … I don't know. I guess we found comfort in each other.'

'How lovely,' Griffin says sarcastically. 'When did it end?'

'When Mark died. We felt so guilty. Angela had … That afternoon, she had told him she was leaving. We were …' He pauses. 'We were together – when he died. That was the last time. We couldn't be a couple after that. I swear.'

'And where were you when Mum died? This morning.'

'What?'

Neil recoils, pushing backwards in his chair, seeking more space between them. Griffin leans forward. His hand reaches for the rucksack between his legs and Neil's eye line follows.

'Where were you when Mum died, Neil?' Griffin repeats, his voice slow and deep.

'I was … I don't know,' he blusters. 'What time did she die? I was probably at work. Or here.'

'I'll tell you where you were. You were at her flat.'

Neil's hand starts to shake, the brown liquor jumping in the crystal tumbler.

'You're not some master criminal, Neil. You signed in. Your name is in the visitors' book.'

'Yes, I was there. But when I left she was fine.'

'And how was she when you saw her?'

'Awake. Confused, but okay. I made her a cup of tea. We chatted. About old times.'

'Are you wondering where the box is?'

'Box?' he squeaks.

'Yes, the box.' Years of interviews have left Griffin with a well-honed calm facade, even when his insides are doing hopscotch. He continues: 'The one you were looking for. That contain the accounts for the first few years of the business.'

'I don't know anything about a box.'

Griffin opens the top of his rucksack. He takes out his extendable baton. Standard issue police kit. He lifts it behind his head, racking it with a satisfying crack.

Neil jumps. He drops the glass with shock, the whisky soaking into the carpet.

'What … Nate … Please …'

Griffin's closer to the door than Neil. He watches the old man's eyes dart. To his only exit. To his mobile phone he's left on the sideboard behind Griffin, out of reach.

'I don't want this to get nasty, Neil,' Griffin says. 'But unless you start telling me the truth …' He leaves the sentence open-ended, as Neil's eyes focus on the baton. Extended to its full length it shines, black rubber grip and shiny steel. Simple, but effective.

Griffin's gaze drops deliberately to Neil's legs. To his knees and shins.

Neil makes a dash for it then, but Griffin is faster and bigger, getting in his way and placing a large hand on his fleshy chest. Neil stops; Griffin can feel him shaking through his palm.

'Sit down.'

Neil does as he's told. Griffin looms over him, the baton lowered by his side, intention clear.

The old man shrinks in his chair. 'No, no. You don't need … You and Cara … And Angela … you were my family. You … You …' Neil continues his bleating as Griffin slowly sits back down. 'I'll give you whatever you want, Nate. Is it money? I have money. In the safe—'

'Shut the fuck up.' He does. 'What did you do to my mum?'

'You have to understand … the company is everything to me. It could never … I could never …' Neil pants, struggling to take a breath through his panic. 'I can't go to prison.'

'What – exactly – would you go to prison for?' Griffin asks slowly. He pulls the chair forward to sit directly in front of Neil. He taps the baton against the leg of the chair, the metal making a satisfying clink against the wood.

'It was only a bit. Here and there. At first.' Neil lifts his hand to wipe his brow, now sweating profusely. He lowers it again with a wince. 'Mark didn't notice. How could he? He was preoccupied with his own problems. And I needed a new car. So I thought … it's a company car, right?'

'And that's what the accounts show?'

'No—'

'Is this a company house too?' Griffin sneers, gesturing around him.

'It … No … It …' he stutters. 'It was just a bit of cash. And then Mark died and it was all mine anyway. What does it matter?'

'It matters, Neil,' Griffin says slowly, struggling to keep his fury under control. 'It matters because my parents are dead, and the common factor in both their deaths is you.'

'I had nothing to do—'

But Griffin's anger can't be contained any longer. As Neil blathers on, he stands up, takes two steps towards the sideboard, then brings the baton down on the tray with the crystal glasses. The tumblers shatter, a spray of shards litter the carpet like diamonds.

Neil jumps with a squeak as Griffin turns his way. He starts to cry. 'I had nothing to do with Mark's death. It was an accident. It was suicide—'

'Make your mind up.'

'It wasn't me!'

Griffin bends down so that Neil's face is close to his. 'What about Mum? What did you do?'

'I didn't … Nothing … I …'

He taps the baton on the back of Neil's chair, a repetitive *chink chink* behind the old man's ear. Neil flinches. Sweat is pouring from his forehead.

'I'm sorry. I'm so sorry,' he begins. 'I didn't …'

'Tell me!' Griffin bellows.

'I didn't mean to. I only went there to collect the files, but as soon as I asked about them, she knew. And she wouldn't shut up. It was like she was back there. In the nineties. She kept on saying, "I'll tell the police. I'll tell Mark." She tried to hit me and—'

'And you held her down.'

'To stop her … A-And …' he stutters. 'Do your worst. I don't care. I deserve it. It was an accident. I didn't mean to … to kill her. I put my hand over her mouth. To shut her up. But … But … She was so weak. She barely struggled. I'm … I'm sorry. It was a mistake. I …'

He's sobbing now, snot pouring from his nose, his face twisted and red, turned away from Griffin. As much as Griffin wants to destroy this man until he's a twisted bloody pulp at his feet, that's not what he's there for. He'll get justice in other ways. He takes a step backwards, his hand reaching for the phone in his pocket.

'And you'll come clean to the police? You'll confess?'

Neil's eyes open. 'I … I can't.'

Griffin raises the baton again and Neil winces. 'I know where you live, Neil. You know what I'll do.'

Neil nods quickly. 'Okay ... I ...' But his words stop in his mouth. His hand goes to his throat, his body shaking. He takes another wheeze in, then looks up at Griffin, fear in his eyes. 'It's ... I ...' He clutches at his left arm, then his chest. 'Call 999,' he manages.

He reaches for Griffin, his mouth open, face red, grabbing at him. He pulls himself to his feet, sways, then his legs drop from underneath him into a pile on the carpet.

Griffin's stunned. He stands for a moment, the man he was threatening to torture moments ago, prostrate at his feet. Then his training kicks in. He drops to his knees in front of Neil and rolls him onto his back. He presses two fingers against his neck, but there's nothing. Cheek over his mouth, he listens – no signs of breathing.

'Fuck,' he hisses. Then: 'Fuck!' He shouts it over and over. This wasn't what he had in mind. He wanted to scare him, get the truth. Not have him drop dead on the plush shagpile carpet.

He interlaces his fingers, places them on the man's chest, and starts compressions. All the while swearing softly. He needs to call an ambulance, but this is his fault. He knows the survival rate is low from cases like this. What then? How does he explain a dead man, this time of night? The smashed glass? The police baton, lying next to him on the floor.

On autopilot he pounds on his chest. Panicking. Mind racing. Until a voice speaks from behind him.

'Nate,' the woman says. 'What have you done?'

Chapter 61

Cara doesn't trust Griffin at the best of times, let alone in the middle of a murder investigation when his mother has just died. She knew that look on his face – the blank expression when logical thought had departed and pure emotion had taken over.

She'd gone home for a while. Read the latest reports, Jamie's observations, planned the next steps in the investigation. But she couldn't concentrate. The spectre of her mother hovered at her periphery, the sorrow too close to the surface, the pile of paperwork that needed to be addressed whispering from her bag. She'd tried to call Griffin, but his phone cut to voicemail. Set to silent, or was she being ignored?

As night fell, she closed the laptop decisively. Stood up and grabbed her coat. She knew how his mind worked – he'd go straight to the source of his problems. To Neil Lowe. She opened her laptop again, logged into the PNC and searched for Neil Lowe's address. Not far away, but Griffin had a head start.

She ran out to her car, driving quickly through the quiet

streets, her worst fears confirmed as she pulled up in the driveway behind Griffin's Land Rover. But nothing could have prepared her for the sight of Griffin bent, doing CPR, over the prostrate body of Neil Lowe.

'Nate,' she whispers. 'What have you done?'

He turns, his face stricken. And it's only then that she sees the extent of the problem. The smashed glass on the sideboard, the decanter upended on the carpet. Discarded, empty tumblers, whisky in the air. A baton, extended, to the side of a chair.

'He just collapsed,' Griffin shouts, pumping on his chest. 'It must have been a heart attack. I … I didn't know.'

'You were threatening him.'

'He killed Mum.'

'He said that?' Cara's hands go to her face as she tries to think. Griffin will lose his job. Be sent to prison. That can't happen. It can't.

'Go,' she says at last.

He turns, confused.

'Go. I'll do that. I'll call an ambulance. I'll say I came out here to see him.' He doesn't stop, and she pulls at his shoulders. He pauses, then backs away.

'What about …?'

'What about the crime scene, you mean?' Cara snaps. She kneels next to Neil, starting compressions. 'Take your baton. I'll make the rest up. Pretend someone broke in. I don't know!' She's shouting now. 'Go. Please. Use my car. Not your fucking truck, it's too distinctive. You were never here.'

He hesitates, then runs out of the room. She waits and hears her Audi start and fade into the distance.

Her arms are aching already. She can't think. She pauses

to give mouth-to-mouth but Neil's eyes are staring, his gaze vacant. She restarts the compressions but her movements slow. She stops.

Neil Lowe can't survive. If what Griffin says is true, he killed their mother. He could tell the police what happened tonight and Griffin would be arrested for assault. False imprisonment. For making threats to kill, if she knows Griffin as well as she thinks she does. That can't happen.

She has lost too much. Her husband, soon to be ex. Noah Deakin – her partner and best friend – locked in jail. Even her children feel elusive to her.

Her parents are dead.

She won't lose her brother. He's all she has left.

She sits back on her knees and waits. She can hear her own heart beating, feel the sweat drying on her back. Her eyes fix on the prostrate man. She counts to a hundred, slowly, then leans forward and checks his pulse. Nothing. No breath sounds.

Nothing.

She gets to her feet and looks at the room with a careful eye. What story would this crime scene show? Smashed glass. A man blundering around in pain, his heart failing. What lies should she tell? Cara rehearses it in her head: Neil is an old family friend. She knew he would be upset about their mother dying so she came here to see him. Just in the nick of time; he was close to collapse. She started CPR straight away, did what she could. Called 999.

There are no security cameras; the doorbell is old school, no way of recording who visited that day. The neighbours are far enough away to ignore a car late at night, and hopefully wouldn't have paid any attention to the time the Land Rover arrived.

341

She picks up the two glasses and carries them to the kitchen, carefully washing them up and putting them in a cupboard. She obliterates any trace of Griffin – wiping door handles, scuffing out the footprints from his heavy boots, walking her own across the pristine tiled floor.

She's a respected DCI, she'll be taken at her word. And why wouldn't they believe her? Her mother's death was ruled natural from the beginning, no debate. There's no reason for anyone to look closer. What motive does she have?

Satisfied at her efforts, she goes back to the body. Starts CPR again, gets her heart rate racing. And then takes her phone out of her pocket.

'Ambulance,' she says, her voice panicked. She describes the scene, what she's doing and waits for the first responders. The men and women who will heroically do what they can to save the man, but will ultimately pronounce time of death.

An unfortunate accident. A man overcome with grief, who fell victim to too many late-night glasses of whisky. Too much good food. He lived a good life, died a sad death.

And nobody will talk of Neil Lowe again.

Chapter 62

Griffin paces his flat for hours. A full glass always seems to be in his hand, but he's constantly drinking, so he must be drunk, must be out of control. The cat has fled out of the open window, confused by his unease. He picks up his phone to call Cara any number of times, but always pulls back. She knows what she's doing. He mustn't raise suspicion. Mustn't do anything to compromise her plan.

But what *is* her plan? He imagines the worst. That Cara's failed, that blue lights will flash outside his window and someone will arrest him. For GBH. For manslaughter. He deserves it all.

At last, he hears a car outside. The unmistakeable rumble of the Land Rover's engine, then footsteps on the metal stairs. He opens the door; she stands there, glaring, then pushes through into the flat.

She picks up the whisky bottle from the table and, finding it empty, reaches across and grabs the glass out of his hand. She downs it in one long gulp.

'What's going on? What's happened, Cara?'

She slumps into a chair next to the table. 'He's dead.'

Griffin collapses next to her, his head in his hands. He lets out a strangled groan.

'What did you expect, Nate?' she snaps. 'He was an old man. Overweight. A drinker, a smoker.' She pauses. 'Dr Ross says it's almost certain he had a history of heart problems.'

'Ross was there?'

'I spoke to him. They'll have to do a PM. A sudden death like that.'

Griffin gets up and heads across to his kitchen, opening the fridge and cupboards.

'Stop drinking,' Cara hisses. 'You've had enough. We're both due at work in a few hours. You've been at home, in bed, remember?'

Griffin stares at her. 'How can you be so calm?'

'I'm not. But I've had a lifetime covering up your shit.' She pauses, gathering herself again. 'Put the kettle on, will you?'

He does as he's told, pours instant coffee into two mugs and carries them over. When she picks hers up he notices her hands are shaking and feels instant guilt. What he made her do.

'Look,' she says. She grasps the coffee cup as if it's a lifeline. 'I forced Ross to give me his best guess and he said heart attack. Natural causes.'

'But I killed him.'

'No, Nate.' Her words are hard now. 'You didn't. Sixty years of bad lifestyle choices killed him. And you were here last night. With me.'

'With you?'

'Yes. We had dinner together. And then I decided to go and see Neil. By myself. To make sure he was okay after Mum dying. Right?'

344

'Right. What did we eat?'

'Pizza. From your freezer. Meat Feast.' Griffin screws his face up. 'And I complained because I wanted something healthy. Okay?'

'Okay.'

But his stomach churns as he sips his coffee. He's killed a man. He's been close to doing so on many occasions, but he's always pulled back from the brink. But this one? This is his to own. For the rest of his life.

He feels hands on his, gently pulling his attention to the here and now. Cara faces him.

'This doesn't change anything,' she says gently. 'You are the same man. Neil Lowe was a murderer.'

'But that doesn't mean ...'

'It wasn't your fault. You weren't to know.' She pauses. 'Did he admit to it?'

'He said he didn't mean to. That it was an accident.'

'Doesn't matter. One way or another, he killed our mother.'

'Yes. He ...' He stops, his voice breaking. He can't cry. He won't. Cara taps his hands softly in a gesture of reassurance and gets up, heading across to his cupboards and opening each in turn. By the time she returns with a packet of digestives he's managed to get a grip on his emotions.

He picks the biscuits up – the best before date is two years ago. Lost at the back of a cupboard. He opens the packet and takes one out. It's soft but edible; the hit of sugar is just what he needs.

'Now,' Cara begins, sitting opposite him and dunking a biscuit in her mug. 'Are you clear on what happened?'

Over the next half an hour they go over the story. Getting their details straight, making sure everything lines up. The reason Cara was driving the Land Rover; what Griffin watched on TV; why she decided to go and see Neil, that evening.

Cara nods with satisfaction when they finish. The coffee is drunk, the biscuits eaten.

'Thank you,' he says at last. 'For everything. Tonight.'

'You're a pain in my arse,' she replies. 'But you're all I've got.'

'Then you're as screwed as me.'

Cara gives him a wan smile. 'One last thing.'

'Anything.'

'Brody. Are you fucking her?'

Griffin considers her question with a final gulp of his coffee. 'I think it's more like she's fucking me.'

Cara nods slowly. 'Fair enough.' She pushes her chair back with a grate on the tiled floor. 'Have a shower. I'll see you at the office in a few hours.'

He looks up to the clock in surprise. It's nearly four a.m. The whole night has passed in a fog.

'Where are you going?' he asks.

'Bed,' she replies, decisively. She gets up, picks her Audi keys from the table and leaves without a backward glance.

He's always admired his older sister. For her policing skills, her strength, her determination. But he's always assumed that she didn't really like him. Thought of him as an annoying wart or a mole – something to be tolerated until it could be removed.

He hadn't realised that she loved him, until today.

Chapter 63

Cara doesn't want to go home. She drives through deserted streets, her heart thumping. Her chest aching. Her head whirrs with thoughts of her mum, her *murdered* mum. Neil Lowe, dead, thanks to Griffin. Breaking the law, covering up a crime.

Miles pass in a second as she pulls up in front of the small, neat terrace. She rings the doorbell and waits.

A light turns on in the hallway. The scrape of the lock being opened, and then Charlie's there. His hair in disarray; he's wearing a grey T-shirt and a pair of tracksuit bottoms. Bare feet. He squints from behind his glasses.

'Cara? What do you want?'

'I want you,' she replies.

He's silent for a moment, and she worries that she's made a mistake. That he'll slam the front door in her face. But then he steps forward, takes her face gently in his hands and kisses her.

He pulls her into the house; she kicks the front door closed with her foot. They kiss again; clothes are discarded. She pulls her shirt over her head, flicks her boots off to a corner of the hallway. Grabs his hand and leads him up the stairs to the bedroom.

She feels different this time. She's had enough of self-doubt, of worry. She just covered up manslaughter for her brother – in terms of risk, sleeping with Charlie falls low down on the list.

She's laser focused, there is nothing else in her mind. She wants him. Wants to feel adored, touched, the feeling of her skin on his. Almost naked, they fall into his bed. Warm from where he's been sleeping, his body hot on hers. He turns towards her; she can see his face in the darkness, the only light trickling from the hallway, his eyes intense without his glasses.

'Are you okay?' he whispers, his lips millimetres from hers. 'Are you sure you want this?'

'Yes, I do.'

He moves away; she misses the intimacy and pulls him back close. 'It's … the other night …'

'I'm sorry about that. It's a weird time. There's a lot going on. This case now, and …'

'I get it.' He moves, his head on the pillow next to hers.

'I'm not normally like this,' she whispers.

'Like what?'

'Weak. Pathetic.'

'You are neither of those things, Cara.' She feels a hand reach; he locks his fingers around hers. 'I've never thought that about you. To deal with the things you have. What you've seen.' He shakes his head; she hears his stubble rasp on the pillow. 'You're extraordinary.'

She wants to be that person – the woman he sees. And that thought is intoxicating. She leans across and kisses him again. He returns it, responding to her intensity. Her whole body aches for this man. This one bit of simplicity. Of goodness. She reaches for him, pulling closer, their legs entwining, their bodies pressed together from hip to toe. Skin against skin, hands everywhere. His fingers— Fucking hell. She wants him so much.

'Have you …' she manages.

'Here.' He pulls away from her, she gives an involuntary groan of frustration. Knickers off, boxers off. The awkward business of the condom, and he is on top of her, her legs wrapped around his hips.

Charlie is new, different. But good different. Something she never expected to feel with someone else again. That desire. She grabs at his back; her legs pull him in with each thrust. Her lips on his neck, his head thrown back as he comes. He collapses onto her, the heaviness of his body reassuring.

He rolls off. 'Sorry … It's been a while.' He pauses. 'Can I …?'

'What?'

'Try and … you know.'

She grins. 'You can try.'

He does. His fingers find her, his mouth. He succeeds, her body bucking with pleasure. And after, as they lie, side by side, sated, sweaty, she thinks, okay. You're okay. This might turn out okay, after all.

Part 3

Paul

His hands shake as he picks up the plastic bag. It's large. No holes. A handy ziplock fastener at the top. Big enough for what he wants to do.

He lays it reverently on the table. He picks up his phone and writes one last text. *I'm sorry. It was us. You know it needed to be done.*

He deletes and rewrites it a few times. His brother will know what it means but he's confident he won't intervene. If anything, he will approve. His one act of bravery. He presses send.

He worries about leaving his brother, alone. Younger, more troubled, in many ways. He's had it so much harder. Paul tried his best to do his part. Meet up. Give him money, clothes, even drugs. Whatever he could. And in the later days, make sure he saw their mum. But he always knew it wasn't enough. None of it was.

It doesn't matter now.

He picks up the bag and carries it to his sofa, the heavy canister in the other hand. He'd debated where; this seems good enough. He can't fail. The shame – if he can't even get this right.

Ever since that day, he's not been able to get her out of his head. Her face, seared into his brain. They'd talked about when. They'd talked about where. But they'd never discussed how it was wrong. How he would feel afterwards. How much Paul would wish to have one more day with her, one more conversation. How he loved to read to her, the only thing he could do in those later days, watching as her face relaxed, her fingers gently laced in his.

Instead, they had left her to die. She was warm and peaceful, yes. But she was alone. And rather than being brave enough to own up to what they'd done, they'd left. Gone to a bloody supermarket, of all places.

He hates himself for that.

He picks up his phone again. He looks at the text; it has been read by his brother. The tiny bold letters confirm it, but there is no reply.

He debates for a second. Types another few words then presses send without thinking. Job done, he picks up the bag and pulls it over his head. Condensation from his breath fogs the plastic immediately, but oxygen is getting in from below. He picks up the hose from the canister and turns the dial to the left. A hiss confirms it's on, and he points the hose into the plastic bag, sealing the ziplock tightly under his chin.

He sits back and waits. The helium is odourless, but he knows it's working from the dizzy swirl in his head, from the relaxation that floods his body. He forces himself to take deeper inhales, each one causing his head to grow foggier, more woozy. His chest is tight; his mind distorts. The Christmas lights outside the window dance, a haze of

354

red and blue and yellow. It would have been his first without her. He doesn't want it.

He struggles to hold the tube and lies down, resting it by his side like a faithful hound. His hand drops; his consciousness fades.

His phone falls to the floor, showing the message he has just sent.

Make him pay. Make them all pay.

It beeps. A reply from his brother that he will never see.

I will.

DAY 9

TUESDAY

Chapter 64

Before the sun is up, as light starts to graze the tops of the cupboards in Charlie's bedroom, Cara lies awake. Thinking. Planning. Next to her, Charlie sleeps, his dark hair mussed on the pillow, eyelashes flickering. He snores gently.

She guesses she had an hour's worth of shut-eye before her brain catapulted her back. This case. She has to solve this case.

She rolls over and slips her hand around Charlie's middle, snuggling up against his back. He's warm and comforting; she likes it here.

'Charlie?' she whispers.

'Mmm?' he replies, but it's languid. He's still asleep.

She tries again. 'Charlie?'

He turns now; half opens his eyes, looking at her through a squint. He smiles slowly. 'Hello.'

'Hello.' She returns the smile.

'Are you okay?' he asks.

She told him about her mother's death last night. In the early hours, in the void between sleep and awake. He was sympathetic, kind; holding her close when she cried.

'I'm fine,' she says now. Not the truth, but close enough. She kisses him. 'What have you got on today?'

His hand edges around, pulling her closer. 'What have you got in mind?'

'Not that,' she laughs. 'Although I would like nothing more than to stay in bed with you.'

'We should.' His voice is husky with sleep. 'What could possibly be more important?'

'The investigation?'

He makes a quiet, disgruntled humph. 'I am at your disposal, DCI Cara Elliott. For whatever you need me for.'

'Meeting at nine? Case review?'

'Absolutely.' He nods sagely, reminding her of a serious child about to forget everything. 'What's the ...' He looks over her shoulder at the clock. 'Not even seven. Do we have time for an additional review of our own?' That hand again, creeping around to her bum, pulling her against him.

He kisses her neck; she runs her fingers through his hair.

'Since you asked so nicely, Mr Mills,' she says, as his mouth works downwards.

An hour later she's in the car, making calls, trying to concentrate on the investigation as Charlie's smile flickers in and out of her head. She holds back an insufferable grin as she thinks about him. Of the promise of things to come.

Ross's bark pulls her back. 'As much as I have more pressing things to do,' he says, his voice echoing over the loudspeaker, 'I'm happy to help in whatever way I can. If only to free up space in my mortuary.'

She thanks him as she pulls up in the underground car

park, breathing a sigh of relief as she spots Griffin's Land Rover at the far end. He's here. Business as usual, she tells herself as she walks up to the incident room.

When she gets there, the whole team is waiting. Griffin and Brody sitting in front of a laptop at the central table; Shenton in the kitchen making drinks; Jamie with Oliver, a long printout laid on the desk. She takes her coat off; Shenton presses a mug of coffee into her hand.

'I don't need to tell you how important it is that we draw this investigation to a close. We have eight victims now. Eight. And that pisses me off. I want to catch this sneaky bastard and I want to do it soon.'

Everyone nods. 'I'm sorry to hear about your mum, boss,' Jamie says. 'You too, Griffin. If there's anything we can do …'

'I appreciate that,' she says, bluntly. She catches Griffin's eye. He's unshaven, black shadows haunting his face, but nothing you couldn't put down to standard grief. He gives her a slow nod. Cara continues: 'But right now my priority lies in this room. My mum suffered from dementia, like Eileen. We need to get justice.'

The door opens and Charlie and Ross come in. Charlie flashes a smile at Cara and sits down, nodding to the rest of the detectives. He's professional, giving no hint of their relationship beyond the walls of the nick. Unlike her, she thinks, aware of her face flushing.

'I've asked Charlie and Dr Ross—'

'Greg,' the pathologist grunts.

'Greg. To join us this morning. The more heads we have at this stage of the game, the better.'

She turns to the whiteboard, ignoring the curious look Griffin is giving her.

'So, let's start at the beginning. Colin Jefferies. Our train victim. What do we know?'

Over the next few hours, they work through every detail on the case. Causes of death, findings from the PMs. The digital footprint from all the phones – internet search history, calls made and received, social media. And the nuts and bolts from the police searches: CCTV footage, ANPR, eyewitness accounts. Anything and everything gets recorded – both up on the whiteboard, and by Oliver, silently typing on his laptop.

At the end of the download, Cara steps back and looks at the board. It's a mess. Leads followed up, resulting in dead ends. Names, dates, and for what? They don't have a single suspect.

She's convinced the key lies in the link between the victims and taps her finger where she scribbled barely days before.

'We know two victims are definitely linked – Ken Laker and his step-daughter Isabel Warner. This can't be coincidence. Oliver,' she says, exasperation now creeping into her voice. 'Where are we on the commonalities? You must have something new, surely?'

'A bit, yes.' He turns on his chair and gestures to the board. Scribbles and random thoughts, nothing connected.

'I started by looking at the shops in the area,' he begins. 'We know they all went to the Tesco, and Kate Avery bought her book from the Dog's Trust—'

Cara lifts her eyebrows, hopeful.

'But no,' Oliver continues. 'Nothing. Kate Avery's father had a licence for the shotgun, none of the others did. Jefferies,

Jessop and Hobbs were all taking the antidepressant, sertraline. But it's common, hardly surprising.'

'Therapists?' Cara asks, pointing to the next line on the board.

'Some of them were seeing counsellors, but all different people, at different clinics across the city. But—' He clamps his hand across his mouth, his eyes wide. 'Shit. Shit! That … that can't be …'

He swivels back to his laptop and starts typing. The whole team stares.

'Ollie?' Cara says. Then louder. 'Oliver! What?'

He ignores her, muttering to himself. 'I should have looked … I knew …' Then he slams his forefinger on the enter key. 'Helpline,' he crows, victoriously.

'Helpline?'

'All of our victims regularly called a local mental health helpline.'

Something sparks – and not just in Cara's mind. Griffin gets to his feet, standing to attention; Brody cranes forward; even Jamie squares his shoulders. Nobody makes a sound.

'How regularly?' Cara asks quickly.

Ollie turns back to his screen. 'Jefferies called it … twice, maybe three times a week. Isabel Warner … only once. Kate Avery called a good few times before she died, Lisa Hobbs … in bursts. And Jessop most of all – at least every day, usually at night.' Ollie looks up. 'Do you think that's significant?'

Everyone focuses on Cara.

'It could be,' she says. 'Ollie, carry on digging. Get as much intel as you can on this place. How long it's been around, who set it up, that sort of thing. Shenton, help him. Was this the helpline the GP's wife was on about? Brody,

360

find out. And Griffin and Jamie, get down there. Speak to whoever's in charge.'

Brody starts to say something but thinks better of it. Her nose is probably out of joint – not being paired with Griffin as she has been for a considerable part of the case – but Cara's not a fan of the two of them working and sleeping together.

Not that she can talk.

Charlie and Ross leave, promising to get in touch if either of them finds anything new, but before he goes Charlie gives her a quick smile. She returns the grin. She goes into her office feeling a hundred per cent better. Is it Charlie, or the promise of a solid lead on the case? Either way, who cares. It's time something good happened in her life.

Chapter 65

Griffin leads the way down to his Land Rover, until his attention is caught by a shiny black vintage BMW parked next to it.

He pauses, running a finger gently along the paintwork, peering through the window.

'It's mine,' Jamie says, meekly. 'Well, not mine. Bishop's. My Corsa broke down and Adam was always saying I could drive it ... so ...'

Griffin gives a low, appreciative whistle. 'What's the engine on that thing? Two litre?'

'Two-point-eight.'

'And the horsepower?'

Jamie shrugs, bashful. 'I don't know anything about cars. And before you ask, no, you can't drive it. It's staying safely here in this car park until it's time for me to go home.'

'Don't you trust me?'

'Hell, no,' Jamie replies and Griffin laughs, at last eliciting a smile out of his colleague.

'Point made. We'll take the truck, but it won't be nearly as fun.'

Griffin unlocks the Land Rover and they both climb in.

'What a beauty,' Griffin mutters, admiring it in his rear-view mirror as they pull away, desperate to get behind the wheel.

The premises for *GetHelpNow* is a short fifteen-minute drive away, situated in a row of shops between a hairdresser and a Co-op. Shenton has called ahead, and a stout, grey-haired woman answers when they knock. After introductions she shows them through to a small office on the far side of the building, past an assortment of people talking on phones, and a kitchen where a gaggle of women are chatting.

The three of them sit down on soft, low chairs, arranged in a perfect triangle.

'How can I help?' the woman asks, her face serious.

She's introduced herself as Mary Staples, the manager of the helpline. She's wearing a navy cardigan, black trousers, sensible shoes – she strikes Griffin as a no-nonsense woman, someone used to getting every penny out of donations.

'Can you tell us a bit about the charity,' Jamie begins, 'how does it work?'

'We're open twenty-four-seven, the lines manned solely by volunteers. I'm the only salaried member of staff, and my job is to keep things running, make sure everyone's trained, and look after the team.'

'How long have you been in operation?'

'Three years. And we've never had to close the lines.' She sits up straight, shoulders back, proud. 'We provide a vital service. If they need us, we're here.'

'Do you keep records of the people that phone in?'

'It's all anonymous. That's important, so our clients know they can share anything.'

'Nobody takes notes?'

'Never.'

Griffin's let Jamie take lead so far – he has a gentle way about him that people respond to – but Griffin can't help but interject.

'Your volunteers – do they share their names? Do your clients know who they're talking to?'

'They use pseudonyms,' Mary replies. 'To protect the boundary between our volunteers and the clients. Some can get …' She pauses, clearly trying to explain in a positive way. 'Clingy,' she concludes, failing.

'So, a client, as you call them, won't speak to the same volunteer twice?' Griffin pushes. 'Ever?'

Mary looks chastened then. 'Well … Sometimes a client will phone and ask for someone specific. And usually we let them. A good relationship can go a long way to help someone open up. Something I'm sure you're aware of,' she adds, with a glare at Griffin. 'And we're a dedicated team, some working long hours, all from the kindness of their hearts.'

'Can we have a list of your volunteers?' Griffin asks.

She visibly bristles. 'I don't want you hassling them,' she says, turning away from Griffin and smiling at Jamie. 'We're down a few as it is. David Hammond, a most lovely man, died at the weekend.'

'We heard,' Jamie says softly. 'We're sorry for your loss. He was a GP, wasn't he?'

'Yes, and a great help to our charity. He would organise events, golf tournaments, that sort of thing. To raise money. As well as spending time on the phones.'

'He sounds like a kind man,' Jamie says, with a gentle

touch to her hand. Griffin has to admire his manner, but then we all have our strengths, he thinks ruefully. Jamie's is getting the best out of people. Griffin's is convincing people to talk. By any means.

That thought takes him back to last night. To Cara, and Neil Lowe. Griffin had kept an ear out this morning around the nick, even had a quiet chat with a sergeant he knew from his days from Response and Patrol. But nobody was talking about the deployment last night as anything other than natural causes, and how lucky it was that DCI Elliott had been there, to give CPR even though it was unsuccessful. She tells a good lie, his sister.

The worry is fading, but the guilt throbs. He had tried to sleep after Cara left, but his brain turned the events over, again and again. What he should have done differently. How he could have saved Neil Lowe. But also, a burn of anger, of justice, that this man had killed his mother.

Accidentally, so he said. But once is happenstance; twice is coincidence. What might he have done in the past?

Thoughts of his father will have to wait. There is nothing he can do now – to go near the office or Neil's house would risk destroying the story they had so carefully crafted last night. He has to stay away.

Next to him, Jamie and Mary are still talking. It seems Jamie's super-power has persuaded Mary to part with her staff roster, a list she's now downloading from her computer. The printer spits out a page and she hands it to Jamie.

'You promise me,' she says. 'Be nice. They're good people.'

'We will,' Jamie says with a smile.

Once they're clear of the office, Jamie passes the list to Griffin and he sits for a moment in the front seat of the truck, running through the names.

'So Hammond did work there?' Griffin says, and Jamie nods. 'All our victims lead back to this helpline. It can't be mere chance.'

'It would explain how our killer knew how Lisa was raped,' Jamie says.

'And how best to target them. Their worst fears. That Jefferies couldn't go outside, and Kate Avery was terrified of getting dementia.'

Griffin opens the page out again, and the two of them look at it in silence. A list of no more than fifty names. And one of them is their killer.

Chapter 66

Ollie needs to get away, take a break from staring at a screen twelve inches in front of his face. DCI Elliott has them raking through the names on the list. Checking criminal records, social media, PNC, RMS – any source of intel they can get their hands on.

But the problem of digging into anyone's history is you can always find *something*. An altercation at the age of eighteen with a bloke in their university halls. A spliff in the wrong place at the wrong time. Photographs on Facebook that should have been deleted.

But this one name, this one man. There's nothing.

At first Ollie assumes his name was changed legally, but there's no listing on deed poll. Not registered for council tax, paying no bills. He spends half an hour going through social media, but it's a common name and there are too many to filter through easily. So he decides on the direct approach.

The team are busy arguing over another name on the list, so Ollie grabs his bag and heads off to the bathroom to change.

Five minutes later he zips his energy gels into his pocket, pulls on his running shoes, and he's on the road.

He doesn't define how far he's going to run, or even how fast. He likes to see how the mood takes him, whether his muscles and his mind yearn for hill sprints, or a long slow amble through the countryside. Today he makes his way north, dodging students as they head to university, past the halls of residence, only stopping to traverse the busy road at the bottom of the motorway.

He enjoys the respite. Data and locations churn in his head, facts and figures he can't pull into a logical order. Normally by this point he's made sense of the case – a taming of the chaos – but this time nothing will pull free. He runs further; he knows where he's heading. To the address that bloke had given.

He's run this area before, many times, but only because he's tracked most of the roads and trails in his home town. A need to explore, when he's been cooped up all day. But today he pays particular attention. He takes a left and finds himself outside Dr Hammond's GP surgery. It's busy, Hammond's death seemingly not important enough to close the place, and he notices a poster for *GetHelpNow* among the usual printed signs. He squints, but there's nothing else out of the ordinary. What is he expecting to find? A killer lurking in the shadows?

Keen not to let his muscles cool he breaks into a run again and traverses residential streets and cul-de-sacs, an address he recognises as Colin Jefferies', then to the impressive block of flats where Lisa Hobbs met her disturbing end. There is no police activity at either, but Ollie is reminded of just how close together their victims lived.

Something must connect them.

His energy is fading and he realises he's three miles from the nick. He needs to go now if he's going to check out this guy.

He pauses for a moment to get his bearings, then takes a left, heading to a less than desirable part of town. Middle of the day, he's moving at speed. He's unlikely to get into any trouble.

He turns down the correct road and slows to a jog.

Cars are parked bumper to bumper in front of the small, terraced houses. The paint is peeling, but the windows are bright. He hears the chatter of conversation and laughter, gets a mouth-watering scent of spices. He counts down the numbers and pauses next to the front gate.

Curiosity twitches. This would make sense. An address right in the middle of their search area – there's even another one of those posters in the window. He should get back to the nick and tell someone. Griffin or Brody. They could have a chat with this guy. Find out why he's using a false name.

But Ollie is here now. What would be the harm?

Ollie has always envied the detectives, with their confidence, their authority. And he likes the team; he wants to do a good job. What if he checks whether the guy's in and if he is, has a quick word? That way he could rule it in or out, save them all some time.

Decision made, Ollie pushes at the metal garden gate. He walks two steps over broken concrete to the front door. And knocks.

Chapter 67

Griffin and Jamie returned from their visit to the helpline with more than Cara could have hoped for – a list of suspects.

The page was photocopied, names assigned and the team got to work. Hours later they've made progress. Sixteen ruled out. Out of the country, in hospital. Even one now under remand, couldn't possibly be their guy. They move on.

Cara manages to keep focused on work. But every now and again a thought creeps in. A memory from her childhood. A regret; a conversation; a shared joke. Followed by the accompanying surge of sadness that her mother is dead. A lurking permanence – this is it now.

She gets up from her desk, for want of a distraction, and heads to the kitchen. But when she gets there, she's completely overwhelmed. This investigation; the loss of her mother; worry for Griffin. It's too much, her head spins.

She places two hands on the wall and rests her forehead against the cool plaster. She screws her eyes shut and exhales in a series of jerky hiccups, trying to compartmentalise her anxiety and stress. One person can only deal with so much. Why does it have to be her? All the time?

Her legs are jelly, her mind is mush. It's not working, and to her horror she realises she's going to cry. She's going to lose it, right here, in the middle of the fucking kitchen, in the middle of a serial murder investigation. She hears footsteps behind her, she doesn't dare turn.

'Cara?'

She feels hands on her shoulders, strong arms pulling her in. She recognises Charlie's voice, his aftershave as she buries her face in his jumper, sniffing and gulping as the tears start. For a moment they just stand there. Her arms wrapped around his middle, him gently stroking her hair until somehow, eventually, she feels strong enough to pull away.

She wipes furiously at her eyes with her sleeve.

'Sorry,' she says with an apologetic grimace.

'You're allowed to cry, Cara,' Charlie says. He hands her a tissue. Clean, neatly folded from a packet in his pocket. She carefully wipes her eyes. 'It's natural to grieve.'

'But here? Now? No.'

She blows her nose and realises that at some point Charlie has pushed the kitchen door shut and they're alone. She smiles, weakly.

'Thank you. Why were you here? Did you want something?'

'I was coming to see you. Well, your analyst.' He holds out a beige file. 'Ollie asked me for the call logs for Isabel Warner. Is he around?'

'He went out for a run. About an hour ago.' She puts a hand on the door, then pauses.

'How do I look?' she asks.

'Gorgeous,' Charlie replies, then winces. 'But your

mascara could do with some attention. Here.'

He takes another tissue out of his pocket, licks it, then gently dabs under her eyes.

'Good as new.'

She knows he's lying, but leaves the sanctuary of the kitchen anyway. Oliver has returned and looks disgustingly healthy and showered after his run. Charlie heads over, leaving Cara to make a beeline for her office.

Inside, she picks up her handbag and checks her make-up in a mirror. Charlie was underplaying the mess: mascara smudged, eyes pink and puffy. She does all she can then replaces everything in her bag.

She feels embarrassed, to have lost control in that way. But Charlie's right. She is allowed to be upset.

She's an orphan. That thought alone makes her glad to have Griffin. Her stupid hulking brother – but family nonetheless.

She's watching him through the window of her office when she spots Ross appear on the far side. She goes out to greet him.

'Twice in one day, Greg,' she says. 'To what do we owe this pleasure?'

'The lab called me. They wanted to compare notes on Peter Jessop.'

'The drugs came back?'

'They did indeed.'

His arrival has attracted the interest of the rest of the team. They gather around as Ross puts a report on the middle table. Brody picks it up.

'Medical notes state Jessop was prescribed olanzapine and sertraline,' Ross begins. 'But the ones found in his rucksack—'

372

'Whatever he was taking?'

'—what you *assumed* he was taking – were no more than vitamin B, and a drug called Roaccutane. Easily identifiable from the look of them. It's prescribed for severe acne.'

Cara looks up at the photograph of Jessop on the board. 'He didn't have acne.'

'Because the drugs were working?' Brody says.

Ross scoffs. 'It doesn't work that well. We're talking a serious persistent skin condition.' He points to the photo. 'This guy had the skin of a dermatologist.'

'What are we saying? Someone swapped out his meds?' Cara pauses. 'Deliberately?'

All faces look at her, with the exception of Ross, who is flicking through his notes. 'That would make sense,' he says slowly. 'Roaccutane has been known to cause anxiety and suicidal ideation, and withdrawing someone's antidepressants and antipsychotics is not recommended, for obvious reasons. Jefferies was drugged with chloral hydrate to get him to the railway station. Ken Laker died from a massive dose of heparin, which nobody would take willingly, even if they were trying to kill themselves.'

'Who would know this? Who has access?' Cara asks.

'A doctor?' Jamie suggests. 'A counsellor? Mental health nurse?'

'Or a pharmacist.' Oliver looks up from his computer, his face white.

Cara stares at him. It makes sense. Someone with access to medical records, who knows pharmaceuticals and drugs. Who has contact with patients; who promises confidentiality and a sympathetic ear.

'Which pharmacy did they use?' she directs to Ollie, who's gone back to his tapping, his eyes flicking up and

373

down the screen.

'They all … Fucking hell,' he says. 'How did I miss this? They all use Randall and Sons. In Chandler's Ford.'

Next to him, Griffin swears, making them all jump. 'Fuck!' he repeats. 'That crafty bastard.' He thumps his hand hard on the table and their coffee mugs jump. 'I knew I recognised it.' Griffin fetches the master list of volunteers at the helpline and pushes it towards her. He points to one name. 'Paul Randall. Brody and I interviewed George Randall on Friday. The man Hammond accused of killing his wife. He's a fucking pharmacist.' Griffin explodes. 'That cunt!'

'And Paul Randall's his son,' Oliver says, his fingers deftly working the keyboard.

'You're kidding me. Go and speak to them. Even better, get them both in here.'

'We can't,' Oliver says. 'Paul Randall's dead.'

Cara knows what's coming next. 'He didn't—'

'Killed himself. Just before Christmas. Stuck a plastic bag over his head and suffocated himself with helium.'

'Fucking hell.' Cara's brain is running a mile a minute. 'What are we saying? That Paul conspired with George Randall to kill his mother …when?'

'November.'

'Then killed himself a month later? Paul couldn't possibly be our guy.'

'But his father could,' Griffin says. 'And guess where his pharmacy is?' He doesn't wait for an answer. 'Around the corner from Hammond's GP surgery, right smack bang in the middle of where all our victims lived.'

'Do you know where that is?' Cara asks, and Griffin nods. 'Well, go back there. You're about to arrest him for murder.'

374

Chapter 68

The bell over the door tinkles merrily as Jamie follows Griffin into the pharmacy, Brody bringing up the rear. Three long strides and Griffin is behind the counter, another two and George Randall has been turned around, face pressed into the wall as his hands are cuffed behind his back. Jamie has to hand it to his colleague – his manner might be abrupt, but Griffin gets the job done.

Jamie studies their suspect. He's pale, confused. Stuttering and incoherent as Griffin recites the caution.

'I didn't kill my wife,' Randall finally bleats.

'It's not about your wife, sir,' Jamie says, and Randall quietens, forehead furrowed as he's led away.

The pharmacy is silent in the aftermath of the arrest. The closed sign is now on the door, customers ushered out to the street; a crowd of onlookers gather, attracted by the blue lights, the police car, the uniforms.

The assistants stand, silent, watching. Uniformed officers have been drafted in for the search and they chat among themselves, waiting for instructions. Jamie scans the rows of boxes and pills, his gaze locking on the computer that

Charlie instructed they bring back to the nick.

'Start with that,' Jamie says, and they do as they're told, unplugging the old machine.

'Who's in charge?' Jamie asks the closest assistant. 'After Randall?'

The pale, thin girl points a finger to the older woman, who raises her hand nervously.

'Mrs Jenkins,' she says. 'Francis.'

Jamie introduces himself. 'I'm sorry to take up so much of your time today, but if you wouldn't mind answering a few questions?' Jenkins nods. 'You can go,' he says to the other assistant. 'Leave your name and address with my colleague before you do.'

Brody waves and the assistant shuffles over.

'Who has access to the computer?' he asks Jenkins.

'All of us. We have logons to the various systems.'

'Which are?'

'The PMR – patient medication record – the information held by the pharmacy, and the SCR, which is information shared from the GP's record, including diagnoses and meds. Only George has access to that one. It needs a smart card and a security PIN.'

'And you can see a patient's entire medical history on there?'

'Not all. Definitely medicines and allergies, but it will often include significant problems or diagnoses, end of life care, or other important information that the GP feels is necessary. Unless the patient has opted out.'

Jamie stares at the computer as it's taken away. So that could be where George was getting his personal details.

'Would it include ...' Jamie's not sure how to phrase this, 'the most personal of information?'

'What do you mean?'

'How someone was raped?'

Jenkins pales. 'Oh, I doubt it. Unless the patient specifically asked for it to be included. And I can't think why they would.'

Jamie can't imagine why, either. He moves on to easier topics.

'Who has access to the controlled substances, like morphine?'

'In the drugs' safe. It's here.' Jamie follows Jenkins into the back room of the pharmacy. Drugs' safe is a misnomer, it's a small white cabinet, with a single keyhole.

'And where's the key kept?'

She points to a lockbox on the wall, number dials on the outside. 'Only George and I have access to the code.' She thinks for a moment. 'But he hasn't changed the combination for a while.'

'But you keep a record? Sign all controlled drugs in and out? Regular stocktakes?'

'Yes, of course.' She reaches over and takes the key out of the box, opening up the safe and removing a scrappy bound notebook, the corners battered. She turns to the current page and Jamie can see lines of records. Drugs in, drugs out.

'Do you do a regular stocktake?' he asks. 'You'd know if something was missing?'

She looks ashamed. 'We've been busy. Last one was … I don't know. Not since that one before Christmas.' She catches Jamie's disapproving look. 'But no one's stolen anything. I don't know what you think George's done, but he wouldn't have. Not George.'

Jamie ignores her comment. 'Take me through how you issue a prescription,' he says. 'Step by step.'

'It's not a complicated procedure. Prescriptions come in either by hand, from the customer, or via the system, direct from the GP. We dispense the drugs. Everything is double-checked by George, everything monitored.'

Jamie thinks of the pills swapped out in their blister packs.

'And George is never here, out of hours. By himself?'

'Never. He leaves when we leave. We have a security system,' she says quickly. 'It records when it's switched on and off.'

'Show me?'

She leads him to the back of the shop, where a panel with numbers sits next to the door. She presses a button on the front and the screen lights up.

'See here?' she says. She prods at the button and a series of numbers appear. 'Last night the alarm was turned on at six-fifteen. Just after we closed. And it was on until eight-twenty this morning, when I turned it off.'

'And before that?'

More presses of the button. 'See? The same. Around opening and closing. Oh—'

She pauses; Jamie looks over her shoulder. 'Midnight?' he questions. 'Why would someone turn the alarm off at midnight?'

'I-I don't know,' she stutters.

Jamie takes over and presses the button a few more times. It's put on again at two in the morning, but the same pattern happens a few nights earlier.

'Who has access to this code?'

'Me and George.'

'And how often do you change it?'

She stops. 'I can't remember the last time. It's— It's been

the same code since I started working here.' Her face turns red. 'Three years ago.'

'Great.' Jamie sighs sarcastically. 'And let me guess, the locks haven't changed in that time, either?'

She shakes her head.

Jamie gives up. 'Go home for now,' he says. 'We'll need you to come into the station later to get a full statement.' Jenkins nods, her face flushed, refusing to meet his eye. She's the epitome of guilt, but he thinks it's more because of the lax security measures, rather than anything sinister. She scurries away and he presses the button on the alarm again, flicking through the recorded times. Brody appears by his shoulder.

'Someone, who knows who,' Jamie says, 'has accessed the pharmacy at night, regularly, for the last few months.'

'Oh, great,' Brody says. She knows, as well as he does, that it doesn't help their case against George. 'But if the stocktake can be believed, they haven't stolen anything.'

'Unless someone was falsifying the stocktake, too. Get those records.' The bloody, cat-mauled features of Ken Laker flash into mind. 'Especially the ones for the heparin.'

'Will do, sarge.' She turns to go.

'And call Charlie,' he continues. 'We need someone to download these records properly from the security system.'

She nods and leaves him to it. Jamie wanders around the back room, looking at the hundreds, maybe thousands of drugs. He finds it odd that this is the pharmacy that he uses. That his own prescription is here. And with that thought, his skin prickles. It will be found, catalogued, along with the search. His colleagues will know.

His conversation with the GP yesterday was brief and embarrassing. Jamie got the sense that the woman wasn't listening, let alone cared. But she prescribed some sleeping pills. So that's a start.

But the prescription was sent here. It should be confidential, but coppers gossip. It will get out – and then how will they see him? It was bad enough being a source of whispers when Pippa was killed, but time has passed and it's old news now. The last thing he needs with an IOPC investigation hanging over his head are rumours of flagging mental health, a man struggling. Even if that is the truth.

He looks to the row of drawers on the far side, letters stuck on in a large font. *A–D*, *E–G*, *H–K*. He pulls the final one open and rifles through with his gloved hands. And there it is. A sealed white packet, his name in capitals on the sticker. He glances behind him, and seeing nobody looking his way, pulls it out, opens it, and slips the packet of pills into his jacket. He folds the paper bag into four and pushes it into his back pocket. Instantly he feels better.

Nobody will know but him.

Chapter 69

Griffin hates this man. Hates that he felt sympathy, a kinship over their shared dead wives. And now he's crying in an interview room while Griffin glares.

Griffin finishes his standard cautions, the tape rolling, while the man snivels into a balled-up rag. The solicitor holds out a tissue box.

'Take your time, Mr Randall,' the solicitor says, throwing a disapproving look at Griffin. He folds his arms across his chest and waits.

The man's been steadily withering since he was arrested two hours ago. He sniffed his way through custody, pathetically saying 'please' and 'thank you' and 'would you mind?' to every question thrown his way. He was wild-eyed and baffled at the arrest for murder, his solicitor grumpy in the discovery meeting before the interview when all Griffin would disclose is that it was nothing to do with the wife.

Yet.

Griffin's itching to add her murder to the list of victims, but they don't have the evidence to support it. Unlike the other deaths. They've spent the last few hours cataloguing the exhibits, prioritising the stocktaking for the drugs they know are involved. And even in this short timescale they've made progress.

Griffin asked to do the interview. Cara gave him a warning look and capitulated on the basis that Jamie's still at the pharmacy, managing the search. But she insisted on Brody being there, a compromise he's willing to accept.

Randall has stopped crying, and his solicitor nods.

'So, Mr Randall,' Griffin begins. 'I am going to take you through a number of prescriptions. And I would simply like to know if you agree that they were issued by you over the last few weeks.'

He lays the green slips out on the table, one by one, all encased in their evidence bags. Randall peers at them as Griffin works his way along.

'We have this one for amitriptyline, tramadol and diazepam, made out to Isabel Warner. Would you agree they were dispensed by you?'

Randall glances at his solicitor who gives a small nod.

'Yes. That's my signature, yes.'

The next: 'Olanzapine and sertraline, for Peter Jessop.'

'Yes.'

'Pregabalin and sertraline for Colin Jefferies.'

'Yes.'

Griffin goes through the rest – for Lisa Hobbs, Eileen Avery, Ken Laker – Ron agreeing, the solicitor growing more confused with each one.

'So all these people were customers of your pharmacy?' Griffin concludes.

'I suppose so.'

'What's the relevance, DS Griffin?' the solicitor interrupts.

'These are all people who died in the last few weeks. And

the one thing that connects them is you.'

'Me?'

'You. What do you have to say about that, Mr Randall?'

'I—' He looks to his solicitor. 'No comment.'

The lawyer looks at the prescriptions. He picks up the one for Eileen Avery. 'I recognise this name. This woman was murdered by her daughter who then went on to kill herself. It was in the newspapers. What could that possibly have to do with my client?'

'Moving on,' Griffin says, ignoring the solicitor. He places a printout on the table. Multiple rows have been carefully highlighted in bright yellow. 'Do you recognise this? It's the download from the security system at your pharmacy. And these ...' he points at the lines, 'are when somebody accessed your pharmacy in the middle of the night.'

'What?' Randall leans forward, squinting at the rows. 'But this is at two in the morning.'

'It is.'

'That can't be correct.'

'It is, Mr Randall. Was it you?'

'No!'

'Where were you at two a.m. on Monday night?'

'I would have been home in bed. That's where I am every night.'

'Is there anyone that can verify that?'

'No! Since my wife died.'

'Pity,' Griffin says sarcastically. He's starting to enjoy himself now. 'Do you know what Roaccutane is, Mr Randall?'

He frowns. 'It's a drug usually prescribed for severe acne.'

'Correct. Do you know some of the side effects of that drug?'

'Er … off the top of my head, no.'

'Let me help you. Dry eyes, dry skin. Headache. Psychotic disorder and suicidal ideation. Do you know where we found this drug?'

The solicitor huffs, interrupting Griffin's fun. 'How could he possibly know that?'

'In a blister pack of pills, prescribed to Peter Jessop. But do you know the strange thing about that? It should have been sertraline, an antidepressant. But someone had carefully opened the pack and replaced the drugs, so that when Jessop thought he was taking antidepressants he was actually taking these. Pills issued by your pharmacy.' Griffin thuds a hand onto the prescription. Randall jumps. 'Did you issue those pills?'

'I …' He glances to his solicitor. 'No comment.'

'Not to worry.' He moves on. 'Why do you keep heparin at your pharmacy, Mr Randall?'

'It's an anticoagulant, it's prescribed to reduce blood clots.'

'Are you aware you're missing two boxes of heparin sodium solution? Twenty millilitres in total?'

'We are? No, I wasn't aware.'

'And do you know where that missing heparin has gone?'

'No comment.'

'Because we do. Into the vein of Ken Laker. Who then died in an excruciating, and incredibly messy manner on the floor of his flat two days ago.'

'But I don't know Ken Laker.'

'You do. You issued him a prescription on this date, see here?'

'But I don't know my customers personally. I couldn't possibly.'

'Does anyone else have the access code to the pharmacy?'

'Just my assistant, Mrs Jenkins. And me.'

'And access to the heparin?'

'It's not controlled.'

'Anyone who works at the pharmacy could have had access to that drug,' the solicitor interjects. 'You have no evidence it was my client.'

'Except only your client has the detailed knowledge about what this drug would do to someone with end stage stomach cancer.'

Randall starts crying again, pushing the snotty rag up against his nose. 'Anyone could google that,' he wails.

'Have you heard of the *GetHelpNow* helpline?'

Randall looks up. 'My son used to volunteer there.'

'Paul?'

'Yes.'

'Did he ever tell you about the people he spoke to?'

'No. Never. Everything said on that helpline was confidential. Paul knew that.'

'And how did Paul die, Mr Randall?'

Randall glares at him, his eyes red raw. 'He killed himself. As you well know, or you wouldn't be asking me that question.'

'DS Griffin,' the solicitor says, interrupting, 'can I have a word?'

Griffin nods and pauses the tape. Brody stays with Randall while Griffin and the solicitor move out into the corridor.

'Can I ask what you're getting at?' the solicitor says. 'You can't possibly be implying that Mr Randall was involved in these suicides?'

'That's exactly what I'm saying.'

'These people all died alone. Surely you're not implying he was anywhere near them?'

'No. But Mr Randall's actions with the drugs he issued directly led to their deaths. He went into his pharmacy in the dead of night, switched the pills they were supposed to be taking, and as a result, they killed themselves.'

'This is preposterous,' the solicitor replies. 'The most ridiculous case I've ever heard.'

But before Griffin can answer him, Shenton comes running around the corner. He's winded, face red, and he stops in front of Griffin.

'It's Ollie,' he utters. 'He's on the roof. And he says he's going to jump.'

Chapter 70

The wind whips savagely across the rooftop, twisting and turning his cries until they sound inhuman. Griffin stands a few metres away, thighs and lungs burning, having taken the staircase at full speed.

The night has closed in; it's dark. Only a floodlight at the doorway illuminates the ghostly spectre of Oliver Maddox as he stands on the edge. His feet rest on the middle rail, his legs leaning against the top as he bends forward. And that tilt is the only thing keeping him in place. He has his arms outstretched; his fingers splayed. And he's singing. 'My Heart Will Go On', by Céline Dion.

Griffin notices Cara arrive out of the corner of his eye.

'He thinks he's on the fucking *Titanic*,' Griffin throws backwards to her. He doesn't dare take his eyes off Ollie.

'He … what?' She strains to hear. 'Negotiator is fifteen minutes out.'

'We haven't got that long,' Griffin replies.

Griffin takes a few steps forward, tentatively joining in with the song. Ollie turns and, catching sight of Griffin, laughs hysterically into the wind.

'You're here, Jack!' he shouts. 'Are you going to save me?'

'I'd like to help,' Griffin calls back. He's alongside him now. He considers his options: maybe sneaking up behind, grabbing him off the railing. But if he mis-times it, even by a fraction of a second, Ollie will go over.

'I don't need saving!' Ollie shouts again.

Griffin starts to shiver, the cold cutting through his shirt. It's freezing up here; Ollie's lips are blue, his skin pale.

'Come down,' Griffin shouts. 'Let's talk in the warm.'

Ollie chuckles again. 'I like you, Jack! But there's no space for you on my life raft. You can go back the way you came. I'm fine.' He stands up straighter and wobbles; Griffin's stomach lurches.

But Ollie just shouts with glee.

'Look at it, Jack! Look at the colours and the sunshine. Look at the rainbows.'

There is no sunshine. There are certainly no fucking rainbows. Oliver is high. Tripping off his tits. Fuck knows what he's taken, but reality has well and truly left the building.

'There's more light the higher you go. I can get to heaven. I can fly.'

He leans forward again. Griffin takes a step closer. He can see over the edge of the building, down to the concrete below. They're on the fifth floor, although they only need a fraction of those. A memory sparks: a man, early in his career, having jumped from three floors up, landing face down on the concrete. His head caved in, body mush; blood and brain spilling across the pavement as Griffin attempted CPR.

Griffin can hear a crowd below. People shouting, their voices lost in the wind.

'How did you get up here, Ollie?' he asks, just to keep him talking.

'I flew!' Oliver pauses, his voice quieter: 'I took the lift. I didn't like the lift.' He looks at Griffin, his pupils dilated, black holes to his soul. 'No rainbows in the lift.' He bends his knees to jump.

'Ollie! Oliver!' He turns. 'I know where there are more rainbows.'

'You do?'

'Yes. But you need to come down from there.'

Oliver frowns. 'Don't arrest me. I don't want you to stop me flying. You'll put me in a cell where the crocodiles go.'

'I promise I won't put you in a cell. I want you to be safe. Come with me. I'll find you more rainbows.'

But Ollie isn't listening any more. He's singing again, his arms outstretched. Griffin takes a tentative step closer. He glances back to Cara. She's watching, the phone clamped to her ear, her free hand over her mouth. She shakes her head, although he's not sure what she's saying. Don't do anything stupid? There's no one coming to help? Probably both.

He looks back to Oliver. He's not paying Griffin any attention, so he edges closer. He's an arm's reach from him now, the boy swaying to and fro on the railing in time with the song.

It all happens in a split second. No thought, just action. Oliver reaches a crescendo, a strange screeching warble as he opens his arms to the empty air. He bends his legs and Griffin realises: he's going to bloody do it. The crazy sod thinks he can fly.

But Griffin's reactions are quicker. His reach further as he dives towards Ollie. His body comes in contact with the railings, a painful knock to the ribs as his hand closes on the

389

back of the boy's shirt. There's a rip; Griffin feels a crack and a bolt of pain charges across his hand, but something holds as Oliver tilts desperately over the edge.

'No!' he cries out. 'Let me fly! I can fly!'

Any moment now the shirt will split and Oliver will plunge to his death. Every muscle in Griffin's arm strains; he grabs out with his other hand but only manages to catch the belt of the boy's trousers. Griffin feels wrenched in two as gravity attempts to take its victim. He pulls as hard as he can to get Oliver back to solid ground, but his muscles shake. He can't.

'Oliver, grab the railing,' he shouts. But his pleas fall on deaf ears – Ollie is laughing, almost wriggling in Griffin's grip.

He can't. But he must. He grits his teeth, holds tight. He can see the concrete five storeys down; his feet are slipping on the gravel. If he doesn't let go, Oliver will take Griffin down with him, but if he does, Oliver will fall.

He feels his grip weakening, and just in the moment when all must be lost, the weight lessens. Uniformed officers lean over the railings, hauling Oliver back; Cara is behind Griffin, her arms around him, anchoring him to the roof.

The boy is struggling, crying out in anger, in frustration as he's forced down, restrained against the concrete. Griffin steps back to safety, shaking, body buzzing. His right hand, the one that first made contact with Oliver, feels stiff and unnatural. He flexes his fingers. A burn of agony follows, accompanied by nausea. He examines his finger in the dim light: it's definitely out of line with the others.

'You've broken it,' Cara says. 'We'll get you a paramedic.'

'I'm fine—'

'You're not.'

Cara leads him away, Griffin cradling his sore hand. Oliver is defeated, sobbing on the ground, uniforms standing guard in case he makes a bid for the drop again. Griffin knows he'll be taken to hospital to be assessed, possibly detained under section 136 of the Mental Health Act.

They arrive back in the office, where the grey faces of Brody, Shenton and Jamie wait. Griffin feels almost weak with shock and exertion. He collapses into a chair, clasping his shaking hands together under the table.

'He's okay,' Cara tells them. Sighs of relief as another woman rushes in. Griffin knows her from the analytics team – their manager.

'I just heard ... Ollie ...' she says. 'Is he okay?'

'He's fine. For now, at least.' Cara encourages her to sit down; she slumps, her face flushed.

'I had no idea that he was suicidal. He always seemed like such a good-natured chap. Eager to please.'

'That's the impression we got too.' Cara glances to Griffin. 'But I don't think he was trying to kill himself.'

The woman looks confused. 'What do you mean? I heard he was on the roof. Threatening to throw himself off.'

Griffin takes over. 'He said he was going to fly. He was on something.'

'Oliver? No!' She's shocked. 'He's the healthiest person I know. Doesn't even drink. He's been with you guys for nearly a week, you must have seen that too. Those ridiculous salads he packs for lunch. The running.'

'He's only young. We all do foolish things ...'

'Not Oliver. There's no way he would take anything. Especially not while he's at work.'

Griffin gets up and heads across to Oliver's workstation. Underneath, his navy blue rucksack. He picks it up and carries it to Cara's office, plonking it on the desk.

'We can't …' the manager says. 'That's an invasion of his privacy.'

'I stopped him jumping off a roof. I'll take whatever he wants to throw at me.'

Using his good hand, Griffin opens the top. Cara helps him; they put gloves on and unload the contents of the bag onto her desk. There's not much. A tattered diary, a few pens. Balled-up tissues. His lunchbox, the remains of kale and quinoa inside. Soggy running gear, scrunched up into a plastic bag. Griffin turns his attention to the front compartment – two energy gels drop out. One raspberry flavour, one lemon.

'He uses them when he goes running,' the manager explains. 'They contain glucose or carbs or something.'

Griffin picks one up. It's unopened; he turns his attention to the bag with the dirty running gear. And the two empty foil wrappers inside. He unfurls one and holds it to the light. He can just see a series of tiny pinholes – in the packaging. He thinks about Peter Jessop – the bridge jumper who believed he was taking drugs that would help him – and imagines someone tampering with the energy gel, inserting who knows what into the mix.

He grimly places it in an evidence bag, anger flaring. It was bad enough when this killer was going for innocent members of the public, but now he's gunning for their team?

It confirms one thing to Griffin. They're getting close.

Chapter 71

The atmosphere in the incident room is muted, tension palpable in the air. Griffin leaves to see a paramedic and returns with his hand bandaged, refusing to go to the hospital.

'They said it's fine,' he mutters. Cara knows there's no point arguing but forces a can of full-fat Coke into his hand.

'You need the sugar,' she whispers. He accepts it without debate.

'This is all so weird,' Brody says. She picks up the evidence bag and holds it up to the light; they're waiting for it to be collected. 'Do you think these have been tampered with?'

'It's the only explanation I can think of,' Cara says.

'Assuming he didn't do it himself,' Brody interjects. 'To throw off suspicion.'

All eyes turn to Brody, Cara's included.

'We don't know much about Ollie, do we?' Brody continues. 'Other than what his manager has told us.'

'What are you saying? That he's our killer?'

'Just a theory.' Brody shrugs. 'This department has a record.'

Cara feels a prickle of guilt. Griffin glares at Brody.

'What?' she says, unabashed. 'It's true.'

'It is,' Cara replies, recovering quickly. 'We can't rule anything out, but let's give Ollie the benefit of the doubt. The guy did nearly throw himself off our roof. What do we know? Have you managed to get anything useful from Mr Randall?' she directs to Griffin.

Griffin scowls. 'He's admitted all victims were customers of his pharmacy, but it's hardly concrete evidence. The security there is deplorable. The alarm codes haven't been changed in years and the keys could have been copied at any time. The search of his house is ongoing, nothing so far. And the uniforms are yet to report back from the pharmacy where they've started a full stocktake.'

'The pharmacy assistant has come in for her voluntary interview,' Jamie says. 'I could find out more from her?'

Cara nods. 'Make sure she's under caution. She could be a suspect.'

'On it.'

They all move to go, but Shenton stops them.

'Do you think …' he starts, then pauses, thinking. 'Do you think that targeting Ollie could be personal?'

'Go on,' Cara prompts.

'Well …' Shenton flushes. 'We know Hammond's death was suspicious – it felt deliberate. Like our killer knew he was talking to us. So, maybe Ollie was the same. Brody's right. Well, not right, but she has a point. If he was targeted, how? He's been here all day.'

'He went for a run at lunchtime,' Cara says.

'Where? Perhaps he found something important. I could have a look on his computer?'

'Do it. Thank you, Toby. Thank you, everyone,' Cara

adds. 'I know it's late, but we're making headway. I feel it.'

The team move off to their various tasks, leaving Cara sitting alone at the table. What happened to Oliver has shaken her; her team could be at risk. It's chilling. That this killer is reaching them, somehow, in the middle of a police station.

And any one of them could be next.

Chapter 72

'I don't think this is necessary,' Mrs Jenkins says, her eyes darting around the interview room. 'I told you everything before.'

'Just a formality,' Jamie replies, plastering on a friendly smile. 'Now if I could finish the paperwork.'

She nods and listens as Jamie goes through the final few cautions for the voluntary interview. Brody points to the form and she signs.

'You're recording this?'

'You'll get a copy to take away. Now, if we could ask you—'

'Is this to do with his wife's death? I thought the police dealt with that in December.'

'This is about a separate—'

'Tell us about that?' Brody interrupts, throwing an apologetic glance at Jamie. 'Did you work for Mr Randall at that time?'

'I did. Yes. Assistants come and go, but the two of us have worked together for ages.' She pauses, lost in thought. 'Not now though. If this gets out.'

'And what do you remember?'

'Poor Mr Randall. He had an awful few years. His wife was sick and getting worse. He had to be by her bedside more and more. Leaving me in the pharmacy.'

'By yourself? How did you dispense the medication?'

'The customers were understanding. They'd drop off their prescriptions, I'd put them together, and then Mr Randall would come in when he could to check them. Very efficient he was.'

'And if someone needed something urgently?'

'Oh, then Paul would help.'

Jamie looks up. 'The son? He was a pharmacist too?' Jamie looks at Brody. She returns his surprised expression.

'Ran in the family,' Jenkins confirms. 'So you know then … that he's dead?'

'We heard.'

'All so sad. Mrs Randall had just died, then Paul committed suicide. Or we're not supposed to put it that way, are we? Committed suicide. Killed himself. Never said why.'

'Did he leave a note?'

'Not that I heard. Such a weird way to do it. But he'd know the best approach, being a pharmacist. And he couldn't get near the morphine, not at that time. After all the discrepancies—'

'What discrepancies?' Jamie interrupts her, but she carries on regardless.

'Mr Randall was devastated after that. He was completely alone. Except for that good for nothing—'

'Sorry, Mrs Jenkins. What discrepancies?'

She stops. 'The stocktake? Didn't I mention it before? That's why you police did the post-mortem. Because of the

397

missing morphine.' She tuts. 'I'd have thought you guys would speak to each other. But he was cleared, wasn't he? Couldn't have done it. Was with Paul at the time.'

'That was his alibi? His son?'

'The son that then killed himself?' Brody clarifies.

'That's the one.'

'Excuse us for a moment.'

Jamie gets up, Brody following. Jamie texts Cara and they wait in the corridor. It doesn't take long: quick footsteps and Cara arrives, Griffin and Shenton with her.

'What's this about missing morphine?'

Jamie relays what they've found out, Griffin flicking through the file in his hand.

'So why didn't they prosecute the wife's murder?' Cara asks.

'Here it is,' Griffin says. 'I pulled the original file after we brought Randall in. It says telemetry on the car confirmed Randall's location on the day, and CCTV at Tesco confirmed both George and Paul Randall were there at the time of death.'

'Both husband and son leave the wife to go shopping? When she's that ill? To me that sounds like they gave her the morphine and left her to die.'

'CPS said, and I quote "it wasn't in the public interest to prosecute".'

Cara sighs with annoyance. 'And now someone's going around killing vulnerable people.'

'But it can't be Paul, for obvious reasons,' Jamie says. 'And I don't believe it's Randall. He's not strong enough to pull Hammond into a tree to hang him, for one. And look at the technology needed on Isabel Warner's case. You're telling me Randall knew how to do something like that? He's not

398

on any social media. He doesn't even have a smartphone.'

The door opens behind them and they all jump. Mrs Jenkins pokes her head out.

'Er, detectives,' she says. 'I couldn't help but overhear your conversation.'

'Sorry, Mrs Jenkins,' Jamie says, trying to persuade her back in the room. 'If you could wait inside—'

'Have you spoken to the other one?'

They all stop and stare. 'The other what?' Cara asks slowly.

'The other son. It's called Randall and Sons for a reason,' she scoffs gently. 'Plural. There were two of them.'

Chapter 73

Cara returns Mrs Jenkins to the interview room. She seems to be revelling in the attention now and pauses, fluffing up her hair.

'Tell me about this other son,' Cara says, sitting down in front of her. Jamie leans against the wall behind, waiting, while Griffin has gone back to speak to Randall. 'What's his name?'

'Younger of the two. Heard he had problems. But I never met him myself.'

'What's his name?' she says again, struggling to keep the impatience out of her voice. She's gripping the edge of the table so tightly her hands ache.

Mrs Jenkins frowns. 'D something. David? No. Donald?'

Cara turns to Jamie. 'Go find out how Griffin's getting on with Randall.'

'No point asking him, honey. George pretends he's dead.'

The door opens and closes as Jamie leaves.

'Why's that?' Cara asks.

'George says it was because he stole from him. Money, jewellery. Even nicked his keys and broke into the pharmacy once. But all he got was a few boxes of amoxicillin.' She laughs. 'Can hardly sell those on the street.' She lowers her head conspiratorially. 'But I think George threw him out because he was ... you know?'

'What?'

'G-A-Y.' She spells it out in a whisper. 'Not that there's anything wrong with that, in this day and age. George was always so set on his sons following in his footsteps – he called it Randall and Sons from the beginning. Talk about the weight of expectation.' She chuckles. 'But then George said he came home early from work one day and this kid – Daniel? Dominic? No. This kid was on the sofa with another man. And they were doing ... *that*.' She whispers the last word. 'Randall couldn't stand it. Kicked him out. Says that was the day his boy died. He can't have been older than fourteen, maybe fifteen at the time. Course, it wasn't long until one of his boys actually did die. The tragedy of that.'

A quick knock on the door and Griffin comes back in. He shakes his head.

'Told you,' Mrs Jenkins says happily.

'All no comments,' Griffin confirms. 'Except to say that both his sons are dead.'

'Mrs Jenkins ...' Cara says. 'Please.'

She scrunches her face up. 'It was kind of Scottish. Dougal. No—'

'Douglas?' Griffin interrupts.

Mrs Jenkins' eyes light up. 'Yes! Dougie. That's what they all called him.'

Chapter 74

Griffin's out of the interview at a run, phone clamped to his ear calling for a deployment to Dougie's address. Patrol cars are dispatched and, while Griffin anxiously waits, he dives back into the interview room where Randall is sitting.

'Your son. Tell me about him.'

The man's face is stubborn. 'I don't have a son. They're both dead. As I said.'

'We know you helped your wife kill herself.' Griffin leans forward, his hands resting on the table, his face almost next to Randall's. 'We didn't bring any charges at that time, but in light of new information discovered today I may feel the need to ask the CPS to rethink. Unless you start talking now.'

Randall looks to his solicitor, who nods.

Randall clears his throat. 'Dougie is the bad apple in the barrel. The one who rots the others, and I'm not sorry he's out of my life. We always had problems with him. As a baby he did nothing but scream. Paul had been an absolute dream, eight hours' sleep a night, but Dougie? Didn't like being picked up, didn't like being left in his cot. Cried, all the time. As a toddler he bit, punched, wouldn't do anything we asked. And school was the same. Even at primary. How often can a parent say that? That their child got expelled from primary school.'

'Why did he get expelled?'

'He inflated the class hamster.'

'Sorry?'

'Inflated it. Sealed his mouth around the poor mite's head, and blew.'

Even the solicitor raises his eyebrows at that one.

'Whole class had to go home early,' Randall continues. 'They told us Dougie wasn't welcome back, but that they'd keep quiet about the reason why, so we could get him into another school. So we did. But it didn't stop there. Reports of bullying. Fights. The lot. His poor mother … What he put her through. The worry.'

Randall swallows hard. 'Then the day I came home to … to *that* … was the day he died. To see that depravity, in my own living room.' He shudders, and Griffin stifles the urge to roll his eyes. 'Mike was my mate from darts. Dougie invited him around and … and … I think he did it to get to me. He knew I'd be home at that time. Poor Mike.'

Mike gets a blow job from a fourteen-year-old, and the kid is the one kicked out? Somebody's fucked up, Griffin thinks, and for the first time he feels a pang of sympathy for Dougie.

'I told him to leave and never return,' Randall continues. 'To his credit, it's the only request he's ever complied with.'

'When was the last time you saw him?'

'In November. At Gillian's funeral. We didn't speak.'

'Did Paul keep in touch with him?'

Randall purses his mouth, tight as a cat's bum. 'I believe so, yes.'

'Did he go to Paul's funeral?'

'I thought he would. But no.'

'And does he have access to your pharmacy? Has he ever been there? Would he know the alarm code?'

Randall pales. 'You don't think … He …'

'Answer the question, Mr Randall. Could Dougie have access to your pharmacy?'

'Y-Yes,' he stutters. 'He could. Yes.'

Griffin leaves the interview room, his mind reeling. He's learned nothing in the course of his career – the old adage of *assume nothing, believe nothing, challenge everything* that Cara drilled into him in those early days was forgotten the moment he met Dougie. All Griffin saw was an unlucky kid putting his life back together. He trusted every word he said. Had that all been an act? His father would like them to believe Dougie was a skilled manipulator, a psychopath from a young age, but did Griffin believe it? After everything he's seen, all the evil, the depravity, Griffin knows it's not that simple.

Cara meets him at the door to the incident room. It's quiet, eerily so, after the bustle and action of the day.

'Go home,' she says.

'But Dougie—'

'He's not at the address you gave us. Nobody's seen him since lunchtime. We've got an alert out. A fresh team are interviewing his housemates. He'll resurface soon enough.'

'And Ollie?'

'In hospital, but the doctor says he'll make a full recovery. He went there, Nate. To Dougie's house.'

'But how?'

404

'Shenton put it together. Dougie's name was on the list of volunteers, but as Dougie Morgan, not Randall. Ollie did some digging, discovered that this Dougie Morgan had no background and went to the address given by the helpline. Somehow, I don't know exactly, Dougie managed to spike his energy gels with LSD.'

'LSD? Fucking hell.'

'Ollie requested Isabel Warner's phone records from Charlie before he went up to the roof. And Morgan was Dougie's mother's maiden name. Ollie must have made the connection.' She places a hand on his arm. 'You look like shit,' she says with a smile.

'So do you. Have you heard any—'

'No.' She cuts him off. 'Let it go,' she whispers. 'Go home. Get some sleep.'

Griffin's about to protest, but realises he's exhausted. Awake the whole night before, he hasn't slept properly in days. He leans forward, gives his sister a quick hug, then leaves.

He notices the vintage BMW has left and hopes that Jamie is getting some rest as he climbs into his Land Rover. He drives almost subconsciously, his mind churning the events of the last few days. Neil Lowe, dead. George Randall, not the man Griffin thought he was. But, Griffin thinks with a sting, who knows what anyone will do when pushed to the edge.

The car lot is quiet as Griffin parks up and walks towards his flat. But even before he gets there something doesn't feel right. He stops, looks around. Nothing seems out of place.

Putting his paranoia down to lack of sleep he trudges down the metal steps to his flat. And it's then that he notices the smell. Chemical, disturbing – it catches at the back of his throat, making him cough.

It's petrol.

His footsteps slow. At the bottom of the stairs, the door is ajar, and he cautiously pushes it open.

The room is in darkness, except for a single beam of light coming from a torch, resting on the table. His hand goes out to the light switch.

'I wouldn't do that if I were you,' a voice says.

The torch is lifted, and a ghostly face appears. A man, sitting at his table, his clothes wet, his hair plastered to his forehead.

'Turn the light on and this whole place will go up.'

Griffin pauses. The man smiles.

Griffin coughs, trying to clear the petrol fumes from his airway. 'What are you doing here, Dougie?' he asks.

Chapter 75

By the glow of torchlight, Dougie's face looks demonic, eerie shadows throwing the contours of his nose and cheekbones into points. He smiles – calm, accepting, gentle. It chills Griffin to the core.

'Sit down,' Dougie says, gesturing to the seat opposite him.

Griffin pauses. A grey glow from the only window reflects off the puddles around his feet, the pooling on the wooden table. The whole place is doused in petrol; if it catches they're both going up in flames.

There's no sign of Frank.

'If you're looking for your cat, he went out the window when I arrived,' Dougie says. 'A hell of a lot more gracefully than I came in.'

'You climbed through the window?' Griffin replies, stalling for time.

Dougie ignores his question. 'Sit. Down,' he repeats, in a tone that tells Griffin this is no cry for help.

Slowly, he obeys.

'What do you want?' Griffin asks.

'My friend told me the police came to the house,' Dougie begins. 'Tried to arrest me. You're searching the place now. Interviewing them?'

Griffin nods. 'What will we find?'

'All the evidence you need. The computer I used to target Isabel. Keys to the other flats near Lisa Hobbs. Enough pharmaceuticals to render the most enthusiastic of addicts happy for months. LSD, oxy, you name it. You'll arrest a few of my housemates, I presume.'

Despite the circumstances, Griffin feels a thrill. He keeps quiet, hoping Dougie will continue his confession.

'What gave it away?' Dougie asks.

'*GetHelpNow*. The helpline. And your brother.'

Dougie nods slowly. 'Paul. Poor sod. But at least he had the guts. To kill himself after what he'd done to Mum.'

'So he did kill her?'

'Him and Dad. They said she asked them to, but ... I don't know. Mum would never have wanted that. She wouldn't have risked either of them getting into trouble with the police, but who knew!' He cackles. 'Who knew that the police would be too stupid anyway? Have you worked it out? How they did it?'

'Morphine?'

'In her insulin pump. Smart, when you think about it. Cut off the insulin and her blood glucose becomes deranged, which means the pump responds with more morphine. An upward spiral. Change it all back when they return. Paul was always her favourite. Ironic that he'd be the one to kill her.' His gaze drifts into the middle distance. He looks so young, so vulnerable, sitting here. Griffin has to remind himself that this is no child. He's twenty-two, and he's killed eight people.

'Why did you do it, Dougie?'

Dougie's focus snaps back. He stares at Griffin.

'Why did you kill Isabel? She was your friend.'

'Friend?' Dougie says with a sneer. 'She wasn't my friend. Spoilt cow. Coming to our house. Smoking our weed and pulling the poor little rich girl act. Sure, she'd had a hard time with her stepdad, who hasn't?' He doesn't wait for an answer, ploughs on. 'Do you know what happened to me, the night my father kicked me out? I ended up down a cold alleyway, shivering. Just the clothes on my back. No money, nothing. Some bloke took pity on me and offered to buy me a drink. Dodgy bar, but I thought okay, what could go wrong. Shall I tell you what went wrong?' His eyes flare. 'I ended up back in that alleyway, trousers around my ankles, blood running down my legs. That's abuse. That's rape. But did I go running back to Daddy? No, I fucking did not.' He juts a finger towards the outside, towards the garage. 'Issy had a father who loved her. Who gave her an allowance, a roof over her head. And she wasted that opportunity by snorting it up her nose. No, she deserved to die. And all it took were a few messages on social media.'

'How did you know how to do that?'

'A screw-up like me, you mean? I learned, I studied.' He scoffs. 'And it helps that I live in a house full of people from all walks of life. Pickpockets, thieves. And computer hackers. Show interest and everyone is keen to share. Even you, Nate Griffin. With your sob story about your addiction. How is that going now?'

He smiles and Griffin remembers the beers given to him on that awful night. And the ones consumed since.

'What about the others, Dougie?' Griffin says, his voice

barely more than a whisper. 'Your other victims. What did they do to you?'

'Me? Who says they did anything to *me*?'

'You killed them,' Griffin says, temper bubbling in the face of Dougie's games. 'You persuaded them to kill themselves. You took Colin Jefferies to a railway station—'

'Colin? A man who hadn't left his flat in years.' Dougie laughs. 'Jefferies was an experiment. One that worked better than my wildest dreams. Who knew he'd fall on the rails. Best thing he ever did, ending up under that train—'

'And Kate Avery? Eileen Avery?'

'Kate Avery's brain would have become riddled with dementia before long, in the same way her mother's had. I just sped up the process. Broke into her house, moved a few things around, took her car keys. Got her brain properly addled. Jessop was a mess, whinging about his schizophrenia. Ken Laker was glad to go, but he was a nasty piece of work. A lifetime of rape and sexual assault. My little favour to Isabel. To balance the scales.' He pauses, smug. 'No way was I letting him go peacefully. You should have seen the look on his face when he came back from raping that girl. Positively salivating.'

'So what about Lisa Hobbs?' Griffin struggles to keep his voice level. 'What you put that girl through? You must have some empathy for her?'

'She would have been in and out of mental hospitals her whole life. Suicide attempt after attempt. What she needed was a big dose of reality to finish the job.'

Griffin's stomach turns. He tastes bile. The complete psychopathy of this man. He has no empathy, no consideration for others' pain. What he's done to all these people.

'We all experience grief,' Dougie snaps. 'We all lose the ones we love. But we don't spend our time moping about it. Make a decision. Move on or move out.' His face turns sad. 'Would you include my mother as one of the victims?'

'We'll charge your father with her murder.'

'But it was my neglect that killed her. I should have fought harder. Fucking Dr Hammond. I would have killed him eventually, but you guys let him go and he seemed so fucking *happy*.' He spits that last word. 'I enjoyed stringing him up, watching him suffer.'

Griffin swallows, choking down the saliva flooding his mouth. *Focus*, he tells himself, his head swimming from the fumes. *Focus*.

Dougie continues, unaware of Griffin's discomfort.

'It was his fault. If Hammond had spent longer attending to the patients that mattered, then maybe Mum would have survived. It took months for her cancer to be diagnosed. And by that time half the options for treatment had gone. It was everyone else that killed her. The people clogging up A and E, the doctor's surgeries with their so-called illnesses. Their *problems*.'

'Their problems were as valid as your mother's. They were ill. They were sick. Just because it's not visible in the same way—'

'That's utter shite!' he bellows, Griffin's argument hitting a nerve. 'Everyone nowadays has autism, or ADHD, or some other made-up illness, invented solely to make millions for the pharmaceutical industry. It's all bollocks. This pathetic black parade of misery and torment. They're the weak. I did us all a service, carrying out my cull. People like Issy. And Colin Jefferies. All he needed was a kick up the arse. I got him out of the house within half an hour—'

411

'You drugged him. You abducted him.'

'No more than he deserved. Than all of them deserved.' He pauses, then reaches into his pocket and pulls out something small and silver. Griffin's heart jumps. A Zippo lighter.

'I should have known that helpline would be my downfall. They all phoned. And I'd talk to them. I'd be understanding, sympathetic to their woes, while all the time delicately prodding them towards their deaths.' Dougie opens the top of the lighter with a click, revealing the flint and the wheel. Griffin tenses. Every synapse in his body wants to leap up, get out of there, but he doesn't dare move.

'You need to tell my story,' Dougie says.

'Tell them yourself.' Griffin slowly reaches a hand forward. 'Give me the lighter, Dougie.'

Dougie shakes his head, then places the Zippo, open, unlit, on the table in front of him. The beam from the torch dances on the dented silver. Tantalisingly close, too far away.

'You're going to tell my story. Or DCI Elliott will, depending on how stupid you are. Try and wrestle this off me and the whole place will go up, you included. But leave me alone …'

His finger reaches to the wheel.

Griffin takes a long breath in. 'I'm not going anywhere.'

Dougie narrows his eyes. 'So be it. That DCI is smart, your sister. I followed her for a while, did you know that? Watched her. But she was a poor candidate for my fun. Kids, husband. Even you to look after her. She'll be sad if you die with me. But I have no doubt: she'll work it out for herself. And then everyone will know.'

'Will know what?'

'That actions have consequences. For people like my

mum. Even after my father kicked me out, she stayed in touch. Sent me money. I took her name, started afresh. And she came to see me once I got settled. Every week, without fail. She loved me, unconditionally. She was the only one that believed in me, that made me feel like … like I mattered. Paul made sure I saw her, even after she got ill. Let me know when the coast was clear, when Dad was at work. And when she died, I knew I had to do something.'

He picks up the lighter, thoughtfully, turning it around in his hand.

'What I did to those people, what I'm going to do tonight – it'll make everyone out there think twice. So the next time they feel a bit off colour, or their tiny delicate head hurts and they demand an appointment with their GP, they'll realise that they are taking that time away from someone who needs it. Someone like my mum. Who was too caring and considerate not to argue when the first appointment she was offered was three weeks away. When she was ignored, pushed to the back of the queue. So yes. They needed to die.'

'That's all this is?' Griffin says, dismayed. 'An argument about the NHS?'

Dougie's eyes flare. 'Not the fucking NHS. It's about society, and how selfish we've all become. About how we all demand everything for ourselves, without a single thought for others. Look at me. I'm hardly the paragon of good mental health. What would you diagnose?'

Griffin stalls for time, deciding whether to play his game.

'Go on,' Dougie prompts. 'I won't be offended.'

'PTSD for a start. Some sort of personality disorder. Psychopathy.'

'Psychopathy's not a diagnosis, but I take your point. And do I go to the doctor? Do I cry for help?'

'You should. We can—'

'No! You can't. There is no *cure*. This is just me. That's why I'm doing it this way. If I let you arrest me, you'll lock me up. Maybe even put me in a psychiatric hospital. And that's more resources, more money that should be going to someone else.'

'Why should you decide who gets that money, Dougie? Everyone needs help. Mentally, physically. It's not up to you. I'm not going to let you kill yourself today.'

Griffin's heart jumps as Dougie holds the lighter out. 'And why not? I'm not stupid. This isn't going to be an easy death, I know that. The agony of self-immolation, as the fire burns my skin away, the pain before my nerves are obliterated. If I'm lucky, I'll die quickly, suffocating as the flames destroy my lungs. But nothing gets more publicity than death by fire.' His thumb hovers over the wheel. 'Why do you give a shit?'

'Why should you get to choose when your victims didn't?'

Dougie eyes him warily. 'It was still their choice. With the exception of poor old Hammond, I didn't put the gun in Kate Avery's hand. I didn't force Issy to down those pills. We all have free will. But some of us choose to take the easy way out. Like your colleague.'

'Ollie is fine, Dougie. We know what you did. We're looking after him.'

'Not Mr Maddox.' He pauses. 'Actually, l kind of liked him. He had a positivity I admired. Stupid idiot. Tracking me down and coming to the house all by himself. I think I convinced him by the end of our conversation. But then he asked to use the toilet, and that energy gel fell out of his pocket so I thought, "Why not?". Live in a happy family of drug dealers and you'll always have a needle and syringe and some liquid LSD to hand – it didn't take long to inject a wee bit inside. What happened?'

Griffin keeps quiet, not wanting to give Dougie the pleasure.

But Dougie shrugs. 'Whatever. I just wanted to distract him. It obviously worked. No, he was fun. But your other one. All that pathetic moping around. After everything he had done – or not done. Couldn't see the killer right under his nose.'

Griffin's blood chills. 'Who are you talking about?'

He laughs: an amused snort. 'See? Useless, the lot of you. I've been building a bomb. All the pieces he needs to self-destruct. People are predictable, more than you would ever believe. A suggestion here, a pointed question there. Thoughts subtly infused into their brains where they niggle and itch. Breed and multiply. Their own minds work against them, they collapse and spiral.

'They don't sleep; insomnia reduces the sane to mush, what must it do to the crazy? Then all I need to do is insert the blasting cap, the trigger, the dead man's switch. And it's over. He'll be at home now, your colleague. Drinking the bottle of vodka I left him, looking for any way, the best way, to numb the pain. He could be dead already, for all we know. Chilling out, up above, with his *poor dead wife*.'

Dougie says these last words slowly. And in one second, Griffin realises what he's done. That complaint. The break-in at the house. A systematic campaign to crack one man.

Jamie.

'You have a choice,' Dougie continues. 'Leave now, and you might be in with a chance of saving him. But carry on talking, try and stop me, and there will be nothing you can do. Jamie will die, and I will burn this godforsaken hovel to the ground, taking you and me with it. That's your choice. That's on you.'

There can only be one decision. Griffin stands up, slowly backing away from Dougie, who holds the lighter in front of him like a talisman. And then he turns, he runs. And as he takes the stairs two at a time he hears the click of the lighter. The whoosh of flames as the fireball follows Griffin up the stairwell. And Dougie's screams as he burns to his death.

Jamie

Jamie can't bear it any longer, surrounded by all these crime scenes, the photographs, the victims. Reminding him of the one thing he is not brave enough to do.

He walks away from work. His mind is dull, bleached of all rational thought. The only sure thing is the knowledge that nothing benefits from him being here. Nobody will miss him, the opposite. He is a burden, for no one to bear.

He drives back to the house. He debates ploughing the powerful BMW into a tree, jumping red lights, but he doesn't want to risk hurting someone else, or even surviving. He waits for the garage to open and carefully parks up, closing the door again with the press of a button. He unlocks the dividing door into the house and walks into the kitchen.

This feeling – this dark, lonely, horror of his everyday – has to end. He needs to do something, anything. Speak to someone. But who? Cara, Griffin, Brody – they're all engrossed in the case. And Cara and Griffin's mum has just died, they have enough on their plate. His mum? Her resulting panic will only make him feel worse. Adam and Romilly … What time is it in Australia? And what can they

417

do from there? They can't bring his wife back from the dead. They can't cure his broken mind, the grief that drags at his muscles, making him tired.

So tired.

Time does not heal. Time only accentuates the guilt, the regret. The birthdays you're not spending together, the evenings you suffer alone. Jamie's had enough.

He tries one number. His doctor's surgery. An automated voice tells him he's in a queue. He waits – five, ten minutes – before he hangs up. He sighs, every cell weary.

He stands in the kitchen, arms by his side, head bent. And that's when he sees it. A full bottle of vodka. And the keys to the BMW.

The car is warm and peaceful. With the garage door closed, he can't hear the road outside, the people that might disturb him. That might interrupt. No chance of that now.

He doesn't remember leaving the vodka there, on the side in the kitchen, but maybe he had. Maybe some part of his addled mind realised the link he needed to make, the plan he needed to form.

He is sitting in the passenger seat. It's felt wrong all day to be in the driver's side: this is Adam's BMW, not his. His natural spot is on the left, alongside his friend. He misses Adam, hopes his mate will forgive him for what he's about to do in his car. But what else is there? Where else can he go? There is no next.

He reaches down and picks up the bottle, resting it between his legs. He takes the packet from his pocket, the sleeping pills he nicked today from the pharmacy. One by one he pushes them from the pack and one by one he

Chapter 76

Griffin drives, his foot hard to the floor. Making calls to Cara, to Jamie, not getting through. At last, 999 confirms units have been dispatched but when he gets to Jamie's, uniforms mill in the road.

'Why isn't anyone inside?' Griffin shouts as he runs closer. The PCs shuffles awkwardly before one of them speaks up.

'Skipper said not to until we're sure it's safe.'

'It's not fucking safe, that's the whole point,' Griffin exclaims, but he doesn't wait for a response. He bashes on the metal garage door. Behind it he can hear the whirr of a powerful petrol engine. He shouts Jamie's name.

There's no reply.

He turns his attention to the house. A few swift kicks and he's in, the lock splintered, the front door flying open. Inside he can already smell the fumes.

He doesn't waste any time. He locates the inner door to the garage; again, locked, but again, nothing that will stop him. He's quickly in.

The fumes slap him in the face. He coughs, a spasm gripping his lungs and he bends double. He backs away, taking a lungful of fresh oxygen, then tries again.

The garage is dark; the open doorway from the kitchen throws shadows around the black BMW. Griffin gropes around to the front of the car, searching the wall for the control panel. He presses the button to open the garage. No response.

'Fuck,' he whispers.

He turns to the car and Jamie, slumped in the passenger seat. His head leans to one side, eyes closed. Griffin opens the door and grabs Jamie's shoulders, shaking him. He moves, groans, but doesn't open his eyes: alive, but only just. Griffin shuts the passenger door then runs around to the other side of the car and throws himself in the driver's seat, silencing the car's ignition. But it's not enough. The fumes hang in the air, suffocating them both. They need to get out – and fast.

Griffin's head is fuzzy. He leans over and shakes Jamie again. Now, nothing.

Jamie's a big bloke, over six feet, no chance Griffin can carry him out of there. Not quickly, at least. He needs another way.

His hand reaches for the ignition. And as it does, his phone rings. He answers.

'Cara? Get everyone out of the way of the garage.'

The car's 2.8 litre engine roars into life.

'Griffin, what are you doing? You're not—'

'Get everyone out of the way.'

He drops his phone into his lap where it instantly resumes its ringing. He ignores it. The engine growls. He looks at Jamie. His face is red, breathing non-existent.

He releases the handbrake and presses his foot hard on the accelerator.

The car bursts through the garage door, hitting it at full power with an ear-splitting crash, tyres squealing on the concrete, a screech of metal against metal. A shard of evening light breaks through as the door buckles in the middle and peels away from the runners. Glass shatters but he doesn't let up, leaving the door hanging in a mess of twisted steel as the BMW lurches forward, Griffin barely managing to brake in time. It lurches to a stop, the engine running, Griffin's heart beating hard.

Shocked faces run to the passenger door. It's pulled open. Air – beautiful cold freezing air – rushes in. It's never been more welcome and Griffin gulps at it, already feeling the fug in his head ease. An oxygen mask is placed over Jamie's face before he's carefully lifted from the car, paramedics checking his vital signs. And then, to Griffin's relief, he sees him stir. His eyes open, he thrashes in confusion but he's alive.

Griffin sits back in the driver's seat with relief. Cara comes up next to him.

'You twat,' she says.

'Like throwing a rock through tin foil,' he replies smugly, but his arrogance barely compensates for his shaking hands, the adrenaline coursing through his veins. 'These old beamers are made of granite. Did what I had to do.'

She tuts, then leans forward and gently touches above his left eye. It stings; her finger comes away bloodied. He's covered in glass from the windscreen, a shard has embedded itself in his forehead.

'Let's get you cleaned up,' Cara says, wearily.

She holds out a hand and he climbs out of the car. He takes a few steps then looks back at the mess. No airbags, no crumple zones, the old BMW did what it needed to do, but it won't be up to anything again soon. The bonnet is bent, headlights smashed. The mangled front is pressed up against the tyres; scratches and dents run the length of the bodywork.

'Look at the state of Bishop's car,' Cara comments. 'You can be the one to explain.'

Griffin nods. Jamie's being moved onto a stretcher, the oxygen mask over his face. His eyes are closed, but his chest is moving up and down in a reassuring rhythm.

'I'm sure Bishop won't complain,' he replies to Cara. 'I just saved his best mate.'

Chapter 77

Cara sits alone in the incident room, staring up at the whiteboard. At the smiling faces of Colin Jefferies, Isabel Warner, Kate Avery and her mother. The victims that started it all.

So many dead. And for what? So Dougie Morgan could burn himself to death, alone, in Griffin's basement flat. There had been no getting out of there alive. The quantity of petrol, the accessibility to the crime scene; they couldn't even get to the body for twenty-four hours after. The curled black husk was taken to the mortuary yesterday, now stored alongside his victims. So much death, for so little.

Griffin and Cara have agreed that Dougie's story will stay buried. Left in the burned-out shell that used to be Griffin's home. There is no purpose in sharing it with the world, no retribution to be sought. Just an insane mission

425

from a disturbed man.

George Randall was charged with murder and put on remand. The pharmacy has closed; he'll never work again. When Cara told him of Dougie's death, he looked up at her, his eyes bloodshot and watery.

'Both my sons were already dead,' he said. 'This changes nothing.'

Cara stands up and carefully takes the photograph of Colin Jefferies from the whiteboard. Randall was right – Dougie's death will never change the outcome, except Colin Jefferies' mother can be assured her son didn't kill himself. Ron Warner knows Isabel had hope in her future; David Hammond's family have justice; Ollie Maddox never intended to jump off that roof.

Cara's going to see Ollie later. He's out of hospital, staying with his mum. Shaken, confused, but alive. He's said he'd like to return to work, and Cara hopes that he will.

There's a knock on the door of the incident room and Cara looks around. To her surprise, DCS Halstead is standing there.

'I was just coming up to your office, ma'am,' Cara says.

Halstead smiles. 'Putting it off?'

Cara looks at her, curious. Her manner is soft, almost contrite.

'The chief constable wants to see you,' Halstead continues. 'To congratulate you on the successful conclusion to your investigation.'

Cara turns back to the board. Removes the photograph of Peter Jessop and adds it to the pile. 'It doesn't feel successful,' she replies.

'How is DS Hoxton?'

'Recovering. But better.'

426

'That's good. Tell him I'll sort that promotion. It should have been done weeks ago. No matter what the IOPC says. And DS Griffin?'

'At home. Taking a few days off before he comes back to the team.'

'Good. I like him. He's a blunt instrument, but useful.'

Cara laughs. 'I agree with that. And have you heard about Lee Goodwin?'

'A good result.'

Unexpected justice has been served. Dougie's flatmates, fearing arrest, turned on each other, implicating a man called Lee Goodwin in a rape from last year. Lisa Hobbs. He used to brag about it, late at night. Spilling the horrific details over a spliff and a six-pack of Stella. The original investigators had been on the right track – an ex-mechanic, a man of impotence and rage. He wouldn't be getting out any time soon.

'We were lucky,' Cara says.

'No such thing. Just good policework.'

Halstead moves to stand next to her. She reaches up and takes the photograph of Hammond down, looking at it. Cara waits.

'I should have trusted you,' her boss says at last. 'You were right.'

'We were both right. It wasn't Hammond. And I didn't trust my own judgement at times.'

'Well, you know now, don't you?' Halstead hands Cara the photograph and turns to leave. 'You're a good detective, Elliott. Nothing changes that. Take a few days yourself. See you on Monday.'

Cara agrees and her boss departs, the clack of her heels fading down the corridor. She goes back to the job at hand

and pulls the rest of the photos down, stacking them in a pile on the table, then wiping the black handwriting off with a cloth until two words remain.

SAVE ME

Peter Jessop's final words. *You can't save me*. And they hadn't. But maybe someone else would receive assistance in their hour of need.

The helpline is still running. New procedures, new checks in place, but they will carry on answering the call from whoever needs them. Whoever asks for help. Cara resolves to do the same. Look for the colleagues that might be struggling; help her brother get sober. As many times as he needs.

'You ready?'

Charlie this time, leaning in the doorway, a smile on his face. She grins back.

'Absolutely.'

Chapter 78

It was his home, on and off, for nearly three years. Where he was at his worst, when Mia had just died. When he was suspended from work and depressed and low and grieving. But now his sanctuary is no more than a blackened shell.

The fire crew have deemed it safe and Griffin ventures down the steep steps, the walls dripping with soot and water, the stench sticking in his lungs. But now he's here he's not sure why he bothered.

There's nothing. The kitchen is charcoal; his sofa reduced to a metal husk. Debris – wood, plaster, brick – lies in piles across the floor. There is nothing recognisable. From the practical to the personal, even the last few photos of his father in the shoebox on the top of his wardrobe: everything he owned has gone.

He stands in the middle of the room and rotates in a slow three-sixty. The light from the dirty window turns everything grey, dull tones reflecting in the puddles on the floor. He wonders why Dougie had chosen this location for his last showdown. Maybe he'd seen a kindred spirit in Griffin, or maybe his urge to destroy brought him here for a last hurrah. A desire to take everything of Griffin's before he went.

Either way, it doesn't matter now.

Griffin would have liked to have seen him in court, but he knows legal proceedings would have been tied up for years. Arguments of diminished responsibility. The laborious process of gathering the evidence across eight deaths to prove what he had done.

The lab has matched the DNA on the rope used to hang Hammond to Dougie's toothbrush. Footwear marks left at the scene correspond to a pair of Dougie's size ten Reeboks. As he said, the computer at the house is the one used to message Isabel. If they dig they would find more – cell tower pings from Dougie's mobile placing him at the superstore where Kate Avery's car was stolen, at the pharmacy at the dead of night – but what would be the point? He's dead.

Griffin's head aches from the events of the last few days. From residual carbon monoxide in his system, lack of sleep, who knows what else. And the choking stench from being here isn't helping.

He marches up the stairs to the fresh air. He's blinking in the bright sunlight at the top when a warm, welcome body wraps itself around his legs. He smiles and crouches down, stroking the length of the cat's warm fur. Frank pushes his head against his leg, purring.

'How've you been?' he asks. The cat looks at him reproachfully. 'Yeah, sorry about the flat,' he replies. 'But you can come with me, if you like?'

He tentatively puts his hands under Frank's tummy, expecting a scratch, but the cat doesn't protest as he gently lifts him to his chest. He carries Frank to the Land Rover,

430

opens the door; the cat jumps to the passenger seat. Griffin gets in next to him.

And, with the cat by his side, Griffin starts the engine and drives. He doesn't look back.

His home is at Cara's now, but he wants to keep busy. Once the cat is settled with a dinner of Cara's best smoked salmon, he drives across town to his mother's flat.

Miles lets him in, a few more trite platitudes and Griffin is heading down the corridor towards the empty cardboard boxes Miles has left outside the door.

'Label them up. A local charity will take them,' Miles had said, used to dealing with such things.

It's the least he can do, Cara already working on funeral arrangements, and he begins with their mother's wardrobe, pulling down wool skirts, warm pullovers, cotton tops, folding them and placing them inside. The smell of his mother is unmistakeable and for a moment he holds a blue cotton jumper against his face, inhaling her scent and remembering all the times as a child when he would wrap his arms around her middle, feel her gently caress his hair, kiss the top of his head. His father may not have been there for him growing up, but his mother always was. He wishes he could have thanked her for that. Told her he loved her one last time.

He gently places the cotton jumper inside the box and clears his throat, blinking hard. He turns his attention to a pile of books, dumping them in with the clothes. Her jewellery next – placed in a separate pile for Cara, along with the more personal items. He keeps nothing for himself.

431

The bottom shelf of the cupboard is packed with dusty photo albums. He rues the loss of the mementos of his father, reduced to soot in the fire, and pulls them out, hopeful. He remembers these from their bookcase at home; their mother with thick packs of photos from Boots spending evenings sticking photos behind the clear plastic covers, carefully labelling each one. At the time he wondered why she bothered, but now he pulls one out and sits on the too-soft bed, resting it on his lap. The first page says *1997 to* – the second year left unwritten. He would have been fourteen, Cara sixteen, and sure enough he opens the first page to a scowling, dark-haired, chicken-legged boy, wearing a T-shirt with Nirvana on the front. Never a fan of being photographed.

Griffin smiles at this kid. So cocky, so sure of himself. The next one is Cara and another girl. Her best friend at the time – Tara, Tanya? Who knows. He fancied some of Cara's friends at that age, not that he would have ever spoken to them. Cara's smiling warmly. Hair over her shoulders, she's wearing flared jeans, soggy at the hem, a dress inexplicably over the top. He flicks a few more pages, and here's one of their father. He's almost facing away from the camera, one hand resting on a car parked in their driveway, looking at something. He's smiling, in a way that Griffin hadn't seen often. Gently, almost lovingly, and with a jolt, Griffin realises his father was looking at him. He's a small figure in the distance, turned away, riding a red bike he remembers all too well.

Griffin stares at it. He's always assumed that he and Cara were a nuisance to his dad. No more than two small people getting in the way of his ridiculous plans and ideas. He rarely took them anywhere or engaged in conversation. Certainly didn't turn up for parents' evening or school plays.

But maybe, Griffin thinks now, looking at this photo – maybe he wanted to, just didn't know how. Griffin remembers how he felt in the grip of his own addiction. His health had been so compromised by the time he went into rehab, so turned hatefully into his own head, that thinking of someone else was impossible. Perhaps his dad had been that way, too.

Perhaps he had loved them. But so ill, the drugs and the bipolar messing with him so comprehensively, that he simply didn't know *how* to love. How to be a father or a husband. It wasn't Mark Griffin's fault. And it certainly wasn't Nate's.

He sighs and turns a few more pages. Photographs are few and far between as two teenagers grow up and refuse to pose. *Christmas, 1998*, one says. The last before their dad died. All smiling around a table. And here's one with Neil.

Griffin cranes forward. Cara has confirmed that the pathologist has ruled it natural causes. A heart attack, as they assumed. So Griffin's off the hook. Neil Lowe paid the ultimate price for what he did to their mum, natural justice has been served. He should move on, but for a moment he stares at Neil's face, trying to work out what he feels. Guilt, certainly. That he brought it on and dragged Cara into the mess. But otherwise, nothing.

He flips another page, finding it blank this time. When his father died, their mother stopped. Lost motivation or less time, Griffin would never know. But before he replaces it in the box, he notices a slip of paper sticking out of the cover. He opens it again and flips to the back.

It's a sheet of old yellowing A4 paper, the formal letterhead for the solicitors across the top. Jagged handwriting – a few words, written in biro.

He gapes at the page, then slumps back on the bed, the note clutched in his hand.

'Oh, Mum,' he says, quietly. 'What did you do?'

Chapter 79

When Jamie wakes, the world is blurry. He blinks; his head aches, a blinding thump behind his eyes. He can see bright overhead strip lights, blue. So much blue. He closes his eyes again, lets his mind drift. The squeak of rubber-soled shoes on lino, a distant murmur of conversation. He is confused but too lethargic to be worried. The world fades.

Next time he opens his eyes it is darker. Quiet. The steady trickle of conversation remains but the voices are closer. A woman and a man. Talking, next to him. The woman stops, footsteps fade away. But there's someone still there, gentle exhales, a rustle of clothing. He turns.

'Bishop,' he says.

'Welcome back.' His friend smiles gently. 'How are you feeling?'

The confusion returns. 'You're here? But how … You're in …' It's definitely Adam. A tanned, tired version, but him. 'What day is it?'

'Thursday night. Cara called. We took the first plane back from Sydney.'

'So, Romilly … She …'

'She's been in. Checked on you while you were asleep. She's at home now. Sorting the place out. How are you feeling?' he asks again.

Jamie lies back, taking stock. His head is thrumming, the exhaustion almost overwhelming. He feels nauseous, but his body is so empty there is nothing to expel.

'Like I've had the flu. But a hundred times worse.'

'You're in safe hands now.'

'You didn't have to come back. You shouldn't be here.'

Adam leans forward, resting his elbows on his knees and looking seriously at Jamie. 'We did. I shouldn't have left you. I didn't realise how bad things were.'

'Bad? I …' Jamie tries to think. He has no idea what happened, how he got here. He closes his eyes, scrunches his face into a tight frown. 'I remember being at home. And … and …' He can't say it. That crushing knowledge that nobody would miss him if he was gone. The guilt, the grief, the pain.

He wants to cry but he's numb. He turns his face away from his friend but Adam reaches out, placing a hand gently on his arm.

'Listen, Jamie,' Adam says. Jamie can't even bear to look at him, such is his shame. 'Romilly and I – we're here now. Anything you need, anything you want. We're here.'

'You don't have to—'

'No, don't give me that. You're family. You were there for me, when I … When I was stabbed. Through all the pain and the rehab and the crap after. I shouldn't have walked out on you. That's on me.' Jamie chances a look now. Adam's face is serious, his blue eyes dark. 'Cara—'

'Oh, God. I walked out in the middle of a murder investigation.'

436

'Cara doesn't care about that. She's worried about you. Besides, it's over. The guy … well. I'll explain later. That bastard,' Adam spits. 'What he did to you …'

'It was my fault,' Jamie whispers.

'He took advantage of you. You were vulnerable, and he made it worse. Getting the Blakes to put in the complaint, cancelling your doctor's appointment. They found footprints near the doctor's car. He was there, in the woodland. Watching.'

'I saw Pippa everywhere. Even her perfume.'

'That was him. When he broke into the house. He'd been following you. Taunting you.'

It all seems so insane. He can't think straight. 'I thought I was going crazy,' he says quietly. 'I thought it was her.'

'I'm sorry, no. Someone messing with your head. And Cara says you can have all the time off you need. Your job will be waiting for you when you're feeling better. And you *will* get better, Jamie. You'll look back on this one day and be glad that Griffin stopped you.'

'Griffin?'

'Yeah. He drove my car through the garage door.'

'He did?' Yet another reason to feel guilty, and Jamie's face falls. 'Is it … okay?'

Adam laughs. 'No, you wanker. It's a complete write-off. But don't worry about that. We're going to need a more family-friendly car now anyway.'

Adam grins and Jamie feels a rush of joy. Something he hasn't felt in a long time.

'You're …'

'Yes. Romilly's pregnant. A few months along, don't get too excited. So we didn't just come back for you. I was getting sick of the spiders.'

It makes Jamie feel better, somehow. He's shattered. He closes his eyes again. But he doesn't want to be alone.

'You're staying, right, Adam?' he whispers as he drifts off, safe as his friend confirms the only thing he wants to know.

'I'm not going anywhere, mate. You're going to feel better. Romilly and I are here, every step of the way. I promise.'

Chapter 80

Griffin sits next to Cara at her dining table, the piece of A4 paper in front of them. He'd presented it to her and she'd read it, before turning to him, astonished.

'Huh,' she'd said.

'Quite.'

And now here they are.

It is a page of their father's handwriting. Confused, rambling, some illegible, but the meaning is clear: when Mark Griffin drove off in his Ford Focus that night, he'd meant to kill himself.

Why, Griffin still isn't sure. He talks about having a mind that betrays him, how he hates being a burden on his family. How he loves his job, but can't concentrate; how he sees the way that Neil looks at him, contempt in his eyes. And he finishes with the words that he knows Cara is focusing on now, same as he did when he read it.

Tell Cara and Nate that I love them.

'So Mum knew,' Cara says. 'Do you think she told Neil?'

Griffin thinks for a moment. 'No,' he says. 'He would have told me. He confessed to killing Mum, why would he

439

hold back on this?'

'And she kept quiet ...'

'For the insurance money?' Griffin finishes. Cara nods. 'What do we do with this now?'

Cara's gaze drops to the page of A4. She picks it up, turns it over, then sighs.

'We get rid of it.'

'Shouldn't we ... I don't know. Submit it to the coroner?'

'What would be the point? Dad's dead. Mum's dead. Why dig everything up now?'

He shrugs.

'You agree with me, Nate. Or you would have put it in an evidence bag the moment you found it.'

She's right. Little was considered around their father's death at the time, case files left mouldering in storage. With the exception of the small notebook Griffin nicked, now burned to soot in the fire. Nobody cared. Not then, not now. But some part of him would like to right some wrong in this whole sorry mess. He's spent a week chasing his tail, debating, worrying about what happened to his dad.

'You know now,' she says, reading his mind. 'Let it go.'

And, decisively, she picks it up and screws it into a tight ball.

He laughs, the gesture so out of place for his rule-abiding sister. She grins then chucks it carelessly over her shoulder. It hits the kitchen floor and rolls to a stop.

In front of them on the table, his phone beeps and they look at it. A message from Brody, the contents mercifully hidden.

'Is that a serious thing now?' Cara asks.

'I doubt it.' Cara gives him a look. 'Her decision, not mine,' he replies. 'She wants to keep it casual.'

440

'Good for you.'

Cara gets up, places a hand on his shoulder and squeezes it. 'I'm sorry that nutter burned down your flat, but I'm not sorry you're now living with me. Did you lose anything valuable?'

'Nothing I can't live without. The important stuff is here.' He means the few boxes of Mia's belongings upstairs, but reaches up and places his hand over Cara's. He smiles up at her.

She grins back, then wrinkles her nose, pulling briefly at his T-shirt. 'But buy some new clothes. You've been wearing that one for days.'

'It's fine.'

'It stinks.' She picks up her bag. 'Do it by the time I get back. And buy that cat some proper food. *Cat* food,' she stresses.

'Where are you going?'

'To right some wrongs of my own.' And with a cryptic smile she leaves him, the front door slamming behind her.

Griffin picks up his phone and reads the message from Brody.

Are you busy?

She's followed it with an aubergine emoji. 'Not subtle, Alana,' he mutters. He starts to reply – he is free, shopping can wait – but instead of apprehension or the excitement he expects, something else twitches in his stomach. Dread. Or maybe, disappointment. In himself? In her? He doesn't want to be this guy – a fuck buddy who jumps when he's called. Many men would love this opportunity, but for Griffin it just feels tired.

He gets up, picking the crumpled ball of paper from the floor and pushing it hard into the bottom of the bin. He can think of his father differently now. Someone who loved him, but was too ill to demonstrate how. He and Cara will plan their mother's funeral. He might even go to Neil's. And that will be it.

He trudges upstairs to the spare room to where Frank is sleeping on the bed, curled up in a tight black furry ball. The cat opens his eyes, watching him, as Griffin appraises his sparse belongings. Everything he was wearing on the day of the fire, and two large brown boxes, brought down from Cara's loft. He taps them, content, then replies to Brody.

I don't want this, Alana. I'm sorry, he sends, then switches his phone off.

He lies down on the bed next to his cat, puts his hands behind his head, and smiles.

Chapter 81

Cara takes a calming breath and rings the doorbell of the nice semi-detached house. The Mercedes is neatly parked on the tarmac; the evergreen hedge is square and precise, the grass short. A half-full bird feeder hangs from one of the trees.

She hears footsteps; the door is opened. Her husband stands there, wiping his hands on a tea towel.

'I didn't expect to see you. I thought you'd be celebrating with your team.'

'I'm not sure there's much to celebrate right now, Roo.' She pauses. 'Can I come in?'

'The kids are at school.'

'I know. I want to speak to you. The restaurant said you were here.'

He doesn't reply but goes back into the house. She takes that as an invitation – or as good as she's going to get.

He walks through to the kitchen, picking up belongings as he goes. It wrenches her heart when she sees them – a hoodie discarded by Josh, a bracelet belonging to Tilly.

'How are the kids?'

'They're good.'

'And you?'

'What are you here for, Cara?'

He turns quickly, one hand on his hip, the other raking at his hair. She knows from fifteen years of marriage that he's angry and trying hard not to show it.

'I want to apologise,' she begins.

'You're going to need to do more than that.'

'And to say that you're right. What I've been doing—'

'Upsetting the kids. Ignoring me.'

'Yes, that. It was wrong. It's been … a hard time.'

His face softens. 'I know that, Cara. I've always known that. I didn't want you to be perfect. I just wanted you to try.' He pauses. Picks the kettle up and puts it under the tap. 'Tea?'

'Yes, please.'

It's something. That he's inviting her to stay. She sits down at the table, and flicks through the pile of paper in front of her. They're drawings, brought home from school by Tilly. Their colours are bright and gawdy. Rainbows, unicorns, people smiling, her name written in neat cursive at the bottom.

'These have changed so much,' she comments.

He looks for a second, then makes the tea. 'She's becoming quite the little madam,' he says. He puts her mug in front of her and joins her at the table. 'Eight going on eighteen.'

'I'm sorry.'

'You said that.'

'How can I put things right, Roo?'

He sighs. 'Take the kids. This weekend. No excuses.'

'Done.' Cara feels a thrill. She can't wait to see them.

'And return my calls straightaway. No matter what case you're working on.'

'I will.'

'And for God's sake, phone the solicitor back about the house. Get it sold. Buy yourself a new one. Somewhere the kids can come and stay.' His face turns serious again. 'But they're living with me.' He pauses. 'For now.'

She nods. 'For now. I'll sort myself out, I promise.'

He looks at her, his face sympathetic. 'What's going on with you? I know we're not together any more, but you can talk to me.'

She turns the mug around in her hand. 'It's ... after everything that happened. With the Echo Man.'

She looks up. He nods, encouraging her to go on.

'I thought I was good at my job. Catching killers. But there he was. Right under my nose. And I'd put everyone at risk. Griffin. You. The kids.'

'You're not infallible, Cara.'

'But I thought I had some certainty in my life. That you would always be there ...'

It's Roo's turn to look abashed. He stays quiet.

'And that ... he ... Noah ... would have my back. But it turns out, he was the one we were looking for all along.'

'Noah was always smart, Cara. You know that. And what he must have gone through. As a child.' She looks up quickly. 'I read some of the coverage around his sentencing. It's no excuse, but ...' His voice trails off. 'I don't want to talk about him. We're here to talk about you.'

'Me?' Cara thought they were done. 'I'm fine. I will be fine. We had a big win this week. It's helped. And Griffin's back on form. He's living with me. For the moment.'

Roo snorts. 'Griffin is not a stabilising influence.'

'I know. But it helps. Having him around. And talking to you.' She reaches out to touch his hand, but he pulls away.

'I'm with Sarah. You know that.'

Her face flushes at his rejection. 'Not that. I don't want that. I meant as friends.'

He nods slowly. 'Okay.' He pauses. 'But as your friend, I should tell you: you need to see someone. To talk. Sort all this properly, in your head.'

Cara frowns. The last thing she wants is a shrink.

He notices her reluctance. 'Please. For the kids?'

She agrees, but only to get Roo onside. For now.

Cara drinks her tea in semi silence, Roo talking about the children, anecdotes from school, and she finds herself laughing along, desperate to hear more about Tilly's defiant argument with the teacher, or Josh's new obsession with owls. But after a while Roo stands and she glances at the clock. Time for the school run.

'Can I come?' Cara asks tentatively.

Roo frowns apologetically. 'I don't think that would be a good idea. But I'll tell them,' he adds quickly. 'This weekend.'

'You promise?'

'I do. Come and get them from here tomorrow. We'll have dinner together, and then they can head off with you.'

She stands up. 'Thank you, Roo.'

They walk to the front door. 'But you'll do as I asked?'

'I will. I'll make a call today.'

He leans forward and gives her a quick kiss on the cheek, waiting at the door as she heads down to her car.

She gets in and gives a final wave as she drives off.

She wasn't lying to Roo. And he's not wrong. She knows that for her own sanity she needs to go and see someone. To talk. To get to grips with her past and everything that happened during those eventful few weeks.

She will make that call. It's just not to the person Roo thinks it will be.

446

Epilogue

The grand red-brick entrance of HMP Nottingham looms in front of Cara. With its huge bright blue door and fake machicolated battlements, it resembles a castle more than a prison.

She shows her identification and is allowed inside. Her bag is searched. The security measures are carried out swiftly and efficiently, and before she has time to change her mind she is escorted through clanging doors to the interview room.

She sits down at the battered table and runs her finger across the scratches and dents, wonders how they got there. Her hands shake. She'd felt sick as she woke up this morning, too nervous for breakfast, but now she regrets it. She feels empty. Her mouth is dry.

She hears noises in the distance, the ring of metal against metal, keys in doors. Footsteps, but no voices. And then she sees him.

His head is shaved, almost to the scalp. Dark stubble across his chin. His eyes are sunken, black shadows underneath. Around one of them is a dirty green smudge, a fading bruise.

She looks away. She can't bear to meet his gaze; he might guess what she's thinking. He always knew her so well. Instead, she stares at her fingers, her nails picking at the edge of the table, scraps of the brittle wood coming away as sawdust. She brushes them off as he sits down in front of her.

He's a metre away. He's still, calm, in the way that he always was. His hands rest lightly on the table. No cuffs. She asked for that specifically. She's not scared of him, only herself. How she'll feel. What she'll say or do.

He was everything to her. Her rock when things got tough. Her best friend, who she thought she knew. It hurts she was so wrong.

Now they're facing each other she can see the trace of old injuries. A small scar in his hairline. A mark across his cheek, puckering the skin. She knows the other inmates won't be kind. A murderer. A rapist.

Ex-police.

He's wearing a grey tracksuit, the sleeves pulled up to his elbows. Lines of silver scars lace the inside of his forearms from his suicide attempt; he notices her staring at them and pulls his cuffs down, encasing his hands inside. A strange, vulnerable gesture.

'I didn't expect you to ever come,' he says. He clears his throat, his voice catching. He's upset. That hits her hard.

For the last few years, she's imagined him as cold. A creature who knew nothing of morality or care. But emotions contort his face. He's battling with something. Regret? Love? She thought that once, to her shame.

'I'm glad you're here,' he says. The corners of his mouth tilt up, just a fraction, and despite herself, she smiles back.

'Hello, Noah,' she replies.

448

If you, or someone you know, have been affected by any of the issues raised in this book, the following organisations offer expert advice and support:

Call 116 123 to talk to the Samaritans, 24 hours a day, or email: jo@samaritans.org for a reply within 24 hours.

Text 'SHOUT' to 85258 to contact the Shout Crisis Text Line or go to www.giveusashout.org.

Contact the Campaign Against Living Miserably (CALM) on 0800 58 58 58, 5 p.m. to midnight every day.

Childline – for children and young people under 19 – call 0800 1111 any time. The number will not show up on your phone bill.

For family and friends who need support after losing a loved one to suicide, please reach out to Suicide&Co on 0800 054 8400 from 9 a.m. to 5 p.m., Monday to Friday.

Alternatively, please speak to someone you trust, and contact your GP and ask for an emergency appointment. Out of hours, please call 111 – they will find you the support and help that you need.

Acknowledgements

This book is dedicated to Dominic Nolan. As well as being an exceptional writer, Dom has been an incredible supporter of my books; he was the first person outside of my editorial team to read *The Echo Man* and his resulting 'essay' was the stuff nervous writers dream about. He fed back on an early draft of both *The Twenty* and this book and his insights prove to be ever valuable. Thank you, Dom.

While we're talking writer friends, thank you to the rest of the Criminal Minds gang – Heather, Rachael, Jo, Kate, Adam, Clare, Barry, Tim, Susie, Fliss, Victoria, Elle, Niki, Liz, Rob, Harriet, Simon and Polly – who keep me company on many a lonely day at my desk. Particularly to Kate Simants, who provided the 'hamster story' (not her, I hasten to add) and Adam Southward for how to ram a BMW through a garage door, among other things.

To my incredible team of experts: I couldn't do this without you. To PC Dan Roberts and Charlie Roberts for everything police based; to Dr Matt Evans for his patience when faced with numerous pages of botched medical jargon depicting horrendous violent acts, and correcting it all without judgement. To Sgt Jon Bates from the SCIU for help with Mark Griffin's car accident; Susan Scarr and SB for talking to me about drugs and pharmacies and how best to make a bad guy suffer; to Joe Allnutt for help on software engineering and image processing; to Laura Stephenson for everything paramedic; to Lauren Sprengel for the trip to HMP Nottingham; to Nikki Wallace for trusting me and sharing your first-hand experience. To you all – thank you. As always, all mistakes are mine and mine alone.

Now to the publishing side. Thank you to Kathryn Cheshire, Julia Wisdom, Angel Belsey, Maud Davies and the rest of the incredible team at HarperCollins-slash-Hemlock. Thank you to my magnificent agent, Ed Wilson, for putting up with my lists and *endless* questions, and to the rest of the team at Johnson and Alcock, particularly Hélène Butler, foreign rights extraordinaire.

Thank you to Soraya Vink and the incredible team for making me so welcome at HarperCollins Holland.

Thank you to Charlotte Webb for the copyediting and Sarah Bance for the proofread.

Apologies to Dannie Carter (@anoveleveningpodcast). She requested to be a murder victim and I just couldn't tempt fate. Dannie – I hope you don't mind being a 'best mate' instead.

Thank you to my family, Chris and Ben and Max, Dad, Susan and Jon, Tom and Mel – I love you all so much.

Endless gratitude must go to the amazing bookshops who get my bonkers novels into readers' hands. I am incredibly fortunate to have a number of bookshops supporting my journey – to mention a few (and I will forget some, sorry!), thank you to the teams at Waterstones Westquay,

Portsmouth, Whiteley, Salisbury, Winchester High Street and Brooks Shopping Centre. Thank you to Robyn and Daniel at Imaginarium Books in Lymington, Sarah at The Book Shop in Lee-on-The-Solent, Antonia at Books on the Hill in St Albans, Steve at P&G Wells, and the team at October Books in Portswood.

Finally, thank you to you, the reader, for picking my books out of the hundreds and thousands of incredible crime thrillers out there. I am nothing without you, and I love hearing all your comments and questions. Do keep in touch on Instagram, Facebook or Twitter (@samhollandbooks.)

And what's up next, I hear you ask? The conclusion to all good stories: the culmination of everything that's come before. The end game. I can't wait to start writing...

KARIN
Slaughter's

CRIME
CLUB

Exclusive to

ASDA

Dear Readers,

I'm always on the lookout for a book which makes my adrenaline spike and the hairs on the back of my neck stand up, so when I picked up *The Puppet Master* by Sam Holland, I was thrilled! Right from the start, we are launched into a terrifying investigation which twists and turns, and sends the reader on a real emotional rollercoaster. And then that ending, what can I say, it's definitely explosive, in more ways than one!

What particularly stood out to me with *The Puppet Master*, though, is the way the characters come to life, so we really feel like we know them. Cara and Griffin are both flawed in their own ways, but I honestly felt like I was living every up and down with them. I can't wait to see what they do next.

I hope you are as gripped by the story as I was.

Enjoy!

Karin

READING GROUP QUESTIONS

Warning: contains spoilers

---

1. The story opens with a shocking scene – did this pull you in immediately?

2. How did you react to Griffin the first time we meet him, and did your opinion of him change as the story went on?

3. How important is it that Griffin is in Cara's life? How does she influence him as a child, and what difference does she make to him as an adult?

4. How do you think Brody and Jamie feel about having Cara as their boss? Would you like to work for her?

5. Jamie is a very complex character – what do you think is next for him after this story ends?

6. The parent/child relationship is central to much of this story. How did this come into play at various points?

7. What was your favourite scene in the story, and why?

8. What did you think of the reveals at the end? Did you guess the identity of The Puppet Master?

9. Crime fiction is as popular now as it ever was, why do you think this is? What do you enjoy about these books?

10. If you had to sum up this book in three words, what would they be?

Q&A WITH
SAM HOLLAND

Warning: contains spoilers

The Puppet Master contains some very dark themes. What made you decide to write a story that focuses on suicide?

I didn't set out to write a book about suicide but was intrigued by the idea of someone gaslighting and manipulating vulnerable people to their deaths. I did a degree in psychology and have always been interested by criminology, particularly the very worst of human behaviour, and writing books with dark themes mean I can dig into this. What drives someone to kill, and kill in this way? What events in their life brought them to this point? It's endlessly fascinating.

This is your third book in the Major Crimes series. How do you think your writing and stories have evolved as time has gone on?

My aim when I start each book is to create a compelling story that readers can't put down, and to tell this through the eyes of characters they love. This hasn't changed, and I hope I've got better with each book. I had a sense with *The Puppet Master* that I was moving to a more psychologically eerie story, and I've certainly enjoyed delving into the mind of a complex and manipulative killer.

My understanding of how the characters think and look at the world has grown over time. Cara, Griffin and Jamie now feel like old friends and I've loved getting to know them as the books have progressed, and how their lives have changed as a result of the crimes they've experienced. Given this fact, I probably should be nicer to them!

Your characters really do leap off the page. Do you have anyone in mind (either in your own life or a celebrity) when you're writing them, or are they entirely from your own imagination?

The way characters behave are totally from my own imagination, but the way they look is usually influenced by someone famous. I'm a visual thinker, and have to be able to 'see' a scene or a character before I can write them, so my office is full of photographs of actors – usually very attractive ones. It's a hard job, this, you can tell!

Do you have a particular favourite character?

It has to be Griffin. I'm a sucker for a dark, damaged, devastatingly attractive detective and Griffin fits that bill! He likes to think of himself as a lone wolf, but he loved his wife and all he really yearns for is human connection, like the rest of us. I enjoyed exploring this in *The Puppet Master*, both through his relationships with Cara and Brody, but also his friendship with Jamie. Those are some of my favourite scenes to write.

What is the most difficult part of writing a thriller, and what do you enjoy the most?

The hardest part of writing a thriller, especially one that revolves around the police, is holding the various strands and clues in my head. I have a whiteboard next to my desk and it's covered in index cards and post-it notes – essentially the structure of the book. It's the only way I can make sense of it and ensure that all questions are answered by the end.

On the flipside of this, it's a fantastic feeling when the book starts to come together; when an ending or a twist appears out of left field and suddenly you know how it's going to work. Writing a book is the best job in the world!

Can you tell us anything about what is next for Cara, Griffin and the rest of the team?

Things don't get much easier for them, I'm afraid. Just as they are starting to relax, a woman drops a disk at the police station – on it is a snuff film, a murder playing out on the screen. The investigation into this death takes them to a shadowy underworld, where people are killed on demand, where huge sums of money are exchanged to play out deepest, darkest desires – mostly illegal, all shocking and violent. The book pushes all the characters to the edge – Cara, Griffin, Jamie, but also sees a return for two of my favourites: Adam Bishop and Noah Deakin. As you can tell – it's a lot of fun!

What do you look for when choosing your next read?

It's rare I don't have at least two books on the go at any one time – there is no shortage of fantastic fiction out there! I particularly love authors that are original and doing something new with their genre – and I will read anything from crime (my personal favourite) to romance or sci-fi. I'm a sucker for a heart-breaking love story. I'm also a big fan of Australian crime fiction and dream to write one of my own one day.

What's the most surprising thing you learned while writing your books?

One of the best things about writing crime fiction is the research, and the crazy rabbit holes you find yourself going down. Over the years, I've read books on everything from haematology and vampires, to undercover cops and assassins, but it was the research into serial killers for *The Echo Man* that surprised me the most. The deaths and murders that some of these killers got away with for years before the police even realised what was going on is shocking. Sutcliffe was interviewed nine times by the police before he was arrested; Dahmer was only caught because one of his victims escaped. I would hope policing has come a long way since then.

After writing about such dark themes, do you have a favourite way to relax?

I live in the beautiful Hampshire countryside, so I spend a lot of my time walking or running my crazy spaniel in the woods. The rest of the time I'm with my family, and I'm happiest when curled up in a comfy chair with a book.

THE NEW WILL TRENT THRILLER

KARIN
Slaughter

AFTER
THAT
NIGHT

One night can change
your life forever ...

**After that night,
nothing was ever the same again ...**

Fifteen years ago, Sara Linton's life changed forever when a celebratory night out ended in a violent attack that tore her world apart. Since then, Sara has remade her life. A successful doctor, engaged to a man she loves, she has finally managed to leave the past behind her.

Until one evening, on call in the ER, everything changes. Sara battles to save a broken young woman who's been brutally attacked. But as the investigation progresses, led by GBI Special Agent Will Trent, it becomes clear that Dani Cooper's assault is uncannily linked to Sara's.

**And it seems the past isn't going
to stay buried forever ...**